Jahleel

S. ANN COLE

LOVING ALL WRONG

LOUD GIRL BOOKS

This is a work of fiction. Names, characters, places and incidents are either the product of the author's imagination or are used fictitiously, and any resemblance to actual persons, living or dead, business establishments, events or locales is entirely coincidental.

Jahleel

For Jahleel and Tiffany...
...because it was never just 'Jahleel', or just 'Tiffany'.
It was always Jahleel and Tiffany,
or Tiffany and Jahleel.
I love you both.

Chapter 1

"YOU ARE SUCH a strong, head-on woman, Kia. You are awesome."

I heard that a lot.

Long before my parents made their unexpected exit out of my life, I used to hear those words. At seventeen, after they died, I heard those words even more. The same words voiced by so many people complimented me all my life.

And I used to agree.

Accepting the credits, I *did* believe I was strong, sensible, driven, mature, sensible (deliberately repeated) and functional. Because I was. Really. Truly. I was all of those things…

Until I met Jahleel Kingston.

1

Alright, I didn't exactly 'meet' him. No, not 'meet', because he didn't even notice me. What I should've said was: until I 'saw' Jahleel Kingston.

Yes, *saw.*

Just saw him.

Glimpsed him at first. Then tripped over my own feet aiming to draw closer for a clearer, unhindered view. Then I gawked at him.

Then drooled. Then hyperventilated. Then I became obsessed, becoming a Jahleel-craving idiot.

A fool. A dumbarse. A dolt. A lummox. Throw what names you will, I readily accept them.

So, the adjectives 'strong' or 'sensible' no longer belonged anywhere near the name Saskia Day. Once upon a time, I *was* a strong young woman, but that 'me' died a brutal death the second I laid eyes on the biggest American arsehole ever, who became the bane of my existence, but at the same time, the love of my life and holder of my happiness.

One glance at him, and he didn't even have to acknowledge me to rob me of my senses, my thoughts, my integrity, my virtue, my pride, my heart and, most of all, my love. Both a blessing and a curse, he took it all, all of me, just by *existing.* Just by breathing.

Jahleel Kingston stole me, claimed me, owned me, just by

2

ignoring me.

FIRST TIME I saw him?

Well, I had just hit the 20, just got me some freedom, and just landed my biggest gig yet. Quite a lot of 'justs' there, yeah? So I'll just throw in 'just fell in love', too.

Just for the heck of it.

Lion T'mar, a major R&B artiste who was sitting on top of the world at that time, was on tour headlining a show in Manchester, England. Being the silver-tongued, miracle worker that she was, my then manager, Lydia, got me the gig to open for Lion T'mar.

That was the catalyst for my career.

Even though the cheers from the audience weren't for me—some wild-haired, tattooed chick they'd never heard of— I went up on that stage and stole their screams, their chants, their hearts and devotion. Confidence on high, I made them *my* bloody fans, too. The nervous, sweaty palms thing? All gone once I was in front of an audience. The rush was too great.

Even as I bounced off that stage, I optimistically con-vinced myself I would hit it large. Soon. One shot was all I needed, and opening for Lion T'mar, I believed, was that shot. Not bragging but, through Lydia's coaching, I was good at making people like me.

Obviously, where Jahleel was concerned, I failed miserably.

The instant I was off the stage, I was bombarded with "Awesome!", "You rock!", "You ripped it up, Kia!" and other praises of that nature. But I hadn't the time to respond as Lydia promptly grabbed my wrist, yanking me through the throngs while ecstatically yammering, "Lion has requested to see you! You did great, Kia. You were magnificent up there."

Struggling to catch my breath, I let her haul me down an ongoing, shadowed hall, still yapping on about how great this was for me.

Security was hefty. Every other step we took, there was some buff, almost impenetrable man grumbling into his earpiece, while I was rushed through, beading sweat, not given the chance to grab a breath, a handtowel or a bottle of water to rejuvenate.

Truth be told, I didn't give two craps about Lion T'mar's music. His music was utter bullocks and degrading to women. Songs along the lines of 'Clap that Big Thang,' 'Lick & Slurp,' 'Glide & Grind,' 'Sit on Daddy's Lips'... Ugh.

Thing was, aside from his music, Lion had a talent for developing highly successful artistes. He recognized talent, and with his unlimited connections and secrets to dominating the business, he unfailingly turned them into stars. He was the hottest thing on the music scene back then. But now, even more so as a mover and shaker—he was my ticket to success.

Lydia stopped outside a door guarded by a man so big and so black, I had to take a frightened step back.

"Help you?" he asked in a rumble so deep, I felt my lungs vibrate.

Lydia told him we were there to see Lion T'mar at his request and he held up a hand, rumbled some more into his earpiece, then opened the door and stood aside for us to enter.

There wasn't a dressing room behind the door as I expected, but a dance room. Wide and open with a long wall of mirrors, laminate flooring, air-conditioner on full blast.

The frigidity of the air-conditioner was much appreciated.

Along with Lion T'mar were six other chaps—his backup dancers. No one was dancing though; each had scattered to his own corner, cooling down in preparation for the show.

Lion, whose back was to us when we entered, fiddling on his phone, turned around with a slant grin on his face.

"Saskia Day," he greeted, swaggering towards me in baggy jeans, graffiti shirt, and one helluva gold chain hitting somewhere near his navel.

Tall and built like a line-backer, he had a smooth, dark-caramel complexion, deep-set brown eyes and trimmed dark hair. Clean, handsome, and unlike his songs implied, no tats, no piercing.

"Lion T'mar," I returned with a nod and a smile, being formal. "It's a pleasure to meet ya'. Thanks for the opportunity."

With a steep raise of his brow, he scolded, "Don't be comin' up in here actin' all nice and formal. Not wit' them tats and shit." He came forward and hauled me into a side hug.

"I was aiming for politeness," I explained.

He waved a hand dismissively. "None of that with me. I like 'em real. And I know you keep it one hunnit. Can tell by the way you sing, girl. Not many opening acts can get the crowd hyped like that. Sure as shit wasn't like that for me when I started. Was a while before I learned how to get 'em crunk, ya know," he flashed a promising grin, "You gon' hit it big."

"That's some faith you have in me, yeah?"

On a chuckle, he waved me off again and started to say something, but I got distracted when the air behind me shifted with the weight of someone's presence, the overpowering scent of male, sweat and some earthy fragrance. A warm palm pressed lightly to my lower back, sending an electric wave up my spine as I was gently pushed forward to make room for the person to pass behind me.

At the mere touch, my eyes inexplicably fluttered closed,

as my mind drifted off. To somewhere inexpressible. A place I'd never been before. It was a celestial journey. Somewhere I would love to go again. And again.

Back to earth, I opened my eyes and glanced to the mirror across the room to get a view of the person whose touch alone made my mind blank. But there was no one there.

I looked to the right of me in the mirror and my eyes got stuck to the reflection of a guy sitting on the floor with his back against the wall, knees drawn up, earplugs in his ears, head nodding to music only he could hear. He wasn't there before. It had to be him who pushed me forward to pass by.

He wore grey sweats, white sneakers, and a red hoodie zipped open, sneaking me a peek of his abs and tattoos.

The hoodie was drawn over his head, so his face was obscure. But it was his hair hanging down the sides of his face under the hoodie that caught my attention. Thick, sandy-brown with sunburned blonde highlights, shoulder length, and *begging* me to rake my fingers through it.

Perfect.

Completely enraptured by the figure in the mirror, I didn't hear when two girls entered the room until one of them stopped next to me to relay some news about the current performance on stage to Lion, while the other, holding a tray of FIJI water, went straight over to the figure I was staring at and handed him a water.

In tiny, butt-cheeks-revealing white shorts and skin-tight blue blouse slit at the front to exhibit her copious cleavage, she was, I hated to admit, flawlessly sexy: petite and curvy with raven dark hair flowing in waves around her.

Red Hoodie glanced up at her, and his white teeth sank into his bottom lip as he pulled the hoodie off his head. But before I got a chance to see his face, Water Girl moved in front of him, flirtatiously jutting her hip out to one side as she said something to him.

With my gaze still on them, I moved sideways like a crab, twisting at every angle, trying to see around the flirty tart, and before I knew it, I was tumbling to the ground in an embarrassing heap.

Faster than a pirate could say "aye!" I was back to standing, pretending my fall was no big deal, even though my ear tips were flaming. Everyone was watching me with concerned expressions. Everyone except Red Hoodie, and that was because the trollop still flirted with him.

"You okay, girlie?" I heard Lion ask.

Reluctantly dragging my gaze from the mirror, I raised a hand to my throat and croaked, "Yeah. Just need water."

Which was the honest truth.

Lion frowned calculatingly at me as he called, "Tori,

bring Saskia here one of those waters, will ya."

Gaze shifting back to the mirror, I watched as Water Girl started to move off from Red Hoodie, but he grabbed her wrist and yanked her lower, so her ear was at his lips. Her cheeks flushed crimson as her tongue licked across her lips at whatever he whispered to her. She nodded and started over to us, finally allowing me to see his face.

Every ounce of air left me. I was immediately desperate for that water. Breath robbed, my world stopped. Heart thudding, I watched him as he watched her bum.

He was...*hot*. Ridiculously hot. Ruggedly hot. No-words-to-describe hot.

Jesus Christ.

Along with his thick, sandy-brown hair, he had eyes so astoundingly gold, they almost seemed paranormal. The sharpest, most conspicuous jawline I'd ever seen on a man. A nose probably too small for a man, and lips probably too full. But everything just worked together. Made him perfect. Flawless. Made him, him.

And made *me* breathless. Never had I seen any man that...alluring. Beautiful. Physically without fault.

In hindsight, I believe the moment I lost my senses was when I fell as I attempted to catch a glimpse of that face. With that fall, my senses scattered from my brain onto the floor, and

I'd never bothered picking them up.

"Um, hullo?"

I belatedly registered a well-manicured hand waving in front of my face—Water Girl trying to get my attention.

Snapping my eyes from Red Hoodie, who'd stopped leering at Water Girl's bum and dragged the hoodie back over his head, I grabbed the bottle of water with a scowl.

Amused rather than snarky, she raised an eyebrow at me before turning to leave the room, exchanging a look with Red Hoodie as she did.

I unscrewed the bottle and downed half its contents. By the time the water helped cool my nerves, and I was somewhat coherent, I noticed how everyone in the room—except Red Hoodie, of course, who seemed to excel at ignoring others—watched me with much amusement.

Pretty apparent I was being too obvious. But I couldn't help it. Like an eclipse in the sky: it's there, blinding, unusual, like *nothing* you've ever seen, and you want to tear your eyes away, but you can't. It's too beautiful. Too remarkable a sight to miss. You. Just. Can't. Help. *Looking*. And so you sacrifice your eyesight in admiration of its beauty.

Leaning over to me, Lion whispered, "That's Jahleel. Also known as JK…my best dancer."

As I began wagging my head, about to lie through my

teeth that I wasn't gawking/ogling, he called aloud, "JK!"

When he glanced up and pulled the plugs from his ears, Lion told him, "Saskia here wanna say 'hi'."

Oh hell.

Jahleel slid his gaze over me for a brief, bored second, muttered, "Hey, Sastia," then made to put his earplugs back in.

"Saskia," I corrected.

"Yeah," he mumbled, without sparing me another glance.

I felt like nothing. No one. For some reason, I wanted him to look at me like he did Water Girl.

"Really, JK?" Lion said, brows raised, looking a tad surprised. "That's the best you can do? What with all your nag—"

Head still down, Jahleel raised his glaring golden eyes at Lion and hissed out, "Gimme a fuckin' break, man!"

Wow, not the wisest way to address the person who handles your pay check.

To my surprise, Lion merely shrugged and looked to me. "Touring gets a bit stressful sometimes. When it does, they get like that."

"Not 'they,'" a voice said from right behind me, "*Him.*"

Swivelling around, I realized one of the other dancers had sidled up to me, unapologetically raking me over with a licentious leer. "Don't mind him, baby girl. He's a natural asshole.

11

It ain't you."

Gag. I hate it when men call me 'baby girl'.

At the sound of the door opening, I glanced over my shoulder and glimpsed the red hoodie retreating through it.

"So, Saskia…" the dancer beside me began.

"Fall back," Lion said to him.

"Why? Because I'm not *JK*?" the dancer shot back. "You know what he's gettin' ready to do, right? And we're on in less than thirty minutes. Why does *he* always get away with shit like that?"

Lion took a step forward and more sternly warned, "Fall. The. Fuck. *Back.*"

The bloke took it with a sniff and walked away.

Lion turned back to Lydia and resumed their discussion, him trying to convince her to let me move to the U.S. This was my career, I should've been on my toes listening, pitching in and seeking favours, but at that moment, I could only concentrate on one thing, one person, while I stared at the now empty spot where he'd sat. I nursed his rebuff, wishing he'd looked at me like he had Water Girl.

Why didn't I catch his attention? Was I not attractive? Were blonds not his type?

Right then, I decided as soon as the sun rose the next morning, I would head to the salon and dye my hair raven black.

Lion sent us off with, "When you hit it big, don't forget it started here."

I followed Lydia out the door, only half-listening as she went on about her plans for me.

As we drifted down the dark hall, my head a flustered mess, I heard a soft giggle followed by a moan, and for some instinctive reason, I stopped and glanced back over my shoulder.

A door on the left was slightly ajar, and as the giggle and moan came again, I inched towards it, as though I were magnetically pulled. When I got there, I peeped through the crack and saw the familiar red hoodie and grey sweats, standing between the parted bare thighs of a woman whom I had no doubt was Water Girl.

She was spread open in the corner on a glass desk, and he was right there between those eagled legs doing something with his right hand while whispering God-knows-what in her ear, which had the magical effect of making her moan, giggle, then moan deeper and beg for him to kiss her.

Blech. I was already plotting her murder.

A firm hand gripped my bicep and dragged me away from the door. Lydia. She didn't reproach me as I expected her to. As if understanding, she instead spoke to me like the mother I didn't have.

"It's okay to see and want. But sometimes you have to know when to *take*. For you, now is not the time to take. Make something of yourself first. Give yourself a name. Make yourself recognizable and respected. So when anyone hears the name Saskia Day, they'll know *who* Saskia is, and won't dare mispronounce it."

I wanted to die a million deaths at that reminder, but Lydia patted my arm and continued as we moved down the hall, "In other words, career first—success, respect, financial stability. Men later. By the time you start recording, traveling, touring, you'll come across tons of fellas who look just like him. Even better than him. You'll have your pick of them, vying for your attention, and you'll long forget there was some chap named Jahleel who once made you fall flat on your face."

I thought she was right. Because Lydia was *always* right.

But after focusing and achieving it all, after I blew up, got a name, became recognizable and respected, after *all* those hard-earned successes, I realized she was dead, dead wrong.

About both things.

One: I never forgot Jahleel. Ever.

And two: becoming famously rotten rich with number one hits slamming the music charts still wasn't enough for Jahleel Kingston to notice me.

Chapter 2

WHAT WAS LIFE like before Jahleel?

Well, I mean, before I knew such a striking fucking creature called Jahleel *existed*.

Life was crap. Stressful. Lame. Difficult.

You'd never believe how exciting being obsessed with another human being could make your life!

It could also be sad and depressing.

Anyway, I'd always been a loner, a struggler, a caretaker, a mother. Not to my own children, but to my siblings.

Sad to admit, *both* my parents were delinquent drunkards. As in, they both left us at home during the evenings to gamble and drank until they were piss-drunk and broke. Until one night their own sins inevitably consumed them in a car accident. They ran themselves off the road. Died instantly.

Did I miss them?

What was there to miss?

We impecuniously grew up on a small farm with my little sister Timberly and my older brother Ferburt—oh Jesus, that *name*! No idea what Mum and Dad were thinking when they named us. For short, I called him Ferbie.

Ferbie, he was kind of a dolt. A dumb-dumb. An imbecile.

Not being malevolent here, he was my brother, after all, and I loved him dearly. Plus I was the only person allowed to refer to him as such. But, he was naturally slow. Three years older than me, but had the brain of a toddler.

Ferbie was twenty when our parents died, Timberly fourteen and me, seventeen. The only family left was our Aunt Lizzie, a thirty-five-year-old self-centred lesbian, the girlfriend of Lydia.

Aunt Lizzie sold the farm, kept the money for herself and jacked us up in her claustrophobic one-bedroom flat, from which she was almost always absent. She didn't care two craps about us, so just as I'd always done since I knew how to spell my name, I assumed the mother role, taking care of my brother and sister.

The role was nothing I wasn't used to since my parents

were never at home once the clock struck 5pm. It was always all left on me. But being the mother became far more cumbersome after they died. I was forced to quit school and take on two jobs: a waitress by day, a flirtatious bartender by night. Some said it was a waste of time and money to send Ferbie to classes, but I did it nevertheless, because I had hopes for him. Timberly, on the other hand, was a nerd. A smarty pants. A know-it-all. Talked a hell of a lot and never shut up. Eyeglasses, cardigan, pleated skirt, but outrageously beautiful— that kind of girl.

And I, I was fucking stressed.

One night, Lydia, in search of Aunt Lizzie, popped up at the flat. When I told her we hardly ever saw Aunt Lizzie, Lydia was appalled. She explained that Lizzie sort of lived with her and disappeared from time to time, but she didn't realize Lizzie had us three crammed in her flat, surviving on our own. After inspecting the apartment, she placed her hands on my shoulders, looked me in the eyes and told me, *"You've been incredibly strong, Kia. But you need help. You need your own life. Let me help you."*

Distressed and close to losing all sanity, I wasted no time being prideful by refusing help when I clearly needed it; I accepted. Aunt Lizzie reluctantly agreed to us moving out of her apartment and in with Lydia.

17

Lydia, a sturdy, muscled butch, was from an affluent up-bringing. She had glossy black hair perpetually pulled back in a tight ponytail, Stygian dark eyes, and a hard, masculine face: squared jaw, prominent cheekbones, crooked nose. Ninety percent of the time, she dressed in black three-piece suits. Lydia was one of those people who, upon seeing her, even if you didn't know her, you felt compelled to tilt your chin in respect, because her very presence declared she was *someone*.

Her surname was Henry—"Henry's" was one of the best-selling tea brands in London, black tea, green tea, mixed tea, the works. Her father's death left her with a large share in the business, so she had a staggering net worth.

She moved us into her grandiloquent, old English country manor in Manchester. Quite a responsibility to take on; three people with no relation to her whatsoever: one lummox, one smarty pants, and one confused, wild-haired, pierced-up young adult.

However, I was grateful for the reprieve, which gave me time to pay attention to who I was, what I liked, and what I was good at. Lydia's takeover didn't stop my two siblings from calling me "Ma", though. Lydia thought it endearing, but I wanted to punch them in the eye each time they called me that. But they never stopped, it was automatic for them. They considered me their mother because I was the one who always took care of them.

Even when we moved into Lydia's home, Aunt Lizzie's presence was still rare. But Lydia didn't seem to care. She became like the mother I never had—in a fatherly kind of way.

After I started taking classes again, I began discovering *me*, noting my profound love for music and my jaw-dropping ability to effortlessly hold notes as long, loud and flawlessly as Whitney Houston.

Lydia thought I had something special. But I thought—I didn't know what the fuck I thought. All I knew was I wanted to be someone better than who I was, better than my background, before I died. I wanted to take care of my siblings so they'd never want for anything, *anything at all* for the rest of their lives. I especially wanted to make life easier for Ferbie so people would never take advantage of him because of his impediments. I had an all-consuming desire for something better, and I had the most amazing person in my corner spurring me on and propelling me in the right direction.

So, when Lydia promised me she would make sure I became something, someone of significance, with a better, easier life...I believed her and held on to that belief. Because I had nothing and no one else to believe in.

WITH A DAVIDOFF cigarette burning to weightless grey ashes between the slim crease of my index and middle finger, I stood on top of the world.

Alright, alright, a slight exaggeration, but I won't apologize for feeling like *Scarface* while he sat in his bubbling Jacuzzi in the middle of his mansion.

My 'on top of the world' meant me standing at the edge of the all-glass balcony of my 10,125 square feet San Francisco home, sucking down the enriching taste of a Davidoff cigarette, staring off at the spectacular vista as the infinity pool below me ran off to nowhere.

From where my hilltop house was pitched in a tortuously exclusive neighbourhood, jutting out its balconies over absolutely nothing and creating the illusion of being suspended in the air, the view was priceless.

At 5:28 in the morning, the sky was a kaleidoscope of soft colours blending uniquely to make a creative artistic statement before the sun turned up its dominating hot heat and melted the sky's beauty, stealing the blend of colours with its blinding shine.

On the norm, I wouldn't be up this early to appreciate the beauteous effects of sunrise, but at 4am I'd slipped out of bed and came out on the balcony to smoke my nerves away because I wasn't able to sleep much.

Throughout the night, I'd tossed and turned from excitement and trepidation, stomach in tight knots, knowing that today, this day, I would see Jahleel Kingston. Face to face. For the first time since I'd last glimpsed him back in Manchester five years ago.

When I moved to the U.S. four years back, I tried with repetitive failure to get near Jahleel, in his vicinity, anywhere I could run into him, but that proved to be as difficult as Trigonometry.

For one, Jahleel lived in San Francisco, and I in Los Angeles. Of course, I flew the short one-hour journey to SF numerous times for interviews, shows, everything connected to my career. But I was never spared the time to investigate Jahleel. Life had been too busy, too hectic.

Had I not been the victim, I would never believe someone could dominate one's mind, thoughts and entire being to such an intense degree even while living life in the fast lane.

But, he did. Not a single day started or expired without me thinking about that guy. Imagining what it would be like to be his. To be touched by him. To be kissed by him. To have him whisper sweet words in my ear.

See, ever since that night back in Manchester, I've been

21

obsessed. All of a sudden, Lion T'mar's music landed on my favourites list. Not because I cared for his crappy music, but because he was connected to Jahleel. I listened to his music daily, trying to feel Jahleel through them. I stalked Lion on YouTube to watch all his stage performances—well, not him. But *him*, the guy with the perfect brown hair dancing in the background—Jahleel.

Each new music video that came out for Lion T'mar, I watched a hundred times over, replaying the parts showing the fierce, gold-eyed dancer—Jahleel. Even if it lasted only for two seconds, I played his parts over and over again or paused the video and just stared at the pixelated version of him.

Before long, I had no more YouTube videos to watch and torture myself with because he quit working with Lion, opened a dance studio, and started his own choreography business, and I had no other means of stealing glimpses of him.

Lion hounded Lydia after our meet at his concert in Manchester, trying to convince her to convince *me* to move to the U.S. and cross over. He assured her he would endorse me, take me under his wing and make me a star in no time. Lydia stayed on the fence about it, and I was flat-out against it, so Lion gave up.

Or, at least, I thought he'd given up. Turns out he decided, almost a year later, to try one last tactic. Why?

Maybe because I, not so stealthily, asked him about Jahleel each time we spoke, or maybe Lydia divulged that I never got over the gold-eyed man who made me fall flat. Obviously, he put all those pieces together, grabbed that knowledge and ran with it.

Lydia handed me her cellphone one evening, a smirk on her face as she told me someone wanted to talk to me. No, it wasn't *him*. It was Lion, of course. When I answered the phone, all he said was, "Move here, to L.A, and you'll only be an hour away from JK. He's still single so you just might have a chance with him. Think about it."

Then hung up.

Did I 'think about it'? Nope. The thought of being just an hour away from Jahleel had me packing my siblings in my suitcase and wheeling them behind me to Los Angles.

How had I not thought about this before? Stupid, stupid, I thought, *so much time wasted.*

Lydia moved with me, but stayed only for about a year before moving back home when Aunt Lizzie landed on her death bed from pneumonia, thrusting me in the trusting care of Lion T'mar.

However, being an hour away from Jahleel didn't mean I got to see him. What Lion didn't prepare me for was the insurmountable amount of work I'd have to invest into 'making it big'.

A heck of a lot. It was never easy. There was no rest. Just work, work, work, day and night, with me surviving on the rush of unwholesome consumptions of energy drinks and adrenaline.

As soon as I hit U.S. soil, he had me doing a reality show, as apparently that was the new and most effective method of building a loyal fan base.

"Hook the world on your raw beauty and down-to-earth personality," he told me. *"Buy fans with true reality."*

Despite my doubts, I went along with it. See, I went along with most of what Lion and Lydia suggested, mainly because they knew the ropes. Also: they never, ever tried to change me, or told me to sing, act or dress like anyone else but myself.

Lion believed in the real me, my real voice, my real attitude and that's who he allowed me to be. Unlike the songs he sang, I later learned the *real* Lion T'mar was a man of morals. He'd never once hit on me. His love for me was genuine, only wanting the best for me and taking pride in watching as I succeeded.

He had a woman, and he worshipped the very ground she walked on. With an über-ghetto name, Twana, she had a bum so big, one saw it before seeing her, along with thick, meaty thighs and perfect perky D-cups. The sceptical side of me inquired, and yep, she was authentic: no silicon, anywhere. That bum, that rack, that tiny waist, all real.

I'd been to tons of parties and events with Lion. Where he went, I went, and I could testify on a stack of Holy Catholic Bibles that I'd *never* seen him so much as flirt with another woman. Everything was all about Twana. Twana was his Queen.

So because of his echt quality, dedication, and commitment to me, I trusted him with my career and rarely disagreed with his suggestions. As a result, most things were smooth sailing because I never put up a fight, followed orders and performed each show, sang each song, delivered each appearance to the best of my ability.

In my mind, I wanted to get 'there' as expeditiously as possible so I could resume my Jahleel chase. And what better way to do that than to push brattiness aside and listen to your mentors who've been in this business since the age of Adam?

By God's good grace, America received me well. Exceptionally well. Everything happened so fast. At such velocity, I hardly had time to realize my life was changing, climbing, growing, as was my net worth.

For a whole year, I had no time to stop and appreciate, because it was all work, no sleep and no play. Until my first album, *Notice Me*, went platinum. An album mostly permeated with songs I wrote while in the throes of Jahleel-craving.

Since then, Saskia Day has been a sensation.

One would think I'd feel different, grow a pride pimple somewhere, knowing I could get whomever and whatever I wanted and to hell with that Jahleel dude. But I didn't. I was, of course, proud of myself. I got what I dreamed of. Ferbie and Timberly lacked nothing, were contented. And because they were contented, I was...somewhat.

'Somewhat', because I still felt incomplete. The one thing—person—I wanted, I didn't have.

It wasn't as though I didn't date other men, attempting to kill my undying and obsessive crush. I had. But no one, *no one*, has ever managed to make me feel how I felt in those few short minutes when I first saw Jahleel under that red hoodie. He stole something from me, a huge chunk, and I would never again feel whole, until I saw him again, even if it's just once, so I could recover that piece of me back from his grasp.

So, I sold my Hollywood mansion and moved to San Francisco. A move Lion was flat-out against. Residing in Los Angles was more convenient and accessible, he'd told me, why remove myself an hour away from the star capital to make things that much more hectic?

Because I no longer wanted to be an hour away *from*

Jahleel Kingston, I wanted to be where he was.

And not even Lion could stop that move. Now, I was near. So close I could almost smell him.

Getting him to take me on as a client was nothing short of difficult.

Jahleel had transcended into one of the most acclaimed dance choreographers in this hemisphere. Lion endorsed him like he was his first born, while Jahleel let his talent speak for itself, and as a result, he was highly demanded. People went to him, not the other way around. And he picked and chose who to work with. That's what made getting to work with him so hard.

He'd accepted me as a client twice last year, and ended up cancelling both times at last minute. Of course, people who *truly* needed a choreographer would've moved on to the next best person. This was their career, after all.

I, however, didn't need a choreographer. My performances consisted of running around on stage in wild bursts of energy or standing/sitting with a microphone as I pour my heart into a soulful, high note song. But pretending I needed a dance routine was the only route to seeing Jahleel face to face.

Earlier this year, he agreed again to take me on but cancelled that meet as well. Frustrating, yeah. But refusing to give up, I tried again, and so far, all was good. Today, Friday April

2nd, I would meet the man who'd owned me, body and soul, for the past 1,826 days.

Unwittingly so.

As the sun rose up in its coruscating glory, burning away the cotton candy colours from the cirrus clouds, I grew more and more anxious. I glanced down and saw over four cigarette butts at my feet. Jesus, I needed to kick this habit before things got bad. Sometime between my parents' death and me quitting school to take on two jobs, I'd picked up smoking and have not been able to quit since.

Outing the current cigarette in my hand, I turned to go back inside the house, snatched up my wireless phone, hiked myself up on a barstool in the kitchen and dialled.

Lion answered in a groggy voice, probably frustrated with me as usual, but he never neglected me. "You callin' me this hour means you freakin' out 'bout somethin'. Wassup, Kia?"

Making a meal of my thumbnail, I whispered down the line, "I'm seeing him today…"

For a passing minute he remained silent, then sighed. "I thought you were over that, Kia."

"I've never been over him!" I exploded, more exasperated with my stupid self than with him. Sometimes I believed I had a dose of Ferburt-ism in my blood. In a calmer voice, I explained, "I don't know how to…"

"Kia," he said in a patient tone. There was the sound of sheets ruffling in the background, like he was getting out of bed. "I know you feelin' him. But, I don't think you should see him…Yet."

"Don't—"

"Hear me out, will you?" he cut me off. "Two things. One, you got a six-months tour comin' up in a few months. JK can-*not* be a distraction. There ain't no time for that. Two, I *know* JK, and he's the biggest asshole you'll ever come across. I love both of you equally, but I just don't wanna see you gettin' hurt… And, Kia?"

"Yeah?"

"He *will* hurt you."

"He won't," I protested, even though I mostly believed the opposite.

Lion sighed. "You alotta' things, girl. Alotta' things I adore and respect 'bout you. But being stupid ain't one of 'em. *Don't* see him."

"Okay. Okay, I won't."

Silence for a good sixty seconds, "I'm bein' serious, Kia."

"So am I. You're right; he'll be a distraction, so I won't see him." Easing off the barstool, I told him, "I'll try catching up on some sleep, then, yeah? Call ya' later."

I hung up before he could utter another word, tossed the

29

phone on the kitchen counter, proceeded upstairs and hopped straight into the shower.

I had every intention of seeing Jahleel Kingston.

Chapter 3

AROUND NOON, I woke up with my towel wrapped around me, my hair damp. Sometime after I showered this morning, weariness caved in and sleep followed.

I was expected at Jahleel's studio by two. My hair was a wild, frizzy mess and my mood was crap. Too many cigarettes.

At this time of day, my house was usually as noisy as a kindergarten classroom. Ferbie lived with me—I went nowhere without him, nowhere. I've always been utterly protective of him and wouldn't brook others making fun of him.

My best mate, Amanda, whom I hired as my hair and make-up artiste so she could move here, resided with me also. She, too, went wherever I went.

I had two American 'friends' Amy and Jamie, who I met when I first moved to the States and started the reality show. Not quite sure if I should label them as 'friends' or 'groupies', but they came through some door Lion T'mar opened and have stuck to me like chewing gum to a shoe bottom ever since.

On numerous occasions I tried getting rid of them, but Lion assured me they were 'cool', and I needed some American girlfriends until Amanda came. I gave them a chance and turned out to like them a bit.

A bit.

Credits to them, they were somewhat allegiant, because they've remained with me throughout the years and never wavered through the ups and downs. Always at my house, yeah, but didn't live with me. Amy and Jamie were loaferish, trust fund brats who lived hour to hour without an aspiration.

When Amanda arrived, she didn't have a problem with them, so I thought, *what the heck*, and we became a pack of four. Not that I trusted them, no, not at all. Lion warned me against trusting people, never to let my guard down, not even once, and never to tell real in-depth truths about myself. As far as trust went, it stretched to Lion, Lydia, my siblings, Amanda and no further.

Along with those people, I had three guards: two home guards, and one outside guard who accompanied me wherever

I go. So, believe me, this house got real raucous at times.

Nevertheless, everyone knew when Saskia needed her sleep, she needed her sleep. My bedroom had its own level and was strictly off limits to other occupants of the house. That was how I managed to sleep right into noon without disturbance. Now, awake, I could hear the cacophonous chattering and jeering downstairs.

Rolling out of bed, I trundled to my massive walk-in closet and decided on something casual to wear. Best if I didn't look as if I was trying too hard. So I went with Chucks, distressed jeans and a tee—the usual me.

My full reflection stared back at me in the closet mirror. The girl on the other side looked wild and wary, with a dash of famous and stinking rich sprinkled on top. Eighteen inches of stubborn, raven black curls, tipped rock n' roll purple at the ends flowed around small shoulders. Cute piercing above an inherently arched eyebrow highlighted big, startling grey eyes on a heart-shaped face. Small nose with even smaller nostrils. Wide pinup-girl lips. Faint dimple on the chin.

At 5ft 8inches, the slender reflection in the mirror had long arms toned from punitive workouts forced on by a grouchy fitness trainer, long neck, coveted super-slim waist, curvy hips and even longer, toned legs. Sun-kissed complexion, glowing.

33

The reflection was only half-pleased with itself, but it turned and vanished from view as I exited the closet room to head downstairs.

The noisy herd was crowded around the breakfast bar chatting about the usual crap. I plopped down on a barstool and glanced at Amanda.

"Make up?" she asked.

"Obviously," I mumbled. "My hair's like a bloody bird nest and my face is bland as Cream of Wheat."

"I don't know what you're talking about," sliding off the counter, she left to retrieve her work kit. "You have no idea how naturally gorgeous you are."

Amanda was the British version of Twana, except her big bum was fake. She got her bum done the minute she landed on U.S. soil; it was something she always wanted to do. Not sure why, though, as her previous one had been big enough, in my opinion.

With a smooth mocha complexion, she was temptingly bodacious. Even if she hadn't gotten the silicon bum and imitated Rihanna's current haircut—that one where one side is shaved off and the other side has long curly hair—Amanda was still a natural beauty. She was more of a Rihanna fan than a Saskia Day fan, and whatever Riri did with her hair, she did, too.

Apparently, I didn't change things up enough. Ever the same ole, same ole with me—chucks and tee, with wild raven curls dipped purple at the ends.

I hated heels with a bitter passion, and even pulled a Kristen Stewart on the red carpet once—ratty chucks, formal dress and messy hair—which resulted in landing on *Fashion Police* as Joan Rivers' 'fashion hoe of the week'. Consequently, I began practicing wearing heels for red carpet events and it was horrible.

Then I decided, fuck Fashion Police! Who gives a crap what they think, anyway? Amanda had glibly answered, "*Hollywood.*" But I disregarded every arsewit who thought they could dictate how people should dress and reverted back to my old self.

While I waited for Amanda, my housemaid, Sylvie, fixed a club sandwich and placed it in front of me with a glass of Crystal Light. Amy and Jamie sat beside me yapping about how "rad" some party was that they went to the night before, while Ferbie perched on the countertop asking Sylvie a million and one questions about things that mattered not one whit to the universe.

Biting into my sandwich, I spoke around a mouthful, "Go grab a shower, Ferbie. We leave in an hour."

"Aye, Ma," he nodded, hopping off the counter. "What

35

colour do ya think I should wear today?"

"What does it matter?" Amy said through a giggle. "Seriously, Ferbie, you need to grow up."

When I stopped chewing and shot her a look, she snapped her mouth shut. She should know by now not to mess with Ferbie when I was around.

"Blue," I told him. "Blue will suit you well today."

He grinned and jauntily walked off. Ferbie was actually good-looking—curly blonde hair that was as wild as mine but never grew past his nape, the exact cat-grey eyes as mine, and an inherently athletic body that reeled girls in like a magnet...until he opened his mouth. Some thought his good looks and amazing bod was wasted.

When Ferbie was out of sight, I turned to Amy with a vicious, "Mess with my brother again, in or out of my presence, and you'll no longer be invited here, yeah?"

Looking chagrined, Amy nodded. She was as pretty as a Barbie. Naturally curly strawberry-blonde hair cropped above her shoulders. Bright, emerald-green eyes and superbly long lashes on an oval face. "I'm sorry, Kia. It's just weird that he's twenty-eight and you're twenty-five and he calls you 'Ma', waiting on your instructions for everything."

"None of your bloody damn business," I hissed. "Leave him the fuck alone."

Amy nodded again as Amanda strolled back into the kitchen with her make-up kit. "He'd make a perfect submissive, you know. Too bad he's not my type. I like them black and strong."

"Even if you were attracted, I'd never let him be your submissive, you kinky fuck."

Amy and Jamie giggled, while Amanda shrugged and set her kit on the counter.

Grabbing my shoulders, she turned me around on the barstool. "Okay, time to make you pretty for—"

I kicked her leg and she stopped, getting what I meant. Since Amy and Jamie weren't privy to my personal business, they knew nothing about my Jahleel-craving.

Close people, usually called "sources" by the magazines, tended to snoop around for dirt to sell to the media all the time, and I was one of those 'celebrities' magazines and reporters had a hard time getting personal news on, because I kept things as private as I could, as trained by Lion. Although Amy and Jamie were rich brats who didn't need to sell dirt for money, I still had a hard time trusting them, so they knew only what I wanted them to know.

Amanda realized her slip up and covered with, "The big meet."

"YOU GOING TO get out of the vehicle anytime this year, Kia?"

Amanda's voice broke through my overworked nerves as I stared out the Jeep window at the two-storey edifice of Kingston's Dance Studios—standing proud and tall in all its weathered, red-bricked glory and opaque, glass facade.

Thomas, my driver/bodyguard, had pulled into a parking space ten minutes ago, and I was still in the back with Amanda and Ferbie, nursing cold feet and rethinking, remembering Lion advising me not to see Jahleel.

Too bad he was back in L.A and couldn't stop me.

Amy and Jamie were sitting in Jamie's convertible in the lot next to us, waiting for me to make a move. Everyone waited for me to make a move. No one made a move without me, apparently.

Shooting Amanda an annoyed stare, I groused, "You're a thorn in my goddamn side."

Looking unconcerned as she inspected her nails, she replied, "You sure *I'm* the thorn in your side, or the guy inside that building who plagues your thoughts so much you can't even take a minute to live?" She glanced up from her nail inspection and pinned me with her blunt stare. "This is stupid and dumb, as I've told you many times before. What're you going to do, go in there and demand that he dates you? What if he already has a girlfriend? What if—"

"Shut up, Manda. You, of all else, are supposed to *support* me, not remind me how much of a berk I am."

She shook her head and sighed. "Whatever. It's going to be interesting to see how this plays out, yeah? Thanks in advance for the entertainment."

Jabbing my middle finger in her face, I wrenched open the Jeep door and hopped out. "C'mon, Ferbie."

Amy and Jamie got out of their car and fell in with my strides, as did Amanda, Ferbie by my side and Thomas, my tall hunk of bodyguard, who led in front. Ben, one of the other guards, also came along and was at the back.

Thomas pushed open the door to the building and we all shuffled in. A burly African American man at the security desk stood up as we entered, his grin being one of those wide starstruck grins I'd grown used to getting. "Miss Saskia Day, Mr. Kingston is expecting you. Follow me."

Plastering a smile on my face, I nodded once and we followed him up a flight of stairs, down a long hall, passing a number of closed doors with music seeping under the creases, until he finally stopped at a door at the end of the hall. "This is your stop. Have a wonderful afternoon." Then he turned and left.

Thomas watched me, waiting for my cue. When I nodded slightly, he opened the door and we breezed in. Cool air-conditioning enveloped me in an instant, reminding me of how hot the climate was.

"Holy *fack*," Amanda whispered from beside me. "Am I in hell or something? I swear to the most high, I've never seen so many hot guys in one room before."

Amy and Jamie giggled like the giggly twits they were, while Ferbie just looked mildly bored. The room was long but wide at the same time, the entire right wall being of mirrors, bright lighting and black marley flooring, everything else was all-white.

There were about seven hot guys, all in black sweatpants and wife beaters, hunched over a laptop, laughing and jeering at something on the screen. As my eyes swept around the large room, there *he* was, back turned to us. He was down at the far end of the room with his cellphone pressed against his ear, though he wasn't talking into it.

No.

He was staring at me by way of the mirror.

As my heart slowed to heavy, ponderous beats loud in my ears, I reminded myself I was someone now, and I needed to act like an important, respected 'somebody', which meant hyperventilating like an adolescent, as I'd done five years ago, wasn't allowed.

Those golden eyes latched on to mine in the mirror and didn't let go. His tongue made a swift pass over his bottom lip and his teeth promptly sank down on it as his eyes moved down my body, slowly.

Oh God, he was looking at me like *that*. The way I'd wanted him to look at me five years ago. The way he'd looked at Water Girl. My heart ricocheted in my chest, and of their own volition, my lips parted and a sigh flowed through.

I must remember to breathe. I must remember to breathe.

It seemed the person on the other end of the phone call felt neglected and nabbed his attention back in, because he suddenly snapped his gaze from me and frowned as he spoke into the phone. "Yeah, yeah, still here. No. What'd you say?..."

At the touch of Amanda's hand on my arm, I dragged my eyes from Jahleel in the corner and turned to her with mild irritation. "What?"

In a low voice so only I could hear, she whispered, "You're being a little too obvious, Kia. Those guys over there, along with Amy and Jamie here, are watching you watch him like you've never seen a man before. Chillax, mate. *You're* the star here."

I glanced over at the men who'd stopped laughing at whatever was on their computer screen and now watched me with amusement instead. Of course, they were Jahleel's dancers, which meant they worked with celebrities frequently. I was just another famous face who didn't faze them in the least. Idly, I couldn't help wondering if Jahleel handpicked his dancers based on looks instead of talent, because those guys were an impressive pack—all taut muscles, drool-worthy faces, exuding undeniable steam.

"Saskia."

At the sound of my name being used so informally, I turned to see Jahleel had ended his call and was coming up to me, right hand held out. My eyes ran over him one last time before I took his hand to shake it, ignoring the tingling warmth between our palms.

He was ruggedly sexy in faded, cut-off jeans ravelling out at the ends, a stretchy white tee with a dog-tag dangling on his chest, dogged grey sneakers and a grey beanie hiding what I knew was amazing sandy-brown hair underneath.

"Jahleel Kingston," I greeted back, shaking his hand and trying not to shiver at the heat seeping from his pores to mine. "So nice to see you again."

Brows furrowing, he tilted his head to the side and gold eyes squinted at me. "We've met before?"

Before I could make a bigger fool of myself, Amanda, ever the woman with control and a brain, came to the rescue by sticking out her hand. "I'm Amanda, Saskia's bitch." She turned and pointed to the others. "That's Amy, Jamie, and Ferburt."

His lips twitched at the corners as though he wanted to laugh, and I knew it was at the expense of my brother's name. But he politely shook everyone's hands. As a matter of fact, the eye-raping person who'd locked gazes with me in the mirror was gone. He was now professional and polite, in an informal kind of way.

Pleasantries done with, he cracked his knuckles and jerked his head to the side. "Come with me." Then to my entourage, "You're free to roam about, but keep off the floor once we start practicin'."

Without waiting for a reply, he turned and started towards his dancers, expecting me to follow. Which I did; I'd follow him anywhere.

Smooth, dark hair laid flat on legs displayed in his cut-off jeans. Ongoing inscriptions tattooed his left leg, running from the side of his knee down to his ankle. The words were too small to read, plus they didn't look like English. There were writings on his right arm also, running from under his short sleeve down to his wrist.

Glancing over his shoulder to check if I was still with him, he stopped on the other side of the room and gestured to his dancers one by one. "Meet Tyler, Sprigs, Mace, Dane, Andre, Leo and Trent. Team A, my main dancers."

After I greeted the hot pack, I mean 'Team A', with a cordial smile and shook each of their hands, they went back to "That's whassup!" and "Crazy, man!" over some dance competition on YouTube that they watched on the laptop.

Jahleel pulled out a small box of Sun Maid Raisins from his pocket, popped it open and tossed a couple in his mouth before putting it back from whence it came. Most men had mints, gum or mouth spray. He had raisins.

Mouth chewing, he crossed his arms over his broad chest and gave me his business face. "Okay, Saskia, I never got a clear explanation of what you were looking for," he said. "So tell me, what exactly do you want?"

You. I've been wanting you for five bloody years, I was tempted to say.

But instead, I was silent. Mainly because, there I was, standing in front of Jahleel Kingston—the opportunity I'd dreamed of since I first saw him. And secondly, because I had no answer to his inquiry. What I wanted from *him,* I had a long list...or scroll. But as a dance instructor...no clue.

To get close to him, I'd used the excuse of wanting a

choreographer, had been purposely vague about what I was hiring him for, and now, face to face, I was cornered. Not that I wouldn't mind being *cornered*, as in, me pinned against a wall by his hips with his tongue in my mouth and his hand down my knickers. But not this kind of cornered where he was about to expose my lie. I hadn't thought this through at all, thinking I could always get by on my name. I was *screwed*.

"I have a six-month tour coming up soon," I started off in my strong, self-assured, 'I'm-Saskia-Day' tone as if I most certainly knew what I wanted. "I need to change things up a bit. There are a few songs that aren't exactly fan favourites that I think would ultimately do well if I amped them up with gripping dance performances on tour."

No idea if what I just said even made sense.

Jahleel raised his eyebrows as he rubbed his chin. "Yeah, I'm thinkin' we probably should've talked more about this before I agreed to take you on."

Oh Jesus, so I guess all I said was a load of bullocks. "Why?"

"We're talkin' about a six-month tour here, Day," he replied in an incredulous tone, as if I was daft. "You got your own dancers for me to train for this tour?"

Uh oh. I really didn't think this through. What the fuck was I doing? God, I was such an idiot.

45

Taking my silence as a 'no', he continued, "My team here can't go on tour with you. We only do 30-day or less tours. However, you could contract some of my other dancers who'll be up for touring. That's the better option."

"Okay, we can do that," I said thoughtfully, masking my idiocy with feigned superiority.

His golden gaze narrowed as he studied me for a minute too long, not lusting, no, just scrutinizing. "I've cancelled on you three times before, and I might do it again, because I get the feeling you're not exactly sure *what* you want and I have too much on my plate to wait around while you figure it out. Plus I hate to believe someone of your status would waste time messin' around. I have zero tolerance for bullshit. Celebrity or not."

"Pardon?"

Ignoring my hand-on-hip attitude, he continued on as if I'd never spoken. "Because I have to audition dancers suitable for your tour, I'll use today to test your fluidity, coordination, and your ability to follow instructions correctly so I can determine just how serious you are about this." He tapped one long, masculine finger on his lower lip as he watched me for another minute, then, "You cool with that, come with me out on the floor. Not cool, then you're free to go."

I looked up at him with disgust on my face (even though

that was so far from the truth), "Anyone ever tell you you're an arsehole?"

He responded with a deep, caressing chuckle that slid over me like silk, and I melted just from that sound. Right then, I wanted, just *had to have*…him.

"No. But I have been told I'm an *ass*hole. On a daily basis." He paused to lick those delectable lips. "I'm an asshole with reason, so the same lips that curse me, always end up praising me, eventually. Not gonna kiss your ass, if that's what you're expecting. Believe it or not, I make less money with celebs than I do with my regulars. Celebs come and go, they rise fast and they fall hard. But regs, regs are constant and steady. Celebs are just good for publicity, and I've got all the publicity I need. So I kiss no one's ass. People find me, not the other way around."

He took a step forward, entering into my personal space, and leaned into me so close, I held my breath so I could feel and hear his. He smelled like sweat, bike exhaust and some earthy cologne being overpowered by something else I couldn't quite put my finger on. *Fuck*, I wanted to fuck him until I smelled just like that. I wanted to feel his weight on me, his skin against mine, his hands on—

"Wanna use those pouty lips you just cursed me with to sing delicious, dripping, deserving praises to my name one day, Sassy? Then follow me."

By the tail end of that sentence, he was out of my face and walking out to the centre of the dance floor.

Two things, my breathing was far beyond erratic as I once again lost control and allowed him to make a fool of me in front of others. Second, he called me Sassy.

He gave me a frigging nickname.

If that wasn't progress, I didn't know what was. So, against my better judgment, I followed.

Remember when I said I was weak and dumb?

I still was.

Chapter 4

To my sweet surprise, the newbie dance tutoring went smoothly. For the most part, Jahleel was professional, as he dropped jokes from time to time to make me relax. But other times, he instructed me to do the most awkward moves, from snake arms to pop and locks—moves made, I believed, strictly for his entertainment.

'Cause Lord knows I had not one rhythmic bone in my body.

But, even though I knew this, I did his silly moves all the same because I loved his laugh. Without a second thought, I would change professions to become a comedienne if it meant I'd get to hear that sound every day.

One would think our semi getting along would've quelled my nerves some. On the contrary, each time we danced too close to each other and his hands so much as brushed my skin, I got so close to hyperventilating, I would call for a time-out and run outside to suck down a Davidoff and calm my nerves.

Back from one of my breaks, Jahleel was explaining the basics of the triangle zone, moving from left to right then forward then a step back to the left again, never leaving the allotted triangle area, when the studio door opened. A lull fell over the room as the loud chattering from Amanda, Amy and Jamie died as they ogled the person who just walked in.

He was a tad taller than Jahleel's six one height, with more of a slim, lean build rather than pounds of muscles. Shoulders wide, hips narrow, arms long. In all-black, he was wearing close-fitted jeans, a long-sleeved T-shirt dragged up at the elbows to show his artsy tattoos on both forearms, and a rosary chain around his neck. Dusty blonde hair was trimmed into a rocker haircut; the sides and back faded low and the front long and tousled, the longer strands falling into his eyes.

He was a sight to behold, and without a doubt, scorching.

When he walked up to Jahleel in a smooth swagger, Ben and Thomas started approaching, but I shook my head and they retreated.

Hot Bod gave a respectful chin lift as he reached us and

handed a disc case to Jahleel. He looked back to me in the same second he registered who I was. One corner of his mouth crooked up as he acknowledged me vocally this time, dragging out a, "Saskia Day..."

Before I could reply, Jahleel addressed him, "All the mixes on here?"

"You got it," Hot Bod's eyes were still on me.

Jahleel eyes shifted between Hot Bod and me. I saw this from the corner of my eye because, frankly, I couldn't take my gaze off Hot Bod. He was...intriguing.

With a faint sniff, Jahleel mumbled, "Lemme check to be sure everything's on here. Won't have a repeat of the last time."

He jogged over to his laptop and inserted the disc while Hot Bod continued to stare me down. In the next second, Amanda was at my side, hand stuck out to Hot Bod, her head tilted to the side—the tilt she reserved for flirting.

"Hi there, I'm Amanda." Her eyelashes did that fluttery thing, "And you are?"

Finally pulling his burning gaze off me, Hot Bod turned his head to Amanda and licked his full, kissable lips. "JK's ride or die."

It was quite possible I heard the hard-as-nails Amanda sigh like a gold-haired fairy-tale heroine, but I couldn't tell for sure.

"So, what do you do, JK's ride or die?"

His lower lip got trapped between his teeth as he chuckled to himself. "Multitalented."

As his obsidian dark eyes shifted from Amanda, they landed back on me, and *he* tilted his head to the side this time, examining me.

An intense silence stretched between us three, until he gave a slow smile and sexily dripped, "You know, I used to date this girl, she was extremely carnal. We had this strong sexual connection to each other, all sex, and there was this one thing about her that drove me wild: whenever she was *deeply, unapologetically* turned on, even by other men, I could tell…"

Trailing off, he dipped his head, smiling to himself as if wondering whether he should continue with his bold and inappropriate overture. For heaven's sake, how did I end up in the middle of this?

"How?" Amanda prodded, all eager and impatient.

Keeping his head lowered, he raised just his eyes to mine, and it was such a fucking turn on, my breath caught and formed a lump in my throat. "Because her nostrils would flare in such a fascinatingly erotic way, around the rims would be flaming red…" Drawing a breath through his teeth, he breathed out, "Just like *yours* are doing now."

Holy fuckaroo!

Was I that obvious? Some boy-toy rock star I'd dated told me that same thing: that my nostrils flared whenever I was turned on. Oh, hell and damnation, I needed to get a hold of myself.

Next, he took the leap and *went there.* Lifting his head, he stared at me dead on and asked, *"Are* you deeply, unapologetically turned on by me?"

Sucking in my cheeks, I flicked my gaze over to where Jahleel was still hunched over his laptop. His head was down, fingers moving over the keyboard but, somehow, I knew he was both listening and watching without being obvious, because he was *too* focused on what he was doing. I stared long enough to see if he would sense me watching him and glance over at me, but he didn't. That confirmed my suspicions. He was waiting, listening for my answer.

Trying to gain some control over my hormones, I retreated a step back from the anchor-heavy intensity levitating in the air. "You always this forward?"

Hot Bod's gaze shifted over to Jahleel and back to me, then back to Jaheel. He nodded to himself as he came to some sort of internal conclusion he chose not to reveal. Instead, he reached over, pinched Amanda on her cheek and winked at me, stating, "I'm just Chad."

53

He turned and swaggered back through the doors.

"Well, fuck me sideways," Amanda said, all breathy. "That was *some guy*. Talk about fearless. The temerity…"

"I need a smoke," I reached in my back pocket for my Davidoff cigs and lighter. As I power-walked through the door, Ben and Thomas promptly followed behind.

Burning two cigarettes back-to-back, I lounged outside Jahleel's complex longer this time, eying the single paparazzi across the parking lot doing a sloppy job at acting like he was just another normal dancer milling in and out of the studio.

The security at the studio was tight for such a casual place. There were three burly men who patrolled the lot round and round as well as security cameras, one being right above my head where I leaned against the wall smoking. Also, two men manned the security desk.

It made sense that he took precautions in ensuring his renowned clients felt safe in their environment, which might be the reason that particular paparazzi lurked outside the parking lot, as the securities must have eyes out for them.

My three mates came outside when I was on my second cigarette, no doubt wondering what was taking me so long. Once they noted I was okay, they started their yap yapping about which guy of the Hot Pack they'd screw without a second thought.

I wanted to hear none of it. I was overwhelmed, I was underwhelmed, I was confused, I was aroused, I was a fucking mess.

I was someone, *someone* dammit! With a name and millions. My crap, I needed to get it together. How did I get Jahleel to notice me, to want me, to come at me like Chad did?

For the most part, he went from polite to arsehole to professional to arsehole again. He wasn't constant, which made it hard for me to know if he was feeling me or not. With his variable persona, I didn't want to flirt to end up embarrassed and pathetic if he rebuffed me.

Flicking the butt of my last cigarette to the ground, I tossed a handful of Tic Tacs in my mouth and sucked them until they melted, getting rid of the horrid tobacco scent before I turned and re-entered the building, the chit chattering following behind. I swear these girls never stopped talking. They talked about everything, and it all ended up meaning absolutely nothing.

Me, I wasn't big on talking. I did better with expressions and actions. The most people heard from Saskia was during my interviews where I was required to talk or when I was in the studio— where I loosened up and went wild.

As we entered the dancing room again, my mood took a nosedive for the worse—a mood I couldn't point my finger on;

maybe anger, maybe jealousy, maybe irritation, maybe frustration... not sure. But I knew for sure I was glowering.

Jahleel stood in the middle of the room with a petite blond. She couldn't be more than five feet one, with a wicked low haircut and a smile that shined brighter than a bonfire on a camping night. Her lips were impossibly red and her eyes were an unusual shade of blue.

If Jahleel hadn't been looking down at her with a softened expression on his face, I wouldn't have felt threatened. But, that look...

It wasn't the look he'd given me in the mirror earlier, and it wasn't the look he'd given Water Girl. No, that was a different look: one of longing, warmth, tenderness and, dear God, *love*. The expression transformed his countenance to an extent where no one would ever believe an arsehole existed behind that face.

No, no, no, no, no!

I thought...I thought he wasn't attracted to blonds. My hair, my lovely blonde hair, I dyed it raven black for this dude! Have kept it raven ever since. So much so, that not many people didn't know I was actually blonde and not raven-haired. Most people thought raven was my real hair colour. Now he was dating, and possibly in love with, a blond?

God, I wanted to kill myself. Such an idiot. When would

I regain my senses? I needed him to give me back all he'd fucking stolen from me—my heart, my brain, my common sense, my strength—so I could move on living my fabulous life of being rich and famous, and stop dogging around over some dude who'll probably never notice me.

Gaining a bit of resolve, I marched towards them, making no effort to conceal my irritation as I narrowed my eyes on Little Miss Blondie. I planned on being a complete bitch, I did well at that sometimes, but before I could get a snarky word out, Jahleel asked, "Ready to go again? Or do you have another pack of cigarettes you got to empty?"

Dragging my glower from Little Miss Blondie, I looked at him and my resolve shattered into smithereens as another piece of my heart chipped off and floated towards him. He was wet with sweat as if he'd been dancing during my extended smoking break, and strands of his hidden hair peeped out of his beanie.

God, he was so much, so amazing, so wanted, *needed,* so desired. By me.

In the midst of my lusting, I noted something had changed in his eyes and in his voice when he asked me that question; it made me prefer the arsehole part of him more than this part. I couldn't quite put my finger on it, but he seemed bitter, irritated, and inexplicably pissed—maybe at me or at himself, I couldn't tell.

Inhaling deeply, I contemplated asking him what I did wrong, why he hated me, and why did he have to be such a jerk, but I exhaled on a sigh, and instead said, "Nah. Done for the day."

He stared back at me with such unhidden hostility, that I half expected him to blast me with a big ole 'get the fuck out!'

Unable to sustain his glare further, I slid my gaze to Little Miss Blonde. "You must be JK's girlfriend, yeah?"

"No," she laughed cordially. "I'm Krissy."

I've never felt so relieved in my entire life, but I didn't let it show. I wanted to hug, kiss and give this girl a million pounds just for not being JK's girlfriend. However, Jahleel obviously had feelings for her, which meant she was still a threat. "And Krissy is...?"

Krissy opened her mouth to answer but Jahleel jumped in with more douchebaggery than before. "Krissy's just Krissy." Arching a caustic brow at me, he bit out, "You weren't clear just now. You're done smokin' for the day, or you're done practicin'? Which?"

If he were anyone else, I would've told him to fuck off eons ago, find something to sue him for, lie on him and screw his career over because he had, honest to God, begun to piss me off. But I was a glutton for pain, so I did neither.

Though I did manage to *hiss* out, "Both."

The *hiss* made him smile; it was the first sign of irritation I'd showed all day. As if satisfied that he'd provoked me, Jahleel said nothing in response, and an awkward silence hung around the three of us, while his eyes studied my face making me all the more self-conscious.

Shoving my hands in the back pockets of my jeans, I contemplated just turning and leaving, seeing that I'd just declared I was done for the day.

I wanted to go, but I wanted to stay. I hated Jahleel's hostility towards me and had an urge to run, but hostility was better than being ignored…so I longed for more.

I was more frustrated with myself than before I came here. Even when he was being a douchebag, I craved more of him. So, instead of walking out, I grappled for a lie to extend my time.

Casting a glance over my shoulder, I checked to see if my mates were still in drool mode. They were. Perfect. I turned back at Jahleel. "Ma' mates back there…say they've heard about ya' and want to see ya'…dance."

Jahleel's smirk deepened, almost resembling a smile. He knew I was lying, but he wasn't calling me out on it.

Remaining purposely staid, I stared back as though I were telling the dead truth. He finally shrugged and tossed over his shoulder, "Jason Derulo's *Breathing*."

Unbelievable, he was *actually* going to do it. Even though he knew it was a lie, that *I* was the one who wanted to see him dance, he was still going to do it. In all honesty, I didn't expect him to. This dude was unreadable as words written in water. He fucking confused me.

Walking backwards, he hauled his T-shirt over his head and tossed it at Krissy, flashing a crooked grin at her. Except for when Jahleel laughed at my dancing, his smile was a rare occurrence, I noticed. But I understood why.

Grins such as his could cause fatal heart attacks in women. A combination of extreme sexiness, extreme arrogance, extreme flirtatiousness, extreme taunting…it was just a truckload of extremes. To simplify, his rare but mesmerizing grin could cause serious heart damage in weaklings, like me, if flashed too often.

Out of the corner of my eye, I saw Krissy grin back at him. I needed to get to know this girl, to determine if the feelings between her and Jahleel were mutual. I also had to figure out my level of competition, and at the same time, pump Krissy for information to use to my advantage.

With that thought, I looped my hand through hers like a bloody pre-teen and dragged her off in the other direction of the room.

She froze up, seemingly surprised by my gesture, but I pretended not to notice.

Jahleel started dancing, and I knew I should be looking at Krissy instead of him when I asked her, "You two close, yeah?", but I couldn't pull my eyes away from a dancing Jahleel. The fluidity, the sexiness...Jesus...

"Yep. We live together."

Live together? That sure as hell got me to snap my gaze to her. "I thought you said—"

She cut me off by holding a hand up and smiling, her plump lips as red as raspberries made her smile a dazzling white. I hated how pretty and exotic she was. "We're, um...His parents adopted me when I was young."

"Oh." For the second time that day, I felt a relief so strong, even my joints relaxed. "So you're brother and sister. Why didn't he just say that?"

With a slight wince, she placed a hand on my shoulder and warned, "Word of advice: if you don't wanna get on his wrong side, don't refer to us as brother and sister."

What? "Why?"

All she offered was a shrug.

Well, that's not weird at all, I thought sardonically. Unless the love I saw in his eyes earlier wasn't love for a sister. He must want her to be more to him. But judging how casual she was about him, the feeling was most certainly unilateral. To her, he was just her brother. Maybe to him, she was his fantasy.

Sucking in my cheeks, lost in thought, I decided then and there to find a way to get him to transfer that love over to *me*. Make *me* his fantasy.

I had work to do.

I turned my attention back to Jahleel who was glistening with sweat as he danced with undiluted passion, as if nothing else in the world mattered but how well he moved to the beat of the music.

His well-defined abs contracted and released with every move, his bottom lip captured between his teeth. The way he moved his hips, those feet, the way rivulets of sweat trailed along the wicked tattoo covering his whole left side from arm-pit to hipbone, the way the big bold 'KINGSTON' across his upper back rippled with each flex of his arms… He is lethal. My attraction to him is definitely fatal. And I wanted him so bad it pained to even look at him.

I chatted some more with Krissy until the song ended and Jahleel made his way over. He halted in front of us and nabbed his T-shirt from Krissy, wiping the sweat from his face. Looking at me, he winked—fucking winked—as he said, "Why don't you go find out what your *friends* think of that performance?"

I. Wanted. To. Scream.

Glowering up at him, I clenched and unclenched my fists, and before I let my mouth say something I'd regret, I flounced off.

Thomas pushed open the door for me as I got up to it, and right before I went through, I cast a quick glance over my shoulder and my eyes unexpectedly locked with Jahleel's. He, too, was looking over his shoulder, straight at me, his beanie off and one hand raking through his hair, looking as exhausted and defeated as I felt.

His golden gaze left mine as his eyes made a swift sweep down my body, before snapping back to my face with unconcealed frustration. With a slight shake of his head, he turned back to Krissy.

Resigned to the failure of the day, I proceeded out the door and out of the building. As soon as I was back in the vehicle with Amanda and Ferbie, I dipped in my back pocket for my cigarettes, only to find the damn box empty.

Mad at the whole frigging world, I punched the headrest in front of me. Amanda pursed her lips and sagely kept her mouth shut as I punched the headrest again and again.

"Aye, Ma," Ferbie strived to calm me by reaching over Amanda to rest a warm palm on my knee.

The loving innocence in his eyes was enough to soothe

me. I loved my brother so much that sometimes I wish there was something, *anything* I could do to make him normal.

Just as Ben began backing the vehicle out of the lot, Jahleel walked out of the studio shirtless, his white tee tossed around his neck. He had one arm around Krissy's shoulders as he talked animatedly to her.

His mouth stopped moving when he spotted Amy and Jamie getting ready to leave behind us. By then, Ben spun the Jeep around and started crawling off the complex with two other vehicles ahead of us. I quickly twisted around in my seat to look out the back window at what was happening.

Jahleel said something to Krissy, then jogged over to Amy and Jamie's convertible—who I suspected were dawdling in the lot because they saw him exit the building. He leaned on Jamie's side of the car and twirled a lock of her auburn hair around his finger, whispering something in her ear. And the bitch giggled like a fucking moppet. I wanted to kill her.

Our vehicle pulled farther and farther away as we drove off the complex. We turned onto the main road, and I could no longer see them.

"Should I dare ask why you're doing this to yourself, mate?" Amanda asked. "Take this however you want, Kia, but this, it's *sad*. And pathetic."

I ignored her words. "Text her. Ask her what he wanted."

"Are you a bloody masochist?"

"Just fucking ask her!" I snapped.

"Sod off! I'm not your fucking bitch, Kia!" Amanda snapped back. "You want me to ask her, ask me *kindly,* dammit!"

Remembering she was a leader and not a follower, a domme and not a sub, a best friend and not an assistant, I turned and flung my arms around her, hugging her tight. "I apologize. I love you. No, you're not my bitch. You're my only friend and I love you. And even when people choose me over you, like what happened with Chad, you don't get jealous and go talking crap behind my back. No, you love me anyways, because that's what friends do, yeah? You're genuine, authentic and I won't ever take you for granted. I love you. I'm sorry for yelling at you."

Amanda seemed taken aback, both by the sudden hug attack and the long-winded apology. I never talk this much and she knew it, so she understood I was being real.

"It's okay, Kia. I love you, too. Apology accepted," she said, hugging me back.

Pulling away, I asked politely, "Now, can you please ask Jamie what JK wanted?"

With a roll of her eyes, Amanda pulled out her cellphone and sent the text message. Seconds later, the phone chirped and she showed me the screen:

Wut d hell do u think he wanted?
Psshh.
Am fucking him 2nite if that answers ur question :)
He's HOT!!
With 3 smoking Ts!!

"Slut," I mumbled as I shoved the phone back at Amanda.

"Maybe you should tell her," she suggested. "I'm sure she wouldn't shag him if she knew you liked him. They're bad but not *that* bad, Kia. You need to give them a little more credit. They've been by your side since you came here, and that spells loyalty."

"No. I don't like them enough to trust them. Let her have her time with him. JK's mine, he just doesn't know it yet. He's my destiny."

"God," she laughed as she shook her head, "I've never known the meaning of obsession until now."

Amanda's phone chirped again. She read it and showed me the screen.

Oh, he also asked 4 Ferbie's #.
(Only God knows Y he'd want 2make frenz with that dumbo.)
*DON'T tell Kia I said that! *giggles**

66

*I told him Kia's very protective of him so he gave me his
card 2give him.*

*But we're going 2 Pizza Hut with him & his sis now,
(sweet!) so we'll catch up with u guys later.*

X

Amanda laughed. "Don't hate me for saying this, but I
think it's the weirdest thing that the only person he made a
connection with in the room is Ferbie. That's something epic
right there."

Though I usually would, I didn't take offense to it, because for the first time in my life, I was jealous of my brother.
When I'd gone outside for my long smoke break after Chad's
visit, apparently Jahleel and Ferbie had 'bonded' through dancing. I was still trying to wrap my head around it. "It seems
Ferbie's better at taking instructions than I am. I didn't even
know the sod could dance."

Ferbie, hearing his name, pulled his gaze away from the
window and remarked, "Aye. JK's real cool, no? I'm thinking
about taking some lessons. What do you think, Ma?"

"I think it's great," I told him. "I'm glad you've found
something you like."

He smiled contentedly and looked back out the window.

Amanda's fingers drummed across her knee and I knew
she wanted to say something but was biting her tongue.

"Manda, what is it?"

She gave me a hesitant look before she queried, "Why not Chad instead of JK? I mean, yeah, JK's like a million times hotter than Chad, but he's a bloody wanker. Now, Chad, you can just feel sexual healing oozing out of him. I swear the room heated up when he walked in. Whew...Plus, he fancies you and he wasn't afraid to show it. I, for one, was bowled over with the way he came on to you at full force without even an hint of uncertainty, knowing you are, well, *you,* and that your guards could've drop-kicked him in a millisecond. He just put it all out there, no beating around the bush, you know." She sighed dreamily. "Swear it, I've never been so turned on in my life. If he had asked me to shag him right there in front of everyone, I would've done it without a thought."

"That was more than obvious, Manda," I agreed, laughing. "I *was* turned on by him, too. Jumping in ma' knickers enough that I probably *would* let him shag me...if he asked politely."

We both cackled.

"But that's all it was. Just sexual. I was turned on by him, and that's where it ended. With JK, it's...different. I don't know how to explain it, but it's like...just being near him sucks away bits and pieces of me, and those bits and pieces *stay* in his possession. He doesn't just make my nostrils flare. No. He makes me breathless, senseless, scatter-brained. He makes me want, he makes me need, he makes me crave, he makes me desire, dream, drenched. He dominates my mind, my emotions, every part of me...only by existing."

Amanda watched me with a concerned expression, and I knew she didn't understand. She never would. No one would. That's the main reason I never talked about it, because people would just think I'm losing it. They would question why someone in my position would bother chasing after some guy who isn't even on my level.

But I fell in love with him before I reached this level. And even reaching this level, my feelings for him waxed instead of waned.

Turning from Amanda's concerned eyes, I looked out the window. "I do wish it wasn't like this. I do wish there was something I could do to make this obsession go away. But...I can't. I've tried and I've failed. Numerous times." Sighing, I let the side of my head rest on the window. "I'm subservient to him. Bound and ensnared. Captured and captivated. Taken and held. It is what it is: Jahleel Kingston *owns* me, and he doesn't even know it."

Chapter 5

ON A GRUNT of pure frustration, I withdrew my hand from my knickers. Not quite sure how it worked for most people, but self-induced pleasure usually sucked for me. Very rarely do I ever manage to get myself there. I'd created a dozen different scenes in my head, which would work for about a minute, then all of a sudden, the scene just melted and the sensation disappeared. Fuck it.

Last time I got laid was over a year ago, not since my last break-up with Oscar holding actor Rick Reese—hot, sexy heartthrob, small dick, undue arrogance, and useless billions that couldn't buy him another inch to his useless dick.

Of the few rich and famous I'd been set up with, none had

been able to satisfy me enough to keep me. But then, *I* couldn't even satisfy me. So, I guess the problem was me then, yeah? I wouldn't be able to give anyone a chance until Jahleel Kingston gave me one.

To check the time, I glanced over at the alarm clock on the nightstand. Minutes to eight. Today wouldn't be as flexible as yesterday was. Yesterday I had time to dally with, but today I had a radio interview at eleven, a charity event appearance at one, two-hour training at Kingston's Dance Studios, then studio time to start working on my new album.

My cellphone buzzed on the nightstand, and I contemplated telling the world a big ole 'fuck you.' Sometimes I wished I could just lock up and hide like a vampire until I felt ready for the light.

Alas, I was Saskia Day.

Reaching over for the phone on the nightstand, I checked the screen. Timberly. *Oh dear.*

Curious nerd that Timberly was, she and a couple of her other nerd friends took some time off from college to conduct their own modern-day voyage, to see every crevice and corner of the world. That Christopher Columbus kind of thing.

I was against her going because, well, whenever she got back—*if* she got back without dying from some disease like malaria, or falling off a giraffe's neck, being trampled by elephants, falling off a kayak and being eaten by piranhas, or getting captured by some extinct caveman, etcetera etcetera—then she would talk three times as much as she talked before. Which was *a lot*—never-ending. No joke.

"Hey, Timber."

"Hi, Ma!" she twittered on the line, ever gleeful.

"How's it going?"

"Great! I know I haven't rung you in a while but it's just that I've been so caught up in this experience. I just settled in with ma' mates to nab a kip and thought I'd ring you to let you know I love you and miss you. And Ferbie. Oh, and Lydia!"

"Ah, we miss you, too, Timber. Especially Ferbie," I told her, my heart warming. "Where in the world are you now, by the way?" I winced after asking that question, realizing it was a catalyst to a ceaseless conversation.

"Oh, Hungary. It's awesome here, Ma. I wish you could be here with us!"

"Glad to know tha—" I started to say, but Chatty Timber's fur had just been stroked.

"Did you know it's one of the oldest countries in Europe?"

I didn't get a chance to answer since her questions were usually rhetorical, as she just blabbered on, answering her own questions. "Yes, yes, it is! Founded in 896 even before France and Germany were found and separated. And in around 1000

C.E, they were also the largest kingdom, bigger than France! And the language they speak is so ace, Ma! It's called Magyar. *Mag-yahr.*" She pronounced, as if I were a high school student who gave a crap. "It was derived from the language spoken by the Huns. And did you know the Rubiks cube was invented by a Hungarian?"

By this time, I was rubbing my forehead, feeling a headache approaching. Why did I answer the phone?

"Yes, yes it was! Invented by Erno Rubik..." —A beep sounded over her chatting, and I pulled the phone from my ear to check the screen. Stacey, my assistant. Saved by the beep.—"...and did you know Hungarians also invented ballpoint pens—"

"Timber, I gotta go," I said, cutting her off. "Work calls. Love you!"

Unable to take another syllable from her, I clicked her off and connected Stacey's call. "Stace. Shoot."

"Hello, Saskia. Good morning," she answered, ever polite. "Two things, Lion T'mar asks that you phone him. He says he knows you are purposely avoiding his calls, but he's not calling for what you think."

I winced. True, I was avoiding Lion's calls because he had the uncanny ability to tell when I was lying. He would know instantly that I went to see Jahleel even though he advised me not to.

"What else?"

"Jahleel Kingston's assistant called an hour ago to apprise you that payments for his services have been refunded, as your hire has been cancelled."

No. Not again!

"Did he say why?" I barely got the question out.

"Just that he doesn't think he's suitable to assist you. He did, however, provide a list of recommendations. I will email it to you in a bit."

I goddamn hated him for making me feel dysfunctional and incapable of sanity and completeness. "That all?"

"Yes."

I disconnected the call. Biting hard on my lip until I drew blood, I reared back and hurled the phone across the room, and watched it bust into pieces.

I fucking *hated* Jahleel Kingston!

AT 3:05PM, AMANDA, Ferbie, Thomas and I strolled into KnockBack Recording Studios. As it was, Amy and Jamie seemed to know my schedule better than I did; Amanda

informed me they were already at the studio waiting for us. With the knowledge of Jahleel shagging one of them the night before he cancelled on me, I wasn't in the mood to see those two.

Why didn't I just give them the boot if I hated them so much, you ask? Because I didn't *hate* them, hate them. I just didn't particularly like them. They were ace companions at times, but more often than not, they annoyed the bejesus out of me. Plus the problem might've just been *me*. Because I had issues. Issues unfathomable even to me. Let's just leave it at that.

Why punish them for loving me?

Ferbie's phone rang as we shuffled into the lift, and my eyebrows shot up in surprise because, well, no one really called Ferbie unless it was me, Lydia or Timberly. He had zero friends, zero associates, zero girlfriends, along with his zero senses. In spite of that, he was quite content with his life, but he was content because I was sure he didn't know any better. Maybe I should've been a little bit easier on him and let him go out on his own sometimes, but I was too afraid of ending up having to murder someone for fucking with my impeded brother.

"Aye," he answered. He listened and his grin broadened. "Ah, ah, life's good...I'm heading to the studio with Ma...No, my sister, Kia...Now?...Why, of course!...okay then. See you."

By the time Ferbie hung up, everyone was staring at him, gobsmacked.

"That was JK," he said to me. "He wants me to stop by his studio to test my dancing skills more. He thinks I got talent, yeah?"

Amanda slowly turned her head to look at me and cleared her throat, but stayed quiet.

"Do you like to dance?" I asked him.

Ferbie frowned and looked perplexed as he answered, "You know I've always liked dancing, Ma."

The hell? Since when?

Not wanting to offend him, I asked, "And you want to practice with *JK*? He cancelled on me, you know."

Ferbie suddenly looked frustrated, which shocked me even more. This guy rarely showed any expression of emotion except for a giddy grin.

"So what, Ma? He dumps you, he wants me. Yes, I want to go because..." He paused and stuffed his hands in his coat pockets, turning away from me with a solemn look on his face. "He makes me feel normal. He doesn't see in me what every-one else sees. He sees talent and purpose and worth. And if that makes someone an arsehole, then, aye, I would love to be an arsehole, too."

Amanda's eyes met mine, wide as saucers. Two chats with Grade-A arsehole Jahleel Kingston and now, all of a sudden, he could verbalize his feelings? I'd never heard him speak so sensibly before. Was he just playing fool before or what?

"Okay, you may go," I reluctantly agreed. To Thomas, "You, go with him. And if anyone so much as breathes too harshly in his face, knock them the fuck out and bring my brother home."

"Sure, Miss Day," Thomas nodded in acknowledgment as the lift doors opened. "Would you like me to summon Ben here in case we're not back before you leave?"

"Ah yes, yes."

I turned and hugged Ferbie, letting him know I loved him before stepping off the lift with Amanda, leaving him and Thomas behind. As the doors closed, I sucked in a panicky breath, wanting to call for him to come back, but Amanda touched my arm and assured, "He's twenty-eight years old, Kia. He might not be as much of a plonker as we think."

"I'm just afraid people will mess with him. I don't want anyone making him feel less of himself."

"And JK is obviously doing the opposite of that. So I guess you can trust him, yeah?"

Then I was angry all over again, Ferbie forgotten. "Don't

even say that wanker's name," I hissed and marched off down the hall to the studio door.

Amanda laughed behind me as I opened the door. "Yesterday you loved him, today you loathe him. I'm having a hard time keeping up."

Chillingly cold air-conditioning attacked us as we stepped into the room. Large, luxurious, and designed to make people like me feel as though we weren't being worked to death when 3am strolls around and we're screaming our lungs out in the sound room, but to make us feel as though we were enjoying the finer things in life.

There was a big black leather couch against the wall where Amy and Jamie were sprawled, giggling and blabbing. A bean-shaped glass table was in front of it with an ice-bucket, highball glasses, two bottles of Grey Goose Vodka and four bottles of cranberry juice. They could drink as much as they wanted, I couldn't.

Greg, my music producer, a 250pound, bald-headed hothead, pushed himself up from behind the mixing board and came over to hug me. "Sup, Kia?"

"Nada. Sorry I'm late. I'll be ready in a min, okay?"

Greg nodded quickly as if it were no big deal that I was late, even though we both knew it was plenty big deal. Studio time was precious, not to be wasted. "Sure. Do yo' thing."

I heard a giggle with the name 'JK' entangled in it come from the area of big leather couch. The masochist in me propelled me in that direction and I plopped down beside the two giggly gals. "So..." I tossed my feet up on the table and leaned back, "How was last night?"

"Energetic," Amy giggled.

Jamie rolled her eyes, seemingly annoyed with her giggling partner. "It was rad. JK took us to the G2K girls' concert, and it was awesome. He choreographed all their performances, and they tore the house down."

After hearing that, I began to feel a heck of a lot better. "That's it?" I looked at Jamie, "You didn't bother shagging him?"

Amanda cleared her throat and leaned forward to pour herself a drink. It was her way of telling me to stop inflicting pain on myself.

"Of course she did," Amy sing-songed in a 'Silly-Rabbit-Trixx-Are-For-Kids' tone.

"*We* did," Jamie ground out.

"So, both of you...?"

"Yeah," Amy piped up. "We got wasted, he took us back to Jamie's place and we banged until the sun came up. Dick? *Huge*. Ohmigod, I want more!"

"Well, you're not getting 'more'," Jamie snapped. "It was

S. ANN COLE

supposed to be just me, not me *and* you."

This was hilarious. And painful. "So, how did you *and* her happen?"

Jamie pointed an angry thumb at her friend. "*She* was trying to get Chad to fuck her. But he wasn't interested. JK explained Chad's pretty selective when it comes to his women—he's hot, but he only beds those he feels chemistry with. Unfortunately, there was no chemistry with this bitch, so she felt the need to sandwich herself between me and JK."

Amy flipped up her 'whatever' hand. "Why wouldn't I? He was more than willing."

Her eyes narrowed at Jamie as if remembering something, then she pointed at her and started laughing. "I forgot this drama: the lead singer of G2K got up in this one's face when JK wasn't around and demanded to know if he was fucking her."

"Lead singer Tiara?" I asked. "He's with her?"

Jamie shrugged. "Seems so. She was all catty and possessive and shit."

Tiara was a good associate of mine. She was flawlessly beautiful. Now I hated *her*.

Jamie and Amy started talking about the G2K concert, but I wasn't listening anymore. Dropping my head back on the couch, I blew out a puff of breath. I was obsessed with a man

80

who was a major arse and a shameless womanizer. And even with that rep, he still didn't want *me*.

Amanda leaned over and whispered in my ear, vodka strong on her breath, "Chad."

I turned to her. "What?"

"You're in love with the wrong one. Chad's the one for you. Not JK."

"Forget both of them," I dropped my feet off the table and stood up. "I'm Saskia fucking Day."

IT WAS 2:37 in the morning when we returned from the studio. Amanda wearily made a beeline for her bedroom, but before I could do the same, I had to take care of my throat. I really worked it in the studio and knew it would be hoarse in the morning if I didn't take precautions now. I headed to the kitchen to mix a concoction of honey and lemon juice—pre-medication.

My cellphone hollered from within the depths of my messenger bag, and I sighed. Only one person would ring me at this hour. Setting my cup down on the kitchen counter, I retrieved my cellphone and answered, "Lion."

"Why the fuck you been avoidin' my calls?"

"I've got a life to live, you know?" I smarted, releasing the phone and keeping it to my ear with my shoulder so I could grab the honey jar.

"And *I'm* a significant part of said life! The one who makes *your* life happen," he snapped. "Two calls you never send to voicemail: mine and Lydia's. We should never have to talk to your assistant. It's just *us*, you ain't got no one else. Always 'member that, Kia."

I knew that, and I never forgot it. It's just that Lion had become such an avuncular figure in my life, I had a hard time being dishonest with him. He could see right through me with this eye that could tell counterfeit from authentic. No man is an island. Everyone in life needs support, and Lydia and Lion were my rocks that would forever be there and never erode. I needed them just as Timberly and Ferbie needed me.

"My head wasn't in the right place, okay?"

Lion made a noise between a grunt and a chuckle, "Went by his studio, didn't you?"

"Yes," I confessed as I stirred the honey and lemon juice, trying to get them to blend together.

Lemon and honey usually took a good, determined whisking for the two to come together as one. Honey was thick and stubborn, wanting to flow at its own slow pace, in its own form, while lemon juice was without form, ready and willing to be used however one pleases—submissive. The sweet flavour coming together with sour, two complete opposites. But when the two coalesce, the ultimate taste was one that could never be replicated, not with any other ingredients. Because only extremely sweet, mixed with extremely sour gave that inimitable taste. Together, they provided a powerful healing.

"Judgin' by your tone, I'll take a wild guess that JK was his usual self."

"He cancelled on me."

"And he hasn't fucked you yet?" He sounded shocked. "That's...kinda off pattern for JK."

"Yeah, well, he shagged Amy and Jamie."

Lion laughed out. "Those two..."

Then he spoke so quietly, I believed it was a thought spoken out loud, not meant for me to hear. "He's still afraid..."

I stopped mixing. "What? What does that mean?"

"Look, I didn't call you to talk about JK. Wanna chit chat about your five-year obsession, do that with Manda. I called to let you know I'm comin' to SF tomorrow. Apparently the G2K girls' concert was through the roof. So their record label is throwin' a celebratory party. Not red carpet, I know you hate those. But just by invite, and we're caught up in the mix."

"Boo! Who cares?"

With the new knowledge that the lead singer of the group, Tiara, was shagging Jahleel, I no longer cared about the G2K girls.

"I don't really care either, Kia. But they're on the top right now, and these are the invite-only's where we *should* show up, if nowhere else. Smilin' and congratulatin' like we give a shit. You're a Brit, Kia. Always 'member that. These fuckers can turn on you in a second for no reason. You gotta work twice as hard as anyone else to keep yourself up there. So put on one of your kickass outfits, slap a smile on your face, and be ready by eight tomorrow night."

"Okay. Whatever."

I pressed off the call and looked down at my sweet and sour coalition.

If only…

Bringing the cup to my lips, I drank it all down, my lips puckering at the taste.

The inimitable concoction that could heal a throat that wasn't even sore yet.

Chapter 6

THERE WERE A heck lot of invitees at the so-called 'invite-only' celebratory party when my usual party crew and I arrived: Lion, his big butt girlfriend Twana, Amanda and Ferbie. Neither of the giggly twats were welcome.

The venue was on the rooftop of Viscas Hotel and was surprisingly ace for being planned in haste after the concert's success. How they managed to get this many celebrities to fly in from wherever to SF on such short notice was beyond me. Unless this was covertly planned before, with optimistic hopes that the concert would be a success—another step to push the G2K girls higher in their fast climb to stardom. Their record label was real shrewd.

As usual, we arrived late, so the party was pumping when we arrived. All-white decor, high-tables and cushy stools, illusory purple flames flickering in large clear vases, potted palm trees in corners, purple cushions and purple psychedelic lights glowed on everyone. Lots of chattering, congratulations and it's-good-to-see-you's behind fake smiles, the usual.

For this event, I got dressed in skin-tight high-waist black jeans, a black bustier bra cropped just below my C-cups to show off my *'Fuck D' Werl'* tattoo on my left side, a studded black leather jacket, and black thigh highs—yes, *heels*. Ugh. Six goddamn inches, too. Curse my stylist.

My hair, of course, was its usual mess of wild raven curls.

Tired of smiling and engaging in meaningless conversation with people fawning over my accent, or how "rad" and "badass" my outfit was, or how much they liked my hair, blah blah blah, I left Lion in the midst of the all the mindless blabbering and found myself an empty table and a stool.

Hating these pretensions as much as I did, Amanda was there with me in the next minute, plopping down on a stool, sipping a *Nuvo* straight from the bottle as I was. Ferbie had disappeared somewhere, but I knew he was safe here.

Even though we were *in* this lifestyle, we weren't exactly *of* it.

We were more laid-back people who'd rather get loose

with a handful of people we knew and were comfortable with, preferably within the confinements of our home. I attended red carpet events because I *had* to. But parties, such as this one, usually took a lot of convincing on my manager's part.

"Ugh. Lawd," I grunted when I spotted Tiara making a beeline to our table.

Tiara Minott—nigh six feet tall in heels. Long, platinum-blonde hair with not a strand out of place. Big, bright blue eyes, and an impeccably white, L.A. girl smile.

In a sparkly silver dress that stopped mid-thighs, showing off her toned, tanned long legs, she was stunning. I used to love how impeccable she was, and I never went without complimenting her. Now, I wouldn't, because she'd given me reason envy to her.

She had what I wanted. Craved.

Laughing into her drink, Amanda mumbled, "What did the poor girl do to you? Except sleep with a man who's *not,* I repeat, *not* into you? Don't be mean to her, Kia. Tiara adores you."

"Blah."

Tiara approached with her blinding smile. "Saskia, you came!"

My manager forced me. "Wouldn't have missed this for the world, Tiara. I heard the concert was a bang, yeah?

87

Congrats!"

She swung her arms around me and hugged me tight. "Awe, thanks. Never in a million years… It feels *so* good to be this high."

Don't flatter yourself, it was only a concert. The real, stressing work is yet to begin. "I know right? You girls are fucking incandescent. No worries, it only gets better, trust me."

She pulled from the embrace, grinned at me then drew me in for another tight hug. "I so totally adore you. You're awesome, Saskia."

Amanda cleared her throat, and I knew she was laughing at my expense, but Tiara took it differently, thinking Amanda felt neglected.

Turning to her, Tiara gave her a hug, too. "Amanda, I'm so sorry!"

"Not a problem," Amanda squeaked.

"*Love* your new haircut, by the way," she complimented.

"Thanks!" she squeaked again, peering over Tiara's shoulder. I wondered why in the world she kept squeaking. It was so unlike her.

A passer-by stopped and touched Tiara, congratulating her. Amanda took the opportunity to lean over to me, whispering, "Twelve o'clock. Ohmi*fucking*god…"

Glancing in the direction she indicated, my gaze immediately clashed with Chad's. In all-black again, he was rather casual for the event, in close-fitted jeans, plain V-neck tee, and a cross pendant chain around his neck. His hair a wild, wild, but sexy mess.

Bloody hell, he was scrumptious.

One elbow on the counter, feet crossed at the ankles, he was leaning against the circular stainless-steel bar right across from where we sat. He kept his head down, creating the illusion he was looking into the brandy snifter in his hand, but his eyes were raised and staring straight at me.

"Shite," I whispered. "What's he doing here?"

Before she could answer, Tiara spun back around from her conversation, caught us staring and followed our gazes. "Chad," she breathed. "Freakin' hot, isn't he? Don't bother looking, though. He's a hard one to catch. *Way* too picky."

Now, this, *this* irritated me. Turning to her, I tried not to sound acerbic, "Heard you're with his best friend, yeah?"

"JK," she whispered to herself, almost like a prayer. Then she spat, "He's an asshole. Fucks around. Total commitment-phobe."

Taking a deep breath, she blinked rapidly, looking upwards as if fighting to hold back tears. "Excuse me," she croaked out, then turned and broke into a jog, disappearing through the crowd. No doubt about to go lock herself in a bathroom to bawl her eyes out.

"Soooo glad I'm over that dude."

Amanda scoffed. "Yeah, right."

Tossing my hair over my shoulder, I said, "I'll prove it", then slid off the stool and started over towards Chad, leaving Amanda with an amused smirk on her face.

Chad kept his eyes on me as I sashayed over to the bar, pulled up a stool next to him and sat with one leg crossed over the other, hip provocatively jutted out. The ole flirt pose.

Chad watched me with a slightly raised brow, gaze traveling from my legs straight up, landing dead on my face. Bringing his snifter of amber liquid to his lips, he took a slow sip, peering over the rim. Then, lowering the glass, he licked his lower lip and asked, "You came over here to flirt with me, Saskia?"

Tossing my hair again—which was so unlike me, by the way—I peered at him from under my lashes. "Maybe."

With a slight shake of his head, he made a disappointed sound and turned his gaze from me, out to the crowd. "You might wanna go back over there, then, because I hate women who flirt."

Splat. I felt as if he just took my head and shoved it into a pile of cow dodo. "What?"

Turning to face me, he dipped one long finger into his drink and absentmindedly began circling it, the cubes of ice clinking against the glass. And I imagined that one long, *wet* finger moving in that same circular movement over my clitoris...

"Flirting is an act," he said, breaking through my inappropriate thoughts. "It's not real. I'm attracted to *real*. Very attracted to women who keep their mouths shut and allow me to read what they want on their faces, in their eyes. Because that's where the truth lies."

Removing his wet finger from the glass, he slipped it in his mouth and sucked it off as if it was nothing. As if women who were watching from afar wouldn't faint at the mere act, wishing it was their finger between those shapely lips. Did he have *any* idea how hot he was?

"I thought you were real, Saskia," he continued in that disillusioned tone. "Guess I misread. Sorry."

He turned and redirected his attention out to the crowd, as if dismissing me.

The hell? Did he not realize who I was? "You're saying I'm fake?"

He took a sip of his drink, and replied without looking at me, "Now? Yeah." Tilting his head to the side, he angled it to look at me without turning his body, seemingly annoyed and

a little ticked. "This," he motioned a hand to indicate my provocative pose, "is being done to prove a point."

Turning back to me fully now, he took a step forward and
leaned into me. "I do a lot of things, Saskia, but playing games
is not one of them." Jerking his head to the left, he said quietly,
"Maybe *that's* where you really want to be?"

I looked to my left where he indicated, and my breath
hitched audibly. It was *this* feeling—this breath-stealing,
mind-numbing, tongue-tied feeling that I *always* got whenever
I saw him that made it damn well impossible for me to get over
him.

I couldn't.

I just couldn't.

At a mere glimpse of him, my heartbeat sped off on a wild
race beneath my rib cage. This was fucking ridiculous!

Why? Why? Why did I crave him this much?

Casual in faded jeans, Timberlands, and a red T-shirt with
a black skull face on the front, he was sitting on an ottoman
across from Ferbie, engaged in deep conversation, hand movements and all. The strangest sight. Who the hell held deep conversations with *Ferbie*?

When he set his drink down on the table between them
and proceeded to move his wrist in some weird circular movement that Ferbie mimicked, I deduced they were talking about

dancing.

"I'm not sure why you'd think tha—" I turned my head back around to see that Chad had vanished. Like smoke.

Jesus, I suck.

Amanda was by my side at the bar in the next minute. "So?"

"He's just as much of a wanker as JK," I groused bitterly.

"What did he say?"

"That I'm fake."

Bursting into laughter, Amanda shook her head. "Christ, Kia, you suck. Big time. How'd you manage to piss off a guy who's so obviously into you, in less than five minutes?"

"I barely got a sentence out!" I complained, wanting to laugh at the absurdity of it. "That man's got bloody issues."

Amanda laughed again and knocked her knuckles on the bar to get the bartender's attention. "Two shots of Coffee Patrón, please."

"Make that a double for me," I added, and the bartender nodded.

Arching a brow, my best friend inquired, "What's up with you tonight?"

"JK," I grimaced, I inclined my head to the left. "I'm going over to talk to him. Maybe facing him with friendly expectations will help me get over him."

"So, you *weren't* over him before, then?" Amanda teased as the bartender placed the shots down for us.

I knocked back the first shot without a wince. "Just shut the hell up." Down went the second one before I slid off the stool and said, "Wish me luck with this one."

I wove through the throngs of people, forcing a smile each time someone stopped me with some kind of gibberish. This made the short journey from the bar to Jahleel a ten-minute trip.

Jahleel and Ferbie maintained their deep discussion as I approached, until Ferbie looked up and saw me. "Aye, Ma. You ready already?"

Jahleel glanced up, and down my body his eyes roved. Then...there it was, the look he had when I walked into his studio the other day. That lustful look: where he sank his teeth down on his full, desirable lower lip and blatantly stared. But just as soon as it appeared, it left as he slapped on a polite smile.

Gah! That wasn't the smile I wanted! I wanted the sexy, crooked smile he flashes at the women he sets his sights on.

"No, no," I waved my hand, "I just came over to say 'hi' to your new mate."

"Ah," Ferbie stood up. "I've got to use the loo. I'll leave you two at it, yeah?"

As Ferbie vacated, I took his seat.

Tossing my clutch on the table, I leaned forward toward the ottoman with my legs apart, elbows resting on my thighs.

Jahleel reached forward for his drink and brought up it to his lips, but I noticed the corners of his lips twitched.

That's when it registered, and I looked down to take in my far too comfortable sitting position, like a guy. For a moment, I'd forgotten I was at an all-eyes-on-you function. But truth be told, this was the real me. It's how I usually sat, or with my legs tossed on whatever piece of furniture was in front of me. Lion hated it, and never ceased to reprimand me for it. The provocative leg-crossed-over-the-knee thing isn't me. Not surprising Chad saw straight through me. Because I *was* being fake; flirting only to prove a point to Amanda.

But it was too late to act coy now. Jahleel would just be all the more amused if I adjusted my sitting position now, so I remained as I was and waited for him to swallow his smile.

When he lowered the glass from his lips, I spoke first, "Can I ask you a question?"

"Shoot."

"Ferbie's my brother, and I love him dearly," I began, "But for the life of me, I can't understand what *you* see in the fella. No one, and I mean no one, has ever held a conversation with him for more than five minutes, if that long."

95

Jahleel chuckled, one coming so deep from his throat, it vibrated and caused caressing waves to surge through me, making me sigh with longing. "He's got talent and he's got depth."

"D-D-*Depth*?" I sputtered with much incredulity.

He nodded, and he was serious as he went on, "You just gotta know how to pick his brain. Ask the right questions to make him dig deep and force him to think; activate his lazy brain. It takes patience. But he's excellent at followin' instructions, and he catches on unbelievably fast." Looking down at his glass, he smiled, "You just need to get him to stop saying 'Aye'. Seriously, who the fuck says 'Aye' except for Christopher Columbus every time he discovers new territory?"

I could see him fighting to hold back a laugh, maybe thinking I'd take offense to it. But when he glanced up and saw me biting down on my lip to hold in my own laugh, we both laughed. I had no idea why Ferbie spoke the way he did.

"Were your parents drunk when they named him?"

For some reason, I didn't take offense to his question, because it didn't feel like he was making fun of Ferbie' slowness. I could tell he genuinely liked Ferbie, and was having fun as a good friend or family member who loves him would. A good-natured tease.

"Maybe," I said, looking away. "They *were* drunks."

"Yeah?"

"Uh huh. My sister's name is Timberly."

"The fuck?" he laughed.

"Then there's my name—Saskia."

The laugh I expected never came, and when I shifted my gaze back to him, he was staring at me with *that* look.

"Saskia is one of the sexiest names I've ever heard."

Except you mispronounced it five years ago...

His stare dropped to my mouth. "And it suits you...more than I think you even know."

Aiming to remain calm, I moved my gaze from him once more.

The look I'd always wanted from him, always dreamt of, I was finally getting it. But, it was too much for me to handle. Too intense. Too demanding. Too probing. He was a lot. A fuck of a lot. And I was just one girl.

In that moment, it dawned on me that even if I won him, I wouldn't be able to contain him. He was a beast, and I didn't have the skills to tame him. I guess, sometimes, it's better to just look, fantasize and don't bother touching.

He cleared his throat. I heard it. The ice clinked in his glass. I heard it. He tried to pull my attention back to him, but I kept my eyes off him, fighting to avoid that penetrating gaze.

Until he spoke. "Chad's here, you know."

When I warily slid my gaze back to him, he'd leaned forward on the ottoman, mimicking my position, elbows dropped on his knees as he watched me intently, not giving me a break from his stare.

All of a sudden, I *didn't* want to be the subject of his stare. Bloody hell, it was unnerving! I'd been begging for it, pining for it, and now I couldn't handle it. Not even a small percentage of it.

"I know," I croaked. Digging for a stronger voice, I cleared my throat. "I spoke with him a while ago."

"You're his type."

"I wish," I scoffed. "He thinks I'm fake."

As if he was expecting a different answer from me, he sniffed and turned his gaze out to the crowd, the skin around his eyes tightening. "Want me to talk to him for you?"

He bit the words out, as though they were hard for him to say.

The hell?

"Yes, actually."

"Saskia," a deep voice called from above me.

I glanced up to see my good friend Zane Zekiel towering over me. Cocking his head, he regarded Jahleel with a frown, seemingly trying to put face to name. "JK, right?"

Jahleel flipped up the deuces in acknowledgment, and I

bit my lip to stop from smiling like a teenager with a crush. He was such a hot show-off in everything he did. His cockiness didn't make him detestable; it made him even hotter and personable.

"Ah man, my ears hurt from hearing your goddamn name so much. Even in the fucking locker room," Zane griped, reaching out to shake his hand. "You should probably have your own reality show or something, man. You're like the single Scott Disick."

Jahleel took his hand and shook it once. "'Cept I still got my balls intact."

Zane laughed out, then turned back to me and joked, "Don't tell me you're crushing on him, too?"

More like obsessed, infatuated, un-fucking-hinged.

But remembering who and where I was, I released a, "Pfffft," being sure I kept my eyes on Zane and not Jahleel.

At that, Jahleel stood up with an, "I'll leave you two", then slipped off into the crowd.

Zane took his place.

Zane Zekiel was a MVP, 4-time Championship Ring holding pro basketball player. Dark-chocolate complexion, hazel-brown eyes, and muscles as hard as steel. I met him at a party like this when I'd first come to the U.S., and he was the coolest person. We exchanged phone numbers so we could chat through IM and sometimes when he was in SF, he'd come to visit me and we would drink booze and talk crap for hours.

"Zane." I grinned widely. "The man who's a *man*."

"I still don't know what the hell that means, Saskia," he chuckled. Passing his eyes down my body, he nodded in approval. "Looking damn good, too."

Mockingly, I waved a hand and tossed my hair like a conceited French tart. Crossing one leg over the other in a slow, provocative manner, I tipped my chin up with an arrogant tilt. "Ohhh, Mr. Zekiel. Youz knowz howz to makez a womanz *blush,* eh? Stopz flirtingz with me. Now, shoo shoo, s'il vous plaît."

Zane tossed his head back and howled in laughter, as he was wont to do whenever I kept up antics such as this. "Faking a French accent with a British accent is the single sexiest thing I've *ever* heard."

Uncrossing my legs, I laughed along with him.

Zane leaned in, "No offense, but you're not my type, Frenchie. I mean, you're fucking hot, no doubt. But, like, white guys' hot. For shit's sake, I'm black, six feet six, with an eight and half inch dick that's five inches in width—you couldn't handle me. I like my women with a big, round ass, thick thighs, D-cups and no gag-reflex...you know this, Saskia."

"Nowz you makez me cry, eh?" I mock sobbed. "You bad,

bad man."

"Cut the crap, crazy," Zane laughed again, shaking his head. "Look, I want you to set me up with someone."

"Who?"

Inclining his head to the right, he nodded over to the bar where Amanda and Twana were talking and laughing. "That girl you're always with."

"Manda? She's my bestest."

"Yeah," he agreed, staring across at her with a ravenous expression. "I've been watching her for a year now; how she moves, her attitude, you know. I've been keeping tabs. And I've decided, I want her. For myself."

"A *year*? Really?" I gaped, disbelieving. "You could've just asked me, you know."

"You would've been biased."

"True," I conceded, nodding. "However, I'm not sure it would work with you two."

Dragging his eyes from Amanda at the bar, he looked curious, "Why?"

"Well, she's kind of, um, dominant," I spared. "A man eater."

Zane dipped his head and smiled to himself, then looked back over to the bar. "I've gathered that much. *That's* why I want her."

"Uh...o-kay?" I dragged out. *How weird*. Most men *run* from Amanda, carping that she's too commanding.

"She lives with you, right?"

"I'd be a mess if she didn't. She's the pep in my steps."

"Great. Make the link, babe." Standing up, he leaned over and gave my cheek a peck. "You're awesome, Saskia. Love ya." Then he was gone.

I watched him with a smile as he walked off into the throngs of people, until the sight of Jahleel wiped that smile right off my face.

Perpendicular to where I was, he sat on a stool at one of the high tables, around twenty feet away from me, and Tiara was perched on his right thigh, yapping off with expressive hand gestures, as though she were spilling her heart out, pleading, begging. Jahleel's arm hung loose around her waist, but his eyes were fixed on me.

Seemed he'd been watching me and Zane, and now his arsehole face was on.

Tiara still blabbered on until he raised his forefinger and pressed it against her lips in a 'shh' gesture. As her shoulders relaxed, she turned her face up at him, and I could tell she was sighing dreamily. *Who wouldn't?*

Taking hold of her chin with his thumb and index finger, Jahleel pulled her face to his and kissed her. A delicate kiss on the lips. The kind of kiss bound to mislead her and make her believe he wanted more from her.

When he drew back, she threw her arms around him and hugged him hard.

Over her shoulder, his stare found me again.

Arse.

Flicking up my middle finger at him, I scooped up my clutch from the table and stood up, deciding I needed a smoke.

This man's attention was all I'd ever wanted. And now that I was getting it, the feeling was overwhelming and bittersweet. Because just like that, he switched from an ace guy I could converse with to a spiteful, detestable bloke.

As I moved off, I glanced back at him to see that devilish crooked grin on his face, the one I wished for earlier. Continuing his taunt, he lowered his head and kissed Tiara's bare shoulder with those coveted lips, while his golden gaze speared me.

Maybe it was the Coffee Patrón mixed with the Nuvo that started to wear on me, or maybe I was getting used to his arsehole-ism, I don't know, but, carelessly, I turned around in the midst of the crowd and flipped him the bird again. Then, crossing my forearms, I slammed them down on my thighs in the good ole WWE 'Suck It' slam.

Jahleel cracked up on Tiara's shoulder, and I bit back a

103

smile. I'd never seen him show so much teeth before.

When Tiara pulled from his embrace and tilted her head back to watch him, I pivoted away and resumed my strides, no longer pissed off.

Jahleel Kingston was screwing with me. Revelling in it. And the stupid, muddleheaded side of me was turned on by it.

Chapter 7

THERE WERE NO more 'run-ins' with the Kingston A-hole for three weeks, as I'd left SF for extended promo trips to Los Angeles, New York and Miami, doing a string of interviews, appearances and guest performances, which temporarily ridded my thoughts of all things Jahleel Kingston.

It wasn't until our group of sleep-deprived, overworked groaners collapsed in our private jet that someone mentioned his name, and I groaned from an entirely different kind of pain.

Twana was scowling at her computer screen as if it repulsed her. She and Lion were coming back to SF with us for a week. A tad more laid back from the craziness of L.A, Lion had begun to love it there. But he couldn't move there as I did because he managed quite a few artistes, and with L.A being the base of everything for stars, he deemed the one hour back and forth 'too much of a hassle'.

Maybe it was, but I was in the same place as Jahleel Kingston, so I could care less about the hassle.

"Can you believe they're considering this fucker JK to replace Andrew Lucas as judge on Dancin' 2da' Beat?" she said, all riled up.

Twana loathed Jahleel with a bitter, bitter passion and got irritated whenever his name came up—or anything about him, actually.

Lion nodded, looking as tired as I felt, eyes closed, head resting back against the seat. "Hmm. I heard."

She gestured to the laptop screen with her long, acrylic-nailed fingers, which were painted a loud commotion of colours, her many gold bangles jingling on her wrist. "But, *why?*"

"'Cause he's good at what he does, T," Lion sounded annoyed. "Be quiet, will ya? I'm tryin' to get some sleep here."

Amanda was fast asleep next to me in the seats across from Lion and Twana, while I was curled up in a C under a blanket, with one eye closed and the other peeking over at Twana.

I, too, wish she would shut up. One, because I wanted to sleep. And two, because I'd been doing so damn well not thinking about Jahleel until she blasted his name.

"I-I just don't understand," she continued, genuinely and inexplicably pissed. "*Why* is he so popular with everybody? What's the big deal? He's just a damn dance choreographer. I don't get it."

Lion's eyes popped open at that, and he wasn't pleasant. A hungry man is an angry man, yeah. But a sleep-deprived man will bite like a fucking shark if you don't let him sleep.

"Because he's shoving his non-famous dick down a lot of famous throats, that's why. Why are *you* so popular, T?"

As she grappled for an answer, he supplied it for her, "Because you're fuckin' *me*."

"That's different."

"No, it's not. Leave him alone, and shut the hell up so I can get some sleep."

"He's the biggest fucking asshole," she retorted. "I didn't think I could hate anyone so much."

"Yeah," unconcerned, Lion closed his eyes again.

Twana remained quiet for a while, thanks be to God, and I started drifting off...

Until she opened her mouth again. "Why do you get so pissed when I throw shade at him?"

Taking a long, frustrated breath, Lion reopened his eyes and leaned forward, staring back at his girlfriend. "One, because JK's my boy; he's like a son to me, two ways. A son, and a fuckin' *sun*. It's people like *you*, with your hatin' and shade throwin', why the world can't be a better place. He shines *bright*, doin' nothing but being the 'biggest asshole' alive who's blessed with enviable talent. And people be in awe, blinding and hurtin' their own eyes. And two, because you always bitchin' 'bout how much you hate him, and you ain't ever gave me a fuckin' reason why."

Lion darted his eyes around the jet, checking if all on board were asleep. Even though he caught me peeking at them, he went on with his shocking question to Twana. "You fucked him?"

Twana gaped at the unexpected question. "Of course not!"

"Do you *want* to fuck him?"

"Are you for real right now?" she angrily slammed her laptop shut.

Lion peered at her closely, reading her. He was so good at that. "Then tell me. Now. Why does his name bother you so much?"

She suddenly looked nervous, and by this time, I wasn't peeking, but staring full-on. If she admitted to sleeping with Jahleel, I was going to jump out of this plane and kill myself. I wouldn't be able to take it. No more.

"Kay."

"*Kay?*" Lion blasted. "Are you serious?"

Kay was Twana's sidekick, who was also engaged to Lion's brother. I hadn't seen her in a while.

"And he treated her like shit afterward," she bit out. "So...that's why."

"Why you mad at JK about a bitch who fucks on her man, T?!" he shouted. "Not even gonna ask if she forced it. JK would never go there. I'm sure of this."

"She did. He was shitfaced," Twana admitted quietly, ratting on her own friend. "You can't tell Dean, babe. *Please.*"

"I'm not supposed to tell my *brother* that his fiancé pushed up on another man?" he asked incredulously. Thoughtfully frowning, he concluded, "That's why JK all of a sudden decided to stop workin' for me?"

Twana lowered her head and whispered, "Yeah. He said you'd never forgive him if you ever found out."

Leaning back in his seat, Lion closed his eyes once more. "Kay's not forgiven. She ain't marryin' my brother."

"Babe, pleas—"

"No reason to forgive JK," he cut her off. "He always said he's an asshole with reason. I'm startin' to get what he means."

I SLEPT FOR 24hours straight when I returned home, as sleep was almost non-optional over the past three weeks. And I had a mere one week to rest before my schedule kicked up again.

Showered, dressed, made-up and killing time before heading out to the studio, I lounged on top of the kitchen island, one leg propped up, the other swinging back forth as I popped roasted almonds into my mouth, Amanda lounged right there with me, shooting down every attempt at convincing her Zane's her perfect match.

Zane had been checking in with me non-stop, wanting to know Amanda's thoughts on dating him. But I wasn't having much luck with her. This much I'd expected.

"Going by looks alone, he doesn't seem like the type of man I can control," she explained, helping herself to a fistful of my almonds. "He's so tall and…intimidating. I don't want to feel intimidated. I want to control. I have to be able to tell him to suck my toes and watch him do it without question or hesitation."

"Looks are deceiving," I muttered, tossing a single nut up in the air and catching it with my mouth. "Like I told you before, when I told him you were dominant, he said, *'That's* the reason I want her', emphasizing the 'that's' very much so."

"And it's the oddity of *that* why I'm all the more dubious. I mean, who watches someone for a whole year to decide if they want to date them or not?"

I laughed at her bewildered expression. "He was choosing you."

"Choosi—" I shushed her, listening.

There was a commotion of loud, zinging, roaring motor-bikes outside the house.

"The hell's that?" I mumbled, hopping off the kitchen counter and hightailing it through the house to the front door.

Opening the door, I squinted against the glare of the sun to make out the people outside my gate.

As the gates jerked slowly open, I counted three bikers. When the gates were fully open, one of the bikers pulled away in a slow and cautious rev down the paved path to the house. The rider wobbled a bit, then stopped. At this, one of the other bikers took off his helmet and yelled out an instruction.

That biker was Chad, his hair a massive chaos atop his head. My heart made a single, hard, and thunderous beat, shifted over to the right of my chest, and sighed... Because, if that was Chad, then the other biker had to be Jahleel.

The remembrance of Jahleel's scent of bike exhaust and earthy cologne attacked me. My heart sighed again, shifting back to the left. My poor, piteous heart.

But that sigh soon turned into a grunt of disapproval as I placed my hands on my hips. Because, if one biker was Jahleel, and the other was Chad, then the wobbly rider had to be—

"Ferbie has lost his goddamn mind," Amanda murmured from beside me.

I'm going to kill all three of them!

Adhering to whatever instruction Chad just gave, Ferbie straightened up and rode without fault this time, coming to a halt in front of the house.

At the gate, Jahleel, with his helmet on, spun his bike around and roared off in a thin cloud of blue smoke. While Chad stood astride his bike, staring at the ground as though lost in thought. He ran a hand through his hair, tugged on his helmet and sped off as well.

Ben drove into the residence a second later, and the gates closed behind him.

Turning to Ferbie, who was now off his green Kawasaki Ninja and grinning at it as though it were a goddamn trophy, I yelled at him, "You bought a bloody bike?!"

"Aye. Just."

"Are you *insane*? It takes training and skills to ride these things," I shouted, marching down the steps. "Also, they're *dangerous*. Do you know the speed at which you'll fly off at

112

this thing in the case of an accident? *Twice* the speed you're riding prior to impact! No one survives a bike accident. The arms, the legs and sometimes even the head gets ripped off the body in a fucking flash! Do you kno—"

"Ma. Ma!" Ferbie grinned at me, "You're starting to sound like Timber."

I frowned at that, and Ferbie laughed and went on, "JK's been teaching me for the past three weeks. He said I was ready and made me ride home on my own. I only slipped up at the front there because I was excited that I finally did it."

"Oh, Jesus."

While we were away, Ferbie opted to remain in SF and do dance training with Jahleel. I wasn't fond of the idea, but I was desperate for him to be normal in some way, so I gave him the benefit of the doubt and left him on his own for the first time since we moved here.

Well, I assigned Ben to him, of course, but still, *I* wasn't there.

Now it became apparent he hadn't been doing dance training alone, but bike training also.

I'm going to murder JK.

"Lend me your cell," I stretched a hand out to him. "I wanna have a little chat with your new mate."

Ferbie took a step back from me. "No."

113

Taken aback, I arched up a brow at him. "No?"

"No," He shook his head to emphasize. "He's the only friend I have."

"I'm not going to curse him out," I cajoled him. "I just want to talk to him."

"Yes, you *are* going to curse him out. And then I'll lose a mate. And I'll hate you for it." He took another step back from me. "You always get overprotective and growly as if I'm so dumb I can't live on my own."

"Ferbie—"

"He took hours out of his evenings, every day, for three weeks to give *me* these lessons. Hours," he stressed, his voice raising. "I'm nothing to him and he gives me his time as if I *am* someone." Taking steps forward this time, he faced me and took my hand in his. "He's a nice fellow, Ma. He wants the same for me as you do."

Ferbie could try convincing me as much as he wanted, I still planned to put Jahleel's head on a bloody pike.

However, I smiled as though I understood, resting a gentle palm on Ferbie's shoulder. "I'm sorry. I had no idea he was such a good person. I understand now. He probably won't answer if I ring from my cell, so may I borrow yours to call him and thank him for taking care of you while I was gone?"

Even though this was what I fought to shield him from,

people taking advantage of his gullibility, I was guilty of it, too. But *my* intentions were pure.

As usual, he bought it. Withdrawing his cellphone, he handed it to me and gave me a hug and a big grin before disappearing into the house.

Turning to face Amanda, I instructed her, "Try distracting him so he doesn't hear me screaming expletives at his new buddy, will you?"

Amanda, all this time had watched us with an amused expression. She wagged her head and mouthed, "Witch," before heading back into the house.

As I walked a distance off from the house, I scrolled through Ferbie's call log. The only numbers there were mine, Jahleel's and Amanda's.

I dialled Jahleel's number, but it rang out and went to voicemail twice. Perhaps he was still riding.

Killing time, I wandered around my water fountain—a naked baby angel with his tiny penis and tinier testicles.

A couple of minutes later, I tried Jahleel again. He picked up on the third ring, but the background was helluva noisy with honking car horns, heavy winds and even a siren. "What's the emergency, Ferbz?"

If I wasn't so pissed at him, I would count the deep concern in his voice as something genuine.

"I'm gonna cut your fucking promiscuous dick off, that's the emergency!"

There was a long pause, then, "Oh shit."

"'Oh shit' is right, you—"

"Hello? Sa-sassy?...Can't hear you...very well! Might wanna...call back?"

This fucker was trying to play me. Did he really think I was that dumb?

"I *know* you can hear me, you lying sod!"

As he started laughing down the line, I fought to hold back a smile.

No. No smiling. I was supposed to be mad at him.

"Listen, Sassy, I'm sittin' at a stoplight and I don't wanna get a ticket." he said. "So I'm turnin' around and heading back to your place so you can yell at me to my face, okay? Be out at your gate."

The line went dead.

No! I couldn't be mad to his face! Could I be a shouty hothead over the phone? Sure. But to his face? I would just melt into a human puddle.

Jesus, why did I call him?

Now with the knowledge he was on his way here, my palms all of sudden got clammy, and my heart was thudding loud in my ears. I contemplated leaving before he arrived, or ringing to tell him to turn back. But wasn't this what I always wanted? His attention? I needed to stop acting like a fucking teenager. Seriously. He was just another human being. Like me. No big deal. *No big deal.*

Growing a pair, I directed my steps towards the gate.

"Miss Day?" I heard Thomas call out to me from the doorway.

"It's okay, Thomas," I called back. "I'm not going anywhere."

Realizing I was missing the LV belt-purse I'd planned on wearing with this outfit, which also had my gate remote in it, I stopped and asked Thomas to go fetch it for me.

I was dressed in a savagely cut-up black, sleeveless tee that showed off a lot of skin and my tats, pencil jeans, and a new pair of black Jordans.

When Thomas returned with my belt-purse a few short minutes later, I latched it around my waist, opened the gate with the remote, and went outside to lean on the right column, waiting for Jahleel.

Well, haven't I been doing this for a while? Waiting for Jahleel? Yep. Five years.

This meaningless wait, however, was different; this time, I was actually *sure* he was coming to me.

The loud zinging from a distance reminded me of the

quietness and seclusion of my neighbourhood. My neighbours sure as hell wouldn't be tolerable of this obnoxious noise on a daily basis, now that Ferbie had a bike and all.

As the noise drew closer and closer, my heart beat faster. When Jahleel turned the corner at the end of my street, my heart collapsed altogether.

Get yourself together, Kia.

Inexplicably, a surprising calm instantly came over me as Jahleel reached my gate and shut off his bike. Kicking down the stand, he threw his leg over the bike, pulled off his helmet and hooked it on the handle.

His thick, brown hair bounced back into perfect loose waves as though nothing at all could ever perturb its perfection—not a helmet, not gravity, not winds or rain, nothing. But Jahleel raked his fingers through it nonetheless, seemingly unaware of how to-die-for his hair was.

Still leaning against the gate column, I must've looked like an enraged baddie to him with my arms crossed, when in reality I was a drooling mess depending on the column for support.

Causal as usual, he wore dark denims, a grey tee with the number 69 in bold red on the front, and black Timberlands. His gold irises seemed almost paranormal under the glare of the afternoon sun.

Reaching into his back pocket, he took out a small box of Sun Maid raisins and tossed some in his mouth, chewing like a kid with his candy. Leaning back on his bike, he crossed his legs at the ankles, crossed his arms and pinned me with his stare.

Can I just walk up to him and kiss him? Would he let me? Would he reject me?

"Let me speak first," he said, calm as you please.

As a go ahead, I waved my hand. It's not as if I was capable of speech at the moment anyway—I was still in drool mode.

"You need to give him a little more credit," he started "Yeah, he's slow in some areas, so much to a point where it seems hopeless sometimes. But for the most part, he's a quick learner. And honestly, I've never enjoyed training anyone as much as I enjoy training him."

"He's not a fucking dog."

"I never said he was," he replied, holding his cool. "Lessons. I'll use the word *'lessons'* since *'training'* offends you so much. Cool?"

When I didn't answer and kept my arms crossed with a hateful scowl on my face, he warned, "Keep actin' bitchy, Sassy, and I'll just fuck you. I like fuckin' bitchy bitches just to watch them cry and beg like the *girls* they really are."

119

My mouth dropped, and so did my hands, balling into mighty fists. How arrogant! "Well, aren't you a nasty bloody wanker, you detestable bugger!"

"What?" he said, scrunching up his face, looking lost. "Sorry, I don't speak British," he added with a careless shrug and continued on with the issue at hand. "If you think I'm a bad influence on your bro', fine, I'll fall back. My advice, however, is that you allow him to get out like he's doing now to keep his brain active, instead of followin' you around like a lost puppy. Hanging around you gives him no hope. The doctors haven't diagnosed him with shit, so there's *nothing* wrong with him. What he needs is patience, not being shut off from livin' a goddamn life."

"How dare you accuse me of—"

"Not accusin' you of anything, Sassy." Pausing, he slid his fingers back through his hair, "You know what, fuck this. I'll fall back."

"Okay, then."

"Okay, then," he echoed, pushing off his bike. He clapped his hands together and rubbed them in a 'job complete' gesture. "So, can I go now?"

He asked the question but was already swinging his leg over his bike.

I didn't want him to go. I'd acted like a bitch when he was,

120

for a first, being nice—a refreshing break from his arsehole side.

And even being pissed off and annoyed with him, I loved the feeling of him being near me. Also, I *needed* to make up with him, or Ferbie might hate me forever for chasing off his mate.

"No," I answered.

Scoffing, he muttered, "Wasn't really askin', sweetie."

Sweetie? Ew. I hated that word as much I hated 'baby girl', and I figured he'd used it condescendingly, not as an endearment.

Pushing off from the column, I made the few steps it took to close the distance between us. Shamelessly, I curled my fingers around the bike handle as a non-verbal way of asking him to stay.

But as if I wasn't there, he reached for his helmet from the other handle, his complexion a beautiful olive glow under the sun.

"What kind of bike is this?" I asked, hoping he'd answer.

Pausing his movements, he set the helmet down between his manly thighs, watching me without a word for several heartbeats. After a long moment of intense silence, his gaze fell to my lips and lingered. "Suzuki Hayabusa."

"Oh," I trailed my fingers against the cool metal,

grappling for something else, anything else to ask. *What can I say to make him stay even a second longer?*

"You give a shit about this bike, Sassy?"

Biting back a smile, I dropped my head and answered honestly. "No."

Leaning in, Jahleel slid a finger under my chin and lifted my face up so our eyes met. "So, can I go now?"

As searing as his gold gaze was, I fought to hold it like a woman. "No."

With a sigh, he dropped his hand from my face, turned his eyes from me, looking off at some imaginary oasis in the distance. His eyes narrowed as he seemed to wrestle with some decision, his wheels churning.

"Fuck it," he muttered under his breath, grabbing up the helmet from between his thighs.

Thinking he was still going to leave, I moved in even closer, contemplating begging him to stay. But I was close enough now that he reached up and jerked the helmet onto my head, shifting my wild curls around so it fit snuggly.

Snapping down the visor, he ordered, "Get on."

What? I looked back to the house—I couldn't just leave.

"Take a risk, Sassy," he dared, revving up the bike. "Get on."

Fuck it.

I pressed one foot on the side pedal and smoothly swung my other leg over, fixating it to the pedal on the other side. Bum sticking out, I leaned forward and wrapped my arms around his middle, ready to roll.

Jahleel glanced over his shoulder, "Didn't even have to give you instructions. You're the real deal, Sassy."

Not quite.

When I was eighteen and a bartender back home, I used to fool around with an outlaw biker. Bad attitude, swore like a sailor, and loved having my arse perched out on the back of his bike.

But I preferred to let Jahleel think I was a 'badass', so I kept my trap shut.

He kicked up the stand, and took off with a jolt and a zing.

Thrilling!

Chapter 8

JAHLEEL RODE AROUND with me without purpose for half-an-hour, and I got the feeling he wasn't sure just what to do with me.

While I could come up with a million things he could do, I enjoyed being pressed up against him while we rode at blink speed, life passing in a blur. So, I relaxed and revelled in the moment, because only God knows if his mood would be this good and tolerable the next time I see him.

One never knew with Jahleel Kingston.

Each time we stopped at a stoplight, he glanced over his shoulder to ask if I was doing alright, and being more than alright, I'd nod in reply.

We ended up in Union Square, where he pulled over at a Levi's outlet on the corner of Post Street, parking at the curb. Getting off at the same time as him, I made to remove the helmet, but he stopped me. "Keep it on."

"What?"

Without answering, he took my hand and tugged me off into the store—me looking like an idiot with this helmet on. He made a beeline to the back of the store, to a section of denim jackets. Releasing my hand, he fingered through a few options before selecting a denim jacket two sizes too big with a black cotton hood attached to the collar.

"Wait here," he mumbled, slipping off through the clothing aisles to the cashier.

He returned with the jacket tossed over his shoulder and reaching up, he took off the helmet and handed me the jacket. "Put this on."

Eying the jacket with disdain, I scoffed. "Pssh."

Biting back a smile, he explained, "I wanna have a drink with you."

"So have a drink with me."

An eyebrow winged up. "Do you want your picture blasted all over entertainment news with some lowly dancer?"

"You're not—"

"Okay," he cut me off. "Do you want it out that you're

sneaking roun' with Tiara's guy? She idolizes you, you know. It wouldn't look right."

A slap to the face. All I could do was stare at him open-mouthed, as he stared back at me, pokerfaced. Again, he was being a dick just for the sake of being a dick. No reason behind it.

There had never once been any kind of gossip linking JK to Tiara, so, clearly, he liked toying with me. It was him who didn't want to be seen with me, for whatever reason. Protecting me, or protecting himself?

"*Are* you Tiara's guy?"

"Next question," he responded without so much as a blink.

Arrgh!

Fists clenching, I resisted the urge to punch him straight on the forehead and grabbed the jacket from him instead.

"This isn't even going to fit," I grumbled, angrily fisting my arms through the sleeves.

As if he was used to people moving when he moved, he stalked off, saying, "That's the point."

Like an obedient disciple, I followed as he made his way back out of the store. "It's not even sexy. I look stupid."

Jahleel suddenly stopped walking, and I slammed into his back. He pivoted to face me, "You're not that girl."

"What girl?" I asked, still peeved.

"The one who tries at being sexy."

Another slap. "So you're saying I'm not sexy, then?" I shouldered past him. "Gee, thanks."

Grabbing my arm to stop me, he spun me back around to face him. "That's not what I meant."

"Tell me, then."

"What I meant was…you're a natural. And your rawness breeds this rabid attraction in…" Pausing, he shifted on his feet, or more like squirmed, "You have no idea, do you?"

Still unsure whether he meant I was sexy enough for him, or if he just admired my non-girly style, I pushed, "Tell me."

He caught his lower lip and pulled it between his teeth, staring at me with this *'I can't believe you're that clueless'* look. Which I was—where he was concerned. I needed to hear the words clear and straight from his lips: *'Sassy, you're fucking hot, and I want you.'*

The muffled sound of DMX's *'What these Bitches Want'* went off between us, and Jahleel frowned as he dipped in his pocket and withdrew his phone. "Yeah?…Shit." He glanced at his Richard Mille. "Aw man, I lost track of the time. Go ahead and start without me. Warm ups, then go over the routines with them…yeah…be there soon."

When he ended the call, I shot him a look of revulsion.

127

"Are you kidding me? *That's* what you have as your ringtone? *Seriously*? Could you be anymore obnoxious?"

"It wasn't me," he protested, still frowning.

"And now you sound like Shaggy," I murmured.

Jahleel barked out a startled laugh, and I bit back a smile. I loved when he laughed.

"Trust me. It had to be Krissy. She's the only one who knows my password. She pulls shit like this all the time," he explained, returning his cell to his pocket. "Look, I forgot I had a two o' clock today. So drinks are off. Gotta make a quick stop by my house for somethin', then drop you home, okay?"

"I can't come with you?"

"Work's work," his tone brooked no argument. "Can I come on stage with you when you're workin'?"

Though my heart plummeted in disappointment, I rolled my eyes and walked ahead of him.

JAHLEEL LIVED IN Pacific Heights, where most of the homes were charmingly attached so close one couldn't swing a bat. They were Victorian-style—which, despite their quaint simplicity, cost an arm, a leg, one eyeball, and a wisdom tooth.

Jahleel revved up a seriously steep hill as though it were

no mean task. Leaving the claustrophobic clutter behind, the hill soon levelled out into a beautiful neighbourhood that rebelled against the rest of the community with its wide roads, modernistic houses and front yard space with driveways. Some real estate mogul was breaking tradition to make a statement, no doubt.

Jahleel pulled over to the curb of a detached split-level, more imposing than I expected, painted grey and white with all its square and sharp angles modernity. A well-manicured lawn flanked both sides, the driveway wide enough to fit more than two vehicles and parked on the left was a red topless, door-less Jeep—a Jeep I couldn't picture anyone else driving but Jahleel.

I climbed off the bike at the same time he did, and he turned to take off the helmet as if I were incapable of doing it myself, mumbling a "Huh".

"What?"

Using his free hand to ruffle my curls, which I assumed were flattened by the helmet, he leaned in, so close I was overwhelmed with his scent of bike exhaust, earthy cologne and...raisins? "I like havin' you behind me on my bike."

He swept a fluff of hair over my shoulder, and I shuddered at the light contact of his fingertips against my skin. "You grip... squeeze...and hold on so well. You don't lean to the side when I make turns, and you don't peek over my shoulder or beg me to slow down. You just hang on and enjoy the ride. It's fuckin' perfect."

Wishing he would kiss me, I held my breath, lips quivering in anticipation. But he didn't. He just kept his luscious lips hovering over mine, his finger idly twirling a lock of my hair.

Right in the middle of this sultry moment, the memory of this same finger twirling Jamie's hair came to me, and my mood vanished, along with my wish.

"Uh, thank you?" I muttered churlishly.

His eyes remained on my lips a minute longer before he stopped touching my hair. He placed the helmet on the handle of his bike and started up the driveway.

I followed.

"How can you afford this?"

I instantly regretted the question. It was the kind that could only serve to spike him straight into a-hole mode.

But surprisingly, he didn't sound offended when he answered, "Parents."

Crap. I forgot his parents were famous Christians. The kind who air weekly on television, convincing millions of people to sow one thousand dollar seeds if they wished to see blessings and prosperity in their lives. I could even remember his father, Pastor Kingston, testifying to being anonymously gifted a private jet. Lucky servants of God they were, eh?

As he turned the key in the lock and pushed open the door, I remembered Krissy saying they lived together. "Is it divided?"

"Yeah," he threw his response over his shoulder. "Krissy's up top. I'm down here."

"Oh." I was relieved they didn't actually live *together*. "Does she—"

"Too much fuckin' questions," he snapped, glancing at me over his shoulder. "Stay here. Be back in a sec." Then he strode off down the hall.

Why did I continue to subject myself to this man's awful treatment?

Oh, right, because I love him. At least, I *think* I did. Or maybe I suffered from a more subtle brain dysfunction than Ferbie. Maybe *all* the Days suffered it, and I just happened to be a tad more sensible than the rest of the lot. That could explain it—why I continued down this path.

I wasn't some obedient child, or anyone's pet, so I didn't 'stay' as he ordered me to. Instead, I wandered down the hall to find it branched into two wings; the left wing ran into the kitchen—which also had a gap entrance by the front door—while the right wing led into a massive living area.

Taking the path to the living area, I concluded there and

then that red was this man's favourite colour. The space was decorated in a theme of red, grey, white and black, with red being the primary colour.

One large, pristinely white rug covered the centre of the hardwood flooring, and a low Chinese-style coffee table sat atop it. Two long, red suede sofas faced each other on either side of the table. Another sitting area was furnished with two grey sofa chairs placed side by side, each with its own round, black leather ottoman in front.

The place looked so spotless and clinical, it was *impossible* to believe the person living there rode sports-bikes, drove around in door-less Jeeps, wore ripped-up jeans and Timberlands, and used the F word like it was a prayer.

He was a bloody neat freak.

I hated those kinds of men. They were the ones who made up the bed the second they rolled out of it, never left dirty dishes in the sink, kept the bathroom dry and arranged, folded the towels, colour coded the closets, and took off their shoes at the front door.

Well, I still had on my shoes, so I guess he wasn't that bad.

A 60-inch flatscreen was installed inside the wall north, and the entertainment centre beneath it displayed neatly arranged CDs, DVDs, and a shitload of pictures with Krissy.

Some of him and her, some just of her. Most were candid shots of Krissy in her natural, unguarded state. One even while she slept, her mouth hung loosely open.

The ones of him and her were casual, faces pressed together with his arm holding out the camera, smiling, laughing, happy. A Jahleel I didn't know. Might never know.

Did I even stand a chance?

Those were the kind of pics he framed, and put on display, candid and open. The only other picture present that didn't include Krissy was one with his parents.

How could she see those and *not* know he regarded her as more than a sister? She either knew and didn't care, or she was just as much of a bitch to him as he was an a-hole to others.

The hairs on the back of my neck stood up—I felt him before he even spoke. "You don't follow instructions very well, do you?"

I spun around and took a startled step back when I realized how close he was, flipping a thumb-drive between his fingers. His jaw worked as he chewed something, and I knew it was his stupid raisins.

"I'm not Ferbie."

"You're right," he nodded in agreement. "He can dance. You're a fish. Even walruses dance better than you."

"Uh, psssh. I can dance," I protested, using my offended

133

face.

With a slight smile, he reached up and softly pinched the centre of my top lip. I moved into it, but before I could get any closer, he nodded over my shoulder, indicating the photos I had just seen. "It's her birthday today."

What the fuck did that have to do with the price of rice? "Oh. You got something special planned, yeah?"

"Yep." He turned to leave the room. "C'mon. Let's get you home."

I was tired of these short, clipped moments with him. I was tired of him kissing everyone except me. Tired of him being with everyone else except me.

Common gossip labelled Jahleel a man-whore who shagged anything with a vagina, yet I constantly fought to get his attention.

I was Saskia Day. I owned the fucking world. I shouldn't have to follow him around, waiting and hoping he'd touch me, or realize that I, too, was a woman with a vagina between her goddamn legs.

And very *willing* to accommodate him, I might add.

As we got to the front door, I reached out and grabbed his hand before it touched the doorknob. Slightly turning his head, he looked at me with his brow raised in question, and I shrugged.

There were no words available, so I tried putting it all in my eyes, because my mouth or brain never seemed to function whenever those gold irises were focused on me.

As he turned fully to me, I let go of his hand. "Sassy?"

My neck heated and my cheeks burned hot as flames, but I didn't answer as he moved into me, backing me up until I was against the wall. He moved in even closer, until the space between us was non-existent.

Yes. Yes. Yes.

Now if I could just get my lips to work. Oh, they would work alright, the minute his touched mine, they most certainly would, like a frog kissing a prince.

"What, Sassy?" he whispered. "What do you want?"

Swallowing past the golf ball size lump in my throat, I sighed back, "Kiss me."

"You want *me* to kiss you?" he asked as his hips pressed against mine, now pinning me to the wall.

"Yes. Please."

"Why, Sassy?" he demanded in a husky voice—a voice I assumed he reserved for moments like these. His right hand came up to brace against the wall, right next to my head, as if he needed a fulcrum, stability, something to keep him restrained.

"Because…" was all I could get out.

S. ANN COLE

"Because…?"

"I just want you to fucking kiss me," I snapped, full of sexual frustration. "You kiss women all the time, don't you? Just do it."

Using his other hand to grip my waist, fingers digging into my flesh, he leaned in even further so his lips were whispering against mine. "I thought you were feeling Chad?"

The hell? How did Chad get into this?

His searing grip on my waist was causing a heavy, un-bearable pressure between my thighs. I wanted, *oh God*, I wanted him. Right now. Right here.

Hooking my thumbs into his belt loops, I yanked him even tighter up against me and raised my face to his, waiting. Waiting for his lips to touch mine. "No. *You.*"

"You playin' games, Sassy," he accused, his cool, minty breath caressing my aching ones.

I tried sounding convincing as I squirmed against the wall. "No, I'm not."

"You think you can have both of us?" he bit out, his mood shifting. "It's me today, him tomorrow? That's how you play?"

He watched my face closely, intently, searching for some-thing. "One minute you want me to talk to him for you, the next you want *me* to kiss you?"

Dear God. He was reading this all wrong. I didn't want

Chad. I wanted him. HIM! Couldn't he see that?

Tipping up on my toes, I tried moving in again to kiss him, but he drew back before our lips met.

I felt like screaming, crying, begging. "You, JK. You. Not Chad."

Lips nearing mine again, he earnestly searched my face. *The hell was he searching for? Just kiss me, dammit!*

"Please. Kiss me."

"No," he whispered, even as his teeth nipped at my bottom lip.

"No?" My breath was coming in airy, ragged waves now.

He nipped my lip again, tugged and released. "No."

Turned up to maximum heat, I frustratingly whined, "Why not?"

"Because I'm not the one you want, Saskia." He drew back.

My thumbs were still hooked in his belt loops, so I yanked him back. "How can you determine that?"

Leaning in close again, eyes to eyes, nose to nose, lips to lips, his mouth moved against mine as he murmured, "Because your nostrils aren't flaring."

What the motherfuckingfuck?

Was he even being serious right now? Really? Because my 'nostrils aren't flaring'?

137

Before I could explain that Chad's theory about my nostrils flaring was total bullocks—even though it wasn't—the moment was aborted by a loud crash at the front door, followed by an eruption of giggles.

Jahleel jerked his gaze to the door, and judging by the look on his face, I knew it was Krissy.

Being too aroused, confused by the nostrils flaring comment, and intrigued at the depth of his feelings for his sister, I didn't look their way, but watched Jahleel's face instead.

"Oh my God, JK, I'm so sorry!" Krissy giggled harder. "I *really* ought to start using my own entrance."

The way she emphasized 'really' meant it wasn't the first time she'd walked in on him with someone.

Jahleel's grip on my waist loosened as he removed his hand and, with said hand, raked his fingers through his hair, closing his eyes. His expression was that of utter confusion and conflict.

Opening his eyes, he turned to Krissy and told her, "I'm sorry" before striding off down the hall.

Me forgotten.

Because, to Jahleel Kingston, Saskia Day was no one, while Krissy was everything.

I wanted to die a million deaths. When would I grow some sense?

"What a fucking asshole," Krissy's companion grumbled, which prompted me to glance over at them for the first time since they entered.

With coal-black, shoulder-length, bobbed hair, the friend reminded me of Amanda, the thick-legged, big booty type. Except she was unmistakably Armenian. Zane would love her.

She tried getting up to her feet from the ground, but kept stumbling back onto Krissy and the scads of shopping bags around them. Going by the dejected expression on her face, there was no doubt Jahleel was shagging her, too—or at least used to.

Jesus, I couldn't take this.

"For the love of God, Marsh!" Krissy barked in a fit of hysterical giggles.

Feeling awkward, uncomfortable, mortified, abandoned and rejected, I shifted on my feet, not knowing what to with myself. If only I could click my heels and disappear.

Krissy looked up at me from where she laid sprawled on the ground, but her friend was pointedly ignoring me, pretending it was no big deal having Saskia Day five feet away from her.

Well, screw her. I wasn't going to acknowledge some plonker who was as brainless as I was to want a fucking scumbag douchehole who was incestuously in lust with his forbidden adoptive sister.

But I opted to be nice to Krissy—not because I cared a damn about her, but because I appreciated her not reciprocating Jahleel's affections, and also somewhat respected her for possibly being the only woman in his radius who didn't turn into a complete lummox over him.

I wish I had her strength, her common sense, her freedom. I wanted to be free. Free from this captivation. Free from loving someone who would never love me back. Free from loving all wrong.

"May I use *your* loo?" I asked her.

"Sure," she chirped in that airy, amicable voice of hers. "Upstairs, turn left."

Nodding, I moved off down the hall, and as I reached the staircase, I remembered Jahleel saying it was Krissy's birthday. That explained the shopping bags.

Spinning back around to her, I forced a smile on my face even though I didn't feel like it. "Oh, happy birthday. Hope it's been good so far for ya'?"

"Thank you," she replied with a smile, and for the first time I detected something not so genuine behind it. "It has been so far."

As I reached the top of the stairs, I heard her friend attempting a whisper, so I stopped to eavesdrop.

"Okay, so, I was trying my damnedest not to look star-struck—you know me and that pride shit—but, holy shitballs, isn't that *Saskia Day?!*"

Krissy laughed. "Yep."

Opting not to hear if they had good or bad to say behind my back, or laugh at my expense at Jahleel's thoughtless dismissal of me, I continued on to the bathroom and locked myself inside.

Her bathroom was impressively huge, holding both a shower and a claw-foot bathtub. Those two weren't lacking for anything, that's for sure. For two normal, casual people, they lived rather large and luxurious. Nothing I wasn't used to, of course. I guess, knowing how hard I worked to acquire all I had, the easy-to-come-by lifestyle of others shocked me every time. Life had never been easy for me, I only ate bread by the sweat of my brow—not that I was complaining.

Closing down the lid on the toilet, I sat and inhaled deeply. I had to calm myself. I needed to put an end to this. The situation was not getting better, but worse. Jahleel was far worse than I anticipated. Too much to bear, too much to tolerate, too much to handle.

Maybe if I started dating again, I could forget about him. Maybe.

Thing is, I never gave myself completely to any of the

men I've dated before, because I hoped for Jahleel. And in those times, I never knew just how awful he could be, and I never considered he might be in love with someone. I was being delusional.

Maybe, with all this sordid knowledge, I could now rationalize with myself and fight, determinedly, to move on from this inane obsession—even though Jahleel would still own a part of me.

I could move back to Los Angeles—because he was the reason I moved here in the first place—and I could go back to being blonde, because he was the reason I went raven.

Maybe, if I reversed everything I've ever done because of him and let go of all the pointless hopes and dreams, the obsession would fade too. Sometimes I wondered if obsession was an incurable illness, if it was actually a phenomenon, or if it was all illusion—dreaming while awake.

Curling my feet up on the toilet, I wrapped my arms around my legs, dropped my chin to my knees and started singing an acoustic version of Christina Aguilera's *Ain't No Other Man.*

Singing was the one thing that could calm my wild thoughts and jumbled emotions right now, and I needed to be calm and relaxed so I could leave this house with some dignity, even if it was feigned.

So I sang and sang over and over again, holding the long, endless trebles, pouring out all my frustration, hurt and pain. By the time I was through it the fifth time, I was feeling much better.

Strength regained, I turned on the tap and splashed some water onto my face and rang Thomas.

"Thomas," I said, when he answered the phone, "Come get me. I'm at—"

"I'm parked only a block away, Miss Day."

A block away? Then I remembered the tracker in Ferbie's phone which I still had with me. Of course Thomas would track it once he realized I'd left without protection. "Okay, I'm coming."

By the time I was outside, Jahleel's sports-bike was gone. He'd left without making sure I had a ride home. Or maybe he forgot about me altogether.

Unzipping my belt-purse, I took out a Davidoff, lit it up, and inhaled a deep drag just as Thomas pulled up to the curb.

The tranquillity the nicotine produced was instant.

Krissy was in a heated quarrel with a drop-dead-gorgeous man I recognized as Trevillo Nelson, a rotten real estate mogul. Her man, I assumed, because parked beside them was a brand-new red Audi TT wrapped with a bow. Birthday gift, it seemed.

Hmm, this must be what ticked off Jahleel while I was in the bathroom and why he left.

A revengeful smirk danced on my lips as I revelled in the knowledge that someone was causing Jahleel hurt as much as he caused mine's and others. Where there's smoke, there's always fire, no matter how small the flame.

I sucked in another drag of my cigarette, feeling a fuck of a lot lighter and freer by the second.

This is the last time, I told myself as I sauntered off and slid into the back of my waiting vehicle.

I. Was. Done.

Chapter 9

ANOTHER FAILED ATTEMPT at self-induced pleasure, I removed my useless hand from my knickers, pressed both palms to my face and stifled a scream in them.

In abject defeat, I kept replaying the scene of the best sex I ever had—with a rock star I dated before I dated the tiny dick actor.

Best sex ever on his tour bus, and also our last sex together as I broke up with him right after we climaxed.

Tex, an undeniably hot and irresistible rock god. His cock, tongue and nose were pierced. He wore eyeliner and was inked from neck to wrist.

He was the one man who I thought, and hoped, could win

me over and eradicate all obsessions of Jahleel—because he was *so* great in bed, and I thought of nothing or no one else when he was inside me.

But that bubble was fleeting, as all of a sudden, all the things I loved about him, that drew me to him—the tats, the eyeliner, the piercings—became repulsive to me, and my Jahleel-craving returned hard. So, I broke up with him.

He loved me madly, and I thoughtlessly broke his heart. For a while, he turned into the male version of Taylor Swift: every other song he put out was about me. Either raging how much he hated me, how much of an abusive bitch I was or crooning how much he loved and missed me.

Blah.

Sexually repressed, I blew a long-winded breath, feeling like I was losing my goddamn mind. I needed a man. I couldn't continue like this. A woman, same as a man, needed to release herself from time to time, and sadly, self-pleasuring and B.O.B's didn't work for me.

Jahleel, of course, was out of the question. And even if he was in the question, he wasn't available, as he was hung up on his sis.

A week had passed since he callously left me at his house. A week since I swore off him. And a week since I spared not even a minute of my thoughts on him—patting myself on the back for that one.

Work helped to keep my mind busy and occupied, and when I wasn't working, my brain was too tired to think, so it rested in sleep. Thus, thoughts of Jahleel A-hole Kingston were non-existent. Of that I was glad. I called that progress.

Nevertheless, I was still sexless, miserable and frustrated.

There *was* someone who could possibly rectify this sexual frustration, but I didn't have his digits, and I couldn't even ask Ferbie for it because he wasn't on speaking terms with me.

When I'd returned from Jahleel's that day, Ferbie was sulking for whatever reason. He then stopped speaking to me altogether; I later found out through Amanda that Jahleel stopped linking with Ferbie, period.

I made it even worse when I told him we were moving back to L.A. Yelling that I was selfish and unfair, he stormed out of the house and I hadn't seen him since.

I knew, however, that he was currently checked into *Palace Hotel,* because I had trackers on him, and I managed both his and Timberly's credit cards, as they stemmed from one of mine. Plus, Ben was keeping a tail on him, so I knew he was alright.

Reaching for my cellphone from the nightstand, I hit up Lion on *WhatsApp.*

147

Me: *You got JK's mate's cell #?*

Lion T'mar: *Yeah...?*

Me: *Send me*

Lion T'mar: *Y?*

Me: *Wadda u care? You're in Dubai! Just send me.*

Lion T'mar: *K. But don't do anything STUPID*

Me: *Am 25. Am allowed 2do STUPID stuff. Fuck fame!*

Lion sent Chad's digits without further reprimand and I programmed it into my phone, my thumb hovering over the call option as I contemplated what I would say to get him in bed with me before the night's end.

A light knocking sounded on my bedroom door, and I looked up with raised brows. No one came to my floor. Not even Amanda. It was the one request of privacy I insisted everyone in the house respected. Intercoms were wired throughout the house, in case of urgencies or emergencies. So there was no need for anyone to ever come knocking on my bedroom door.

Before I could move to find out who was so presumptuous, the knob turned, and the door swung open.

My heart skyrocketed, blasting a crashing hole through the ceiling.

Jahleel.

He strolled into my bedroom as though it was the most normal thing on earth. As if he slept here, in my room, every night and was only returning home.

"What the fuck?!"

"Shhh," he shushed me, pressing his forefinger to his lips.

"Don't shush me!" I snapped, jack-knifing up in bed. "You're in my bloody *bedroom*!"

Like a lion strutting proudly in the jungle, he crossed the wide span of space towards me, dressed in all-black: jeans, plain tee, biker jacket and Timberlands, dog-tag dangling on his chest. His facial hair had grown some, but instead of making him look bummy, he looked extra yummy.

Hell and damnation. I was doing so well, *so well*, for the past week. Now this sonuvabitch just had to walk through my goddamn bedroom door!

"You continue to shout, your guards will hear and throw me out on my ass." Pausing for effect—because he was so *fucking* good at this—he dipped his chin and asked, "You *want* them to throw me out, Sassy?"

This guy deserved an award solely for being him, for existing. "H-How?"

"I admit," he held up his palms in surrender, "I use Ferbz to my advantage sometimes."

"He's come back home?" I asked hopefully.

Jahleel nodded. "Did some moves, splits, back-flips, moonwalks, the whole works, while Ferbz hummed the *Mission Impossible* tune. Easily slipped past your men in the pool room. We bad."

Wondering if he was being serious or facetious, I stared at him open-mouthed, but when his lips twitched at the corners, I knew he was messing with me.

"Don't make me laugh. I don't like you very much," I angrily responded, sliding back down under the covers as I remembered what I was up to before he came in. My knickers were still wet.

"I know," he admitted humbly.

Coming up to the bed, he sat down on the edge and leaned back on the headboard beside me.

He was being so casual as if he did this a million times. Not even looking around the bedroom, as though he'd seen it all before. No, he was looking down at me.

"I came to apologize for the other day. I shouldn't have left you there like that. But a ton of shit was going on in my head, and I probably would've taken it out on you, so I left instead."

"Really?" I shrieked incredulously. "You break into my house to *apologize*? You couldn't just, uh, ring me? Text, even?"

Flashing that heart-stopping crooked grin of his, he slid down from his sitting position and stretched out beside me on his side. He extended his arm and rested his head on it as he fixed his eyes on mine. "Okay, you got me. That's not the only reason."

Jahleel Kingston was lying next to me, *in my bed*. Insouciant, like he belonged. A week ago, I hated him. Five minutes ago, I was about to call his best friend over to shag me. And even though I had convinced myself I was doing it because I needed sex, I knew, deep down, I only wanted to spite him.

But now here he was, with those unreal gold eyes, that amazing hair framing his face, and those tempting lips I still wanted to feel on mine. Here he was, reminding me *he* was who I longed for, *he* was who I wanted, *he* was who I belonged to.

"What else, then?"

"Well," he dragged out. "For the past five days I've been in the Big Apple working with Ray Phillips. For the past five days I've been moody, a supreme dick to my team. For the past five days I've been craving something, something I can't quite put my finger on.

"For the past five days, I kept hearing an acoustic version of Christina Aguilera's *Ain't No Other Man* playing over and over in my head. For the past five days, I've been thinking about nothing, nothing at all..." he trailed off as his gaze lowered to my lips, which were now parted and hustling for breath, then he brought his gaze back to mine and breathed out, "...but you."

My breath came in sharp exhales as I fought to pretend I was unaffected, but it was barely working. He heard me singing in Krissy's bathroom? I wasn't even singing loud, so he had to have been standing outside the door, listening.

"Breathe, Sassy," he soothed, a faint smile on his lips. "Breathe."

Busted.

Taking a deep, calming breath, I asked, "So, what are you saying?"

"I'm not sayin' anything," he replied faster than I could think. Right. He didn't want me to get the wrong idea. "Just wanted to see you for a second...to figure out if you're what I've been craving."

Turning over on my side, I tucked my clasped hands under my cheek. "Am I?"

"Not sure."

"I want to be..."

Emitting a long, deep sigh, he remained quiet for a long while, watching me. "Maybe...I can give you some of me."

"Some?"

"Not the way you want, though."

"You mean, like commitment?"

"Definitely not that," he demurred with a firm shake of his head "But I mean, I can be...friendly with you, I guess? Just not intimate."

"What would be the bloody point of that?"

"To feed my own selfishness?" he whispered warily. "I like your company, Sassy. And I *love* havin' you on my bike."

"But you don't wanna shag me?"

"No."

Flipping over onto my back, I tossed my hands up in exasperation. "Un-fucking-believable!"

"Don't think I'm not attracted to you, Sassy," he put in. "I am. You got no fuckin' idea how badly I'm attracted. But if I go further, I'll hurt you. I know me. *I will.*"

"You sleep with *everyone* without giving a flying fuck that you'll hurt them, no?" I shouted. "Just say it. Just say you're not attracted to me and stop lying to make me feel better."

"Everyone," he echoed, sounding offended.

The truth offended him? He didn't like hearing out loud

that he was a man-whore?

Jahleel reached a hand out to my face, pressing his palm gently on my cheek. When I turned to face him, he held me in his stare and asked with a serious expression, "Why, then, do you want to be one of many?"

Not knowing how to respond, I only stared back at him.

Of course, I knew I was a prat for chasing down one of the biggest womanizers I've ever met. I mean, *who* does that? Sensible women would run in the other direction—unless they were groupies or doormats. And with how I've been behaving of recent, I might as well fall under one of those categories—doormat, no doubt.

With Jahleel pointing it out, it came clear how dumb I was. He was giving me foresight into the future and giving me an out, sparing me from heartbreak, and I was in an apoplectic rage about it.

Sighing, I reached out and trailed my fingertips along his incredible jawline. His facial hair was smooth and silky instead of scratchy. He was damn well perfect. "Okay. I understand."

As I was about to move my fingers over his lips—lips I'd never get to kiss—he caught my wrist. "This is intimate touching," he whispered. "You have no idea what a simple touch like this could lead to."

Oh, God, this was going to be hard.

Scrunching his nose, he sniffed once and brought the hand he still held up under his nose and sniffed again.

My face burned with embarrassment, as that's the hand I'd had stuck down my knickers.

That damned crooked grin of his popped onto his face as he cocked an eyebrow at me. "What did I interrupt?"

Yanking my hand from him, I trained my eyes up to the ceiling, mortified and unable to look at him. But he knew, so it didn't make sense lying. "I had a hectic day. I was trying to release some stress."

His grin was so palpable, I didn't even have to look. "You may proceed…"

"What about not being 'intimate'?"

"Just observing here," he remarked, "Never mind me."

So I wasn't allowed to have sex with him, but I was supposed to be all uninhibited porn star Masturbating Saskia for him?

"It never works, anyway. So, whatever."

"What'd you mean?"

"I can't make myself come."

"You serious?" he asked in disbelief.

"As a heart attack."

"Wow. That last boyfriend must've been damn good in

bed."

"Not the last boyfriend," I corrected. "The one before the last."

Tex, whom I mentioned earlier, the rock god who gave me screaming orgasms. Up until this moment, I hadn't considered he was probably the one who ruined all other orgasms for me.

Silence stretched as Jahleel said nothing for a while, and I wondered what he was thinking. After an eternal moment of quietude, he whispered, "Where do you want me?"

Dragging my gaze from the ceiling, I glanced over at him. "What?"

Taking a hold of my hand, he lifted the covers and guided my hand down into my knickers, being careful not to let his fingers brush so much as a hair on my skin. Leaving my hand there, his withdrew his hand from under the covers. "Now, close your eyes, and tell me," he ordered. "*Where* do you want me?"

Ohhhh, he meant in my fantasies. How arrogant to think I fantasized about him, which I did, but still.

Complying, I cut off sight and circled my middle finger over my clit. "A confession booth, in a medieval Vatican."

"A w-what?"

"A confession booth," I repeated. "You know, where

people go to confess their sins."

Silence, then, "You're fuckin' kiddin' me, right?"

One eye popped open and glared at him. "Hey, this is *my* fantasy, okay? So shut up and talk."

"I'm confused. Am I supposed to shut up or talk?"

"JK!" I growled.

"Okay, okay," he laughed. "Carry on."

When my one eye closed down again, he asked, "What am I doing?"

"You're the priest on the other side, in your black robe and white collar, hair slicked back, and I'm confessing that I've never had my bits eaten before."

Jahleel was quiet, so I went on. "You say, 'Such a sin, such a shame, such a waste'. And I say, 'What must I do, Father? This sin is so...heavy. So burdensome."

Still silence. I continued. "You say, 'I could wash your sins away, Maiden.' And I say, 'How, Father?' Then you open a small trap door in the booth, stick your head through, flick your tongue out and say, 'With this. Lift your gown and let me wash away all your dirty little sins.' Oh, I'm a nun, by the way—"

At the sound of a heavy thud, I stopped talking and opened my eyes.

Jahleel wasn't on the bed.

When I propped myself up and leaned over the side of the bed, Jahleel was there on the floor clutching his stomach with one hand. He had stuffed his balled fist in his mouth as he fought to stifle his laugh.

Fucker fell off the bed laughing.

"Ha. Ha," I grumbled.

Removing his hand from his mouth, he let the laughter rip. "Sorry, Sassy, but, what the *fuck* was that?" He laughed even harder, looking up at me from the floor with glistening golden eyes. "Are you fuckin' kiddin' me? *That's* where your mind goes when you fantasize?"

"Stay down there and laugh, bloody wanker," I snapped, flopping back onto the bed.

Jerkily getting to his feet, he shook his head, "No wonder you can't come. That shit's hilarious."

"Everybody's fantasies are different, nitwit."

Jahleel regained his place back beside me on the bed, closer this time. Me under the covers, him on top of them. "Just let me do the talkin' this time, okay?"

"Okay," I agreed, because I seriously needed to come.

Having Jahleel so close to me—his breath hot on my face, his scent shrouding me—caused major turmoil inside.

"Take off your underwear," he ordered.

Sparing not a second, I dragged my knickers down and

finished kicking them off with my legs, perfectly comfortable with the idea because Jahleel couldn't see me under the covers.

"Now, spread your legs."

I complied.

"Even wider."

I did that, too.

"Close your eyes."

When I closed them, his breathing suddenly turned raspy as he started, "You're in a room...painted a deep, dark red. Nothing's in this room but a black chair wrapped in smooth silk, fixed in the centre of the room. Perched on this chair, Sassy, is you. Naked, legs spread wide, nipples hard, dripping wet, breathing ragged. But you can't touch yourself, you're not allowed to. You're waiting..."

"On you," I finished for him, my fingers gliding in and out of my now soaked core.

"Yes," he husked out, sounding a bit like he was struggling. "You want me there?"

"Oh, God, *yes*," I moaned out.

"Well, call me into the room."

"JK."

"Can't hear you," his voice was hoarse. That made me even wetter.

"JK."

"I'm near, but you have to call louder."

"Jahleel fucking Kingston!" I all but screamed as I buried two fingers deep inside myself, hips lifting up off the bed. "Please. Come. Touch me."

Long silence, then, "Am I there?"

"Yes," I mewled.

"Where am I?"

"Kneeling between my legs."

"What am I doing, Sassy?" he breathed on me, his lips were right at my ear now. "*Tell* me."

"You're licking me...ohmigod..."

"Go on..."

"Your hands, those strong hands are gripping my thighs, spreading them wider apart, and even wider...I try to touch you, but you deny me. Why can't I touch you, JK?" I complained through a deep moan.

"What do I do next?"

"You've gripped my waist and hauled me to the very edge of the chair, and now you're licking me again and...oh, God...Oh, God...Oh fucking god!!!"

I teetered on the brink as Fantasy Jahleel ate me like there was no tomorrow.

"Tell me what I'm doing, Sassy," Jahleel commanded harshly in my ear. "I *need* to see."

"You-You're flicking my clit with your finger. Flick, then lick, flick then lick…oh fuck…Don't stop…Don't stop…"

By this point, I could barely breathe let alone talk, but I struggled through my ragged breaths as Jahleel's own harsh breathing in my ear spurred me on. "You slide two…two…two…oh sakes…two fingers inside me and finger-fuck me, not hard…you're gentle…so very gentle…You lean in and cover my clit with your mouth and—"

It hit me hard, and I jolted, arching up off the bed, my body rigid as the waves of my orgasm crashed over me, rippling on. Biting down on my lower lip, I moaned loud and deep in my throat, riding out the waves.

Too soon the euphoria died, and piece by piece, I came back to earth.

When I opened my eyes, Jahleel was off the bed and on his feet, watching me, hands in his pockets and making no attempt whatsoever to hide his hard-on.

"You're leaving?"

"Yes."

"Wait. No," I begged. "Stay. I want to do that again."

"You wanna come when you masturbate, that's how you do it," he said with a small smile. "No more medieval confession booths, priests and nuns."

"Okay." *How do I get him to stay?*

As he turned to leave, I couldn't help asking, "You're going to shag someone now, aren't ya?"

He stopped and turned slightly, glancing down at the bulge in his jeans. "Well…yeah."

Extremely grateful for his honesty, yes, but I hated that it hurt *so damn much*. I wanted much more than what he was offering, even if I would end up heartbroken in the end.

Fiddling with the hem of my Cami tank, I lamely whispered, "May I ask just one favour of you?"

"Shoot."

"Could you…" I hesitated, knowing it was fool of me to ask this, but swallowed the ounce of sense and dignity I had left, and got it out, "Could you at least pretend she's me?"

He caught his lower lip between his teeth and watched me for a beat before answering, "That's the intention, Sassy."

Then he turned and slipped through the door.

I stared at the door long after he'd gone through it, praying, hoping, he would come back in and tell me he'd changed his mind.

When a solid twenty minutes passed and I realized he wasn't coming back, I burrowed myself under the covers, and for the first time in a long while, I sobbed.

Jahleel was hurting me by trying not to hurt me.

It fucking *hurt*.

Chapter 10

THE NEXT MORNING, I was frozen.

Standing in the kitchen with a glass of orange juice in hand—a glass of orange juice I'd poured out around fifteen minutes before and had yet to take a sip. Immobile, mindless, I just stood there, staring into space, with my lower back propped against the counter.

Amanda came dragging into the kitchen, yawning and rubbing her face. Upon seeing me, she stopped in her tracks, observing, but respecting the silence.

Until she broke it. "Oh crap."

Eyes fixated on a sugar jar on the counter across from me, I spoke like a zombie. "I was doing so well, Manda. Have you heard me even utter his name at all over the past week?"

"No," she cautiously replied.

"I haven't thought about him either. I was ready. Ready to leave here for good. Ready to forget it all. Ready to move on. Ready to call Chad over to fuck me ten shades of purple."

Silence.

Amanda stood patiently and waited for me to gather my thoughts and enlighten her regarding the funk she'd just found me in. "But no. He couldn't let me be. He just had to come here like a thief in the fucking night and steal back everything!!"

Drawing back my arm, I launched my glass of orange juice across the room with all I had. Glass splinters and orange liquid shattered everywhere when it smashed through the glass-faced cabinet door. "Jesus Christ, Kia."

Whirling around, I jabbed an angry finger in her face, as though *she* was the captor, the heartbreaker, the womanizer, the game-player, the bloody thief. "Every-goddamn-thing! All my strength, all my sense of worth, all my thoughts, all my dignity. My fucking heart! He stole it all back. As though none of it were ever mine to begin with."

I moved into her space and her face, levelling eye to eye with her. In that moment, she was Jahleel Kingston to me as I barked out, "I hate you. I hate you. I hate you. I hate you. I.

Hate. You!!!"

"Okay," she crooned calmly, quietly, understanding. "You should."

Stepping around her, I stomped out of the kitchen and bumped into Ferbie, who wore a concerned expression on his face. "Aye, Ma—"

"Sod off, Ferbie!" I screamed at him. "And you might want to stop saying 'Aye' like a darn pirate if you want to become a part of the bloody Hot Pack!"

Sidestepping him, I bolted upstairs, shut myself in my bedroom, sank to floor, and bawled.

I was so weak.

After acting like a complete nutter earlier that morning, I wiped my pathetic tears away some hours later and got ready for the day. I had far too much to do to be acting a fool.

Refreshed and revived, I headed downstairs, reading through a load of emails my assistant forwarded to me for approvals or rejections.

My team was all ready and waiting for me, except Amanda who was sitting at the glass coffee table that happened to be covered in diamond jewelleries. A stumpy man with receding hairline, dressed in a black suit, was standing over her, hands gentlemanly clasped behind his back.

"What's all this?" I asked, sauntering into the living room.

With a throaty laugh that had nothing to do with humour, she answered, "One word: *Zane.*"

"Blimey!" I cheered, clapping my hands together and grinning with excitement.

"Kia!" she berated. "I haven't even agreed to be his girl-friend or anything. All I agreed on was to go on *one* date with him. Next thing I know, this fella shows up telling me I'm supposed to pick whatever I want from this collection?"

"Well," I considered, plopping down in the sofa-chair across from her. "Diamonds are a girl's best friend, no?"

"It's overwhelming," she stared bedazzled at the glitz on the table.

Were I a diamond girl, I would've been all over that collection. I wore that kind of jewellery only when I had to, but in my opinion, they're pointless fripperies. With the exception of custom-made thumb rings, I only wore leather cuffs and chokers.

Snapping my fingers at her, "Oh, you tosser! Just pick something quick before the giggly sluts get here," I said. "Better yet, pick some*things* in case you decide not to go on a second date. That way, it won't be a complete waste. You'll have diamon*ds* for your effort."

With a shrug, she laughed humorously this time and

began making her selections.

This was Zane's manner, he wanted Amanda, and he wasn't a man easily deterred. He was going to buy, force, charm his way right to her heart.

My cellphone pinged on my lap. A text message from the thief:

JK: *C U 2day?*

I didn't even bother entertaining the possibility. One, because I hated him, and at the moment, the last thing I wanted was to see him so he could shred me to pieces again and steal more from me.

Two, due to spending the majority of the morning shedding unnecessary tears, my day was now squeezed tight with no breaks, so I couldn't see him even if I wanted.

And three, I knew better than to place myself in the path of the wrecking ball named Jahleel Kingston.

Me: *Busy.*

I turned my attention back to Amanda who'd chosen over six pieces of jewellery, a wicked grin now dancing on her lips.

"I think I get what he's trying to convey," I commented,

speaking in favour of Zane this time. Both of them are cherished mates, and I wanted them to be together.

"What?" she asked, slipping a dazzling cuff around her wrist.

"Diamonds are forever…"

At that, she glanced up at me, understanding. "So he's two feet in," she concluded. "Head and heart."

"Exactly."

Now, if only Jahleel would…

I ended that thought as soon as it began. Saskia Day was too fly to be daydreaming anymore.

THE DAY ENDED in a crash after consuming too much guarana. Couldn't go a mile further, but had too much energy to sleep.

Amanda wasn't there for me to annoy, as she was out on her date with Zane. Ferbie was in his room snoring. And I couldn't smoke another Davidoff, because I had to cut down to burning one cigarette per day due to the upcoming tour.

Unbelievably so, I resorted to ringing Timberly for conversation's sake, but after thirty-minutes of her non-stop babbling about world facts no one gives a crap about, I decided I wasn't *that* bored and ended the call—while she was still talking.

Amy and Jamie giggled as much as Timberly talked, so I could care less for their company.

As a result, I landed up on the kitchen counter with a whole chocolate cake in front of me, digging in with a fork. Yesterday I had a craving and asked Sylvie to bake me one, but looked at it with disgust when I returned home this evening, wondering what the hell had I been thinking. With the tour coming up, I needed to stay in shape more than anything else. Plus my fitness trainer would strangle me.

But Sylvie knew my moods better than I did, so instead of binning the cake, she left it where it was.

Now with nothing to do, I was indulging. Baked just the way I loved chocolate cakes: extra moist and slathered with too much melted chocolate.

As I forked another chunk of carbs, sugar and all that's forbidden into my mouth, my cell pinged and vibrated across the countertop, declaring a text message.

JK: *Up?*

Oh Jesus. This chap.

The sensible part of me cautioned me not to respond, but

169

I couldn't help myself. I blame it on the chocolate and guarana.

Me: *Yes*

JK: *Gate*

He was outside?

This guy's no joke. He arrived first, asked questions later.

Pushing up from my stool, I glanced down at myself to inspect my attire. I was in white Long Jane pyjamas and red socks. A blotch of chocolate stained my bosom area, looking like a new-born did a number two on me. I contemplated changing but decided it didn't matter what I looked like since we weren't intimate.

On the monitor by the door, I pressed the button for the gate and once it started its slow open, I left the front door open and went back to sitting in the kitchen, schooling my features and posture into a semblance of indifference.

But on the real, I was hypersensitive, ears perked up like a watch dog's as I listened to the turbulent roar of his bike…the silence after the engine was shut off…the click of the front door closing …the mild thuds of hefty Timberlands against marble tiles…

The kitchen was the first turn off on the left after entering the house, so I figured he wouldn't miss me sitting at the counter, as the archway was high and grand. But he walked past the opening, and I listened as his footsteps stopped abruptly, then re-directed to the kitchen, after he registered he'd glimpsed me in passing.

When the hairs on the back of my neck stood on end, and my skin prickled with a million sharp stings, I knew he was standing in the archway, watching me.

Refusing to acknowledge his presence—outwardly, of course—I kept my back turned, forking too much cake into my suddenly dry mouth. The silence was so loud and unnerving, I wished he'd just say something and stop boring holes into my back.

Then I heard his footsteps moving across the tiles again, until he was next to me, easing down on a stool.

"I was expectin' a warmer welcome than this," he commented in a quiet voice.

"Maybe if you hadn't already stole in last night, you would've gotten one—a tour even."

Okay, so indifference was a major failure, and out came irritation, annoyance and anger.

"Fair enough."

From the corner of my eye, I could see his gaze transfixed on my face, while my attention was transfixed on the cake sitting on the counter. Searing heat crawled up my neck and

171

settled into my cheeks, burning, and I knew without a doubt they were crimson red.

Did he enjoy flustering women with his intensity? Sheesh.

After a minute of ignoring while he stared me down, he stood up. I breathed a relieved sigh in anticipation of his imminent departure. A mere minute of him, and here I was, a weak mess.

But then I heard cabinets opening and closing, and soon he was back beside me with a plate, a cake knife and a fork. Reaching over, he sliced a chunk of my cake and scooped it onto his plate. Casual as you please: *Oh, never mind me, I do this all the time. Enter celebrities' houses, locate their utensils with easy grace, and help myself to huge chunks of their chocolate cakes.*

With a cocked brow, I watched as he took out a small box of Sun-Maid Raisins from his pocket and sprinkled a couple onto his cake, then proceeded to shove a forkful into his mouth.

So far, I've concluded two things about Jahleel: he was addicted to raisins, and his favourite colour was red.

"Do you just walk around with a box of raisins in your pocket all the time?" I inquired.

"Yep." He forked more cake in. "You baked this?"

"Pfft," I scoffed. "I'm crap at baking. I love to cook,

though. Give me any recipe and I'll cook it to perfection, but baking pastries is always a cock up for me."

"It's not that hard."

"Says who?"

Smirking at me, he shrugged.

"You cook?" I asked doubtfully, disinclined to believe him.

"Krissy and the kitchen are vicious enemies…So, yeah."

Why the hell did he have to bring her name up? *Gah!* I wanted to scream. Hating that he ruined the moment with her pestilence of a name, I said nothing else.

He must've sensed the change in my mood, because he cleared his throat and made an effort in changing the subject. "We spoke briefly about your parents once, but you're usually evasive with conversations about your life before now in your interviews. Why's that?"

Feeling full and little queasy from eating too much cake, I set my fork down and pushed the cake in Jahleel's direction.

It was true, I never speak of my parents or my life back home to anyone. The only reason I released that bit to Jahleel about my parents being drunks was because I was blinded by lust and rat arsed with alcohol.

"You watch my interviews?"

Expressionless, he watched me for a beat, then took up the

cake cover and lowered it over the half-eaten chocolate pastry on the cake dish, before he stood and walked to the refrigerator. My eyes followed him as he scanned the contents in the fridge and came back with two bottles of Perrier water, handing me one as he sat back down.

"So, you gonna let me in or what?" he prodded.

He did all of that moving to the refrigerator and back to avoid answering *my* question. To evade admitting he watched my interviews.

"My life before now was nothing beautiful, JK. *Now* is beautiful. Even this very moment. Right here. That's why I live in the now and forget the past."

Jahleel swivelled around on his stool so his back is against the counter. He stretched out his feet, crossing them at the ankles as he drank his water. Waiting.

Simplistic as usual, he wore seriously faded jeans and a plain white tee. Hair perfect, eyes a mesmerizing shade of gold. His facial hair trimmed, but not shaved off. Maybe he was trying a new look?

Shaved or unshaved, he was devastatingly hot.

Fighting to understand what was going on here between us, I watched him wordlessly for a moment. What was his game? What did he want? He was willing to give *none* of himself, but he wanted me to give him more of me, on top of all he'd already stolen. Could he not see how unfair this was?

Fool that I was—for him—I gave him more. "I grew up on a small farm..."

We talked for close to two hours as I told him all about my hard-knock life before now. He had a crap ton of questions, like he was a fucking reporter or something, and I answered them all, because even if he was an undercover reporter, I didn't mind if it was *him* putting my laundry out there.

Besides, talking to him felt good. And there he was, in my house, genuinely listening with his ears wide open. He was interested in me. In my life. In who I was. What I came from.

He wanted to know it all. He wanted more. And I gave him all he wanted, praying he'd ask for more than...details.

Feeling drained and exhausted, I stood up and stretched, "I better get to bed."

I watched him as his gaze stayed locked on my bosom as I stretched. His eyes finally swept down my body and settled on my red socks. He couldn't stop a smile as he brought his eyes back up to my face and found me watching him.

"Not ready to go yet," he declared. "Why don't we watch a movie or something?"

Bloody frustrated at this point, I planted a hand to my hip and used the other to gesture between us. "What the hell is this, JK? Tell me. Are you still trying to figure out if I'm what you're craving?"

Recognizing I was on to his game, he looked away, his jaw working back and forth. He looked back to me and answered honestly, "Yes."

Getting up from the barstool, he approached me and reached out his arms as if to hug me or something, but he abruptly drew back and shoved his hands in his pockets, restraining himself I assumed.

"Look, I'm leavin' tomorrow for a couple of days," he sounded frustrated with himself. "Concert in Vancouver, video shoot in Chicago. And I just… I just don't want the same thing that happened in New York to happen again. Need to stay focused on my work, if you understand."

"Oh, so you're just here to get your platonic Saskia fix, then, yeah?" I caustically bit out. "Because God forbid your mind should stray and think about *me* while you're working."

His lips compressed, trying to conceal a smile, while I glowered at him, daring him to laugh, because if he did, I would be sorely tempted to knock him upside the head. That's how intolerable it all was at the moment.

"It doesn't make sense to you, Sassy," he explicated, "but it does to me."

With a resigning sigh, I dropped my eyes down to our feet, red socks to Timberlands. "You're selfish, JK. You want and you want, but you don't want to give."

"I know I am." He moved in closer, but didn't touch me. "You're not, though."

You're hurting me, I wanted to say. But I didn't, of course, because I was a coward. Afraid to lose something I didn't even have.

"You fancy a fuck?"

He took a surprised breath. "Sassy, I told you—"

"I know, I know," I responded through a loud laugh as I turned and started out of the kitchen. "I guess we can hang in the movie room, then."

We jaunted down to the movie room in silence. How long could this platonic thing go on before I lost my blasted mind, I wasn't sure. How on God's good earth could he expect a woman to be alright with no intimacy when he looked like...*that*? He had cockiness abound, so I was sure he knew the effect he had on women. Downright ridiculous and a tease, that's what he was being.

My movie room was in dark grey with blood-red carpeting and five rows of extremely large semi-circular black couches. We opted for the middle row and I began scrolling through pay-per-views while Jahleel toed off his boots.

"How about *Ratatouille*?"

Jahleel paused his doings to shoot me a look. "Fuck no."

Shrugging, I resumed scrolling until his boots were off and he was on the couch.

"Stop. That one. *The Green Hornet.*"

I scrunched up my face. "Nuh uh. I tried watching that crap once and couldn't even make it to the end. Those two are idiots."

He laughed and I resumed scrolling.

"This!" I chirped. "*Alice in Wonderland* with Johnny Depp."

It was now his turn to make a face. "Seriously?"

With a roll of my eyes, I continued scrolling and whispered under my breath, "Off with your head".

Jahleel chuckled. "Heard that."

As I scrolled past the movie *300,* he stopped me again, "Never got around to seeing that one."

"They are mortal punks in briefs and capes. What's the point of having a cape if you have no superpowers and can't fly?" I murmured without even bothering to stop. "*Despicable Me 2,*" I said, selecting the cartoon. "I've never seen part 2."

"Okay, this isn't workin' out. At all," Jahleel griped. He leaned over and snagged the remote from me. "You go for mediocre shit, aka *cartoons*, and I'm into action movies. So, let's find somethin' in between. Deal?"

As if I could ever disagree with anything he says, I

nodded.

We ended up agreeing on *Transformers 3*. We both had seen *1* and *2*, but never got around to seeing *3*. So it was perfect.

Drawing my knees up to my chest, I clasped my hands and stuffed them between my thighs to focus on the screen and keep from attacking Jahleel.

The night before, when I'd touched his face, he'd pulled my hand away and let me know that was considered intimate touching. So without being sure what exactly was allowed with him, I thought it better to keep my hands to myself. But it was oh so frustrating, because all I wanted was to jump him and kiss his lips off his face.

I could feel him staring at me, but I pretended to be engrossed in the movie.

"Come here," he said after a while.

Slowly turning my head, I looked at him with a blank expression. Bringing his feet up on the couch, he shifted so his back was against the handle and stretched out his arms to me.

He wanted me to crawl between his thighs, lie on his chest, and cuddle...

Don't go, the sensible part of me warned. But the stupid part of me went, laying my head on his hard, but warm and cozy chest.

Loosely circling his arms around me, a clear sign he was making no commitments or promises, he whispered, "Comfortable now?"

"Quite."

But what was shocking to my ears, was the warhorse speed at which his heartbeat galloped, contending with the wild, erratic beats of mine. This man, who was supposed to be the master of calm, composed and casual.

"Why's your heart beating so fast?"

I felt his shoulders move in a shrug, as if it was nothing. "Dunno. It always beat like that when I'm around you."

And with those words, my heartbeat out-ran his, hurling my breathing into the frenetic zone.

Seizing a fistful of my hair, he gently tipped back my head so he could peer down at my face. "Breathe, Sassy, breathe."

I narrowed my eyes. "You can't say things like that to me and expect me to be all calm, cool and collected like you."

Tilting his head to the side, his expression became one of sincere confusion. "What? You asked me a question and all I did was answer."

"You could've lied!" —He either didn't get it, or he was purposely playing dumb. —"You could've said it was the side effects of drinking too much energy drink or...something. Anything but *that*!"

Jahleel bit his lip and studied me for a beat, no doubt thinking I was loony. "Sassy, you don't wanna hear the truth, don't ask me. 'Cause I will give it to you straight."

Expelling a huff, I resignedly dropped my head back down to his chest.

As he sighed and curved his right leg over my left leg, I glanced down at our tangled legs and noticed for the first time that he was wearing red socks.

"You're wearing red socks too," I pointed out the obvious.

"The only colour socks I wear."

Extraneously, I stated, "Red's your favourite colour."

"You're observant." I heard the smile in his voice. "What's yours?"

"Black."

"Black's a shade."

"Thanks for the bloody correction, Professor Stinking Kingston," I snapped. There was nothing I hated more than being corrected.

"You know," he opined, humour lacing his tone, "you can be a real bitch sometimes."

"Says the biggest arsehole I've ever met in my entire life."

"Hey now," he dragged out with a lazy laugh, "No one's ever seen *me* do the WWE Suck It slam in public."

I punched his arm. "Put a sock in it."

"That was *epic*."

I pinched his steel-muscled bicep this time. "I said, *shut up*."

"Ow," he groaned, rubbing the aggravated area. "Now you're being abusive."

Feeling too relaxed and snugly to argue, I gave him the last say, and we both turned our attention back to the movie. But I wasn't really watching, because I found listening to the tattoo of Jahleel's heartbeat far more entertaining than giant robots on the big screen.

Before I knew it, I was fast asleep.

Chapter 11

THE WEEKEND FOUND me in the back of a limo with my team, giggly sluts included. We were headed to the grand opening of 'Nth', Chad's new club.

Chad booked me through Lion to make an appearance at the opening, even though he could've simply *asked* me to be there. I guess he was approaching things from a professional angle, as I was merely one of numerous celebrities scheduled to attend.

The intent for 'Nth' was to make it the next best celebrity hot spot in San Francisco. Lion divulged to me all of who was on the guest list, so there was no doubt 'Nth' would succeed in its objective.

At first, I wondered how it was possible for a man with no status to have such a tall celebrity guest list for a simple club opening. Surely, it couldn't just be because he was a fine specimen.

Well, I later learned Chad *does* have a status, one I hadn't been aware of. The chap was wealthier than a lot of the celebrities who would be there.

When I posed said question to Lion, he looked at me as if I were a numbskull, then gave me a quick bio of Chad.

Age twenty-nine, the name was Chadrick Pavlov Niiveux, as in the car brand Niiveux.

You know how you almost never see a TV commercial for some vehicles—like, let's say, Rolls Royce—but when you *do* see a commercial, it's more like an intense mini movie rather than a commercial, which is usually aired during the Super Bowl or one of those grand events when the whole world is watching?

Well, Niiveux falls under that category: the type of car where its worth was known and therefore didn't need commercials and marketing—'whenever you can afford one of these bad boys, just come and get one.'

Niiveux was governed by three brothers, one being Chad's father, the other two his uncles. Stemming from Niiveux were two other brands: Velocity, which was a line of sports cars, and Prominent, a variety of affordable models.

Niiveux originated from Russia, so yes, Chad's part-Russian, his mother's American. Being the only son, Chad was heir to his father's shares and also a trust-fund baby. He had two sisters, Sveta, who's a world-class runway model, and Tashenka, a normal trophy wife to some oil tycoon.

He and his famous model sister were the only two Niiveuxs residing in the U.S. Sveta, because of her career, and Chad, because of some older woman he was infatuated with in his new adult years and followed her to the States. He never bothered moving back home when she left him. He now remained because of his new friend JK, and because of his preference for the low-key lifestyle in SF, compared to his previous high-profile status as the most eligible bachelor sensation in Russia.

Here, in SF, he was a quiet investor, sticking all ten fingers in untold organisations, and also co-owner—with his 'ride-or-die' Jahleel—of a chain of high-end strip clubs spanning from here to L.A.

Although he aimed for a low key, nondescript life as much as possible, people who mattered still knew who he was, enough that his celebrity guest-list for his club opening was extensive.

That was as much as Lion told me, but I had the feeling

he was holding back a lot more. There wasn't anything or anyone Lion didn't have the dish on.

Speaking of, I hadn't heard from Jahleel since our movie night on Tuesday. I woke up the next morning in the movie room, curled up on the couch alone. Jahleel was gone, no word, nothing.

Now it was Friday, and not even a text message from him. Guess he figured out I wasn't his craving. I didn't sweat it, though, as I was getting a little stronger and learning to focus on work instead of him. If he could do it, state point blank that he wanted to focus on his work and not me, then fine, I could do it, too. With him being out of state working, he wouldn't be at the opening tonight, and for me, that was a good thing.

As the car pulled up at the venue, my mind came back to earth and I heard Ferbie talking like an unintelligible arse again to Twana, "...been workin' with 'em for a while now. Not far from doin' shows with 'em soon."

Ever since I'd yelled at him, he'd been speaking in that manner, and it was starting to grate on my nerves.

"Why the hell are you eating all of your pronouns and 'ings?" I snapped. I couldn't take it anymore.

Ferbie looked at me, confused, as the giggly sluts burst into a fit of giggles. "You told me to stop speaking the way I did, Ma."

Oh, dear God. "But I never said you were to speak like *that.* It makes you sound illiterate!"

Tugging at his collar, as if he was everything hot men were made of, he asked, "So you sayin' JK is eelite—ileeeter-um, what does that word mean?"

"Oh, Christ," I mumbled, as everyone else tried and failed to stifle their laughter.

Lion turned his head and glanced out the window, hand hiding his mouth. "We should probably hit the red carpet."

Jahleel was right, one needed patience with this fellow, and that's something I didn't have at the moment. "It means you're a buffoon, a dunce."

His face drooped in defeat as he muttered, "Oh," and I instantly regretted my harsh, insensitive words.

As everyone filed out of the limo, I kept my hand on his as a sign for him to wait. When everyone was out, I took his hand in mine, and he let me. But at the faint sound of his sniffle, my heart plummeted.

"I don't know who or what you want me to be, Ma," he said softly, his face looking out the window. "I try so hard to be the best I can be, but you never seem to notice. A fool isn't supposed to know he's a fool...but this fool knows. I see it in the way people look at me and hide their laughs. It's hard. I tried and failed to explain to JK, the one person who

187

understands me, but he says he already knows how I feel. He explains it in a way I couldn't."

"What did he say?"

"He says it's like when you're out-of-control high and you know you're high, doing stupid things and making an arse of yourself. And you can see people laughing at you, but you have no control over it, yeah? You try to walk and you fall over. You try to speak and nothing makes sense. Because you're high, and being high is not like when you're drunk and can stick your fingers down your throat, hurl, and feel better in five minutes. That high stays with you and screws with your head until you go blank. Except that my kind of high is per— perp—...shite, I can't pronounce the word he used." His face fell again.

"Perpetual?"

He turned to me look at me then. "Yes, yes, that's the word."

Squeezing his hand, I prayed to God he would forgive me. "I apologize for being mean just now, okay? You're not illiterate."

He nodded, looking unconvinced.

"You're *not*, Ferbie," I stressed urgently. "It's just that, you have a heavy accent, and speaking like the hot pack just doesn't fit. Don't try to be like anyone else, just be yourself."

"And you'll still love me?" His voice sounded hopeful, and I wanted to kick myself a thousand times for making him think I didn't.

"I'll *always* love you, Ferbie."

His good ole Ferbie grin returned, and he hugged me hard. "I love you, too, Ma."

Relieved, I pulled from the hug and grinned back at him, "Now, let's go party like rock stars, as the Americans say it."

NTH'S ROOF WAS on fire. Wickedly designed in futuristic aesthetics, the facility was a semi-circular three-level club, with no dance floor, but with booths big enough to fit at least twenty people each, circled all the way around the club, eight party booths per floor.

A huge, round glass bar stood in the middle of the first floor, and that bar had steel posts that supported a replica of the floor bar, which was suspended in the air for the second-floor patrons. The second bar had steel posts that acted as a fulcrum for another bar for the third-floor patrons. Almost sci-fi like, it resembled one big, round glass and steel tube zooming all the way up to the third floor, with sturdy glass paths

leading to the bars. Amazing. It gave off the impression of being ten years into the future. Looking around, admiring, I
could tell a lot of work and thought went into building the club.

Though I rarely enjoyed myself at parties, all of us were
long past tipsy, as the opening turned out far more fun than we
anticipated. Even Lion, who was more of watcher than doer at
parties, was doing the 'bump and grind' with his girlfriend.
Maybe something was in the drinks.

With the brilliant idea of booth partying, other celebrities
didn't feel obliged to walk around flashing fake smiles in people's faces. It was set up so one could just raise their glass in
an "I see ya" hail and continue on partying with their mates.
Even so, Tiara had found her flawlessly beautiful arse in my
booth and was clinging to me like a leech.

How do you tell someone who idolizes you to bugger off?
Oh, right, you can't.

I hadn't seen Chad since I arrived, and I assume he was
probably avoiding me, seeing that I was 'fake' and all.

Amanda got up from where she was sitting on the other
side of Tiara—who was sitting between us—and came to sit
on my other side, effectively putting me in the middle.

"Bloody hell," Amanda grumbled, "that twat just won't
shut up about how much of a cheating 'douche' her so-called
'boyfriend' is. Seems he bonked another one of the G2Ks'.

They're at war over who he wants more. That's why she's here and not in their booth. Jesus Christ, my ears hurt with that bloke's name. I wish someone would just shoot him dead already."

"And I don't want to hear about him," I whispered back. "So get your arse back over there."

"Nuh uh."

"Maybe I should tell her that I, too, am trying to get into her boyfriend's pants then, yeah?"

"Do what you must to get rid of the chatterbox," Amanda said with a careless shrug. "Don't care."

What the true status of Jahleel and Tiara's relationship was, no one knew. She called him her boyfriend, he acted single. He did whatever he wanted, she bitched about it. Maybe she was as delusional as me? Well, no, because she was *actually* with him. All I've had so far were fantasies.

"*Shite*," Amanda all but breathed into my ear.

Following her gaze, my sight landed on Chad, standing at the end of the booth partition, talking in Lion's ear.

Shite was right.

Chad looked scrumptiously delicious and was a sight to behold, as he put his casual appearance aside for tonight and opted for sleek.

In a well-tailored suit, all black with a white jacket fitted neat and close to boast his slim waist, he was impeccable. Men in suits didn't usually appeal to me, but when it was done like that, closely fitted to outline every devastating inch of his frame, well, what's not to admire?

Chad was lean, slender some. He didn't have hard, prominent, well-developed brawns like Jahleel, but for his body type, lean was correct. The black shirt under his white jacket was unbuttoned far enough to display the dash of hair on his chest as it caressed the white-gold cross pendant nestled there. His hair wasn't messy this time, but slicked back, sharpening every hard feature of his arrestingly handsome face.

Wow.

Once Lion and Chad finished talking about whatever, Lion moved back to sit with Twana, while Chad unhooked the partition and entered the booth.

Our booth was a riot with both Lion's team and mine jammed in it, so when I saw Chad stop and frowned, I knew he was trying to figure out the best way to get to who he wanted without disrupting anyone.

Leaning down, he said something to Amanda, who then nodded and leaned over to me. "Brace back a bit. He wants to get to Tiara."

Why her? Ugh! This poor girl was inadvertently making me hate her more and more.

Begrudgingly, I pressed back into the seat, and Chad stretched across Amanda and me so he could talk to Tiara.

Hearing Jahleel's name in the whispered exchange, I probably should've been eavesdropping, but my head was swimming with Chad's scent. His cologne wasn't loud, just subtle enough to blend with his natural masculine scent.

YUM!

While he was still engaged in his conversation with Tiara, I moved forward a little bit to sniff in more of his amazing scent.

"You are *such* a creep," Amanda giggled from beside me.

I ignored her, thinking that I wanted this man more than I'd initially thought. Or maybe I was drunk and feeling neglected because I haven't heard a word from Jahleel in days, yet he could send messages to Tiara. To hell with him!

Chad moved back from Tiara, and as he was passing by me, I involuntarily gripped his arm, stopping him.

As if he'd been hoping to get in and out without having to acknowledge me, he sighed deeply and audibly as he, in slow motion, turned his face to mine. Our lips were less than an inch apart, our noses practically touching, our eyes staring into the other's, grey to black.

He said nothing, neither did I.

It was just him breathing into my mouth, me breathing

into his, the noise of the club and the people in it fading into quiescence. When his stare dropped to my lips, I moved in, closing the tiny gap between us, and touched my lips to his.

We remained like that for a moment, lips together, no one making the first move. He was hesitant, maybe he was thinking, had doubts. But I wanted him…I think.

Making the decision for him, I moved my lips against his, coaxing, and he obliged, kissing me back. Not hard, not hungry, just savouring.

Abruptly, he broke the kiss and narrowed his eyes in thought. Bringing his lips around to my ear, he whispered, "Fifteen minutes. My office. Third floor, left turn before the bar path. "

Then he drew back and left without a backward glance.

The silence receded and the noise of the club came back full volume. I became aware of more around me than just Chad's scent, lips and mesmerizing dark eyes. I also could feel all eyes on me.

All eyes except Lion's. His attention was directed out to the club, a sign that I had an angry manager to deal with later.

"What in the world was *that*?" Tiara asked, mouth agape.

"You've never seen two human beings kiss before?"

"But-But," she stuttered. "I didn't know you two were dating!"

"We're not dating. There's a *huge* difference between dating and fucking, you know?" Hell, yeah, that was a jab at her.

"So you're fucking him?" she queried excitedly.

The hell was she excited about? *I'm in love with* your *boyfriend, sweetheart.*

"No, I'm not." I waved her off. "By the way, what was that about just now?"

Tiara slumped back in the seat, looking apprehensive. "JK's pissed as shit at me."

Now this sounds juicy! "Aww, what happened, babe?"

She wrung her hands in her lap like a teenager in trouble. "I-I kind of named him as my beau in a magazine interview when asked about my relationship status."

"So what? Isn't he your beau?"

"The truth?" She sighed dejectedly. "No. He was explicit about what he couldn't offer and what he could—which is nothing but casual sex. *Great* casual sex, I might add. But it isn't enough and I want more because he's *so* amazing and I was tired of getting just bits and pieces of him. So I figured, well, maybe if I started doing all the things he was afraid of doing, like commit, maybe he'd go along with it, you know. But all that has been counterproductive so far." Letting out another long sigh, she asked, "How do you make yourself stop loving an unapologetic asshole?"

S. ANN COLE

Here was my opportunity to throw her off him. "What kind of car does he drive?"

"Jeep," she answered. "One with no roof or doors. He also rides a bike."

"Hmm," I considered in an ominous tone, pretending to be in deep thought. "That's not good, hun."

"What do you mean?"

"See, you can tell a lot about a man by the clothes he wears and his mode of transportation," I rambled, making crap up. "I've seen how JK dresses. He doesn't care. Now you say he drives an open Jeep and rides a bike, right?"

"Right."

"What do you get from that, hmm? A vehicle with no doors or roof, a bike with even less."

Take the bait. Take the bait.

Tiara twisted her lips thoughtfully, then her eyes widened, "He doesn't like to be confined or caged in. He needs room to breathe. He needs multiple exits so he can get out quick. Which translates to no-commitment."

Look at that. The wench actually drafted something sensible from the load of bullocks I dumped at her feet. "Exactly."

"So, you think I'm just wasting my time?"

Patting her thigh, I told her, "If you want my honest opinion: yes. You can do so much better."

Amanda was tugging on my other arm, so I turned to her, "What, woman?"

"What did he say?" she demanded with eager eyes.

"He wants me to meet him in his office in fifteen minutes."

"To shag?"

I shrugged. "I dunno."

"Would you shag him?"

"*Well*...he smells bloody awesome."

"Looks awesome, too." She grinned in agreement. "So?"

"So, what?" I played dumb.

"Are you going?!" she snapped, seeing through my game.

"I dunno!"

Except, I *did* know.

Fifteen minutes later, I turned the knob on Chad's office door. He was waiting for me, perched at the edge of his desk in the centre of his disorganized office. Opened boxes of knickknacks were piled about. Seemed he hadn't gotten around to sorting out this part of the club yet.

Closing the door, I leaned back against it, hands still grasping the knob.

The heat and intensity Chad exuded was all-encompassing in his stance with his arms crossed over his chest, legs crossed at the ankles, eyes hard on me.

197

Keeping a distance, I waited for him to speak first.

"I don't do public displays," he broke the intense silence, an edge to his tone.

"Me neither. Sorry about that," I apologized, not sorry in the least. "You mad?"

"Yes." His shoulders jerked up in a shrug. "But I'll get over it." Then he added so quietly I almost didn't hear him, "You tasted so good…"

"You too." *Lame, much? Grow a pair, Kia!*

"Why'd you do it?"

"Because you smell amazing?"

"I take daily showers," he deadpanned. "Twice a day, actually."

"You're being a jerk."

Sighing, Chad uncrossed his hands and pressed them palms-down on his wooden desk. "Saskia, I'm feeling you, on a serious level. And I think I've been pretty damn obvious about it too. But you must know, JK's my brother. I love him, respect him, honour him. So I would never do anything to fuck him over."

Releasing the door handle, I flung a frustrated hand up in the air. "The bloody hell does JK have to do with *anything*?"

"Everything," he acknowledged, and there was this edge to his voice again. "Because you want him, and you want me.

That won't work, Saskia."

"Right. Except, *he* doesn't want me, so what's the point of this conversation?"

I was far beyond tired of hearing Jahleel's name now, to be honest. Who would've thought, right? But Jahleel didn't want me and there was nothing I could do to change that.

Chad smelled amazing, looked amazing, and I wanted to shag him. Not a relationship, no. Just a fuck. That's all. So, how the hell did Jahleel fit into this again?

"Listen," Chad pushed off of his desk and smoothed out his already straightened jacket. "I'm not touching you again unless you promise me you won't go chasing after JK. If you're mine, you're mine and you're marked. I don't share my women. Not even if it's casual."

As he made his declaration, he strode over to me, and now he hovered over me—tall, hot and downright beautiful.

I curled my fingers into girl fists and kept them stiff at my sides to restrain myself from grabbing his face and bringing his lips down to mine. I stopped myself because I wasn't sure if I could do what he required.

See, there were times when I hated Jahleel and wanted nothing to do with him or even hearing about him. Then, there were times when I couldn't function at all until I found myself asking someone, anyone, about him.

At the moment, yes, I hated him. But I knew without a doubt in a day or two, I would be singing a different song.

Even though he swore not to touch me again, Chad raised his right hand to my face and gently traced his forefinger around my nostrils that were no doubt flaring. "So?" he prompted.

"Huh?" I stalled, my breath picking up at his touch.

"Tell me, Saskia. *Please*." The timbre of his voice deepened as he husked out, "I'm dying to taste you again."

My chest rose as I inhaled to speak but before I could, my cellphone pinged. Of course, I didn't have to check it right now, but it was an excuse to not answer Chad right away.

With a frustrated sigh, he took a step back when I retrieved my cellphone from my pocket. There was a text message from none other than Jahleel on the screen.

JK: It's not working...

"Just go," Chad ordered in a quiet, though strained voice.

Did it make sense refusing to leave when I knew I couldn't give him what he exacted? No. So I turned to leave his office, my mind immediately off him and his amazing scent, and instantly fixated on Jahleel.

After an entire week, he messaged me. Just like that, it felt as if it had been only last night since I'd fallen asleep to the rapid staccatos of his heart. Nothing mattered anymore but him, because he messaged me. He was letting me know the platonic Saskia fix he made the visit for last Tuesday wasn't working.

I was still on his mind.

Meandering down the walkway with a silly grin, I tapped out a text.

Me: Sorry 4 being such a pain in the head.

*JK: Like a bad migraine that no
amount of aspirin can drive away.
Sucks.*

Me: Gud thoughts or bad?

JK: Always good ;)

Me: How so? We created no memories.

*JK: That's what daydreams & fantasies r 4.
Wanna call 2 hear ur voice but am in a club.*

Me: Me 2. Wish u were here.

JK: Wish I was there.

Me: I want u, JK.
More than what u r giving.

JK: U need 2 get outta my head.
Can't concentrate. Keep seeing ur lips.

Me: No can do.
Either am in ur head or am in ur bed.
Choose.

JK: Sassy...

Me: Do u want me?
Say yes...
fingers crossed

Me: Not going there.
TTYL

I was scowling at my cellphone, heading back to our booth, when I was grabbed by the arm and yanked to a corner. I raised my startled eyes up to Lion's infuriated face.

Oh crap.

"What did I tell you 'bout public appearances?"

"I wasn't thinking."

"Clearly!" he barked at me. "How much do you know 'bout Indija's personal life?"

Oh Jesus, we were back to this again. Always making me feel like a high school student to bring his points across.

"Only what she wants the public to know," I answered.

Indija was a world class vocalist, greater than I could ever imagine to be, idolized by each and every music artiste there is, male and female alike. Lion believed she was the epitome of what every female artiste should be, so he was forever pointing out her perfection to me. He wasn't aiming to change me into her, no, because she was a paragon of class and elegance. I was the complete opposite—raw and intense. But he used her to illustrate how keeping one's personal life personal positively impacted one's career progression.

"Right," he concurred approvingly. "Why?"

"Because the world's attention is on her as a product, her music and her hard work and not on her personal life, because her personal life is none of the world's business. Personal means *personal*."

"So you *do* listen when I speak then?" he patronized me.

"I'm not a dumb twat!"

"Then stop fuckin' actin' like one!" he barked back. "What happened earlier with Chad, never do shit like that again, you feel me?"

Because I knew I acted like a dumb twat, I didn't argue. "Yeah."

Nodding his head in the direction of Chad's office, he continued, "And on to your personal life, stop bein' a fuckin' chicken head with those two friends."

Did he just call me a...?

My hands balled into fists as I bit out, "*Chicken head*? You only call women you're disgusted and repulsed with chicken heads."

One shoulder jerked in a callous shrug as he dipped into his pocket for his cellphone. "I call it like I see it, Kia."

Closing the space between us, I stepped up and chucked him. He barely budged. "Fuck you, *Lion*!"

Dragging his attention from dialling on his cell, he looked at me and inquired, "Who are you?"

"What?"

"Who the *fuck* are you?"

Spine growing stiff, chin tilted up, I answered, "Saskia Day."

"And who the hell is Saskia Day?"

"World renown, inimitable, one-of-a-kind pop/rock artiste, who, in a short span of five years, is sitting on 4 Grammys, 102 other awards out of 240 nominations, two platinum albums, and a net worth of 149mil, *for now*—because I'm only climbing, not sliding. I have the world by the balls. Women want to be me, girls idolize me, boys masturbate to my pictures, and men daydream of me as their woman. I've got *real* talent and I work *real* hard for every goddamn thing I own. I.

Am. Saskia. Day."

Three thirds of all that was said with feigned confidence, but I didn't want Lion to think I was letting him down, so better to fake it than face it.

He lifted his unattended hand and grabbed my face so his eyes were glaring straight into mine. "Remember that the next time you try to pull a stunt like that again. You can lose it all in a flash if you don't watch what the fuck you're doin'. Feel me? "

His grip on my face tightened when I tried to move. It wasn't to hurt or dominate me, but to discipline me as a caring guardian would, ensuring I got it through my thick scull.

"Also remember, before you decide to jump in Chad or JK's bed and make a complete ass of yourself—like your friend Tiara who's sendin' her reputation to shit when her career's just blowin' up—JK and Chad were born into wealth, so they can do whatever the hell they want 'cause they got nothin' to lose. But you're workin' for yours. *Protect* what you've got and strive for more. Don't throw it all away for a fuck. It's *not* worth it."

It'd been a while since Lion chastised me like this, because I rarely mess up. Lion was good at keeping his artistes in line and making sure there's never any scandal surrounding our names. He wanted the music to be the focus. Even my 'reality' show was scripted to control the message.

Now seeing how monumentally pissed off he was, I realized I've been acting a fool for too long and he felt it was time to bring me back in line.

"Okay," I humbly agreed. "I'm sorry if I embarrassed you."

"Not me, Kia," he exhaled on a sigh, releasing his grip on my face. "Just yourself."

Chapter 12

"WHAT'S WITH THE walk?" I asked Amanda before chocking a spoonful of Haagen Daz Rocky Road into my mouth.

Once again, I was sitting in my kitchen bored and eating junk food bound to give me a few unwanted pounds. But whenever I was bored, all I did was eat.

We were leaving in a couple of hours for London Fashion Week, and Amanda just came home, limping some, though sporting a stupid grin.

Straight to the refrigerator, she plucked out a cold bottle of water and sucked it down in one go before answering, "Zane."

"Huge cock?"

"Enormous."

I burst out laughing, nearly choking on my ice-cream as I remembered Zane telling me I'd never be able to handle him. If Amanda couldn't, then I most certainly wouldn't have been able to because Amanda could handle just about anything and anyone.

Pointing the sticky spoon at her, I inquired, "What's with the resident grin then?"

"Best shag of my life. And the thought of knowing he's *mine...*" She grinned even wider and started out of the kitchen. "I'm gonna pack."

My cellphone pinged, vibrating in a dance across the kitchen counter. Glancing at the screen, I sighed.

JK: Home?

He'd never messaged or rang me back after our brief texting exchange the night before, and I didn't bother thinking about him or Chad, not with the harsh reproof Lion had given me.

If he was questioning my whereabouts, then he had to be back in SF.

Me: Yes.

JK: *Gate.*

Despite the urgent need to hurl from overeating, I shovelled in yet another spoonful of Rocky Road, licking the spoon clean before heading to the front door to open the gate.

Leaning on the doorjamb, I waited for the sound of Jahleel's bike but didn't hear it. Instead, I saw the bright headlights of his red Jeep speed through the gates, swung around the water fountain with inexplicable aggression and came to a screeching halt right at the steps to my house.

Jahleel jumped out without shutting off the engine and bounded up the stairs two at a time. As he approached, he held his arms straight, and his fists opened and closed at his sides. His jaw was clenched, hard and ticking, as he glared fixedly at me.

The man looked enraged.

Watching him warily, I stood straight in the doorway, unsure of what to expect.

Jahleel marched right up to me, reached up and around to grab me by the back of my neck and slammed me up against him. Before I could register what was happening, his lips mashed down on mine.

He kissed me. Kissed me painfully hard.

And I couldn't kiss him back because it was his kiss. He

209

controlled it, manoeuvred it, and wasn't giving me permission to reciprocate. Purposefully.

It felt like as soon as it started, he ripped our lips apart and pushed me back from him.

"There!" he shouted, slicing a hand angrily through the humid night air. "I fuckin' kissed you! Since you want to be kissed so fuckin' badly, Sassy. There it is! You're marked!"

Then it dawned on me what this was all about: he'd heard what happened with Chad. Even so, what the hell did it matter? We weren't together. He told me straightforwardly that we couldn't be together! Now he was all enraged because I kissed his friend who was more than willing to give me exclusivity?

My head was spinning. I was at a point where I was just about tired of his confusing, contradicting mind-fucks.

Leaning back on the doorjamb, pretending I didn't give a heck, I shrugged. "He marked me first."

He responded by loudly grinding his teeth, but I held my footing. "That's what you *think*." He closed the distance once more and leaned into my face, his gold eyes now a haunting dark shade. "You won't do *anything* like that again."

Obstinately, making no promises, I declared, "I'm not yours."

For a quick second, he faltered, his gaze lowering to the ground, then he lifted determined eyes to mine again, "Say you won't."

Voice firm and unwavering, I repeated, "I'm not yours."

"Say. You. Won't."

He wouldn't make promises to me, but he was trying to force me to?

Cheesed right the hell off now, I stomped my foot for emphasis as I yelled in his face, "I'm not fucking *yours*, JK!"

Suddenly his hands came up and cupped my face, and I flinched, anticipating another hard and aggressive hold. But this time, his touch was gentle as the pad of each thumb sweetly caressed my cheekbones. Tipping my chin up, he slowly lowered his lips down to mine and kissed me... soft and promising, here but absent, felt and unfelt.

I had no idea what it meant.

Anger gone from his voice, he softly entreated, "Say you won't, Sassy. Say you'll wait. Please."

Sighing, I gave in, because, let's face it, I didn't stand a chance. "Okay, I won't. But," I added, frowning, "what am I waiting for?"

As he was about to reply, he abruptly turned and began coughing violently. He tried to control it, but the coughs kept coming, each one harsher than the one before. He finished bent at the waist, palms on his knees, taking steadying breaths in and out.

Worried, I put my hand on his shoulder, softly inquiring, "You okay?"

Shrugging me off, he used one hand to push me away from him. He straightened and got out, "Gotta go," before he immediately began coughing again.

Afraid of getting pushed again, I stood grounded and watched as he jogged down the steps and drove off one-handed while coughing into the other closed fist.

"Well, that was entertaining," Amanda laughed from behind me. "A bit anti-climactic, though, don't you think? Pretty sure that's not how it happens in romance novels. He was supposed to storm off like an 'alpha badass', no? That exit was *way* too mortal-like for my taste."

Turning, I glowered at her, but she quickly held her hands up in surrender, grinning from ear to ear. "But hey, who am I to talk, right? I'm so thoroughly fucked, I can't even walk straight."

I struggled to not laugh, but her grin was so wide, I couldn't help it, and we both ended up cackling.

THE NEXT TIME I thought about Jahleel was five days later—

within the very second I landed back on U.S. soil on our return from London Fashion Week.

The whole time I was in London, I was too busy-bodied and tired, with a helluva dinner meetings and parties to get through, and much catching up to do, so I was never spared a second to text or call him.

On the other hand, he didn't try calling me either, so why sweat it, right?

When we got home, everyone was tired, cranky, and grumbling about jetlag as they dragged themselves off to bed. But I was restless and suffering from insomnia, plus it was a mere five minutes after eight.

I wanted to see Jahleel. I *really* wanted to see him. But I tried ringing him for about an hour to no avail.

My fingers twitched for a cigarette, but I had to stay disciplined and keep to one a day, with my tour coming up.

Next, my lips tingled at the memory of Jahleel's kiss, both the hard and the soft. Oh God, I wanted to be near him.

Frustrated with the entire world and my own pathetic life, I rolled out of bed and donned a white *Peace* tracksuit, dragged on a pair of brown Ugg boots and slung my messenger bag across my shoulders.

Thomas spotted me coming down the stairs and set his mug of coffee down on the table, heading out the door before

213

I was at the bottom of the stairs. By the time I was outside, he was holding the Phantom's door open. "Where to, Miss Day?"

"I have no idea," I mumbled as I slid in the back. "Just drive."

Except I *did* know where I wanted to go, and apparently Thomas did, too, because he drove me directly to Jahleel's house.

Was I that transparent?

Jahleel's house was dark, not even the outside lights were on. But both his Jeep and bike were parked in the driveway. Maybe he was out with his friends or...

Retrieving my cellphone from my bag, I messaged him:

Me: *U shagging?*

Around five minutes passed with no reply, and I was just about to tell Thomas to take me back home when the phone pinged.

JK: *Y?*

Me: *I wanna see u*

JK: *Bad night*

Me: *Y? U shagging?*

JK: *The word is 'fucking'*

Me: *Am British, arse!*

JK: *U R living in America now & here we say FUCK & ASS*

Me: *K. Whatever. U 'fucking'?*

JK: *No*

Me: *Well, I wanna see u…*
Plz.

There was a long pause before he replied:

JK: *Told u it's a bad night. Awful.*
But if u insist…
Remember where I live?

Me: *Already outside :-)*

JK: *K. Door's open.*

I told Thomas he could leave then slipped out of the vehicle and sailed up the dark driveway. Somewhat giddy, I had a lot of ideas running through my head of how this night could turn out in my favour.

When I turned the lock and opened the door, the house

was so dark I couldn't see my own hand. Fumbling for my cellphone, I turned on the flashlight app and shone it along the walls for light switches.

One was right next to where Jahleel backed me up the last time I was here. I flicked it on and the hallway illuminated.

No sign of Jahleel.

Ambling down the hall, I took the right turn I knew would lead into the living area. This room was dark too, but with the light pouring in from the hallway, the switch was easy to locate.

That's when I spotted mortal-Jahleel, balled up on one of his humongous red sofas, a thick red blanket covering him from the neck down. He looked half-dead, his face pale, his nose red and aggravated, his eyes vacant and droopy. His mouth hung lax as he breathed though his mouth.

The coffee table was drawn up to the couch within reaching distance, and it was littered with tissues, empty water bottles, cough syrup, Nyquil and aspirins.

Seeing Jahleel like this was a little hard to take in. I was used to him being all hot, sexy alpha male, exuding sheer arse-hole-ism. Now here he was, sick and locked up by himself in a house darker than midnight, without so much as moonlight shining through the windows.

"Jesus, JK," I whispered as I knelt down in front of the

couch and pressed my palm to his forehead. He was burning up. "How long have you been like this?"

He opened his mouth to speak, then weakly lifted a hand from under the blanket and touched his throat.

"Thirsty?"

He nodded.

"Be right back," I pushed up from the floor and rushed to the kitchen.

The entire top row of his refrigerator was stacked with FIJI water, yet he was thirsty. Nabbing two bottles, I returned to kneel in front of him.

He was too ill to hold the bottle himself when I tried handing it to him, so he motioned for me to bring it to his lips. He drank until the bottle was half-empty, but he had to stop to breathe deeply through his mouth.

As I pulled the bottle away, he slapped my wrist and beckoned for more. I wanted to laugh, but I figured the moody Jahleel Kingston wouldn't take that too well, so I put the bottle back to his lips and watched him quaff the other half.

"Like an oasis in the fuckin' desert," he breathed, closing his eyes and settling deeper under the blanket. "Thank you."

"You've been thirsty for a while?" I asked him, brushing a damp lock of hair from his sweaty forehead.

"All day." He had no voice, literally breathing out his

words.

"You haven't had anything to eat or drink all day?" I asked in disbelief.

Concentrating on breathing through his mouth, he didn't answer, he just laid there listless.

"I assume you have the flu, yeah?" Probably picked it up when he was traveling for work.

"Since I got back."

"You've seen a doc?"

He barely inclined his head, looking like he was on the verge of falling asleep. But not having eaten anything all day, maybe even days by the looks of things, he could very well be dozing off to eternal sleep.

"Gave me a shot…Said to get lots of rest and drink lots of fluids. But I keep gettin' worse…Weaker…Can hardly walk…Stuck here." He took another deep, through-the-mouth breath. "Feels…like I'm dyin'."

Tracing my fingertips along his sharp jawline hidden under days of facial hair, I spoke past the dryness in my throat. "It only feels like you're getting worse because you've been taking medication without eating."

A miserable sound came from his throat as he pushed my hand away. "I just want…to get better. Tired of feelin' like this."

There were a heap of questions I wanted to ask. For starters, where the fuck was Krissy when he needed her? But I figured it was best to get some food in his system first.

"Would you like some soup?" I asked, even though it didn't matter what answer he gave because no way in hell was I leaving until he was better.

As he reached out for the tissue box, I handed it to him. Feebly pulling one out, he sneezed into it and tossed it among the pile on the floor. "If you...want to."

"Yes." I emphatically nodded, "I want to."

"Okay," he breathed out again, snuggling further under the blanket, his eyelids lowering down. "Just gonna take a nap."

Then I panicked. What if he took a nap and never woke up? Maybe I was being dramatic, but still.

"No, babe," I whispered. "Don't go to sleep just yet, okay? I'll be quick with the soup."

No answer. I jumped up in dismay and switched on the television, thanking God when I saw he had Netflix. Moving at super speed, I looked for a movie he would love and settled on that suck-arse movie *The Green Hornet*, remembering he wanted to watch it the other night.

By the time I turned back to him, he'd already dozed off.

"Look, JK," I said, shaking his shoulder and waking him

up. "The Green Hornet is starting."

I knew I sounded pathetic, like a mother trying to coax her children into eating their vegetables, but for some reason, I was afraid of him falling asleep, because he looked God awful for having just the flu. I had no knowledge of how long it's been since he'd eaten, but it was apparent he'd mixed or taken too much medication in the hopes of getting better quickly.

His eyes flickered open and he looked up at the sixty inches of television screen in the wall. "Thought you said they were idiots."

"They are." I smiled. "That's why *you'll* be watching them, while I cook."

When I saw the movie had stolen his interest, I stood and headed for the kitchen.

"Raisins," he croaked out, as I stepped into the hall.

"Okay."

After searching all the cupboards in the kitchen for raisins, I found a 10kg cardboard box with Sun Maid Raisins written on the side. *Bingo.* Except it was empty.

Someone was out of raisins.

When I relayed the bad news, he groaned out, "Oh. God. Now I'm *really* gonna die."

Biting my lip to hold back a laugh, I went back into the kitchen, called Thomas and asked him to pick up a restock of raisins, a couple of *Haliborange* Vitamin C tablets and a gallon bottle of Orange Juice.

Slinging off my messenger bag, I tossed it on a nearby stool and set about preparing soup for Mortal Jahleel, all the while thinking I would do just about anything to get A-hole Jahleel back.

THANKFULLY, JAHLEEL WAS lost in the movie and hadn't fallen asleep by the time I got done with the soup. Knowing he hadn't eaten anything but pills and cough medicine for…who knows how long, I made the soup substantial with Irish potatoes, leeks, chunks of chicken breasts, carrots, string beans and okra. On the side of the tray, I put two warm, buttered slices of garlic bread, and a small box of raisins.

"Can you sit up?" I asked him as I set the tray down on the now cleared coffee table.

I had multi-tasked and cleaned up the living area while the soup simmered.

"I'm not fuckin' cripple, Sassy," he muttered grumpily as he struggled to sit up, which he barely managed to do.

Men and their stupid egos.

When he was in a semi-upright position, I set the tray

across his lap and left him to it, turning to tolerate this crap of a movie.

At the sound of a weak harrumph, I looked around and found Jahleel staring at me expectantly, food untouched. "You're not goin' to feed me?"

I made a face. This man was so confusing. "You just said you're not cripple, yeah?"

"Can't lift my hands…" he said, staring at my lips. Because he was so pale and bleary, I couldn't tell if he was messing with me or being serious.

My initial plan was to feed him, of course, but then he'd snapped at me, so I aborted the idea. Even infirmed, he was a pain in the backside. Turning to face him, I sidled closer and took up the spoon.

"Raisins," he whispered.

"You want raisins in your soup?" I looked at him in utter disgust.

When he nodded, I shrugged and tossed the raisins in and stirred the soup before lifting a spoonful to his mouth. He cooperated throughout the feeding process and ate more than I expected him to. I fed him the garlic bread, and he ate both slices like it was nothing. Just how long has it been since he'd eaten?

"Either I'm really, really hungry," he mumbled around a

mouthful of garlic bread, sounding livelier, "or that was the best soup I've ever tasted."

Lifting the tray off his lap, I placed it on the table. "I think it's the raisins."

When he was done and settled back down under his blanket, eyes instantly drooping, I finally asked, "How long has it been since you've eaten?"

He took forever to answer, but he did. "Two days."

Christ. He'd laid here on the couch for two days, sick to death, and called no one for a hand? What the hell was this man's problem?

"Where's Krissy?"

The sigh that came was deep and solemn, "She's never here anymore."

"Did you try calling her?" I asked, not too sure how I felt about scratching into his Krissy wound. "I'm sure she'd drop whatever she's doing if she knew you were ill, JK. You want me to call her?"

"No." He shook his head and closed his eyes. "Doesn't matter. She'll choose him."

I didn't know how to respond to that, except, at least he knew what it felt like to be rejected. However, I couldn't imagine his sister not caring that her brother was lying near dead in a dark house alone and helpless.

"Even if you're sick, half-dead?"

"Yes. You don't know her."

Wow, if that's the case, I hope someone runs her over with a bulldozer. "And your parents?"

"Africa."

"What about Chad? You called him?"

"Russia."

Without a doubt in my mind, I was positive Jahleel had a ton of people he could call but chose not to. He had a business that required him being there in the flesh daily to train and choreograph people. I knew he talked to his workers there to let them know he would be out and assigned someone to be in charge—or else they would've come searching out of worry.

Plus, though he didn't answer my phone calls, he messaged me back perfectly well, so he could've messaged someone for help if he needed to. But no, he was playing Macho Man, thinking he could chew down a mixture of pills each day and get better all on his own. He was now worse and so infirmed he was stuck on the couch and couldn't get up even for a drink of water.

Who does that?

Jahleel was off to sleep before I could say another word. Hearty soups could be somniferous.

I went about cleaning up.

By the time I was done, the crash of my London trip sank in and my lids started closing down on me. I turned the lock on the front door, switch off the hall and kitchen lights, and went back into the living room. I collapsed on the twin red couch opposite Jahleel's.

Reaching for the remote, I switched off the television, and before I knew it, I was out.

Chapter 13

A DEEP MOAN formed in my throat as I neared the edge. His fingers were inside me, his lips were on me, his teeth nipped me, his tongue licked me. His body heat seeped through my hungry pores, and I was tipping on the edge.

"Oh, JK, make me come," I begged with a voice thick with desire.

In response, he sucked my nipple into his mouth and pressed his fingers deeper inside me. *His* fingers, *JK's* fingers, were inside *me*.

The thought alone…Oh, yes…Just as I was about to explode, I woke up.

Gah! I effing hate when that happens!

Sure, waking up at the climax of a dream works well when you're about to die, or falling off a cliff. But it's not pleasant to wake up at the climax when you're about to *climax*!

Keeping my eyes closed, I tried forcing myself back to sleep, back to the dream, but failed miserably. When I opened them, I was on my back with my right hand buried down my knickers, stroking over my wet, sensitive folds.

Disgusted with myself, I removed my hand and looked up at the ceiling and sighed. How ridiculously pathetic was my life? How desperate for an orgasm does one—

Wait, this ceiling with grey crown mouldings wasn't mine... The events of the night before registered in that moment and I remembered where I was.

In slow motion, I turned my head to the side and met Jahleel's golden gaze, watching me. The flickering heat of his gaze caused a flush to crawl up my neck and settle into my cheeks, stinging me there.

Despite the heat of his eyes, he was shivering under his thick red blanket, and I could tell he was hugging himself to feel warmer. Panicking, I was on my feet in a nanosecond, almost tripping as I crossed the room towards him.

"Bloody hell," I swore, tucking the blanket tighter around him. I wasn't exactly sure what to do. The place was hot, I was hot, and he was shivering. "Are you okay?"

227

Jahleel gave me a look, which proved not even illness could abate his arsehole-ism. He would die being an arse. "D-D-Do I look ok-k-kay?"

"Okay, um…" I trailed off, looking around for...what? I wasn't a damn doctor!

Espying his cellphone, I snatched it up. "I need to call your doc for instructions on what to do. What's his name stored as?"

"S-steve Hopk-k-kins."

"Password?" I asked when I tried using the phone and found it locked.

Aiming to control his shivering, his eyes flicked up to mine and remained there as he spelled the code out, "G-R-A-Y."

Gray? His password was gray? Weird.

Tapping in the password, I located his doc's number and dialled as I jogged off into the kitchen to set the kettle on the stove.

When I finally got through to Dr. Hopkins, he assured me the shivering was nothing to panic about, as it was brought on by high fever and would subside soon. He began barking over the phone in sheer frustration about instructing Jahleel not take any other medication than what he'd prescribed…and on and on he went.

Keeping the phone a distance from my ear, I located Jahleel's bedroom. There was a guest bedroom at one end of the second hall, and the Master bedroom was at the other end.

I pushed open the master bedroom door and was taken aback at its vastness, tuning out Dr. Hopkins. The room was so neat and spotless, I was afraid to touch anything.

His bed was as big as mine, and my bed was custom built. The headboard was covered in blood-red suede material, the furniture being polished cherry-wood. An ivory chaise sat at the foot of the bed, and the floor was carpeted in a fluffy cream, looking so comfortable, I wanted to lie down on the floor and fall asleep.

Not a thing was out of place. What a neat freak.

Remembering my purpose for entering the room as the doctor's voice droned on about the temperatures of the body, I searched for a closet door and saw none. There was a bathroom door though, and when I opened it, I spotted another door, like a Jack and Jill, but this other door led into a closet.

A massive closet.

Finding what I was searching for, I picked up one of the many red blankets stacked on a shelf, and returned to the kitchen.

The kettle was whistling, the doctor was *still* talking and Jahleel was probably still shivering. I turned off the stove first.

229

Then said goodbye to the good doctor, keeping the most important points in mind: keep him warm, give him lots of fluids, no more meds for 36 hours, and most of all, *don't* bundle him up in blankets—lucky I heard that bit, because bundling him up in blankets was my initial plan.

As I made to set Jahleel's cellphone down, a message icon floated onto the screen. No sound. It was on silent.

Chewing on my lower lip, I wondered how unethical it would be to spy... But then again, I've never been an ethical girl. Have you seen me? I'm a bloody rock star.

Just saying.

I entered Jahleel's password and unlocked the screen again, as it had automatically locked when I disconnected the doctor's call.

96 unread text messages. 298 missed calls.

Christ, who's *this* popular?

Going against the good, angelic voice in my head, I scrolled down over the messages without opening them so he wouldn't know I spied. But I could see the names of the senders, and the first couple of words in each message. There was a truckload of female names, and messages that started out like, *'You've been on my mi...'*, *'Hey, hot stud! I miss...'*, *'Why are you ignori...'*, *'When can I see you aga...'*

They were endless, and I was tempted to delete them all

so he wouldn't see them. The good, angelic voice got through to me somehow and I left them. He would know if I deleted them anyway.

I did, however, opened each of Tiara's, read and deleted them. All were of her apologizing and begging him not to leave her.

Babii, please.

Just pick up the phone... or text me back.

I'm sorry. I didn't mean to force anything on you. Don't end this.

Please. I CAN do casual, I'll take whatever I can get from you.

Just don't end us.

Blech. Whiny floozy. Delete. Delete. Delete.

Then I took special note of my messages in the midst of all those other messages. The others came in mere seconds before or after mine, yet *my* messages were the only ones opened.

This had me reeling for a second. He purposely ignored everyone, but answered mine? Well, he did ignore my phone calls and it took some time before he texted me back, but still, he replied. To me.

This calmed me some, and I felt all warm and tingly

inside. With that, I stopped the spying and deleting and set the phone down on the kitchen counter. Humbled.

Moving back into the living room, I leaned over Jahleel and swept off the blanket. When he glared up at me with the wish of me dying a slow, painful death in his eyes, I hastily explained, holding up the blanket as a protective barrier, "Your doc says this is bad."

Wrapping his arms around his body, he nodded in compliance. "D-Did he t-t-talk your ears off?"

That made me laugh, because the doctor did talk a lot about details and processes, giving explanations that were highly irrelevant. "I've got a sister who talks in a continuum, so I'm immune to chatty people."

He gave me a shaky smile. "That's w-why I never call him. D-Doesn't know w-when to shut the f-fuck up."

Still A-hole Jahleel even in fits of shivers… I *love* him.

"Be right back," I told him, moving off. "I'll make you breakfast."

"N-no," he stopped me. "Lie down with me."

Looking down at his still irresistible body, clad in grey sweats, red socks and white tee, I hesitated.

What if I took advantage of the situation? Did he know what he was asking? Did he know how obsessed I was with him? Even now? What if I laid down there, manipulated his

232

feeble state, and ended up riding him, debilitating him further?

Noticing my hesitation, he coaxed, "Please."

Well, he said 'please', so…

I removed my hoodie and tossed it over the back of the couch, leaving on my white Cami tank and lowered down next to him, curling up.

"Hug me," he ordered quietly.

Oh, dear Lord, help me.

Sidling up closer, I tucked one arm under and around him, and the other over him, pulling him close. He was flat-iron-hot, yet he was shivering. Amazing how the body operates, huh?

"It w-will stop s-s-soon," he whispered. "Happened s-same t-time yesterday morning."

"But I need to get you something warm to drink, JK."

"Wait…" he trailed off, staring at my lips, it looked like he wanted to say something else but decided against it. "Just wait…"

Somehow, I knew he wasn't talking about me waiting to make him coffee. I didn't know how I knew, but I just did.

Wrapping my arms tighter around him, I pressed flush against his body, and we stayed like that for a while, watching each other, until his shivering gradually eased.

Jahleel moved even closer, and so did I. Our noses

touched, though still platonic.

His fire-hot breath touched my lips, "Aren't you afraid of gettin' sick breathing in my germs?"

Smiling, I shook my head the best I could with our tight space. "*Haliborange Vitamin C Tablets.*"

"What?"

"Each morning, I drop one in a glass of water and drink it," I explained, like I was telling a secret. "Vitamin C, it strengthens your immune system. As long as you take it religiously each day, you'll never get a cold or flu another day in your life."

When he raised a brow, I claimed, "Well, it works for me. Swear by it, I haven't fallen ill since I was a teenager."

His smile illuminated our tiny area. "Guess I need to try it then."

"Yeah," I grinned for no reason whatsoever, "I bought you some."

We fell quiet for a while, until his shivering stopped altogether. As I shifted to move, he said with a half-smile, "You moaned my name...You were dreamin' about me..."

Mortification seeped in again, and I dropped my gaze downward as heat crept up my neck. Why the hell did I have to wake up with my hand down my knickers when I was at *his* home? Seriously, I needed to get laid ASAP. This couldn't be healthy.

My abashed expression wasn't enough for him to cease the torture. "A dirty dream, too, by the looks of it."

"JK," I whispered, avoiding his eyes, "stop."

Reaching a hand up between us, he drew the tip of his forefinger up the side of my neck. "When you're embarrassed, your neck flushes a beautiful shade of red..." His finger continued trailing up over my chin and settled on my left cheek. "And, very slowly, right before my eyes, that lovely flush of colour creeps up to your face, then gathers and settles here and here..." He tapped my cheek on the other side, then settled back on the left. "Here it turns into a full-on blush, giving new meaning to the term 'rosy cheeks'..."

Now, what did I say to that? Were we still in platonic mode or what? Had the arbitrary lines been blurred?

Oh, how I wanted the lines to not only be blurred, but rubbed right out.

"Breathe, Sassy, breathe," he whispered with his wicked crooked smile. "It's just fascinating to watch, that's all."

Untangling myself from around him, I leaped to my feet and shot him an accusatory glare, pointing a stiff finger at him. "Don't tell me to fucking *breathe!* You always do and say things like that to me, then you tell me to *not* be affected."

Shifting over onto his back, he looked up at me, still

235

wearing that damned grin. "You're right, I shouldn't be *tellin'* you to breathe. You'll either breathe or die."

"I don't want to *breathe*," I shrieked, flinging my hands up in the air. "I want you to take my goddamn breath *away*! I want to pant and fucking scream, not *breathe*!"

Jahleel leaned up on one elbow, looking semi-normal, though still a bit pale. "You get excited too easily, Sassy. I say a couple of words, and you go all wide-eyed and asthmatic on me."

He purposely, deliberately, wilfully, completely spoke around all I just confessed, refusing to acknowledge my desire, my need, my craving for him. Jesus Christ, he was exasperating!

Catching my lower lip between my teeth, I tried to calm down. "Because you're *you*, JK," I retorted in defense of my actions. "Is that so hard to understand?" *I'm in love with you, douchenizzle!*

One shoulder moved up in a shrug as he simply responded with, "You're *Saskia Day*."

Sending my eyes heavenward, I waved a dismissive hand at him and made to exit the room. "Whatever, man. I'm going to make breakfast."

I ignored his chuckle on my way out.

As slowly as he was recovering, the infuriating a-hole in

him was coming back. Well, did it *ever* actually leave?

WHENEVER I WASN'T working, the place I spent most of my time was in the kitchen. I loved to eat, even though at this point in time, I had to maintain a diet to be in shape for my upcoming tour. But aside from 'preparing for tours' diets, I dwelled in my kitchen, cooking and eating until surfeited.

Jahleel's kitchen, like mine, was a dream to be in. Very rarely did one find much of anything in a single man's kitchen except beer, water and overnight takeout. But Jahleel's kitchen was stocked, piled and loaded. He must cook a lot. In his kitchen, I was like a kid in a candy store.

For breakfast, I prepared a hearty meal of baked beans, thin-sliced ham, poached eggs, mushrooms, sausage and toasts.

Just as I poured a cup of coffee for Jahleel, he appeared in the second entryway of the kitchen, propped on the wall with one hand. Refusing to acknowledge him, I moved the mugs to the tray and dunked a Lady Grey teabag in my cup. I was still in hate mode.

"Gonna use the bathroom," he unnecessarily announced.

I focused my attention on the task at hand and apathetically responded, "Thanks for the update."

"Aren't you gonna help me?"

That got my notice, and I glanced up at him standing there, eyes twinkling with mischief and a repressed smile. In my judgment, he seemed perfectly capable of going to the bathroom himself. The man clearly took pleasure in screwing with me.

"Sure," I caustically stated, "You want me to hold your *penis* while you *wee-wee*, too? Shake it after, yeah?"

"You're the worst caretaker ever," he pouted, lips twitching as he struggled not to smile.

"Piss off, JK,"

"Someone's in a bitchy mood," he grumbled as he shuffled off.

When he was gone, I allowed myself to smile, knowing he couldn't see. I was still obsessed, of course.

BY THE TIME Jahleel returned, his face somehow fresh and revived as if he had healing water running from his taps, breakfast was set up on the coffee table in the living area so he could eat from the couch.

"Wow…what a spread," he commented, nodding at the food as he sat beside me on the couch. Picking up a piece of toast, he bit in, and while chewing, said, "You're amazing, Sassy. Thanks again."

Stuffing food in both corners of my mouth, I ignored him.

"Still in bitch mode?"

No reply.

On a shrug, he gave up and dug into his breakfast, eating every last drop of food on his place. When the plate was clean, he looked at the cup of coffee on his tray and frowned.

As I lifted my cup to my mouth, he asked, "Can I borrow that for a minute?"

Befuddled, I paused and frowned at him. He took the opportunity to steal the cup from my fingers and sipped my tea.

"Lady Grey," he muttered, nodding in approval.

With my cup, he leaned back on the sofa, pulled up his feet on the couch like a five-year-old, picked up the remote and switched on the television.

"Um," I dragged out, looking at my confiscated cup and back to him, "what's wrong with your coffee?"

Eyes on the television, fingers working the remote, he absently replied, "I don't drink coffee."

"Then why do you have a coffee maker and a 27ounce bottle of Folgers in your darn kitchen?"

239

"Krissy."

I'd thought it odd finding boxes of Twining's tea in an American kitchen. They were supposed to be coffee lovers, but I didn't pay it much mind at the time. I just assumed he was a coffee drinker instead of asking. "So, are you going to give me back my tea?"

Without looking at me, he shooed me off with the remote, "Get your own."

Batting down the urge to punch him, or kiss him, or rape him, I cleared the trays and washed the dishes.

I poured two glasses of ice-cold water and dropped two of the Vitamin C tablets in each to dissolve. Mine was quaffed in one go. I brought Jahleel's to him, setting it down on the coffee table. "When you're done with that, drink this. All of it."

"Yes, Ma'am."

The doorbell rang just then and I started for the door, knowing it was Thomas.

Jahleel's voice stopped me. "You're leaving already?"

When I swivelled back around, he was watching me from under his lashes—a look I was positive he used whenever he wanted to win one over. He wanted me to stay.

"No. That's Thomas dropping off clean clothes for me," I told him. "I'm staying until tomorrow...if you're okay with that?"

"Yeah, yeah, of course." He sounded relieved. "But, don't you have shit to do?"

"Yes, but I had my assistant shift around a couple of things on my schedule so I would have today free."

"Ah." He sipped his tea and peered at me over the rim, eyes devilish. "Well, you're welcome to stay, but you have to stop being mean to me…"

My mouth opened and closed like a sock puppet as I gaped at him, stammering, "I-I-*I'm* being mean to you?"

"You were being a bitch earlier."

"You were being an arse!"

"Oh," he mumbled, choking back a laugh. "My bad."

"*Really*, JK?"

Did he have to be such a thorn in my side? And why did I fall even more in love each time he acted like this? Maybe I loved it when he screwed with me as much he revelled in it? Not to mention the way he taunted with such seriousness, making it hard to tell whether he was messing with me or not.

"Bad manners to keep someone waiting at the door, Day."

Mouth still agape, I stared at him, searching his face for something, anything which hinted he was being humorous, but found nothing. He was serious. But he couldn't be. He was a damn good actor, that's for certain.

Doing the only thing I could think of since words were

S. ANN COLE

failing me, I flipped both middle fingers up at him, spun on my heels and flounced off to answer the door.

Thomas had a damn suitcase, and I took one look at it and knew Amanda had crammed it with a crap ton of extraneous items. She could be a tad extra at times.

After giving me a quick brief on what was going on at home, Thomas left and I proceeded with my suitcase down the hall. Stopping at the entrance to the living room, I popped my head in. "I'm gonna shower, okay?"

"Thanks for the update," he said, mimicking my earlier response.

"Is…" I hesitated. "I'm only telling you because I want to know if there's anywhere I'm prohibited from going?"

Slowly, he turned and peered at me over the edge of the couch. "You serious?"

I nodded.

"Sassy," he said, most patiently assured, "You came over and found me on my last leg and stayed without being asked. You're solely responsible for me being better. You've been making your way around here taking care of me as if you've lived here all your life. And *now* you ask me this?"

He turned and directed his attention back to the television. "You wanna clean a fuckin' drawer out and make it yours, I'm not stoppin' you. You fit. Perfectly."

I stared at the back of his head, gobsmacked. Now, now what was *that* supposed to mean? Was he being literal or just bringing a point across? Surely, 'getting a drawer' with Jahleel Kingston couldn't be *that* easy, especially since he was refusing to sleep with me at all cost.

First it was that enraged kiss, then the promise he forced out of me, and now this? His mixed signals were confusing. Maybe he truly wanted me to be his platonic friend, but one who didn't sleep around?

I don't know. I honestly didn't know what his deal was.

Dragging along my suitcase, I headed to his bedroom.

The sensible part of me assured me he wasn't being literal about the drawer statement, so I wheeled my suitcase over to a corner in his bedroom and popped it open.

As suspected, it was stuffed with a lot of crap, including a long strip of condoms situated on the top. That damn Amanda. What part of platonic did she not understand?

Selecting a black Bob Marley tee, red Nike shorts and frenchies, I tossed them on the bed, grabbed my toothbrush and shower gel, then stripped down as I made my way into the shower.

Gratefully, there were no pictures of Krissy on this side of the house, or I'd be forced to ruin them. The bathroom was all-white and glass, extra pristine, creating the illusion that it was larger than it actually was, with the only colour being the red towels and washrags on shelving, and a vase of red roses on the centre of the vanity.

A large tub sat on one side of the bathroom, a long rectangular-shaped shower on the other side. After cleaning my teeth at the sink, I opted for the shower.

Around ten minutes passed after I showered but I lingered under the soothing shower as I tilted my face up under the warm water.

Had to admit, I enjoyed being in Jahleel's shower more than my own—not because it was better, but simply because it was *Jahleel's shower.*

At the sound of the shower door sliding open, I stilled. The hell?

Snail's pace, I opened my eyes and turned around, the water still beating down on my head. I stopped breathing altogether. I forgot how to.

What were the mechanics of exhaling and inhaling again? How exactly did the lungs work? Would I die if I didn't breathe? Because, at the moment, I couldn't. Not with Jahleel standing in front of me.

Naked. Bloody *naked*. Not with a flaccid cock, either. Oh no, that sucker was standing to attention, saluting me: 'Ma'am, yes, Ma'am!'

"W-what are you doing?" I managed, running my eyes all over him.

I didn't know where to look first. Jesus Christ, he was even hotter naked.

A very well-defined V shape went right down into his smooth brown curls. His abs, good God, his abs were rock hard and conspicuously boastful; it was like you could reach out and pluck one off his stomach. His pecs round, formidable. Shoulders, broad and intimidating, now that they weren't downplayed by a simple T-shirt.

In fact, naked, his body was a lot different than one would guess: taller somehow, wider, stronger...the way he dressed in casual, rugged wear, did indeed deemphasize his physical per-fection.

It was all quite a lot to take in, especially when he moved in closer until his dick was touching my leg. One arm reached around me as he picked up his body wash and squeezed some on his wash rag.

"Showering," he answered to my long-forgotten question.

We were a hair's breadth apart, his cock still touching my leg as he watched me with his washrag in hand. But I was too occupied drooling over his body and the warmth of his dick head against my inner thigh to care about his intense gold gaze.

This man here, he was real. Real hard. Real fierce. Real

hot. Real sexy. Real tempting. Real torturous. Just fucking *real*.

Moving in closer, I lifted a hand to feel the smattering of hair on his chest, but as quick as a wasp, he slapped my hand, leaving a sting behind.

"Don't touch me," he asserted gently.

"W-w-*what*?" I stammered, taken aback. "*You* came in here, buddy."

Reaching around me, he wet his rag under the shower and began lathering his skin, keeping his eyes on my face and no-where else. "First off, this is *my* bathroom. Second, I haven't showered in three days."

"You couldn't wait until I was finished?"

"For some reason, I grew pretty desperate for a shower all of a sudden. Felt intolerably dirty, you know?" Smiling se-cretively, he shrugged. "You were takin' too long."

"I want to touch you," I said, not in the mood for his games.

"No."

"Well, then, you can't touch me either."

He held up his hands, "Not touching you."

Arching a brow, I cocked my head to the side and slowly lowered my gaze down to where his dick rested comfortably against my inner thigh.

He, too, tilted his head to the side and commented, "Oh, that...that has a mind of its own. What it does or doesn't do is not on me."

"So, does that mean I can touch *it*, then?"

He bit his lip and shook his head.

"This sucks," I grumbled, turning back around under the shower.

Except it was harder this time, knowing there was a naked Jahleel behind me, and my core was wetter and hotter than the water spraying from the shower above us. I was exponentially aroused and needed to have an orgasm, lest I explode.

I felt Jahleel's washrag passing over my bum, soaping it downwards. "You've got a curvy—"

Fast as lightening, I spun around and shoved him hard against the chest. He moved back a mere inch. "Don't touch me, you spiteful, torturous, son of a dicksucker!"

"It's son of a pastor, actually," he corrected, grinning.

"This is not a joke, JK!" I shrilled, feeling like crying. "You can't keep doing this to me. I'm human. And of the opposite sex. With a vagina. A vagina that desperately needs this monster against my leg inside it!"

"Calm down, woman," he chuckled. He handed me the washrag, "You can bathe me, but that's all."

My scowl deepened. "How exactly will that have me

screaming your name in ecstasy?"

"It won't," he replied, smile melting as seriousness supplanted. "Platonic, remember?"

Waving a hand between us, I hissed, "*This* is not platonic."

"This is my kind of platonic," he shrugged, nonchalantly, "As long as you don't touch, *touch* me."

Out of fight, strength and words, I reached up and started soaping his shoulders, down to his pectorals, as platonically as I could manage. "You're not being fair."

"I know," he whispered, all serious now. "But it's for your own good, Sassy."

I lathered him in silence, taking my own sweet time, even though I could feel his eyes on my face instead of my body, studying, searching for who knows what.

Taking pleasure in admiring every inch of his body, I slowly soaped the intricate tattoo designs on his side. A swirl of vines and thorns and something resembling an open Bible choking in the midst of it.

Moving across the hardness of his abs, I soaped the inscription on his left arm that started from his shoulder down to his wrist. I'd never gotten the chance to see his tats up close before. The inscriptions were a jumble of questions being repeated over and over, from shoulder to wrist:

Why don't you ever speak to me? Is it because I'm bad? What can I do to be good? Will you talk to me then? What is faith? Is it real? What's my fate? Are you real? Why don't you ever talk to me? Is it because I'm bad? What can I do to be good? Will you talk to me then?...

On and on it went. When I sneaked a peek up at him, he was still watching me. Was this tat about Krissy? I wanted to ask, but I was afraid it would ruin the moment, and the opportunity of soaping Jahleel Kingston's naked body would be lost.

"It's not about her," his spoke above me, somehow knowing the thoughts in my mind.

Guess he figured out that *I'd* figured out he had feelings for his sister. "What's it about, then?"

"Nothing I wanna talk about."

The tone of his voice told me to let it go, so I dug no further and continued soaping him until I reached his cock. The thing was fucking beautiful. I estimated it to be over seven and half inches long. Perfect.

As I took him in my hand, I peered up at him from under my lashes for permission, and he shrugged, saying, "You've got to soap all of me, don't you?"

Lowering my head to hide a smile, I gently moved the sudsy rag over his wide, engorged head, red with blood. Using my other hand to glide the soap down his venous length, I

S. ANN COLE

sighed at its steely hardness beneath my fingers.

Above me, I could hear Jahleel's breathing faltering as I moved my palm over and down his length and back up, before circling my thumb around the underside of gorgeous head.

This hard, beautiful thing needed to be in my mouth. Inside me.

I must have been soaping that particular area of his body for too long, because I heard his ragged voice command, "Move along now, Sassy."

"Boo," I whined, letting go of his dick and soaping his hips, down his thighs, spending little time on his legs, lest I be tempted to slip his cock in my mouth.

I paused only long enough to study the tattooed inscriptions on his right leg, but it was written in Greek, so I came right back up and tugged him under the spraying shower with me, taking him by surprise.

He laughed out when his body collided with mine. "Whoa!"

The water beat down on us, washing off the soap.

Reaching up, I put my arms around his neck, and he surprisingly let me. Water droplets dripped off his long lashes, his hair was plastered to his forehead, and his full, sculptured lips were parted, as he seemed to be recovering from something, somehow.

He was beautiful. Did he know I was in love with him? Obsessed, even?

I wanted to hug him until we became one, crawl into him, feel everything he was feeling, make our hearts coalesce and beat as one. How was it possible for me to love him this much when we have few to no moments together? When I knew not much about him, except the obvious? When we haven't shared much of ourselves with each other?

Was it him I was in love with? Or was I obsessed with the *idea* of being in love with him?

As he watched my lips, I could see the deliberation going on in his head. He wanted me, too. Of course he did. His cock said it all. But for some unknown reason, he was holding back. He wanted me, but he didn't. He wanted me, but he wouldn't take me. Not even for casual sex. He offered casual to others, and offered me platonic. Why?

"I want to suck you off," I blurted.

He didn't seem surprised. "Platonic."

"Okay, well, I want to kiss you."

"Platonic."

"Just one, small, tiny kiss."

Clamping down on his bottom lip, he tried to hide a smile. "Oh, one small kiss can go a mighty long way…"

"Nope." I shook my head. "You kissed me last week,

remember?"

"That's different," he countered, "Now we're naked. Wet. Aroused. Nothing's stoppin' me from sliding right inside you."

Oh. God. That sounded so good. Tempting. The heaviness between my thighs grew more unbearable by the minute.

Sighing, I looked down at his live and erect cock nestled between us. The sight alone made me feel like climaxing. "Aren't you afraid of getting blue balls?"

At that he chuckled, his smile so radiant that I had to smile too. "Sassy, every time I walk away from you, I walk away with a raging hard-on. So I'm used to it by now."

Frowning, I chewed on my lip as I thought about this.

Okay, so he wanted me, like, really wanted me. But he was denying himself. That was the baffling part. I wasn't playing hard to get, I was more willing than a hooker on the street side.

Because I was tired of busting my brain, I just asked him, "Why, JK? Why won't you sleep with me? What's the big deal?"

Moving in even closer so his body was flushed against mine, he answered, "For me, *you* are a big deal."

Huh?

Before I could get another word out, he spun me around in one quick motion and backed me up against the marble-tiled wall, moving in so his dick glided along my folds.

"Hmnh," I moaned.

Him, against me, wet, sliding…felt amazing.

"I've got a confession to make," he whispered.

"Yeah?"

"I'm obsessed," he admitted even quieter.

With me? Ohmigod, with me? "With…?"

Tilting up my chin, he studied my lips, passing his thumb across them. "Your lips," he breathed out, "I love them. I'm tortured by them." Touching a finger to the centre of my top lip, he continued, "This little pointy pout here, it does things to me. Especially when it's wet, like now."

He leaned down and kissed the spot he touched, then drew back and watched it in fascination as if waiting for something to happen.

In this case, I wasn't sure what Jahleel expected to happen. They were just lips, and they wanted more of his kisses.

The thought was barely completed when he dropped his lips back down on mine. Hard and ravishing, his tongue chased around mine, and applying more pressure, he kissed me even deeper as if he couldn't contain himself any longer. Cupping my face and holding it in place, he made my mouth his.

Oh God, yes. I'd never been kissed like this before, hard and controlling, but profoundly passionate.

Undulating my hips, I rubbed my centre up against his erection, moaning in his mouth as pleasure heightened and intensified in my veins.

With a deep, throaty groan, he slowed the kiss, bit my lip, hanging on to it for a bit before he released it and dropped his forehead to mine. "Because I'm not ready to be owned yet."

Lost and confused, I stared up at him, wondering what he was talking about.

"That's the answer to your question," he filled in, pushing away from me. Far away.

And I felt bereft, like I'd lost something monumental here and now.

Jahleel turned and opened the shower door. "C'mon."

Chapter 14

I STOOD STILL with my back against the wet tiles, watching Jahleel through the shower glass as he nabbed a towel from the shelves and began towelling himself, his back muscles rippling with each move, the KINGSTON inked across his upper back unsteady with each flex, his waist slim and narrow, he even had lower back dimples like a bitch. I wanted to lick him all over, suck him, ride him, lock my legs and arms around him… *le sigh.*

What did he mean by 'not ready to be owned'? Was he intimating that I had the power to claim him, own him, make him settle? How could that possibly be when I was such a tongue-tied, dim-witted klutz around him? That couldn't be

S. ANN COLE

what he meant. He'd been dropping these confusing lines and signals, making me more and more confused each hour—

"Sassy," he called, dragging me from my reveries. "C'mon."

Worn and wearied, I pushed off the wall and went to him. The sound of his voice, I'd follow it anywhere, anytime, any day, even down into the pit of hell. As long as he'd be there, I wouldn't mind burning in eternal flames.

When I got to him, he leaned back on the vanity, and in one swift go, he wrapped the towel around me and yanked me into him, tucking the towel ends in at the front. Reaching over to the shelf next to us, he grabbed a hand-towel and ordered, "Turn around."

As I did, he snaked an arm around my waist, pulled me even closer to him and used his right leg to nudge between my legs so they shifted wider apart, causing me to shift down lower, my back to his chest.

Just as I was about to ask him what he was doing, he began drying my hair with the hand-towel. A simple thing it was, yet it made me feel cherished.

"They become submissive when wet," I heard him comment, dissevering my thick load of wet hair into sections to dry it better.

"What?"

"Your curls," he explained. "Dry—they're wild and rebellious. Wet—they're tamed into finer curls and flow together."

This moment, I was loving it.

Jahleel Kingston was towel-drying my hair, and most of all, being nice. To me.

"Which do you think suits me best?"

"Both." I detected a smile in his voice. "When wild, you look like a complete badass. When wet, you look innocent and young and virginal. Makes me wanna fuck your mouth, come on your tongue and dirty you up."

"Oh jeez…" I muttered under my breath, which had him chuckling.

After a long pause, he divulged, "But neither are my favourite…"

"No?"

"No."

Tossing the hand-towel on the vanity, he slowly turned me around to face him. "Grammy Awards. Three years ago. You won Best Album. You wore this sexy, sexy red dress. Split came all the way up to here."

He moved a hand down between us and dragged a finger up my left thigh to remind me where the split had stopped, which was far past mid-thigh. "Your hair was longer than this. It was straightened and parted in the centre so it flowed down

257

both sides of your face. And when you looked into the camera, those striking cat-like grey eyes…" His reminiscing trailed off and he shook his head, while I gaped.

Who knew three years ago he was watching me on television and found me attractive? Who knew he'd even remember, in detail, how I was dressed?

"I can't even remember what I was wearing yesterday, let alone three years ago."

Eyes roaming over my face, they lingered on my lips for a moment before he reached out and touched the same spot he'd touched in the shower. "I do."

Pushing me back a few feet from him, he turned and took up the damp hand-towel and tossed it in the laundry basket. He also took up my toothbrush I'd left tossed messily on the vanity with water droplets around it, and the toothpaste cap open.

I interpreted his diverted attention as a sign of dismissal and started out of the bathroom as he set my toothbrush upright next to his in the holder, closed the toothpaste cap, grabbed a rag and began wiping down the vanity.

Neat freak.

When I stepped into the bedroom, my suitcase that I'd left open and spilling in the corner was zipped closed and standing upright. My dirty clothes I'd stripped off while heading to the bathroom was picked up off the floor, folded in a neat pile, and placed on the seat of his armchair opposite my suitcase. And the clean clothes I'd thrown on the bed were arranged.

Christ. The guy was a walking, talking contradiction. How could someone who wore ragged ripped jeans, rugged boots or ratty sneakers and T-shirt all the time, rode a bike and drove a roofless, door-less Jeep be a compulsive neat freak? How on earth was that even possible?

I sat at the edge of the bed moisturizing my legs when Jahleel sauntered into the bedroom naked, casual, carefree and comfortable in his skin.

Did he even care that I was an orgasm-hungry woman in the presence of a man I've been wanting, dreaming, fantasizing about for the past five plus years?

He made a beeline to his dresser, pulled out white boxers from the top drawer and donned them. When he glanced in the mirror and caught me watching him, the forgotten bottle of moisturizer suspended mid-air, one leg crooked up on the bed and the towel draped between my thighs, a small smirk formed on his lips and he winked at me.

He turned and came over.

Snatching the bottle from my hand, he sat down beside me, squirted some moisturizer in his palm and began moisturizing my leg.

What *the hell* did I ever do to get on his good side? And how long would it last, exactly?

"You always this easily distracted?" he asked my leg, his fingers doing more massaging than moisturizing.

"If you had *any* idea how badly I want you, you'd stop being so casual with your dick out."

"What you gonna do, rape me?"

"Molest, sexually harass, sexually assault, gag, bound… Seriously, don't tempt a horny woman."

He chuckled as he raised his eyes to mine. "You need to get over this…me."

"What if I don't want to?"

The last of my sentence came out in breathy sigh as Jahleel's hand smoothed up my inner thigh, causing his thumb to make a light brush against my folds. With his other hand, he tapped the side of my thigh as a signal for me to switch legs.

"You should," he encouraged.

Contented, I watched as he once again squirted lotion in his palm to moisturize my other leg. "You still think you'll hurt me?"

Fingers doing that massaging thing on my calf again, he replied, "Didn't say I *think*."

Nodding in understanding, I stated, "You know."

"*You* know, too."

"Yeah," I agreed, resigning myself to just enjoying this cherishing side of his nature while it lasts.

Abruptly, he turned his head and sneezed, then coughed. He sneezed again, and soon he began coughing uncontrollably. With a grunt of annoyance, he got up and started pacing the length of the room in irritation.

Of course, he'd mistaken his return of vitality as being all better.

"You have to give yourself at least forty-eight more hours of rest," I told him, getting up from the bed to stop his pacing. "You only started recovering a few hours ago."

"I fuckin' hate this," he carped, flopping backward onto the bed.

Who on earth liked being sick?

Getting dressed in a quick minute, I attempted to distract him, "I'll go fix you a club sandwich, okay?"

"Not hungry," he grumbled, then reached out his hand to me, "Come. Watch cable with me."

"After starving yourself for two whole days, you need to—"

"For fuck's sakes, Sassy, just get the fuck over here and stop actin' like my mother!"

"Fuck you," I spat and turned to power-walk out of the room.

But he was quicker than me. Hopping up from the bed, he caught me around the waist and dropped back on the bed with me.

He swept my hair to the side so his mouth was at my ear, and hissed, "Just so you know, I don't care for Bitchy Sassy. She makes me want to do wicked, evil, nasty, degrading...*things* to her."

I wiggled in his arms and he loosened them only long enough to switch around so he was on top of me, smirking.

"Maybe I should start being Bitchy Sassy more often then, yeah?"

A sudden hardness pressed against me. Hell. He got hard in 0.2 seconds flat. Lowering his face down to mine, he nipped at my bottom lip. "Why?"

Before I could form a cognitive thought, he moved so fast it took me a moment to realize my shorts were off and my legs were forced wide apart.

Taken by surprise, all I could do was stare up at him, panting, anticipating...

"'Cause you think being Bitchy Sassy will get you this?" He whipped his dick out of his boxers, shifted my knickers to the side and pressed his wide head at my soaked entrance.

"Oh, God..." I mewled, impatient to feel him surge inside me, filling me.

But he kept nudging me, teasing me, and I kept wanting, needing and wasn't getting. *Come in...Come in...*

Lifting my hips, I tried to force him past the entrance, but he swiftly drew back and tucked himself back inside his boxers, then straightened my knickers.

The hell?

"You're not fuckin' gettin' it," he firmly stated. "So quit being a bitch."

This man...Arrrgh! "And you need to quit being an arse!"

"It's ass."

"Piss off!"

"It's fuck off."

I pushed at his chest, fighting to get the arsehole off me, but he wouldn't budge. "I *really* don't like you."

"And I know a lie when I hear it," he said, promptly following it up with a deep, long, but torturous kiss.

I simpered and melted into him, my legs submissively wrapping around his waist, hands going around his neck. I could totally do this kind of platonic, as long as it meant I would get unexpected and sporadic kisses such as this.

Too soon, he ended it, pushed up on his elbows and looked down at my dazed face.

"Now," he whispered, "will you relax and watch crap TV with me? I like havin' you near me."

Dumbly, I nodded, and a complacent smile crawled onto his face as he shifted me up further to the middle of the bed, grabbed the remote and switched on the television.

A CHOKING WARMTH woke me.

Indolently, my eyes whispered open and it took me a minute to remember where I was. And with whom.

I was in a tangled, fever-hot heap with Jahleel Kingston—his right leg sandwiched between both of mine, one arm crooked around my waist, the other hooked under and around my neck, with my face pressed against his chest. I was being held on a tight leash, with little to no breathing space, forced to inhale whatever air he exhaled.

There was no cognitive memory of how we ended up in this heap, except that I'd dozed off watching a *Sons of Anarchy* marathon with him.

Being as quiet as I could, I untangled myself from the white-hot man-heat, snuck out of bed and sleepily strolled out to the kitchen.

The sun's glare had faded outside the windows, heralding the inevitable darkness called night, so I decided I might as well start preparing dinner. No matter what the gold-eyed man in the next room said, he had to eat.

It had been a while since I'd taken care of anyone, what with Ferbie and Timberly not so dependent on me anymore. It was the other way around now, as I had the world at my beck and call. So much that I'd forgotten how much I enjoyed giving, helping, taking care of. Now, I was back in my zone.

As I was sliding a baking tray with two stuffed Cornish hens into the oven, music came on over the integrated speakers. Jahleel was up.

But I didn't see him until around half-an-hour later when I was striking up a Davidoff while leaning against the kitchen counter. Just as I lit up the cigarette, it was snatched from my fingers. Turning, I saw Jahleel behind me, his fingers crushing my cigarette into a painful mess of tobacco.

"Hey!" I yelled, slapping my palm down on the counter.

"You need to quit."

"You're not the one to say I quit," I shot back. "Look, I only get to smoke one cig per day now with my tour around the corner. Back off."

"Not while you're here."

"Really, JK, I need to take at least one draw or I'll go crazy."

"Go crazy."

Snatching up the pack of cigarettes off the counter, I started moving down the other side of the island to leave the kitchen. "Fine. I'll smoke outside."

By the time I got to the end of the island, Jahleel was there, his bare chest in my face. "What about the food? It'll burn, 'cause I won't check on it."

"Let it burn, then."

"And what will I eat?" He licked his lips. "You?"

Slowly drifting my eyes from his chest and up his face, I hissed, "You really like to play, don't you?"

Jahleel was like a heavy-current river you can't get around, and if you tried crossing it, its depth and wild, swift rush will swallow you up whole and whisk you off to somewhere beyond your control, taking the final decision of your destination out of your hands. No woman stood a chance with him.

Biting his damned lip—which I now realized was a teasing habit of his—he slanted his head to the side, one eyebrow raised, and I stood there wondering what the hell that look was about, until our silence made me aware of the song playing over the speaker: Goapele's *Play.*

How bloody apt.

To think I wasn't even paying attention to the music when I said that. But, of course, he thought differently.

"You don't like that I like to play?" he asked, mischievousness flashing in his eyes.

"No," I snapped. "That's the point. You have too many curves and intricacies. I want you to be *straight*."

All that was a waste of breath, because he wasn't even listening to me, as his hips were already moving to the music. He was wearing a white pocketless sweatpants riding dangerously low on his hips, his defined V starting from his hipbone and disappearing down below the sweatpants.

Hell and damnation, I wished he'd stop moving his hips to the rhythm like that so I could continue being irritated instead of distracted, and go get my smoke fix. I needed to forget about the ball of fire in front of me.

Jesus, why did he continue to do this? Torture me?

"JK," I whispered, forcing my eyes away from his V. "You know how you look. You know how I feel. You know what I want. *Stop* fucking playing with me and this platonic thing will work out fine."

Still, he wasn't listening, as he snagged the cigarettes and lighter from my hand and tossed them aside. They bounce off a wall and fell to the ground.

Clasping my hips, he roughly yanked me up against him, urging my hips to move in sync with his. For a brief moment, I wondered if he forgot I couldn't dance. Not even a little bit.

S. ANN COLE

A brief moment was all I was allowed to wonder, because before I knew what was happening, I was being lifted up off the floor quite effortlessly by my hips, and placed up on the kitchen island.

To a sharp base drop of the music, he ripped my legs wide apart with a swift, yet smooth move, and next he was easing up on the island, moving in so that I had no choice but to lower back on the counter. He kept coming forward, slow, to the flow of the music, and I kept slithering further up on the island until we were in the centre.

What was he going to do? Dance on top of me?

Seizing my arms, he raised them above my head and left them there, slowly dragging the tips of his fingers down my inner arms, down my sides to settle on my hips again.

There was a passionate expression on his face as he listened to the music and made his every movement match the rhythm. He wasn't even looking at my face, he was watching my body and his hands on my body.

In his mind, he was dancing. In my mind, I was being seduced.

Non-platonically so.

Lifting my Bob Marley tee up to my breasts, he touched the spot where the tee was bunched up with one finger and trailed it down my stomach, face intense, like a sculptor admiring his work of art.

Next, his tongue touched said spot and followed the path of his finger, stopping at my navel, where it dipped inside and swirled.

I moaned and sighed at the same time, as searing, aching heaviness settled within.

Without lifting his head, Jahleel flicked his eyes up the length of my body to meet mine peering down at him. Eyes still on mine, he pushed my thighs far, far apart, all in tune with the music. Then moving his head to the left, he licked his tongue down my inner thigh, traveling down and around to the erogenous area behind my knee.

"Hmmmnh," I moaned again, as he switched over to the other thigh and did the same.

Drawing up on his knees, he lifted my right leg up with him and, oh so gently, ran his fingertips along my sole.

One would expect that to tickle, but with the gentleness of his touch in the right way, at the right spot, I was letting out another long-winded moan, frustratingly aroused.

The song dimmed in volume, signalling its inevitable end, and I knew once Goapele stopped singing, Jahleel would stop dancing. That thought frustrated me even more.

"Just fuck me already!"

At that, three things happened: the music ended, the oven

beeped, and Jahleel's phone rang from somewhere in the house.

End of.

I wish he had just let me go smoke the damn cigarette.

Crawling up over me, bottom lip caught between his teeth, he brought his mouth to my ear and said, "*That* was playing. I plead not guilty to any other alleged 'playing'."

He shifted and hopped off the island, sauntering out of the kitchen just as Neyo's *Say It* came over the speakers.

Did he always put on these kinds of music whenever he had women over and 'played' with them like he did me just now?

With each touch of his hands on me, each press of his lips on mine, thinking about him with other women was starting to hurt. It never used to. I used to feel crazy jealous, yes, but not hurt.

Being here, being with him, spending time creating memories to think back on, was downright stupid. A death-trap for my poor, piteous heart.

Why was I doing this when I knew it would never be more than what it was? When I knew Jahleel would never be anyone different than who he was?

Amanda's right, I slid off the kitchen island and turned off the oven, *I'm a frigging masochist.*

Finding my pack of cigarettes and lighter where he'd tossed them on the floor, I scooped them up and stormed through the front door, slamming it with a loud bang. I didn't want to think about which slut he was talking to on the phone in the other room.

More than ever now, I needed a smoke.

Chapter 15

"Oh, wipe that miserable look off your face. Another fifty frames and we'll be out of your hair," declared the photo shoot director, Derek.

He stood behind my chair in the makeshift dressing room, watching me with queer fascination as Amanda dabbed my face with dramatic make-up. Extra-smoky eyes, long fake lashes, exaggerated eyebrows, ruby red lips, the works.

"Hallelujah?" I wearily proclaimed.

Having been at this acrobatic photo shoot in L.A for the past six hours, changing hairstyles, make-up and outfits, and being instructed to twist and contort my body into positions I didn't know were possible. I was hungry, knackered and most of all, sexually repressed.

For the past eight days, I've been stuck in L.A with events too close together for me to fly back and forth to SF. But the main reason behind my miserable temperament was, of course, *him*.

The longer I was out of SF, the more distant I felt from *him*, and the more I missed something we didn't have. Something we didn't share.

It was dumb, I know. But I liked keeping my imagination alive.

Derek flashed me a wide grin that wrapped around his face, walking away as some distant voice called for him. He loved me, loved working with me, and always wore that broad grin whenever I was around.

Truth be told, most people just inexplicably loved me. A warm, automatic love, just as most people would automatically love a precocious prodigy.

Sometimes I thought it was because of Lion—the man was possibly the world's most loved person—and sometimes I thought it was because he'd trained me well. My facial expressions, smiles and comments were, half the time, stark contradictions to what was truly going on inside my head: nasty, boorish, mocking thoughts. One could never tell based on my outer appearance.

273

"So," Amanda swept the blush brush over my cheeks as she opened up the conversation.

She was transforming me into Cat Woman. My hair had been straightened and gelled back into a tight ponytail, my nails were painted black, and I was dressed in a butt-tight, faux leather onesie.

"...you've been unusually tight-lipped since you spent those two nights with...you know...*him.*"

Pulling at the faux leather sucked onto my thigh, I ignored her and that topic. Again. True, I hadn't spoken of him at all and didn't want to, but my thoughts were right there.

"One would think you'd be in a better disposition after that dream-come-true sleepover, yeah?" She went on, digging. "What? Was he a disappointment? Was he awful in bed?"

"I wouldn't know," I mumbled.

"W-what?" Amanda stopped working and shot me an incredulous stare in the mirror. "You wouldn't know?"

"Right."

"So, you're telling me you spent two nights in that debaucher's bed and there was no sticking it in the poi-yoi?"

As always, whenever she referred to sex as 'sticking it in the poi-yoi'—which made no sense whatsoever—I snickered.

"You know how a man would refer to a woman as 'cock-tease'?" I asked.

Amanda laughed in answer.

"Well, JK's a cunt-tease."

"God blind me," she exclaimed, shaking her head, disbelieving. "That whore? *Tease*? Really?"

"Really."

Resuming her work, she measured, "And here I was thinking he was bonking you in fifty-five different positions over there."

After Jahleel's 'playing' that day, I tried making things as innocent and platonic as possible for the remainder of the evening. Whenever we sat down to eat, watch television or sleep, I made sure there was descent enough space between us.

No fool, he realized what I was doing, and instead of giving me a hard time, he went along with it. But whenever I caught him watching me, he had this small, impish smile on his face, as he kept some private joke to himself.

I ignored it, ignored him, and consequently got through the night without combusting from sexual frustration.

The following morning, I woke up before him at 6am, whipped up some breakfast and stuck it in the microwave for him. I wrote a note, left it on the kitchen counter and fled.

Being in that house with him, receiving his touches, kisses and nothing more, was more than I could handle. And even though I could've altered my schedule to stay there with him until he was better, I didn't.

Because staying with Jahleel in that house amounted to self-torture.

I wanted him too much, and the whole platonic thing was bullocks. Without hesitation, I'd have traded places with Tiara any day to have casual sex with Jahleel, taking the unfaithful A-hole that came with it.

The more time I spent around him, short and clipped as they were, the deeper and harder I fell.

"Ready for you, Saskia," Derek's voice broke through my reverie.

Pushing all thoughts of Jahleel Kingston aside, I got up and went to be the superstar I was.

SUSPENDED UPSIDE DOWN from the ceiling, the twisting belts created the illusion I was a pro at this acrobatic thing. I flexibly splayed my legs in positions I knew would look helluva sexy in the leather Catwoman outfit as I made fierce expressions for the camera.

Somehow, in the midst of the camera flashes, the rapid-fire directions from Derek, and the flurry of movements beyond that, I managed to see *him:* Plain black tee, black jeans, red ball-cap and Timberlands. Standing with his legs apart, arms crossed, he watched me.

This sod. How the hell did he...?

Ferbie. It had to be.

Shifting my gaze from the *fucking perfect* sight that was Jahleel Kingston and ignoring the immediate change in the pace of my heartbeat, I professionally—amping up the provocativeness—posed for the rest of the frames, disregarding Derek's directions altogether and doing my own thing.

No doubt, those last frames would be my best frames, as the presence of the man in the red ball-cap standing behind the director spurred me on.

When the photographer was finished, and I was lowered from the ceiling for the belts to be removed, Derek rushed over and hugged me, kissing both my cheeks. "You, my dear, are awesome."

"Thanks," I answered absently, peeping over his shoulder at Jahleel whose attention, by then, was directed at Derek's petite assistant. He had one side of his lower lip caught between his teeth as the girl flicked a pen between her fingers over and over, flirtatiously talking in quiet tones to him about God knows what.

It wasn't the assistant's flirting with him that ticked me off, it was that the doucheholecocknozzle seemed to be

277

genuinely interested in her words.

"Who's that?" I asked Derek, nodding over his shoulder, pretending not to know who the steam-emanating, Timberland-wearing hot stuff in the red cap was.

Derek turned halfway and glanced in the direction of Jahleel and his assistant. "Oh, JK? He rents the studio across the hall. He comes over sometimes when…" Trailing off, he turned back to me to examine my expression. "You don't mind him being on the set, do you?"

I didn't mind in the least.

His presence, in fact, made me perform better, knowing those gold eyes were watching me. But I had to pretend I did mind. I was trained well.

"Of course I do," I snapped. "Anyone can easily snap a pic and leak the photos."

Understanding, he nodded, and gestured to the side indicating the representative of Nixx Magazine. She and the photographers were engaged in animated conversation as they clicked through the photos on the monitor, fawning over what was usable and what wasn't. "Gracie doesn't mind. If anyone should worry about photos leaking before the magazine is out, it's her. Besides, JK's cool."

One eyebrow winged up at his choice of adjective. Other than Ferbie, he was the only person I've ever heard refer to

Jahleel as 'cool' instead of 'asshole'.

As the crew disconnected the last belt from around me, I muttered, "So unprofessional," and walked off.

Out of the Catwoman outfit and back into my distressed jeans shorts and Batman T-shirt, I plopped down in the chair at the makeshift makeup station and let Amanda clean the makeup from my face, while I thought of all the things I could eat in my starved state, keeping my mind off Red Ball-Cap who was somewhere in the room chatting up a dumb tramp.

Amanda gave me no hell about Jahleel's presence on the set. She knew it wouldn't help mentioning his name while I was: one, tired. Two, hungry. Three, sex starved. And four, pointlessly, ridiculously, helplessly and hopelessly in love with him.

I was only partially free of makeup when Amanda stopped cleaning and shoved the alcohol-scented cotton into my hand, ordering me in her ever-dominant voice, "Clean."

As I started to tell her I was the one who paid her to work, not the other way around, she tilted her head to indicate Jahleel who, undetected by me, was now with us.

Amanda moved off and Jahleel settled in the chair next to me, dangling his forearms over the flimsy chair arms.

Leaning closer to the mirror, I resumed the task of removing layers of makeup from my face. "If I didn't know any better, I'd think you're stalking me."

In the mirror, I watched as his eyebrows shot up. Of course, that was a low blow, even for me. If anyone was doing any form of stalking here, it was me.

"I rent the studio across—"

"I know," I clipped, choleric—the PMS kind of choleric.

Even though I pretended to focus on removing my makeup, I was aware of his every move, blink, breath. My peripheral vision was sharp. As of recent, everything became sharper, keener, when it came to Jahleel.

So, under his ball-cap visor, I didn't miss his eyes as they swept swiftly over me, fast enough so a less acute person would miss it. Those eyes came back to me in the mirror, but he would never catch me watching him. Nuh uh.

"Your eyes are blue," he stated the obvious.

"Contacts. Clearly."

"You were Catwoman." He shifted unnecessarily in his seat. A ploy to garner my attention, but I continued to focus on my reflection. See? I was getting used to his games. "Grey or hazel would've portrayed it better. Your eyes are already grey. Cat grey."

"The director wanted a blue-eyed a Catwoman. Not my call."

"I don't like it."

"Don't buy the magazine."

Seriously? He was a dance choreographer. What the hell did he know about expressionistic portrayals of fucking cats?

Jahleel kept quiet for a while, but I felt him drilling holes into me. Until the comment, "I see we have Bitchy Sassy to-day."

The last of my makeup removed, I threw down the messy cotton pads on the vanity and turned to face him. "What do you want, JK?"

He drew a breath as if to speak, but his eyes shifted to the cottons on the vanity. Blinking, he brought his gaze back to me, tried to speak again, but his attention moved back to the cotton pads. Helplessly, he shook his head and leaned forward, scooping up the messy cottons off the vanity and disposed them into a small waste-bin.

Wow. OCD much?

Sitting back, he sighed and looked at me full-on, no longer distracted by the heap of dirty makeup-stained cottons. "A note on the counter?"

"Nine days later?"

He brushed the back of his fingers against the shadowed scruff on his face. "I've been busy."

"Like you are now?" I questioned. "You don't live in L.A, so you must be here for work. Yet, you're on *my* set."

Eyes on mine, light-gold to artificial blue, he informed me, "I have no business in L.A."

Was he saying he came here to see me and not because he was working in his studio across the hall? He was here because of me?

"You had a craving?"

Pleading the fifth, he stood up and came over to me. I watched him, wondering what he was about. Cupping my face, he slightly tipped my head backwards and ordered, "Stay still."

Next, he used his index finger to gently stretch up my eyelid while using his other index finger to slide the contact off my eyeball. Resting the fragile thing on the back of his wrist, he switched over the other eye and did the same.

Stepping back and turning to the vanity, he located the contacts case and set each one in its rightful place, poured solution inside and closed it.

When he was done, he sat back down in his chair and looked at me with a satisfied smile. "There now. There's my grey."

I didn't even bother asking how he knew to remove contacts.

"You're crashed," he pointed out.

"Very." I pensively looked down and studied my black

desert *Clarks* for a moment then looked back at him. "You never called."

"Sorry," he answered, unrepentant, "I was offended."

"Offended?"

"'Breakfast in the microwave. Raisins stocked. Never skip Vitamins. Rest for another twenty-four hours, at least. Get well soon. Sorry I couldn't stay longer.'" He quoted the note I left on the counter.

Now hearing it repeated verbally, I had to admit it did sound a bit cold and distant. But, well, what else did he want me to say?

"I don't see how I offended you, JK."

"'Sorry I couldn't stay longer.'"

"I couldn't."

"You *could*."

Backed in a corner with no plausible lie, I shifted my gaze to my desert Clarks again. "You wanted me to stay?"

No answer came from him, but I knew it was because the question was a stupid one. Of course he wanted me to stay with him! Or else he wouldn't have taken offense to my abrupt leave.

"I've missed you," I confessed to my Clarks.

A finger nestled under my chin and elevated it so I was looking at him. "What exactly have you missed, Sassy?"

S. ANN COLE

His expression was one of curiosity, test and confrontation, as though wondering what was there to miss about him when we were nothing to each other and spent little time together creating memories, or moments to miss.

There was nothing to answer with, because I, in truth, didn't know *what* I missed. Except that I missed *him*. All of him. Him being a walking contradiction. His playing, his teasing, his eyes on me…as they were at that moment.

Those unique gold irises studied me. Sandy-brown waves of his silky hair suppressed by his cap, the visor created a light shadow over his face, lending him a brooding bad boy look. I itched to take off his cap and ruffle his hair until it bounced back into free, unsuppressed impeccability.

When he realized I was speech-impeded, unable to answer him, he leaned forward, elbows on his knees, and asked, "You did *Twelfth Night* in school, Sassy?"

"*If music be the food of love, play on',*" I quoted.

Nodding, he asked, "What's your take on Orsino and Olivia?"

Huh? "Um, I dunno…Orsino was obsessed and madly in love with Olivia. He…spent his time lying around daydreaming and fantasizing, listening to music and spewing poems about love, pining for Olivia. Often he would send Cesario to deliver his proclamations of his love for her…I…I don't know…"

"And Cesario always failed to get through to Olivia, right?"

"Right."

"And what did Orsino do about this so-called love and obsession *himself*?"

Was I in high school or something? "Nothing. Lay around and pine because he was obsessed with love, all things of and about love, and the concept of desire and need."

"As a highly respected nobleman with a title, 'Duke' Orsino, what *could* he have done?"

"Gone to her himself and demanded her?"

I guess I answered correctly, because he leaned back in his chair and studied me for a moment before asking, "So, tell me, do you think he was really in love/obsessed with her, or did he just like the *idea* of being in love/obsessed with her?"

Tired of getting drilled, I rubbed my eyes and whined, "I don't *know*, JK. I usually got C-D in all things Shakespeare."

Maybe there was a point somewhere in all of this, something he was trying to tell me, but I was too hungry and knackered to rack my brain further about Shakespeare's mindfuck of plays.

Leaning forward once more, he whispered with a steady air of confidence, as someone not fascinated with an idea, but with the real deal, "Let me tell you what *I* miss, Saskia: I miss those wide, passive, all-consuming grey eyes looking at me. I miss that puckered point on those perfect full lips. I miss how your nostrils flare, the way they turn bright red around the rims when you crave having me inside you. I miss those long lashes, how beautifully dark they are, the way they fan your cheeks when you sleep. I miss your silky-smooth skin sliding against mine. I miss your raspy voice. I miss watching you dream about me, whispering my name in your sleep. I miss cuddling with you, laughing with you, teasing you, pissing you off. And most of all, I miss watching your heart."

Holy crap.

Sucking in a sharp breath, I got out, "Watching my heart?"

"Yes," he said definitively, leaning further over to me.

He pressed two fingers to the base of my neck where my collarbone parted, leaving that soft little dip.

"Right here," he whispered. "I watch your heart right here. Your skin is so delicate, that whether your heart beats once or twice, skips a beat or pounds erratically, this little dip right here moves in sync. It's fascinating. You're a rare treat, Sassy."

Lost for words, I stared back at him. Who knew he was so attentive to detail? So…aware? Half the time he seemed not to give a crap about anything. Yet now he was telling me he missed watching my heart? How the hell do I respond to that?

I fought to keep my breathing under control so my 'heart' wouldn't rat on me. But it was pointless, because he would know I was trying to 'hide' my heart. Maybe I should start wearing scarfs. But then, my nostrils also ratted on me, so should I start wearing gas masks, too?

Jahleel dipped his head and chuckled lightly at his own private joke, then glanced back up at me. "You hungry?"

Oh, how bloody hungry I was. Raw. Rabid. "Yes."

As he stood up from the chair, his eyes read mine, knowing damn well I wasn't talking about food. "Gather your bearings, fair lady," he joked, still with his secret humour. "Meet you outside."

I watched his retreating form as he navigated through the room and spotted Derek's assistant arch a brow at him. Right as he was about to pass by her, she scuttled to his side. She grabbed his bicep to stop him, speaking the words of a slut no doubt, fluttering her lashes at him.

Feeling eyes on me, I glanced over to Derek and found him watching me with a smirk. Indeed, I'd pretended I didn't know Jahleel, then snapped at Derek for harbouring him on the set, next I was hyper-bloody-ventilating with him in a corner. Sure, anyone with half a brain would've figured it out.

With a roll of my eyes, I waved off Derek and looked back to Jahleel and the eager hoe.

Once Jahleel started his famous lip biting thing, I shot up from the chair and gathered my motherfucking bearings.

Chapter 16

I MET HIM outside the building.

Straddling a wicked green and black Ninja bike, motor running, he waited.

My ride was right behind him, Thomas holding the door open for me.

Mindful of the last rumour of me having a Russian boyfriend a couple of weeks ago when I kissed Chad publicly, I contemplated my choice of transportation, as rumours would only escalate if I hopped on Chad's best friend bike and go…where?

Glancing around, I spotted one paparazzi. A stocky old baldy, camera raised to his face, snapping.

At the feel of a hand pressed into my back, urging me in Jahleel's direction, I turned my head and to see Amanda. Making the decision for me, she snagged my duffel bag and hissed, "Stop trying to be perfect for Lion all the time. Get wild sometimes—like a superstar with tattoos and purple streaks would—and tell the world to sod off. We're right behind you."

She was gone before I could respond, jumping in the back of the Escalade. Thomas closed the door behind her, seemingly knowing I'd go with Jahleel despite my hesitation.

Dicking around on his phone, Jahleel waited with easy patience. He, too, knew I'd go with him in the end.

When I traversed over to him, he took the helmet and raised it above my head, warning, "Might feel a bit uncomfortable with that ponytail" before jerking it on.

The ponytail bump pressing against the cushy interior of the helmet was annoying, but not uncomfortable, so I gave him a thumbs-up as he watched me for signs of discomfort.

Understanding, he jerked his head to the side in a manner that meant 'get on'.

Climbing astride the bike, I wrapped my arms around his middle, thighs pressed up against his, chest to his hard back, heart thudding just because it was *him*.

Jahleel revved the bike once, then turned his head to the side and asked over his shoulder, "You forgot for a minute, didn't you?"

"Forgot what?" I asked, voice muffled through the helmet.

"That you belong here."

"On the back of your bike?"

Revving once more, he replied, "And wrapped around me," before zinging off down the main.

ALTHOUGH JAHLEEL DIDN'T ride as manically fast as the last time—probably so Thomas could keep tail of us—the ride was disappointingly short. In no time, he was careening onto a complex on Olympic Boulevard.

"A bowling alley?" I questioned once I was off the bike.

"Rented for the day," he explained, kicking down the side stand before getting off.

"Is there food, at least? Because I don't think these weak arms can afford swinging a bowling ball right now."

"Sassy," he said with a surprising amount of patience, "I know you're hungry, I know you're exhausted, I know you're sexually frustrated. Yes, there's food inside. No, you're not here to bowl. You're here to eat and relax…"

"And what about the sexual frustration part?"

291

He studied me for a beat, the corners of his mouth ratting on his fight to suppress a smile.

Looking at him now, hale and healthy, well-rested, well-fed, confidence intact, almost immortal, one would never believe a few weeks ago he was the complete opposite. Now, he looked untouchable, unflappable, every bit as drool-worthy as he'd been before I walked in on Mortal Jahleel.

And I loved him both ways.

Thomas pulled onto the complex just then, and Jahleel glanced over his shoulder at the vehicle, then back at me. "We can visit the sex toy shop afterward." Tugging my ponytail, he jerked his head to the building. "C'mon."

I wanted to tell him I had enough B.O.Bs to open my own toy shop and none of them worked. My fantasies were warped. But he was already walking a few paces ahead of me, leaving me to catch up.

When we entered the building together, I stopped dead.

Everyone from my circle was there, from Lion to Zane— eating, drinking, laughing. A mini party.

Before I could start asking questions, Amanda came up next to me and kissed my cheek. "A stress-free get together. You deserve it." Then she went off, slapping Twana on her bum and melding into the cheery chattering.

Turning to Jahleel, I arched up a brow. "You did this?"

He shrugged. "Manda called me first, then Lion. Said you've been workin' straight with no breaks and was grumpy, miserable and snappin' at everyone. And for some ungodly reason, they thought *I* should do something about it."

Disappointment crept in as all the excitement seeped out. "So, you're here, did this, because they asked you to, then, yeah?"

His gaze narrowed on me, flickered to the klatch of people, then back to me. "I'm here and did this, because I *wanted* to."

Typical guy answer. I shook my head, refusing to even waste energy on answering to that, or even rolling my eyes.

The loud, unmistakable cackling of Amy and Jamie got my attention. They were raising their bottles of beers to me in salute.

After giving them a forced smile, I turned back to Jahleel. "Why are they here?"

Confusion clothed his features. "Aren't they your friends?"

"You fucked *both* of them."

Jahleel scraped his teeth over his bottom lip in irritation, cast a glance in the giggly sluts' direction then back to me, head slanted to the side. "So?"

Moving in close to him so we were just a hair's breadth

293

apart, I tipped up on my toes, eyes almost levelling with his, and hissed, "Fuck. You."

Pointing to the ground, Jahleel leaned in even closer, our noses almost touching. "I just marked an imaginary threshold. Bitchy Sassy doesn't cross it, got that? Unless you want me to drag you into one those bathroom stalls and fuck you so hard, you won't remember who or where the fuck you are when I'm done. Pain, roughness, humiliation, abandonment. I already warned you how I feel about bitchiness."

The first time he said it, I thought it sounded hot, even contemplated being a bitch more often to see where it would get me with him. But now, recording his seriousness, I realized it wasn't meant to sound hot, neither was he joking about it.

He honest-to-God didn't like bitchiness.

I drew back. Lowering down from my tippy toes.

Congratulations to me, I've successfully dragged A-hole Jahleel to the surface, after things were going so well, I blew it all to hell.

In spite of that, I *was* pissed about being in the same room with women he fucked, so, maybe I didn't really give a crap if he was irritated.

My eyes roamed around the vibrant room, searching for Chad. Jahleel wouldn't invite him after what happened, would he? Of course not.

When I saw no sign of the irresistible part-Russian, I figured it was safe to make my revenge play. "I do hope you invited Chad. It's been a while…"

At the same time those words left me, I felt the air shift as the presence of someone came up behind me.

Jahleel shot me a look I couldn't read, nodded at the person behind me and grounded out, "Enjoy," before stalking off.

"What are you doing?"

At the voice, I spun around and bumped right into Chad.

Shite. Jahleel *had* invited him.

Chad was dashing as usual, semi-formally dressed. Dark denim, white V-neck T-shirt and a single-button grey blazer, securely buttoned, fitting his narrow build to utter perfection. A rosary chain around his neck. His rock star haircut was no more, as his dirty blonde hair had grown out. Unclipped, untrimmed, tucked behind his ears.

Dangit.

"What?" I asked, once I was done drinking him in.

"You're using my name to piss him off," he said without acrimony. "Not cool."

"Fuck him," I said, waving a dismissive hand.

"You did?"

"No." I laughed nervously and smacked his shoulder. He caught my hand.

"But you want to?"

I looked at his hand holding mine, his artistic tattoos peeking out from beneath the sleeve of his blazer. A dust of blonde hair trailed from his wrist and faded out inches above his pinky finger, which had a gold snake ring wrapped around it.

That...hand.

Crap on crap, I was a mess.

"What I want," I composed myself and tore my eyes away from his hand, "is some food in my stomach. Like, right now. I'm starved."

"Well, then," he said, smiling now. "Let's get you fed."

Pressing his palm flat on my lower back, he led me over to a large, rectangular, industrially designed bar. The ongoing countertop was laden with trays of pizza, barbecue ribs and wings, French fries, tacos, all the standard junk food.

Stomach rumbling at the sight, I grabbed a plate and loaded it up with everything, while Chad retrieved two bottles of Corona and popped them open.

Looking around, I opted for seats closest to where Jahleel lounged in the midst of my small but boisterous circle of people. Appearing unperturbed, he was relaxing next to Lion who chatted expressively about God knows what.

This was supposedly a stress relieving get together for me, but who the hell paid me any attention? No one. Except Chad.

I found a seat facing away from them, but close enough so I could overhear their conversation. Chad took the chair next to me, slightly turned so he partly faced them.

Once we were seated, I scooped up some avocado dip with a potato chip and crunched into it, probing around a mouthful, "Okay, spill it. What's going on between you two?"

Face expressionless, Chad replied, "Pardon?"

Scooping up more avocado dip, I crunched again. "I don't know you that well, but I do know you are precise, exact, far from impetuous. A few weeks ago, you wouldn't have touched me so possessively without being sure where my feelings lie. You're still not sure, yet you're acting out of character. To prove a point to someone? That someone being JK?"

Taking a sip of his beer, he watched me for a beat, one brow raised. "You're right in that you don't know me. Not many people do. And you obviously don't know *him*, either. My brother and I, we respect each other. We don't do the 'prove a point' thing. Whenever there's a...let's say, common interest, we allow nature to take its course."

Pointing a French fry at him, I called him out, "That's not what you're doing right now and you know it."

Chad dipped his head smiling to himself. Without warning, he snatched the French fry from my fingers and popped it into his mouth. "Okay, I admit. Right now, I'm fucking with

297

nature."

I couldn't help grinning. "Trying to sway the wind a little in your direction?"

Dropping his forearms to his knees, he leaned over so dangerously close I could feel his breath on my lips, hot, with a fading scent of peppermint. "You kissed me," he breathed out. "*You*. Kissed. Me." His head shook once. "You should've just let me be. You shouldn't have given me a taste. Because now, I want *more*."

Breath trapped in my throat, I watched his lips, parted, pink, enticing, as I waited with eager hunger for him to kiss me. But he didn't.

Even though my back was turned to Jahleel, somehow, I felt his eyes drilling pissed-off holes in the back of my head. But, to hell with him for being an insensitive bugger.

Forcing the trapped breath from my throat, I regained the ability to speak. "I think I need to get some food in me…before I pass out."

Chad leaned back and waved a hand at the loaded plate. "Eat."

The next second, his cell rang from inside his jacket pocket, and he eased it out to look at the screen. "Gotta take this. Be right back," he muttered, as he got up and disappeared to a quiet corner.

Resisting the urge to look behind me, I dug into the plate of greasy junk food and perked up my ears to eavesdrop on the joyous chattering behind me.

Twana was gossiping about her sister's boyfriend who was supposedly the biggest douche on the planet. Apparently, the couple was going through therapy because he was closed off and erratic. Twana was convinced he had some dark past eating away at him.

Lion, who knew the man personally, was laughing, saying the man only agreed to his girlfriend's inane therapy idea to appease her, but nothing was really wrong with him. He was naturally a douche. Twana, Amanda, Amy and Jamie took turns throwing in their opinions on how all fucked-up men had dark, tragic pasts.

Jahleel was quiet throughout it all. Until he spoke.

"That's the thing with you women. You always think there's some psychological explanation for why a dude acts the way he does. You always think you can 'save' him, 'change' him. But really, most men come into the world as jackasses and assholes and will die as jackasses and assholes. Hard as you try, they can't be *saved* by some *girl*, no matter how good she can ride or suck a cock. No matter how pretty, sexy she is. Sex is just sex. Looks fade. Feelings vanish as if they were never there. Shit goes deeper than that."

There was a pause, long quietness, then, "Some assholes, you just have to *wait* for them. Don't try to work on them or fix them. 'Cuz that shit can't be forced. Wait for them to decide to *live* life and not just *have* it. Not just keep it to themselves, refusing to share it with someone else. Because when they do decide to live, they won't just share their life with you. They'll give it to you completely. Giving themselves over to be fully and wholly *owned*."

There was a moment of silence, then all at the once, the male voices erupted, "Word!!"

And the rowdiness resumed.

Chad came back at that point, reclaiming my attention.

We ate, laughed and chatted about things that didn't matter. He was simply amazing, and I could see myself wanting him for more than sex. Too soon, his phone interrupted us again and he answered, speaking in Russian. As the conversation went on, his face grew taut, his voice was curt and riled, sounding like someone different. Someone dangerous.

"You still gonna be here about an hour from now?" he asked when he hung up.

"Not sure. Why?"

Getting to his feet, he buttoned his blazer. Sexy fucker. "Something I gotta go take care of."

I gave him a thumbs up. "If I'm still here in an hour, I'll

text you."

Head cocked to the side, he asked, "You got my number?"

"Yep."

"*How?*"

"I got my sources."

He stared me down, a strange gleam in his eyes, one I couldn't fathom.

Scaring me straight, I was compelled to let on who I got his number from, so I spared, "Lion gave it to me."

The strange look left his eyes at once, and he nodded then leaned over to kiss my cheek. "See you later, then."

For some eerie reason, I decided to watch him as he walked away. He was still Chad.

But by the time he got to where Jahleel had drawn his imaginary threshold for Bitchy Sassy, Chad's smooth, suave posture disappeared, and he suddenly seemed taller, superior, shoulders squared, back straight, like someone with unlimited authority and power.

Amazed, I watched a Chad I didn't know disappear through the exit.

Just then, Amanda occupied Chad's vacated seat. Glaring at me.

"What?" I snapped.

"You know I'm Chad's biggest fan," she said. "But what

you did this evening? Not acceptable."

"I'm no sub of yours, Manda," I told her. "So I don't give a rat's arse what you think is acceptable or not."

She slapped her palm down on the table between us and I fought back a flinch, pretending to be unfazed. The woman could be scary sometimes.

"This wasn't put together by 'us'. Me, Lion, none of us got nothing to do with it. All we were told was where and when. *He* rented out this whole place. *He* paid for everything. He did all of it for *you*. And then you spend the entire evening flirting with Chad?"

"JK's a *friend*. That's what he says he wants. So I don't think it should matter who I spend my time with."

Lips compressed, she leaned back in the armchair, glancing around the room. "He left, you know?"

"Why?"

"Don't know." Her hard onyx eyes returned to drill me. "Why do *you* think?"

"You don't intimidate me, you know," I bluffed.

"You're my best friend, Kia. My job is not to 'intimidate' you, but to wake you the fuck up."

"He invited the giggly sluts," I pouted stubbornly. "I was upset. He didn't care."

Amanda stared at me like I was loopy. "They're your

friends."

"He shagged them both."

"You just said he's only a 'friend', didn't you?"

"I *love* him!" I yelled, hands fisting. "You know that!"

"Keep your damn voice down, will you?" Amanda glanced around room, making sure no one was eavesdropping. "Look, you need to quit dicking around. It's either JK or Chad. Choose *one*. Trust me, you don't want to be the whore who wedged two friends apart. Or you'll be the one hated in the end."

Pushing up from the chair, she jerked at the bottom of her blouse to straighten it like the head bitch in charge and told me, "Now, get off your arse. Everyone's waiting on you to pick a team so we can start bowling."

As people tended to do at the sound of Amanda's voice, I moved at her command, following her to the shoe shelves.

My cellphone vibrated against my thigh in my shorts pocket and I eased it out. Text message from Jahleel:

Remember your promise.

Chapter 17

A TERSE, LOW ding sounded when I pressed his doorbell.

Bathed in a warm glow created by simple brass sconces above either side of the door, I released the ringer and stuffed my hands into my back pockets. I glanced down at the red and black weatherized mat beneath my sandal covered feet that displayed, 'Goodbye' instead of welcome.

Typical Jahleel.

I knew Thomas was somewhere nearby keeping watch on me without making me aware. But I was aware.

Forty-eight hours had passed since the stress-relieving get together Jahleel threw for me. Aside from his single text reminding me of my promise—never to kiss anyone again, like

I'd done with Chad—I hadn't heard a word from him.

Not like I expected to. This was his style. Especially after Chad and I isolated ourselves from everyone at the get together that *he*, Jahleel, threw? Even worse so.

I returned from L.A just this afternoon, did some vocal training, went home and slept like an Olympian. Later I woke up around 8:30pm with Amanda and Ferbie gone, loneliness in my bed, and one person on my mind.

I knew if I rang or text him he wouldn't answer. Or would he?

Jahleel Kingston was unpredictable like that, yeah. So I snatched up my Mercedes car keys and left on my own to circle Jahleel's home. Three times, but his bike wasn't in the driveway.

Determined to wait him out, I drove around the city, listening to P!nk, with no Davidoff to smoke. When I circled a fourth time at 10:34pm, his bike was on the lawn and lights glowed from the windows on his floor. The top floor was dark, and Krissy's Audi was gone, so I swung right into her spot and strolled jauntily to the house.

I had no idea if he had a girl with him, and I didn't care. All I knew was I wanted to see him.

Mannerless sod that he was, he kept me waiting for a few long minutes after the doorbell sounded, before he finally opened the door, wearing white, low-swung, drawstring sweatpants and nothing else. His skin damp, hair wet and slicked back from his face as if he'd ran out of the shower to answer the door.

He didn't look surprised to see me. Just blank. Wet. And heartbreakingly beautiful.

He said nothing. I said nothing. He didn't invite me in. I wanted in.

"You're not going to invite me in?"

"You kept your promise?"

"What if I didn't?"

"I won't invite you in," he said, shrugging.

The mere action caused a lone drop of water to fall from a strand of his hair, land on his shoulder blade, and slowly trickled down the inked inscriptions on his arm. Battling down the urge to lean in and use my tongue to stop the trickle of water in its track, I longingly watched as it flowed into feebleness and melted somewhere on his forearm.

When I looked back at him, he was watching me eyeing the lone trickle of water on his arm.

"What does it even matter if I broke my promise?" I asked him. "*You* just want friendship."

"It matters because it doesn't matter that I just want friendship."

What? "So, you want to possess me as a friend then, yeah?"

"I'm not a fuckin' demon. I don't want to 'possess' any-one," he bit out. "I just respect people who keep their prom-ises."

"But, if I kept my promise, that would mean I'm staying loyal to you, even though we don't have a sensible or benefi-cial relationship."

Jahleel raked his teeth over his lower lip, and I noted it as something he did whenever he was getting irritated. "That's the whole point of promises."

"But we're not in—"

"*Did* you fuckin' break it or not?!" he barked at me.

My head jerked back at his unexpected explosion.

No, he didn't look angered or deranged, just restrained, as if there was something he was struggling to hold back, some-thing he was itching to do, and this roundabout conversation was getting him nowhere.

Taking a step towards him, staring into his depths, I pro-nounced the answer he wanted loud and round. "No."

I registered no sigh of relief or relaxed shoulders, no change of stance, because the next thing I knew, he yanked me across the threshold, slammed the door shut and pushed me back against it, his lips unerringly connecting with mine.

His kiss was hard and eager, expressing exactly how I felt.

Sighing into it, I made to circle my hands around his neck, but he caught them both and moved them back to my sides, still ravishing my mouth.

When I tried to pull away, he trapped my lower lip with his teeth and reeled me back in. Fool for him, I submitted again. But still, he wouldn't allow me to move my hands to touch him when I tried.

"No," he mumbled.

Fighting to be free of his captivating kiss, I cleaved my lips apart from his and wriggled my arms. "Stop. Let me go."

At once, he released my arms, but his chest was still pressed up against me, pinning me to the door, his lips moving in to meet mine again.

Bringing my palms up, I pressed them against his chest and shoved him. "Stop."

The man was immovable, my feeble shove did nothing.

Digging for deeper strength, I shoved him harder, and he took a step back, staring at me ravenously, breathing ragged.

Jahleel was a sight to capture when he was turned on. Abs contracting, chest slightly heaving, lower lip sucked into his mouth...

Thinking sensible for a first, I ignored the ball of steamy hotness in front of me, because all this intensity and arousal awakening was just a tease that would lead to nothing further than cuddling. Turned on as he was, Jahleel wasn't going to shag me.

He wanted to fuck around. I wanted to fuck.

"You can't keep doing that!"

"You don't like it when I kiss you?"

He started to move in again, but I shoved him back.

"You know I do," I panted in response. "But that's *all* you're going to do." Moving forward, I shoved him again and he took another step backward. "I'm only human, JK!"

Again, I shoved him, and again and again and again, taking out my frustration on his defined pecs. With each push, he took a step back, letting me, giving me the illusion that my puny girl hands were moving his hard wall of a body.

"I want you, JK." *Push.* "I fucking need you." *Push.* "Take me, please." *Push.* "Just fucking take me." *Push.* "Please."

As if he'd had enough, he caught my wrists to end the pushing, hauled me in flush against his body and pressed his face in the curve of my neck, his erection hard as stone against my stomach. "Sassy..." he breathed. "I want to."

"Then do it," I breathed back. "I'm yours to take."

As he sighed into the crook of my neck, I felt his tongue against my bare skin, making me shudder. "It's...complicated.

I'll hurt you. If I didn't care for you, I would've given you what you want already. I'd have taken what I crave."

"You're already hurting me."

"Not as much as I would if I..."

"Is this about Krissy?"

He didn't answer so I tried to pull free. But he held me tight, still kissing my neck, weakening me.

"She doesn't want you, JK."

He said nothing.

"She's in love with the mogul. That's clear as frigging day."

He said nothing, but ceased the kissing.

"If she lets you think otherwise then it's because she selfishly wants to keep you on a string—"

"Stop!" he hissed, but refused to let me go, as if afraid I'd leave. "I don't wanna talk about her."

"But you want to keep me on standby in case she doesn't want you, yeah?"

"What? I'm not keepin' you on standby," he denied.

"You want to keep me as *what*, then, JK?"

Pulling back a little, he found my eyes and held them, his gold irises warm and assuring. "I just want to *keep* you."

"I'll get attached."

"I'm selfish."

"It already hurts."

"I'm sorry." He held me tighter.

"I can't," I whispered, cleaving away.

He pulled me back in. "Please."

"Please, what?!" I yelled in his face. "Please understand? Please be a masochist? Please sit on the side and wait while you pine for your *sister* even though I want you for my god-damn self?"

"Neither."

"Then please, *what*, JK?"

Bringing his hands up to cup my face, he leaned in and kissed me gently, softly, pleadingly. "Just please."

Oh Christ, I was getting nowhere with him.

I took a step back away from his aura and gathered my scattered thoughts, summoning common sense from its sleeping chamber. "Look," I began, "I'm sexually attracted to Chad, it's undeniable. With him, I get more. He's not complicated and he's willing to give me all of him if I keep from you. Choosing him is sensible, sane and salubrious."

"But you don't feel anything for him."

"Feelings can grow."

With a sniff, he took a step back from me, too. "Fine. Just know I take promises seriously. Once they're broken, that's it." He motioned to the door with his hand. "Close it on your way out."

He turned on his heels and stalked off, disappearing around the corner at the end of the hall.

Long after he left, I stood staring at the spot he'd been in.

How unfair was he being? Or maybe I was overreacting? One thing was, he never actually admitted to anything about Krissy, I just drew assumptions and took his silence as confirmation.

He wanted me. Of course he did. Chad's statement about them having a 'common interest' stated as much. But he also wanted his non-blood sister, to the extent where he was reluctant to get too involved with me in case, somewhere down the line, Krissy decided she wanted him, and he would end up leaving me for her. Thus hurting me.

And he wanted me to understand *that?*

I didn't. I couldn't.

He hadn't stopped himself with Tiara. He hadn't stopped himself with Krissy's best friend. He hadn't stopped himself with anyone. Hell, he even leaned over Jamie's convertible and sweet-talked her into hooking up with him while Krissy was standing right there.

So what the heck was the deal with me? Could it be that he wanted me as deeply as he wanted her? That he didn't just want to shag me because he could, but wanted something more, making him afraid to take the risk?

My gut told me Krissy wouldn't go after Jahleel. If her feelings were mutual, she hid them well, because I'd never seen her look at Jahleel with nothing more than sisterly love.

Which brought the question: would I be making a terrible mistake by going with Chad? Knowing it would be solely sexual on my side?

There wasn't the emotional, all-consuming, all-encompassing, overwhelming, senses-gone-wild pull with him like I had with Jahleel.

For me, Chad was irresistibly sexy, intense, mesmerizing, with this air of promise that he would give the woman lucky enough to land in his bed fucks she'll never forget. Suave, calculated and in control, from arousal to orgasm. Safe.

But I craved the rawness of Jahleel, the starvation, the unpredictability, the greed, the push and the pull... I just loved him overall. Ever since I fell flat upon seeing him all those years ago.

I stalked him around the world and had come this far, this near, this close, only to do what? Find out he has a hot best friend and choose him instead?

Hands stretched out at my sides, I glanced back at the door, then down the hall, indecision looming overhead.

Decision made, I turned towards the door, making the few

steps it took for me to get a hold of the doorknob. The little latch on the knob locked with a click when I flicked it down. I pivoted away from the door and started down the hall, switching off the lights as I went along.

Taking the right to where I knew his master-bedroom was located, I noticed the door was left ajar, light from the television flashing through the crease. I slung my messenger bag from across my shoulders and quietly pushed his door open.

Jahleel sat up in bed, back against the headboard, legs stretched out and crossed at the ankles, laptop opened on his lap, the glow from the screen reflecting on his face. A face that ignored me.

Even as I meekly walked into the commodious master bedroom, silently stepping across the cream carpeted floor and setting my messenger bag down in the red suede armchair, he didn't look up at me.

He'd known I wouldn't leave. Couldn't leave.

Sidling to the other side of the bed, I sat on the edge and undid the straps of my sandals. I stared at the muted television, airing *Hell on Wheels,* and contemplated what to say to him.

I came up with nothing, so I crawled up onto the bed and balled up next to him, my head at his hip, eyes peeking at his computer screen.

Still, he didn't acknowledge me, sifting through a stream

of emails forwarded by Kayla M., his gangly ginger assistant. Some looked like proposals, some were schedules stretching into months ahead. Boring, boring, boring.

Resigned to him not speaking to me out of vexation, I closed my eyes and inhaled his scent. Fresh. Water and bar soap. No bike exhaust, cologne or raisins, his usual scent.

I began drifting off into a light sleep to the sound of his fingers as they tapped against the keyboard. The tapping stopped, and I heard the laptop close with a soft click.

Soon, I felt him slide down next to me.

I wasn't sure if he thought I was asleep or not, but his arms came around me and pulled me closer into him.

As he swept a lock of hair over my shoulders, his fingertips brushed my bare skin, and he kissed the spot his fingertips touched.

In a voice laced with a mixture of disbelief and relief, he whispered, "Somehow, you have the power to hurt me."

At his words, my eyes opened and locked with his stare. He knew I was awake. "JK, I didn't—"

"Shh," he hushed.

Now I felt bad. Did I feel this awful when I broke my ex-boyfriends' hearts because I couldn't commit to anyone except fantasies of the man who now held me? No. I'd felt nothing because I didn't care, and I'd warned them not to get attached.

Now I felt like crap for saying something I knew I didn't mean even as I said it.

"I'm sorr—"

"Shh," he hushed again. "Just be with me tonight."

"I've missed you," I whispered.

"Me, too."

No more words were exchanged, just our hot breaths mingling, slowing, syncing.

Right there in his arms, the way they held me, I felt something. Somehow, I got the impression those arms had been waiting for me to enter them for years. Waiting to curl around the form and curves of the one woman they longed to hold. *Me.*

But then again, I've always been delusional.

I AWOKE TO the distant sound of a door handle turning. My eyelids lazily lifted in time to see Jahleel as he entered the bedroom. Dressed.

By 'dressed' I mean cut-off, hem-ravelled jeans, simple grey tee, white sneakers and a red Nike sack-bag on his back, hair pulled back in a messy ponytail bundle with an elastic band.

Yum. I'd give the world to wake up to this grungy hotness every morning.

"You must be really tired," he commented as he moved across the room towards me, sliding the sack-bag off his shoulders.

"Huh?"

My voice was hoarse and unwilling to speak, just as unwilling as I was to get out of bed. All I desired at that point was to roll over and sleep for a decade—if Jahleel would get in with me.

Setting the bag down on the bed, he sat down beside me, explaining, "It's afternoon."

Wow. I slept past noon. Good thing it was a free day.

"You went out," I noted.

"Yeah."

When he offered nothing more, I sat up and leaned back against the headboard, studying his attire again. "Work?"

"Yeah."

Did I have a right to question his whereabouts? Maybe not, but he was too reticent at times. I wanted him to open up to me more. "On a Sunday?"

"It's the only day that's clear on Zeff's schedule."

"You're choreographing Zeff?"

"More like training," he offered. "He sucks at live perfor-mances, we all know. So he wants to do somethin' different for his upcoming awards performance."

"Jesus, who *aren't* you working with?"

His signature crooked grin appeared. "You?"

"I have better advantages."

When he raised a brow, I shrugged, saying, "Dude, I just woke up in your *bed*."

That made him chuckle.

"You got more clients today?"

"Nah. On Sundays it's just Zeff in the a.m. Why?"

Hearing movements coming from the top floor, I glanced up at the ceiling. "Krissy's here?"

"She lives here, you know," he said, sounding irritated all of a sudden.

Dragging my eyes from the ceiling, I narrowed them at his unreadable face for a second then flipped back the covers and slipped out of bed. "Okay...I guess I'll just go, then."

"Why?" he asked, pushing up to his feet.

"Because..."

I didn't have a rational reason, except I didn't want to see Krissy because she was suddenly my rival. "Because I wouldn't want her to see us...you and me..."

Realizing I sounded like an idiot brimming with the low

self-esteem of a woman who didn't know her worth, I spun and made a beeline for the bathroom.

The unexpected sight of my toothbrush still in the holder next to his startled me for a second. *Wow.*

Grateful for a teeth cleaning device, I snatched it up, squirted on some toothpaste and commenced the simple mechanic of cleaning my teeth.

Jahleel materialized in the bathroom doorway a second later. "Sassy, Krissy's my..." he trailed off and I knew why.

He couldn't say the word 'sister'. Krissy herself told me he loathed referring to them as brother and sister. Of course he did, because he desired to rip her knickers off in a manner that would make him feel incestuous.

"You're actin' like she's my wife and you're my mistress. It's one building, but two homes. Her place is upstairs, and mine is down here. What goes on down here has nothing to do with her."

"She uses your front door instead of hers," I reminded him while I looked at myself in the mirror.

"Because I've never asked her not to."

"Or because she wants to keep tabs on you," I pointed out, then posted a question, "Or is it you on her?"

Silence stretched between us, with just the sound of toothbrush bristles scouring my teeth and the tap water running.

From the corner of my eye, I saw his shoulder slump as he leaned to the doorjamb and propped against it.

"Stay," he said after a while.

Leaning over the sink, I spat toothpaste suds out of my mouth. "I can't. Honestly."

"Why?"

Deciding he should wait for my answer, I rinsed out my mouth and purposely tossed my toothbrush on the vanity. I proceeded to sloppily wash my face and made sure water drop-lets splashed everywhere, especially the mirror. After I used a handtowel to pat-dry my face, I flung it down on the vanity.

When I turned to Jahleel, he was focused on the mess I created. He jammed his hands in his front pockets, and I laughed to myself, knowing he was itching to clean up the mess.

"Why?" I repeated his question. "Because if I see your *sister*, I probably won't be able to stop myself from punching her in the throat. Why? Because she's in my fucking way."

He looked away from the untidy vanity to me and said quietly, "She's not."

"Not what? Your sister, or in my way?"

As he tried to respond, his eyes drifted back to the vanity. I almost drew blood biting my lip to keep from laughing, but I had mercy on him and stepped to the side.

Blockage out of his way, he moved to the vanity and wasted no time in cleaning up the mess.

When the vanity was all clean, I let my laugh manifest. "How can you dress like *that* and be *this* person?" I laughed harder. "It doesn't make any sense!"

Jahleel turned to me, a frown on his face as if he'd never considered it before. His eyes roamed around the impossibly spotless space: not a towel out of place, no water stains in the shower or on the floor, all clean and arranged.

Leaning back on the vanity, he stuffed his hands back inside his pockets and shook his head, laughing at himself. "I was raised in a perfect home. My parents were perfect in everything they did. I hated it. It wasn't for show, it wasn't for appearance; they were *naturally* perfect. I know this because I wasn't trained by them to be this way. The mannerisms just came through.

"Because I hated it so much as a child, when I went out on my own, I did everything differently. I rebuilt myself, from my speech to my style. I rebelled against who I was and how I was raised, trying to shake the perfectionist ingrained in me. I didn't want to embrace my parents' life. I wanted to be who *I* wanted, not who they thought their so-called God wanted me to be."

With a pensive frown between his brows, he bit his lip and

looked down at his carelessly thrown together attire. "I've managed to change about eighty percent of who I was. But"— he waved a hand in acknowledgement around the bathroom— "as you can see, some things can't be changed. You are who you are."

I blinked at him. Unsure of what to say. Sure as hell did not expect so much insight from him—sincere words, that would ultimately make me more knowledgeable about who *he* was. Truly was.

I must have been quiet for a long time, because he moved in close to me and circled his arms around my waist. "Stay. The house feels different when you're here. I can't explain it."

"I don't want to run in—"

"You won't. She's getting ready to go out with her billionaire. Probably even gone by now."

My skin tingled with warmth where his hands rested on my waist, and I swallowed hard.

Fact was, Asshole JK was gone, and right now, in front of me, I had the man asking earnestly for me to stay with him. Something I never thought would happen with *him*. So, should I let my jealousy of Krissy chase me off? Heck no.

I was Saskia Day.

"Okay," I whispered, looking at his lips, wishing he would lean in the few inches it would take to kiss me. His kisses were usually impulsive, and I never knew when they were coming. "So, we're just gonna stay in?"

"Well, with you being *you*, there's not much we can do in public without it being reported everywhere."

Moving in closer to his embrace, I picked at an imaginary lint on his tee. "You were with Tiara and I've never seen anything about you two in the magazines or on the net. What did you do?"

"Fuck."

"That's all?"

"Yes," he answered. "And I wasn't *with* Tiara. I just fucked her because she wanted to be fucked."

"She wanted more than that and you know it, JK."

He shrugged. "I didn't have more to give."

"*I* want to be fucked."

"I want more than that."

Gaze fixed on him, I searched his face for sarcasm or jocularity, but he was dead serious. Once again, I was thrown in a ring of confusion.

I had no idea where we stood, what our relationship was, what the hell was going on between us. But, the good thing, we were getting somewhere. Slowly. But we were moving forward. And I was clinging on to that with hopeful claws.

"Well," I whispered, "I have more to give."

Chapter 18

JAHLEEL GRINNED, AS if he just won some great gamble. "Now, can we make use of the few hours we have left in this day before Monday creeps in and it takes another week or two before we see each other again?"

"Okay."

In an entirely new mood, he seized my hand and pulled me out of the room. "There's something I've wanted to do."

"What's that?"

"Draw you."

I frowned. "Draw me?"

"Yeah."

Making a right out of his bedroom, he walked to a door at

the end of the hall, one I'd assumed to be a storage closet. But when he turned the knob and opened the door, it revealed a stairway leading down to a dark basement.

"This is my secret," he whispered conspiratorially before he entered.

"Is this the part where you start telling me you're into kinky BDSM whips and chains?" I asked, letting him tug me down the stairs. "Because I'm most definitely not interested in even *trying* that. Nope. Nope. Nope."

Jahleel gave a low, deep chuckle. "Sorry, but I don't have the time, energy, or inclination for that kind of lifestyle. I prefer vanilla, thank you very much."

"Glad we agree on that," I said, then I scoffed and rolled my eyes, and Jahleel chuckled harder, because knew what was coming next. "But then again, I'm not even getting vanilla from you, so—"

Jahleel's full-on laughter cut me off. Yep, he definitely anticipated that response.

At the bottom of the stairs, he stopped and kissed my nose. "Could you, for once, stop thinkin' about sex and just enjoy being with *me?* You've seen what my dick looks like. There's no mystery left."

"It's hard not to when you look the way you do." *And the way it feels when you touch me, stare at me, breathe on me, kiss me, ask me to stay... It's hard to even concentrate when you're near.* "And yes, I've seen what your dick looks like. It's fucking beautiful. A work of art. But I wanna know what it *feels* like. Inside me. Inside my mouth. I want to taste your c—"

"Sassy!" he stopped me, his expression a mixture of restraint and pleasure. "Fuck's sake...I already have a hard time controlling my dick around you. Stop."

Giving me no chance to respond, he let go of me and moved off into the darkness. At the sound of a click, the room lit up from a bright hanging bulb.

Bewildered, I glanced around the room. A large portion of the wooden floor was covered with white bed sheets, and on top of them were scattered sheets of sketches. Sketches of pointless, random things. Flawlessly done, might I add. Some were half-finished, some placed in frames and propped against the wall.

The entire room was in white, like an asylum—save for a massive oak desk stretching along the wall on the left, with a group of large pencil cups holding paintbrushes, scissors and all different shapes and sizes of pencils. Little jars of bright colour paints were stacked up on each other.

Next to the desk was a wooden high stool and an easel. To the right of where I stood, was an antique ornate chaise lounge, ivory, with intricate gold finishes—certainly not a piece of furniture one would expect to see in this guy's possession. The room held nothing else, and was spotless, the statement chaise lounge being the focal point of the room.

"You're an artist?"

"I'm not qualified to be called that," he replied. "I just like to sketch when time permits."

"Crap?"

He laughed. "Things I find interesting. Things that pull me to draw them."

Sliding my gaze to the sketches on the floor, I pointed to one of an ordinary coffee mug, a little dove in the middle. Nothing special about it. "That's just a mug, JK."

Following the length of my tattooed hand to where it pointed, his smile faded, something sad replacing it. He toed off his sneakers and stepped on the sheet to pick up the sketching.

"When I was ten, my parents used to take us regularly to see this girl they supported in the hospital. She was dying of cancer, our age. During one of our usual visits, while we were there talkin' to her, she passed away. In front of us, in the middle of our conversation. I'd never seen anything like it. She just closed her eyes and never opened them again…."

Holding up the mug sketch, he went on, "She was holdin'

this mug when she died. Not with coffee, but with green Jell-O—she loved that. The mug fell from her fingers and broke into four pieces instead of shattering. Krissy cried. I picked up the pieces and brought them home with me. Kept them in a box for years. Don't ask me why.

"When I started sketching, I glued the pieces back together and sketched it with the cracks. A year later, whenever I looked at it, I would get sad and angry. Angry about that little girl not having had a chance to live. So I got rid of the cracked sketching and re-sketched it without the cracks. Made it perfect. As everything should have been for her."

And there I was feeling like a load of crap for criticizing. "I'm sorry."

He shrugged it off as no big deal. But it was.

"Do all your sketches tell a story?"

"Nah. Some are just crap as you say."

Scanning the sketches again, I pointed at one with a headless girl.

She stood on what looked like a stage, a mike in her hand. Out of the pencil-shaded darkness beneath her, came crafted hands, raving for her. No faces, just hands in the darkness. Her headless figure above them, held the mike at her side in a confident stance, owning the world.

Had it been in a gallery, viewers of the sketch would wish

to know more about the girl, as her posture was so strong, sure, undaunted. They would use their imaginations to envision her face, placing it on women with similar body types. Some might get pissed at the artist for drawing such a powerful sketch, yet leaving the one person with the power, headless. Faceless, though with so much power.

"What about that one?"

Setting down the mug sketch, Jahleel turned to look at the one I indicated. Something flashed across his face, too fleeting to recognize, but I noticed a difference in his breathing, his eyes narrowing. After staring at the sketch for a long while, he shook his head. "It's crap."

"Bullocks," I retorted. "Anyone can see it tells a story."

"An incomplete story," he admitted. "That's why she's headless."

"What is it?" I prodded.

Sighing in reluctance, he took up the sketch and looked at it as if he were reading from the traces of his pencil. "I saw her some time ago. I committed her face to memory and sketched her. I saw her some time after that; her face was different, but the rest was the same. Committed her to memory and re-sketched her with her new face. Saw her again. Her face was different and this time, she was different. Committed her to memory and re-sketched her: new face, new person. But, as

329

soon as I was finished with that sketch, I looked at it and knew when I saw her again, something about her would be different. So I immediately re-sketched her. Headless."

"Do you think you'll complete it whenever she's constant in your eyes?"

Head still lowered, he raised his eyes to me. "Yes."

Thrown by the intensity of his stare, I laughed nervously. "You sound as twisty and peculiar as all those other artists."

The humour missed him, as he set down the sketch and walked over to me. "No more storytellin'. I came down here to sketch you. So let's get to it."

"How do you want me?"

He led me over the chaise lounge. "In the exact position you woke up in when you slept over on the night I was sick. I've wanted to sketch you ever since. Think I outlined and shaded you with my eyes a hundred times before you woke up. Your moans and whisperings of my name while you slept was my music."

Ah, the morning I woke up with my hand down my knickers. I'll never live that down. Heat percolated my cheeks. "That was embarrassing."

"It was unforgettably sexy."

Grasping the hem of my tank, he pulled up to take it off, and I raised my hands, allowing him to drag it over my head, tossing it on the scattered sketches on the floor.

He moved in, the heat of his body clashing with mine, created unbearable steam. His chest pressed against my breasts as he circled his long, muscled, tatted arms around my hyper-sensitive torso, and though I hoped it would be a tight, sensual hug, it wasn't, because his fingers landed on the hook of my brassiere and undid it with one skilful flick.

His hands came back around, pulling off the brassiere at the same time. My breath spiked with anticipation.

Throughout the entire process, his eyes stayed on mine, as he seemed to find immense pleasure in building my hopes up, only to deflate them. The brassiere got tossed in the same direction as the tank.

As he hauled his own tee over his head, his warm bare chest now against my aching, hardened nipples, I had to ask, "Are we still sketching or...?"

That damn crooked grin popped onto his face as he took a step back from me and pulled at his cotton tee again and again until it was in shreds. "Told you to stop thinkin' about sex, Sassy."

"Are you even serious right now?"

How could he expect me *not* to think about sex while we were both half naked?

"Take off your jeans," he ordered, shaking his head, grin

still present.

When I did as he asked, he positioned me to his desire on the chaise lounge, strategically draping his ripped-up tee over me to his liking, one of my breasts covered, one perfectly exposed from the shreds of material.

When he was satisfied, he backed away to the high stool and picked up his sketch pad and a pencil.

"Should I stick my hand down my knickers, too?" I joked.

His laughed easily. "If you feel the need…"

Then the sketching began.

Tick. Tock. Tick.

The thing was, I wasn't big on sitting still for long periods of time, especially without a smoke or music, so in no time, I was bored.

Jahleel was intensely focused, quiet, the only sounds between us being the faint scratching of pencil lead against paper.

"I feel like that girl from *Titanic*," I muttered, breaking the ear-splitting silence.

"Except she laid still for Jack," he uttered low under his breath, pencilling away. "She was perfect."

"And I'm not?" I shot back indignantly, forefinger idly poking at the chaise cushion.

"Fuck no," he replied, laughing now. "I think you've

scratched a non-existent itch on your right thigh about ten times in the last five minutes."

My eyes went heavenward. "Okay, I probably should've told you I'm not good at keeping still."

"No shit," he agreed.

"Maybe if there was music or something...?"

Eyes never leaving his pad, he mumbled, "My whole life is music and movements. This is where I come when I wanna wind down."

His brows pulled together, two soft creases forming between them as he held the sketch pad out at arm's length and examined it. "But I think I can tolerate *you* singing. My choice."

Glad to! Beats lying here in silence. "Which one?"

He lowered the pad and began sketching again, taking a few minutes before answering, "Coming."

The name of the song came out so low, I almost didn't hear him. Funny how he chose that song. It was about him. The whole award-winning album was about him, as a matter of fact. But that particular song was a retelling of the first time I ever saw him. 'Coming' was a number one hit right off the bat.

"You like that one?" I fished. "It's an oldie."

"A favourite," he confessed. "Now sing so I can sketch."

Watching his strong hand manipulate the pencil into a smooth flow across the pad, I cleared my throat and sang a song he had no idea was written for him.

A bout of shouts
A bright white light
A fresh false start
Shining, blinding, recognizing

A grab of a wrist
A kiss and a smile
A promise for more
Bigger, better, forever

An obscure beauty
A red colour of love
A fool of me, no senses
Tripping, falling, gaping

Ignore what the eyes can see
Ignore what the heart can feel
Ignore what the world says to be
But please, please, don't ignore me

Because I'm coming
I'm on my way
I will be there
Don't give my heart away

I'm coming, coming
Stray not too far
I will be there
Don't love while we're apart

Wait, wait, wait,
I'm coming for your love

You, You, You,
Will give me all your love

Long after I finished the song, neither of us spoke. Jahleel kept his head lowered as he sketched. I avoided eye contact for fear I might reveal the truth: that rich and famous as I was, I was also a pathetic stalker who was obsessed and irrationally in love with him.

The silence now was different. It was a contented, peaceful silence. A quietness that, instead of being fidgety as before, I now succumbed to. I closed my eyes and envisioned how different this day would be if I was the one who could have chosen what we'd do. The sex we would be having... And on those futile imaginations, I fell asleep.

EVEN AS I slept, I felt him. My eyes flicked open to see Jahleel sitting at the edge of the chaise, watching me with an amused expression. It took me a moment, while I yawned, to realize my hand was down my knickers again.

"Oh crap."

Jahleel flashed me a half-smile and I didn't bother removing my hand.

"I ruined the sketch?" I asked him.

He held up two separate sketches. One was half-complete with me awake, and the other was complete with me asleep, hand down my knickers.

The completed sketch was awe-inspiring. Faultlessly done. Vivid even without colour. Even my curls looked as they would in a camera snapped image.

"Wow," I whispered, "You're really good at this."

Nodding at the compliment, he set the sketches aside. "I need to feed you."

"I want to come," I blurted. My dream had left me in a

semi-aroused state.

"You didn't come in your dream?" he asked, a smirk on his lips.

"I don't remember."

"Well, sorry about that." He made to get up, but I grabbed his arm to stop him.

"Please. Make me come." As he started to protest, I pleaded, *"Please."*

Staring at me for a long moment, he gave in. "No sex, okay?"

"I know."

Moving between my thighs on the chaise, he took off my knickers, spreading my legs apart; one crooked on the top of the chaise, the other hanging off the edge.

Wide open, wet and wanting in front of him.

He removed the ripped-up tee and tossed it to the ground, leaving me completely naked, heated, squirming, waiting for the first touch of his fingers.

Lowering down on top of me, he braced his jeans covered erection against me. His navel kissed mine, his abs kissed mine, his chest kissed mine, and his lips hovered above mine—no kiss.

Flexing his hips so the friction of his erection made me moan out, he whispered, "My hands are yours. Tell me, what

337

do you want me to do with them?"

As he circled his hips again, I whimpered, "Anything. Anywhere. Just touch me."

Easing back a fraction, he ran his fingertips down my neck to my nipples, passing his thumbs over them in gentle circles. An indescribable sound left me at his touch.

"Is it me you're hot for, or anyone else would do?"

"Yes. Just you. Always."

My breasts mourned the loss of his touch when his hands left them and smoothed their way down my stomach, down my pelvis and settled on my inner thighs.

"Lie," he refuted. "You just want to come. And I just so happen to be the man in the room."

"Fuck you, JK."

The words were meant to be venomous, but came out in panted moans instead.

Jahleel ignored the curse and brushed his knuckles against my sopping folds. "You expect me to believe it's just me?"

With the question, he caught my clit between his thumb and forefinger and rubbed.

"Oh God!" I cried, almost exploding into something unexpected. "It's always been you, JK."

"Oh, for fuck's sake," he hissed as he drove two fingers inside me, making me cry out in sheer pleasure. "Wasn't it just last night you were ready to choose someone else?"

As his fingers moved in and out of me in a smooth, slow rhythm, a familiar tingle crept up the back of my knees, alerting me that my orgasm was near.

"I wouldn't have," I told him in a mewl. "You know it."

"I don't know jack-shit," he shot back before I even got the last word out.

Removing his fingers from inside me, he caught hold of my clit again.

Half-conscious, half-consumed with pleasure, I gazed up at him through hooded eyes. "Are you still mad at m—"

"Shut up," he cut me off, then squeezed my clit again, commanding, "Give in, Sassy. Now."

As he fingers applied pressure, my body yielded to his command and I spiralled into a loud, writhing mess. "JK...Ohmigod, JK!"

Jahleel pressed his palm over my folds, keeping it there until I calmed. Getting up from between my spread thighs, he fetched my clothes and handed them to me.

Sprawled out on the chaise, clenching with desperation to feel that part of him inside me, I resorted to begging, "I know you said no, but, please, just this once—"

"Aren't you hungry? Sure you are," he cut in, his mood a bit off, eyes avoiding mine. "I'll head upstairs and fix you

339

something."

"JK—"

"Every girl just wants to *fuck!*" he erupted, surprising me. "All of you, the same. You all just wanna fuck me because I look or act a certain way. None of you really want to know *me*. Women claim they want 'more', but I don't give them shit, because their definition of 'more' is for me to tell the world I'm *with* them so they can slap a label of ownership on me, even though they know nothing about me, except the length and width of my dick, or the flexibility of my waistline. Tiara? The same. She was obsessed with my cock and that's it. Naming me as her boyfriend in a high-profile magazine, when I'm pretty sure if they asked her my date of birth, she wouldn't have a clue."

Glancing wildly around the room, he shoved a furious hand through his hair. "I wanted you to be different. *Convinced* myself you were different. But the only difference between you and the others is that I actually want *more* from you. Yet I have to fuckin' force it out of you.

"I'm tryin' to share parts of myself with you that I've never shared with anyone else. Not even Krissy knows I sketch. But you don't want more. More bores you. You just want to fuck. Like the rest of them. So you can say you've fucked me. Because apparently I'm some type of achievement? The popular face of the season? What? I dunno. I'm still tryin' to figure that out.

"You don't seem to care about protecting your emotional state or what I could do to it. See, I'm an asshole, and I know I'm an asshole, and I wanna get the most out of you *as a person* before I fuck you and end up doing or saying some fucked-up shit, as I tend to do. Because when I do, you'll want nothing more to do with me. And that will be that. But at least I'll have memories like what I've tried to create today to hold on to. I wanna know that the moment I slide my cock inside you, you'll know *whose* cock is inside you. Not just my name. But absolutely everything about the man who's on top of you. Fucking you. Sharing himself with you."

He threw his arms out. "My efforts here are futile, though. You're disappointingly just like the rest. A woman's definition of more is evidently different from mine. Or maybe I'm the one who's the bitch?"

Shirtless, barefooted, my cum on his fingers, he turned and strode out of the basement.

Halfway up the stairs, he stopped, stood there for a moment, before slowly turning to calmly say, "You have me, you know. But you're not ready for me." Pausing, he bit down on his bottom lip pensively, then went on, "You have the power…But you're not yet constant."

Then, he was gone. While I laid there, mouth hanging open at his explosive tirade.

What the fuck just happened?

Chapter 19

I GOT ATTACHED.

As if being obsessed and in delusional love wasn't enough, now I went and got a-friggin-ttached. As in, I needed to hear from him, whether via text message, phone call or email, before I started and ended each day.

He wasn't complaining yet. And I was making the most of his non-complaining compliance. Not after his harangue when he accused me of wanting him solely for sex.

Unable to refute his postulation without giving off I was a stalker and a creep, who had obsessed about *him* and not his cock for over five years, I didn't address the topic that day after I joined him in the kitchen. Instead, I stopped bringing the conversation around to sex all the time and gave him the 'more' he wanted.

We spent every free time our busy lives afforded together. Doing unbelievably mundane things in unbelievably mundane places. But every moment spent with Jahleel was, for me, extraordinary. More didn't bore me. That was all in his head.

I already lived an extraordinary life, doing extraordinary things. Jahleel, he was the equanimity I needed. The balance. The ordinary in my over-the-top life. He wasn't a normal guy, but he managed to live his life that way. Got no idea how he did it, but he made everything seem natural.

I loved him.

Our favourite hangout spots were down in his basement, where we ate crap, got drunk, talked about nothing and fell asleep locked in each other's arms. Or in my theatre room, where we cuddled and watched movie after movie, 'til we fell asleep.

Weird enough, cuddling and watching television was one of his all-time favourite things to do. Not usual for men. But here I had Jahleel, a complete movie addict.

Want to calm him? Just put on a good movie and he'd just immediately go placid.

Nature taking its course I see...

Too bad I'm not there to fuck with it.

I will, though.

As soon as I'm back on U.S. soil.

Don't reply

I smiled at Chad's message as Amanda steered the vehicle into Jamie's neighbourhood.

Don't reply. Such a muted command.

Not that I would've replied anyway. After getting so much closer to Jahleel, more than I ever thought possible, I was being prudent in not frigging it up.

For all I knew, Chad was testing me. He'd said it himself that he would never do anything to screw Jahleel over, so if he was positive I was in Jahleel's corner, he wouldn't come after me.

Amanda steered the vehicle down Jamie's street. We were both knackered. I had spent the day in a bloody hotel suite, doing back-to-back ten-minute interviews for a truckload of magazine journalists. Question after question. Most of them repetitive. Ennui didn't even begin to describe it.

After that, on to training and rehearsals.

We'd expected Jamie to show up at the studio, but she never did so Amanda and I decided to swing by to check on her. More Amanda than me, as a matter of fact. If it were me alone, I would have directed Thomas to take me straight home. But one of Amanda's functions was to provide rational, thoughtful behaviour to my life. So Thomas took Ferbie home, while we set off for Jamie's.

The night was a windy one. Wild winds. The clouds, a bloated puff of coral meets tangerine, covered the sky in one uniform colour. Not a single star dared to peek, and the moon's shine was non-existent, hidden by swollen clouds biding their time before they unleashed their wet wrath over the city. The thunder grumbled on, rattling the earth, but had yet to release its growl, its roar.

One of those nights perfect for dragging on a pair of thick socks and curling up under a thick blanket with a large cup of hot chocolate, your significant other nuzzling your neck.

But such a life was for the contented poor, wasn't it? For-tunate as I appeared to be, I didn't have a significant other to curl up with whenever the rain decided to pound in unrelenting showers.

For the past two hours I'd tried ringing Jahleel to no avail. So shower and bed it would be for me tonight.

Amanda pulled up outside Jamie's, while I mindlessly scrolled through text messages. "Go check if she's breathing," I mumbled. "You stay longer than two minutes, I'm driving off."

346

"Shite," I heard Amanda mutter under her breath.

Before I could question the reason, she swung the car into a neighbour's lot to make a U-turn. "Her car isn't here. So she's not home," she rushed out.

"I told you this was a waste of tim—" I stopped short as Amanda got the car around, me on the opposite side now, able to see what she didn't want me to see: Jahleel's bike parked in Jamie's driveway.

"Stop the car."

Amanda ignored me and kept driving.

"Stop the bloody car, Manda!"

"Why?" she demanded. "So you can go make an arse of yourself?"

Reaching over, I grabbed the steering wheel and tried turning the car around, while Amanda fought to regain control of it. The car swayed from side to side, until it swerved up on someone's lawn and ran over a garbage bin, careening back onto the road.

"Alright! Alright!" Amanda yelled. "You trying to get us killed, you daft cow?!"

"Turn. The. Car. Around!!!" My shrieks reverberated through my temples.

"Get your fucking hands off the steering wheel then, yeah?"

347

I spared her one last don't-fuck-with-me glare before I removed my hands from the wheel.

Slamming the car in reverse, she furiously hit the gas pedal, and the car sped back down the street. She stopped with a sharp hit to the brakes at Jamie's curb.

Amanda got out of the car faster than me, getting in my face. "I'm coming with you to ensure you don't do anything dumb."

Ignoring her, I tried to get around her, but she pressed a firm palm to my chest, stopping me. "Just remember, he's *not* yours. He has no obligation to you. He owes you *nothing.*"

When I said nothing, she glared at me with those hard, intimidating onyx eyes, making sure I got it.

Being obdurate, I glared back at her, but it wasn't long before I sighed and gave in. "I know."

"Good. We're here because we were worried about Jamie and came to check on her."

"But that's the truth," I pointed out.

"Exactly."

We walked up the driveway to Jamie's cute, brick-faced bungalow. As usual, her door was negligently left unlocked, which made it easier for me to catch them in the act.

I heard the groans first, coming from the direction of her living room.

We turned off the first wing to her living room. Jamie's auburn mane was dangling over the edge of her lime-green couch, as her head was tossed back on it. Because the couch faced away from us, I couldn't see much else.

"Be gentle, JK," she moaned out.

A cocktail of raging emotions laced through me at her words, his name, and rendered me immobile, speechless.

Picking up on this, Amanda stepped forward. "Jamie?"

Jamie's head jerked up at her name, and she slightly turned to glance over the edge of the couch at us. "Oh, hey, Manda. Kia," she casually greeted, as if she wasn't in the middle of getting pleasured by my...not my...*my*...Jahleel.

"We were worried and—" Amanda started and stopped when Jahleel's head popped up over the edge.

Our eyes connected and I inhaled a sharp, painful breath. We stared at each other for half a minute. His expression held no apology, no remorse, his hair falling devastatingly deliciously into his eyes.

Arse.

Amanda grabbed my hand and tried to pull me out. "We'll just go and—"

"You're still fucking her?" I impulsively directed at Jahleel, unable to just walk out like it was nothing. Not when my insides felt lacerated.

349

The arsehole's lips curved up in his signature crooked smile, and he slightly shook his head before disappearing behind the couch again.

As I prepared to make my way towards the couch, Amanda pulled me back, while Jamie just stared, brows raised.

"So you're just going to ignore me?" I questioned the out-of-sight Jahleel. "You know what, raisin dick, I'm Saskia D—"

"Shut up, Sassy," Jahleel's voice calmly ordered from behind the couch.

With one sharp tug, I pulled from Amanda's grip and power-walked towards the couch. "You don't get to tell me to shut—" I skidded to a halt when I rounded the couch, words and movement arrested.

Jamie reclined fully clothed in a white Capri and pink top, and her left leg, which had a huge red burn on the calf, rested in Jahleel's lap. He knelt before her, applying some kind of ointment on the burn.

Well, wasn't I the idiot.

But then again, he was here at her house. Maybe he planned on shagging her. What the hell was he doing here?

"Bike burn," Jamie explained. "Hurts like hell." She dropped her head back on the couch and groaned unhappily. "I'm freakin' scarred!"

Jahleel quietly screwed the cap on the tube of ointment and put it in his drawstring bag lying on the floor next to him, before asking Jamie, "Where's your bathroom? I need to get this shit off my hands."

Jamie grumpily groaned out her response, "Down the hall. Turn right. And if you see God on the way there, tell him I said 'thanks' for fucking up my life."

"It's just a burn, drama queen. The scar will fade in about, say, five years." Jahleel stood up and tossed his bag over his shoulders, chuckling. "Until then, yeah, you're blemished. Just like the rest of us."

Jamie flipped him the bird and he laughed out. "You're welcome, James."

He moved past me as if I wasn't even there.

As he disappeared out of the room, I moved in front of Jamie.

"The hell was that about?" she asked before I could question her. "Are you two, like, dating or something? Because if you are, Kia, I would never, ever do anything to—"

"How did this happen?" I cut her off, indicating her scarred leg.

"JK and his stupid bike," she grumbled. "Why can't he drive a car like normal people?"

Getting impatient, I waved a hand at her. "I can see it's a

goddamn bike burn, Jamie. I'm asking how you ended up on his bike in the first place."

Jamie's eyebrows shot up, and she studied me for a second, a smile creeping onto her face. "Holy shit! You are *so* doing him. All possessive and jealous—"

"*How* did you get on his bike?" I snapped. "You were going to shag him?"

Jamie waved me off, unfazed. "He treated me like ass shit after the one time I 'shagged' him, so *NO*. Definitely not."

Her lips curled in displeasure as she regarded her leg. "I had car trouble this evening, that's why you never saw me. My car broke down on the road. Something about the radiator, JK says. He was speeding by and recognized me. So he turned around and came to help. He called a wrecker for my car and offered me a lift home. My ass has never been on a bike before, so when we got here, I came off on the wrong side and burnt my damn leg on the exhaust pipe. Freaking thing."

Bringing her apologetic green gaze up to mine, she held up her hands. "He only offered to put some crap on the burn for me because I was freaking *the hell* out. Nothing else, I swear."

As mollification replaced indignation, I nodded. "Yeah."

Control freak Amanda assumed the position Jahleel had been in, taking up Jamie's leg to examine the burn.

The distant sound of the front door closing snagged my attention.

He was leaving.

While Amanda and Jamie were going coo coo over a boo boo, I breezed out of the house, hoping to catch Jahleel.

He was about to swing his leg over his bike when I got outside. "JK!"

Surprisingly, he stopped at my call. Turning to face me, clad in his usual simplistic denim and cotton, he waited for my approach.

"You were just gonna leave without a word?" I asked once I reached him, tugging at the hem of his tee.

Both arms shot out from his side, the jingling sound of his keys carrying off on the cold night winds. "What do you want me to say, Sassy?"

Moving closer into him, I touched my hand to his chest, his heartbeat pounding under my fingers. "Nothing. You don't have to say anything. As long as you're with me, near me, that'll do."

His eyes lowered to my hand on his chest, then back to me. "You shouldn't do this out in the open Sassy, or we'll end up on front pages. And I know Lion well enough to know he'll shit a brick if your name gets caught up in a 'dating two best friends' scandal."

He was right. Lion was, at the moment, pissed at me. But I was used to him being pissed, because he'd been getting pissed at me quite a lot ever since I moved to SF. Oh well, I'd just have to bear it until I got what I wanted, what I came to the States for, who I got rich and famous for: Jahleel Kingston.

So, on that resolution, I didn't stop touching him. Instead, I closed the sliver of space between us and brought my other hand up to his chest, taking fistfuls of his tee in my grasps. "I don't care about Lion or the world. I care about *you*."

A drop of wetness hit my cheek and we both looked up at the sky that had started drizzling. The clouds were now a darker orange, angry tinges of red here and there, huffing and puffing. Any minute now, they were going to blow.

"If it makes you feel any better," Jahleel said, dragging his squinted gaze from the sky and back to me, "I haven't been with anyone since I was sick."

Wow, that's impressive. "I'm sorry, I wa—"

"I only crave you, Sassy," he talked over me. "So, you see, I've been starvin' myself—because, obviously, I'm not feedin' my desires."

"And Krissy?"

"I only crave you," he slowly repeated.

Oh God. "So are you sayin—"

"*You.*"

As if we couldn't have gotten any closer, I lurched hard against him and tipped up to connect our lips. Caught off guard, he stumbled back a little and chuckled in my mouth, but I didn't stop kissing him. I was too fucking happy. No more Krissy dilemma! He was all mine.

Mine.

The drops from the sky were getting fatter, stinging our skin like wasps.

One splatted on Jahleel's forehead and trailed down his nose as he tried to pull away. "Sassy," he mumbled, trying to pry our lips apart, but I was greedy. "I have to go before the rain. Bike, remember?"

The fat plops of rain came faster, as if to spite us.

Amanda rushed out of the house, jingling the car keys. "Break it up, world's weirdest couple! Rain's coming."

"Come home with me," I begged him.

He began to decline, but the rain came down faster, working in my favour.

"It's risky to ride in the rain, JK. And, clearly, this one's going to be torrential."

Jahleel squinted up at the sky, his bike, then the house, before acquiescing. "'Kay. Lemme ask James if it's okay to park my bike in her garage."

Far from getting enough of him, I kissed him one last time

355

before letting him go. He jogged off to the house, while I ran to the car where Amanda sat behind the steering wheel, impatiently waiting.

"Okay, I'm *very* confused. Are you two shagging or not?" Amanda inquired the second I got into the car.

"No, we're not. Platonic, somewhat."

"So, basically you guys just kiss and feel each other up like you're in high school?" she asked as she flicked on the headlights to reveal Jahleel's hot bod moving his bike into the garage. "Hell, even back then I was getting penetration."

"It's complicated, Manda."

"Clearly."

Jahleel left his bike and ran back to the car, opening Amanda's door. "I'm behind the wheel, Mandy."

"Like hell!" she argued. "And do you always just slap a nickname on everyone you meet?"

"Yeah, because I *can*," he said impatiently. "Out."

Amanda wasn't used to being bossed around. But there she was, complying, unsnapping her seatbelt and getting out of the car even as she fired, "I've got bigger balls than you, you know."

Laughing, Jahleel gave her a once over, regarding her lifted chin and squared shoulders, her confidence and air of dominance. "I've no doubt about that, Mandy. No doubt at all."

Ducking into the car, he adjusted the seat to his comfort, and as soon as Amanda was settled in the back, Jahleel peeled off from the curb. And, as if it had been waiting for us all to take shelter, the rain instantly *poured*.

Chapter 20

CURLED UP AMONG scads of pillows on a puffy cream comforter laid out on my bedroom floor, I shoved a spoonful of chocolate-chip pistachio ice-cream in my mouth as the rain cascaded in a loud torrential deluge outside, the thunder rolling, growling, roaring. Lightning flashing through the darkness.

As I was wonted to do whenever it rained, I'd drawn back the drapes from the sliding glass doors to watch the rain beat down on the city, the sky a beautiful coral despite its windy rage.

Jahleel sauntered from the bathroom, a white towel slung low on his hips, his damp hair finger-combed back from his face, his abdominal muscles contracting with each breath, his calves strong, toned, fucking sexy.

I sighed around another spoonful of ice-cream, ogling him from the floor as he stopped, looking askance at the bed bench where he'd left his clothes.

"I gave them to Sylvie to get them washed and dried for you," I told him.

As though he hadn't noticed me there before, his gaze dropped to me on the floor. A brow arched up. "Something wrong with the bed?"

"Nope," I said, scooping in more ice-cream. "I always do this when it rains. It's amazing to watch."

He continued over to the bed bench and retrieved his cell-phone, doing god-knows-what on it, while he groused, "We should've gone to my place. I smell like a bitch with all that flowery, fruity shit you have in there."

"Hey, I have to at least *smell* like a woman, okay? Else people are gonna start wondering…"

The tell-tale sound of a Samsung Galaxy powering off sounded as he tossed it in his bag. "Your hair, I've always tried to place that scent. Now I know. Coconut. With a '*burst of* lemon citrus."

The way he emphasized 'burst of' as though they highly annoyed him, had me giggling.

"No joke, Sassy," he said, chuckling at my mirth. "All your products in there are burstin' with something. Marketers can't come up with a less trite description for their products?"

"Why should they? Women like having things bursting—or squirting—all over them."

Jahleel shook his head as he walked over and joined me on the floor—me, partially naked in a lacy nude boy-leg and sheer bra-top. Placing a hand on my bare stomach, he leaned over and touched his lips to mine, ever so gently, then propped back on a pillow and stole the container of ice-cream from my hands.

"You're right," he muttered agreeably. He stared out the glass doors at the rain and spooned ice-cream in his mouth. "This is nice to watch."

I sidled closer and lay my head on his stomach. We fell into comfortable silence, watching the rain's downpour outside. Under the towel, I could feel his erection hard as steel, but by now I knew he wouldn't act on it. How he managed going without sex for so long was beyond me.

Whenever we were together like this, in a matter of seconds, I'd be in a state of dizzying lust and arousal, which usually resulted in me asking him to make me come, which he would do with just his fingers. But I was learning to live with it.

The sensible side of me warned me not to take comfort in his vague admission of being over Krissy. Because if he was, why abstain from sex with me still? In addition, he hadn't actually told me he wanted a relationship. I was still locked out and confused about 'us'.

All I knew was whenever we were together, we fit. Words weren't needed. We could lay in silence for hours, just soaking in each other's warmth, then walk away feeling whole and complete. Fulfilled and satisfied. Until we saw each other again.

Sexless, yes, but it was with *him*. Jahleel Kingston. He'd shed his asshole veil for me and let me in…somewhat. And I was clinging, grabbing, scraping for what I could get from him.

I loved him.

Trailing a finger along the tattoos on his side, I broke the silence. "Are you ever going to tell me what the inscriptions on your arm and leg mean?"

His voice came out raspy from being quiet for so long, "Like I tell you each time you ask, it won't make sense to you."

"And like I keep telling you, I still want to hear."

He claimed it wasn't about Krissy, but I had a hard time believing that. Who else could it be about?

"Someday, then."

"How about tonight?" I pushed. "It's going to be a long one."

Chuckling, he set the now empty ice-cream container aside. "Okay," he agreed, sliding down the pillow and shifting so my head was on his chest instead of his stomach. "It's about God. The end."

"What?"

"Exactly."

I tilted my head back to peer up at him. "No, I mean, what do you mean it's about God?"

"I don't know Him," he said with an easy shrug.

"And you want to?"

"My parents taught me about Him since I had the ability to understand. I know all the stories of miracles and works of wonders. I can probably quote the Bible verbatim. But Him, I don't know. He never talks to me or give me guidance like my parents said He would. So…yeah."

After a moment of silence, I agreed, "You're right, I don't understand."

"I told you."

Thing was, I wouldn't know how to even go about having a conversation on such a topic. My life was too busy, and I've never taken the time out to get to know a God, let alone talking to one. So I backed off. His tattoos were his, with his own personal, incomprehensible, meaning behind them.

"Hey, your tats aren't straightforward either," he pointed out. "I think I might've figured out what some of the images you've hidden in the ink along your arm symbolizes, though. The two skulls represents your parents. The joined hearts wrapped with barb-wire represents Ferbz and Timber on a leash—your leash. The microphone and music sign, represents your career." He slid a finger under my chin and tipped it up to see my face, asking, "Am I right so far?"

Astonished at his unerring reading of my tats, I barely got out, "On point."

Lifting my arm, he studied the tats and pointed at the last image on the lower part of my inner arm, watching my eyes carefully. "I've never been able to figure out what this one represents, though. From what I can make out, it's a red hood over an obscure face. What's that about?"

You.

But I didn't divulge that secret. Instead, I took a few minutes before answering, searching for a better way to explain it, while Jahleel waited patiently for my answer, a suspicious gleam in his eyes. "It represents what I hope for."

"And what do you hope for?"

"A man in a red hoodie?"

He let out loud laugh, then all of a sudden got serious,

saying, "'Kay, I get it: Faceless Hoodie Guy is to you what Headless Singing Girl is to me."

"Something like that…"

Jahleel moved, and the next thing I knew, his mouth was on mine and I was on my back, him crowding on top of me. He groaned deep in my mouth and pressed his erection against me, an agonizing yet arousing sound vibrating in his throat.

There was no choice but to kiss him back, because, sure, we've kissed before, a lot, but now, he was *claiming* my mouth. With a certain greed. A deep need. Moans and ragged breaths against my lips…*something was happening here.*

"Saskia," he breathed my name in quiet reverence, like a prayer.

Using one hand to grip my face, he roughly tipped it up and directed his lips to my neck, dropping kisses like hot fire-balls. Latching on to soft skin right above my collarbone, he sucked hard, the sting from it a unique taste of pleasure. That was definitely going to leave a mark.

But I was his to mark.

Releasing my flesh, he rose up above me and poked his thumbs through the sheer bra-top, ripping it in two. With an impassioned expression, he cupped my breasts, gently rolling my nipples in the centre of his palms. As if I could've gotten any wetter, I did.

He'd never been like this with me before. So different. Possessive, earnest, intense. I was left with letting him do whatever he wanted with me. And hoping this new attitude meant we were finally going to *be* together, because a finger orgasm sure as hell wouldn't suffice tonight. Not with all this heat and passion, with how intensely hot he was making me. This was different. Better end different.

Jahleel's hooded gaze drifted back to my face. "You're all kinds of beautiful, Sassy. Crazy fuckin' beautiful."

"Are we—" I tried to catch my breath. "Are we—"

"Are you mine?" he asked in earnest, eyes a blazing fire.

"I've always been yours, JK."

"Well, yes."

"Exclusive?" I begged. "*Please...*" *Don't hurt me*, I wanted to add.

"Yes," he promised, before dipping his head to suck a nipple into his fire-hot mouth.

Back arching, I moaned and squirmed beneath him, an unstable mess, impatient to have him.

Swift, adept and pleasure-loaded, his tongue flicked over and around my nipple, giving it a sharp nip before moving over to the next to deliver equal pleasure, his hand kneading the other.

Leaving my nipples to quiver for more of his mouth's wet

heat, he kissed and licked a sweet, tantalizing path down my abs.

"Have thought about runnin' my tongue down these packs over a million times…" he whispered.

"You dreamed of something you've always had."

Jahleel hooked his thumbs in the side of my knickers, sliding them down my legs. He removed the towel from around his waist, his cock springing up. Stiff, hard, red and ready.

I licked my lips, aching to have it inside me. I couldn't wait. No. No more waiting.

But Jahleel pushed my legs wide apart, smoothing his hands down my inner thighs, his lower lip trapped between his teeth.

I just wanted him to enter me, but knowing the unpredictable sod he was, I bit my own lip to keep quiet. I was trying not to come from the way he was regarding me, my body, with reverence—with the gentle but scorching touches of his hands, and the sight of his beautiful cock pointing readily at my entrance.

Sliding down my body, he put his lips in direct line with mine below. I stilled, waiting, anticipating, until I felt the heat of his breath blowing on my clit, slow and controlled.

My hips thrust up on their own, aiming to make contact with his mouth, but he dodged, blowing gently on me, making me bloody tormented, wild, writhing without a single touch.

"JK…"

"Yes?"

"Please…"

"Please, what?"

Mild humour coloured his voice, and I was reminded of his penchant for screwing around with me. Frigging demon.

"JK, please," I urged.

He paused, his lips so close. "*What* do you want, Sassy?"

"I want…I want…" *Oh God.* "Fucking suck me! Lick me. Eat me."

The amusement was still there when he said, "All you had to do was ask," and sucked my clit into his mouth.

My hips jerked up off the bed at the long-anticipated move. "Ahhhh, yes."

Releasing my clit from his deep suction, he flicked it about with his tongue, driving me insane. I kept thrusting up my hips, trying to grind on his mouth, but he pressed his palm down on my pelvis to keep me stable. With his free hand, he slid one finger inside me, then another, his tongue beating a steady tattoo on my clit, his fingers working in perfect symphony.

It wasn't long before I felt the familiar tingle creeping up the back of my knees, the tell-tale sign my orgasm was near.

When Jahleel withdrew his fingers from me and used his forefinger to flick the über-sensitive tip of my clit—one, two, three times—an unheralded orgasm ripped through me like a frigging copper bullet. Busting me into smithereens.

I came *hard*. Long. Loud.

As he was used to doing, Jahleel kept his palm flat over my folds until I was calmed.

Coming back up above me, he gave me a quick kiss before setting his wide, engorged head at my entrance. "Birth control?"

Still out of breath, far from recovered, I nodded. "Injection."

"My check-up was clean last week. You?"

"Yes. I'm clean," I fussed in impatience. "Just fuck me. *Please*."

As he pushed in an inch, he paused, took a steadying breath, then asked, "Slow or hard?"

"What?" I breathed, semiconscious.

"How do you fuckin' want me, Sassy?" he growled. "Say it. Quick."

As starved as I was for him at the moment, I wanted to savour him, so I told him, "Slow."

"Shit," he grumbled under his breath, sounding like he hoped for the opposite.

His hips flexed and his dick moved farther and farther in, taking me, claiming me, filling me, sealing *us*. When he was fully inside me, he stilled and took another breath, eyes closed.

He needed a minute.

Bringing my hands up to his chest, I moaned at the feel of his hard muscles under my skin, because now I was free to *touch* him—something I was restricted from doing before.

As he began moving slowly in and out of me, I rubbed my thumbs over his taut nipples.

He stopped and stared at me. "If you keep doing that, Sassy, I won't be able to go slow. You have no idea how bad I've wanted you."

Like a chastened child, I moved my hands down to his abs instead while he flexed his hips in and out, eyes hooded, expression strained, as if going slow was a difficult task.

Wrapping my legs around his waist, I brought my hands up around his neck and pulled him down to kiss me, unable to believe this was even happening. Jahleel Kingston was on top of me, inside me, fucking me. I've dreamed a million dreams about what this moment, should it ever happen, would be like. And even with a million dreams, a million fantasies, this was a gazillion times better.

Right this moment, I was living my dream. My dream was never to become a rich and famous superstar. My dream had always been to make love with Jahleel Kingston, have him fall in love with me—as backward as it sounded.

I pushed up against him, wanting to get closer, wanting to crawl inside him.

Too soon, he broke our kiss, pulling out of me and eased up onto his knees. "I'm sorry. I've tried. But I can't do slow."

Grasping both my legs, he bent them and pushed them down to my chest.

"Yessss…" he whispered, looking down at me open wide and exposed for him. "Wrap your arms around your thighs to keep them there."

When I did, quivering for him, he positioned his head at my entrance once more, then, lifting his darkened gaze to mine, plunged deep inside me, while I screamed out like a bitch…his bitch.

Then he moved, not rushed or frenetic, but deep, hard and steady. Each thrust harder than the last, each thrust paving its path, branding me, bruising. His eyes remained on mine, reading me, as he moved fluidly, deftly, calculatedly, fucking me like fucking was art to him. Like it should be done precisely, properly, perfectly, without falter.

A deep, feral groan sounded in his throat, his eyes shuttering down as he lowered on top of me, forcing me to let go of my thighs.

Burying his face in the curve of my neck, he moaned incomprehensible sounds against my skin, until I felt him marking my flesh again.

"Ohhhh, God," I whimpered as I felt another orgasm on the horizon, moving in on the ocean waves.

Before I could register his intentions, Jahleel pulled out of me and flipped me on my side in one smooth, experienced move, as if I weighed nothing, causing me to let out a squeal at the sudden and unexpected change of position.

Getting behind me, he hitched up my right leg in the crook of his arm and wasted no time plunging into me from behind.

"JK!" I cried out, holstered in euphoric pleasure.

"Mmnh?" he groaned in response, plunging into me over and over without pause, dragging me *there*.

"You feel...so damn good inside me."

"Mmmmmnh," he groaned again, lost in his own nirvana.

"You own me, Jahleel."

"I know, babe."

With that, he flexed his hips up and into me, then kept himself buried there, no movements, just our harsh breathing, me teetering on the brink, and him...up to something.

Suddenly he did an indescribable gyration of his hips and touched something, *somewhere* buried deep inside me, and the most intense, profound feeling had me garbling out

371

unintelligible words, unsure of how or what I was feeling.

Out of my body, out of my mind.

He did it again, and I let out a long mewl like a cat, because I couldn't understand what the fuck he was doing or what the fuck I was feeling.

Again he did it, and I unexpectedly came with a loud, unladylike growl, my toes curled tightly, my fists balled, as an unprecedented feeling lanced right through me, splitting me in two, wounding me up tight like a coil and then springing me free.

My orgasm roiled on forever. Unwinding and never-ending.

Jahleel didn't start moving again until my muscles relaxed, even though my heart beat wildly and erratically in my chest, as if I had just outran Usain Bolt.

"W-w-what the *fuck* was that?" I squeezed out.

Ignoring the question, he began pounding me from behind, his groans getting louder, his grunts deeper.

Soon, his fingers sank into my flesh, gripping my arm, as he again buried his face into the crook of my neck, his pumps getting faster, wilder.

With a muffled "Saskia" into my neck, he made one deep, hard slam into me and stilled, his warmth flooding me, his cock pulsating, his breathing harsh against my skin, his heartbeat hammering against my back.

When he was back to earth, he released my leg from the crook of his arm, slid out of me and flipped me over to face him, brushing my wild ripples over my shoulder.

"Being inside you," he breathed against my lips, "is heaven."

Unable to speak as yet, I passed the pad of my thumb over that bottom lip he was always sinking his teeth into. It was slightly swollen, with fresh grooved marks of his teeth imprinted, as he'd no doubt sank his teeth onto it when he came.

His eyes slit open, limp damp hair falling down into his face, beads of sweat on his forehead, breathing far from returning to regular.

He was beautiful. And now he was mine. He promised me exclusivity. He gave himself to me.

With that thought, when our breathing returned to normal, I found myself saying it...because, at this point, why not, right?

"I'm in love with you, JK."

Breath held, I watched as his eyes closed down at the confession, his jaw tightening. He didn't want to hear it. He didn't want to face it. He was shutting it out.

Letting out a clearly forced laugh, he said, "I've been here before."

373

"What?" I asked in confusion.

"You women," he said lazily, reposed. "Sleep with me once, and the next thing I know, you're spouting off love confessions."

When I stiffened in his arms, he opened his eyes. They were hard and empty. The fire and passion just there minutes ago, gone.

"You are the biggest arse I've ever met in my entire life."

Voice flat and devoid of emotion, he responded, "Then why'd you let me fuck you?"

"I just told you why…" I whispered, so low I barely heard myself. I couldn't… I couldn't understand what was happening.

"*Why?*" he demanded with a cruel edge, meant to make me feel like nothing and nobody. "Why the fuck would you do that, stupid girl? Why go and ruin everyfuckingthing?"

Enraged and hurt, his words twisting a knife deep into my heart, I took a breath, ready to light him up with a string of expletives, because I was hating him so much at that moment. How could he just switch on me like that? Be so loving one minute and so cruel the next?

Before I could start my diatribe, Jahleel drew back and held up a hand. "Look, I'm not in the mood to argue. Besides, it's fuckin' rainin' and I don't even have a vehicle here to get the fuck away from you."

Tears sprang to my eyes, and I tried to find the strength to hold them back so he couldn't steal anymore of me, so he couldn't win. But the weak part of me, the part that belonged wholly and completely to the man verbally hurting me at the moment, couldn't hold the tears in. Instead, they flowed out in endless wet streams down my face, while Jahleel watched me without emotion. He was unmoved by my tears, as if he'd seen it all before.

"You're...h-hurting me," I sniffled out.

Getting up to his feet, he shrugged. "You were warned."

As he turned and started towards the bathroom, I stood up and yelled at his back, fat tears rolling, nose running, "I hate you! I fucking *hate* you! I wish, oh how I wish I never fucking knew you. At all."

He stopped when those simple words penetrated whatever wall he had up. He stood there for a moment until he shook his head as if clearing it and his shoulders fell.

A raging demon entered me and I ran to him and began pounding my fists on his back, screaming how much I hated him.

When he turned around, he gripped my arms to stop my flailing fists. I immediately saw arsehole Jahleel gone and replaced by the Jahleel who had just made love to me. His eyes were soft and apologetic, his posture defeated, his voice humbled, "Sassy, stop. You don't mean that."

Holding on to my dignity (even though we were both butt naked), I stubbornly raised my chin and jerked from his grip, taking a few steps back. "I meant every word, JK."

"Yes, you do. The words from earlier. But not these words. You don't hate me."

As he took a step in my direction, I moved back and pointed an angry finger at him. "Don't you dare! Don't you bloody dare!"

But my warning went unheeded as he moved in swift and smooth, grabbed my face and kissed me deep. I tried to fight him off, but he kept my face firm in his hold, forcing me to accept his kiss.

When he realized I wasn't giving in, he ripped his lips away and wrapped his arms around me in a way that trapped my arms at my sides, in case I was still inclined to fight.

"I'm sorry," he fiercely apologized, "I'm sorry."

"No, you're not!" I barked in his face. "You're right! You are what you are: an arse! I don't want you anymore! *I don't want you.*"

Forcefully moving me to the bed, he pushed me back on it, and before I could lurch up, he braced down on top of me, pinning me. "You're right and wrong. I'm an ass. But I truly *am* sorry, Sassy." He dropped apologetic kisses all over me, kept me restricted. "I never meant any of it. Don't say you hate me. I'm sorry for hurtin' you."

He kept kissing me everywhere. Soft, tender, soothing kisses. "Babe...please...Am I forgiven?"

Even though his kisses were wiping away my hurt and anger, replacing them with love and passion, I said nothing.

I must not give in. I must not give in. I don't love him. I do hate him.

Jahleel moved a hand down between us, and before I could stop him, he pushed into me.

I tried to suppress a moan, but it weaselled its way out in a satisfying, "unhhhhhh."

"I'll go slow, babe. I'll go slow," he soothingly whispered, dropping his forehead to mine, genuine apology evident in his eyes, his expression. "Please, forgive me. I-I...I am... Forgive me, Saskia."

My eyelids fluttered down as he moved slowly in and out, a peaceful calm settling over me. Even if he didn't want to hear it, and even if it was stupid of me, I was in love with him and I couldn't help it.

So when he flexed deep into me with a pleasurable flow, asking once more, "Am I forgiven?" I reopened my eyes, locked them with his and answered with a foolish, but unapologetic, "Yes."

Chapter 21

JAHLEEL WASN'T NEXT to me when I woke up the next morning. But, uncharacteristically, a short note was left on the pillow next to me:

Have an important early meeting. Took Ferbz's bike.
Last night? Unforgettable.
I'll ache for you all day.

P.S I'm still sorry.

Folding the note until it was a minuscule piece of hard paper in my palm, I tossed it in the nightstand drawer and slugged out of bed. I remembered the hurt from the night before, but it was fleeting, considering he spent the rest of night trying to make it up to me.

I heard his apology, I felt it, and I saw it.

I wouldn't try to find an excuse for his behaviour or try to justify it. But I could forgive. And he was forgiven, sin forgotten.

Just like every other morning for the past 5 plus years, this morning was no different: I woke up madly in love with Jahleel Kingston. Not only that, but I was flat-out happy.

It had taken a long time, but the feat was now accomplished. Jahleel was now mine. *My* man. We were in a relationship. An exclusive relationship. And though it was kiddish to believe in promises, I believed him when he promised me he'd never hurt me again.

There was just one thing hanging over our heads: My tour. Which was in two weeks. The timing couldn't have been more off. After finally coming together, I was about to leave him for six months.

Yep, believing in exclusivity and promises was definitely foolish.

I HAD A long day of rehearsals. Planning and training stretched out before me, so I spared no time grabbing a shower, donning sweatpants, cropped tank and low-top Chucks. I bundled my mass of hair atop my head, snagged my messenger bag and sunglasses and headed downstairs.

Amanda and Ferbie were already dressed and waiting, messing around in the living area. Or more like Amanda messing with Ferbie.

My beloved brother was looking fresher, sprightlier, happier than I'd ever seen him. Of late, he'd been MIA quite a bit. Ever since he bought that darn bike, he'd been attracting female attention like ants to crumbs. Apparently, chicks dig guys who straddled bikes.

I came home tired one evening and saw two girls I didn't know from Adam lounging in my living room. No need to ask if I went radge on Ferbie.

Since then, he spent most nights out with his groupies. At one point, I'd gotten paranoid that he might be squandering his money to impress these girls, but when I tracked his spending, it was used mostly on hotel rooms and food, far below the daily limit I gave him. When I ask asked him about it, he only spared, "JK taught me the works."

Whatever 'works' JK taught him kept him sensible, so I let him be.

"I see you've remembered your address," I greeted Ferbie, skipping up to him and throwing my arms around his neck. "Give me snog!"

Grinning wide, he kissed both my cheeks before pulling from my tight embrace.

"Ma," he said with a determined expression as we headed for the door. "There's someone who wants to meet you."

My gaze shifted to Amanda who had her lips folded, holding back something, then back to Ferbie. "I have no time for your opportunist biker babes, Ferbie."

"No, no," he protested quickly. "Madame Viper isn't like that."

A startled laugh got caught somewhere in my throat, while Amanda smacked Ferbie on the back on his head.

Ferbie yelped, "Ow!" at the same time I squeaked, "Madame Viper?" at the same Amanda reprimanded, "You don't go around calling her that, you plonker!"

As Ferbie started to speak, Amanda put her hand over his mouth to shut him up, then apprised me, quietly, "Your sycophantic brother has found himself a Domme. Ten years his senior who is—for all things beyond my understanding in this weird world—*insanely in love* with him."

My eyes narrowed on Amanda. "You took him to that bloody freak club, didn't you?"

"It's not a 'freak club'," she defended. "And he was annoying the crap out of me one night about being bored, so I tagged him along with me."

"And now I'm supposed to just accept that my brother's a submissive to some senior citizen called *Madame Viper*?"

Ferbie tried to speak behind Amanda's hand, but she pointed a firm finger at him. "Shut up."

I smacked her hand from off him. "He's not *your* sub, so don't put your hand on him or talk to him like that!"

"Right, because if my sub ever mentioned me by my play name in public, I'd beat him black and blue."

Oh Christ. This whole thing was absurd.

"Anyway," Amanda continued in topic, "Whether you want to accept it or not, Ferbie is naturally submissive. Sade is only thirty-eight and, by some miracle, she's smitten with him."

"Am I supposed to believe that?"

Amanda waved her hand in the general direction of the door. "The proof is outside."

Casting her a glare, then one at Ferbie, I marched out of the house.

Parked next to the water fountain was a brand new, matte black Lamborghini.

"Wow. She bought him a Lambo... Don't you think this

is a little extreme?" I muttered to Amanda who drew up beside me.

She shrugged. "Sade's filthy. Her late husband was an Internet Billionaire. Everything went to her. Plus she was well-off before him."

Turning to Ferbie who was standing on the other side of me, I asked him, "Are you happy?"

His grin blinded me. "Aye, Ma. More than ever."

Oh, so he was back to saying 'Aye' now. *Ole Madame Viper must love that.*

I moved in and hugged him tight, whispering in his ear, "That's all I ever wanted for you."

Thomas rolled up with the Phantom and stepped out to open the door for us.

I gaily clapped my hands and rubbed them together. "Okay, let's kick the hell out of this day."

As I made my way to the car, Amanda grabbed my arm, letting Ferbie go ahead of us. "With that bounce in your step and that dimple which only comes out when you're super-duper-deliriously-happy, I take it some sticking it in the poy yoi finally went down last night?"

As I tried not to grin like a goof, I replied, "Maybe?"

Amanda raised a brow. "So? How was it? Does he live up to the hype?"

Emitting a Cinderella sigh, I murmured, "No words, Manda. I have *no words*," and bounced off to the waiting vehicle, Amanda laughing behind me.

"YOU FUCKIN' FOCUSED?"

I flinched and grimaced at the familiar voice. *Lion.*

Mouth latched on to my water bottle, I twisted around in the direction of the voice. He stood behind me on the stage where I sat at the edge, legs dangling, as I took a break from tour rehearsals.

Impeccably and uncharacteristically dressed in a sharp charcoal suit, his stance was neutral despite his hard asked question.

"Don't I look focused?" I croaked out.

His eyes widened a fraction, and his worried expression took over his features. "The hell's wrong with your voice?"

I didn't want to see him freak out, so I turned back around, telling him, "I might have pushed a little too hard on a note during rehearsals?"

"Jesus Christ," he muttered.

"Look, Lion," I twisted around to assure him, "no need to freak out, okay? Nadine says I should just lip-sync through rehearsals to prevent it from getting worse. No big deal."

With a sharp shake of his head, he glowered at me. "You're *not* focused."

But I knew what his real worry was. Jahleel. Me being less focused on work and more hung up on Jahleel. Me blowing off the tour at last minute. Me giving up…everything.

"Trust me, I'm *very* focused." And high. And ecstatic. And euphoric. And in love.

After giving me the glare down for another long minute, he had no choice but to take my word for it. He came over to sit beside me on the edge of the high stage and threw an arm around my shoulders, our legs dangling.

All the occupants of the vast room were slumped in a seat somewhere, either stuffing their faces with crap food or fiddling around on gadgets.

"What's up with the suit?" I asked Lion, motioning up and down the length of his body with my water bottle.

He regarded his attire with distaste. "I sat in on a huge meeting with a friend this mornin'."

Good friend here in SF and not LA? Hmmm… "This JK, yeah?"

Instead of answering the question, he inquired, "Things

385

workin' out with you two?"

"I love him."

"And this is a secret?" he said, laughing.

Toying with my water bottle, I stared off in the distance at nothing. "He doesn't want to hear it."

Lion's arm tightened around me. "You just blurted it out, didn't you?"

When he got no response from me, he bumped me with his shoulder, saying, "JK's not that kinda man, Kia. You have to be patient and wait for him. You try to shove somethin' like that down his throat, he won't know if he should chew it slowly, swallow it whole, or savor it on his tongue. So his first response always will be to spit it out."

"*Wait*?" I whined. "I've been waiting for over five years."

"So it shouldn't hurt you to wait just a little longer, right?" he said, pushing his point.

"He agreed to exclusivity…" I trailed off and dropped my gaze, studying the peace sign on my sweats. "But I'm going on tour in two weeks. For six months. How can I be sure he'll remain faithful to me?"

"He won't," Lion stated. As simple as that. "This ain't a romance novel or a feel-good movie with perfect people in perfect relationships, Kia. This is real life where people have needs that, most of the time, they give in to."

Lion's straightforward words knocked a gasp out of me, and the back of my eyes burned with threatening tears.

Squeezing his arm tight around me, he continued, "Hol' up, now... speaking as a man who's been there and done that, I'll tell you this: a fuck is just a fuck. Some time, while you're away, he's gonna feel like fuckin', and he *will* fuck. But, if you're in his heart, his mind, his thoughts, no matter what bitch he's fuckin', *your* face is the face he's gonna see."

"But...But I've *never* seen you cheat on Twana. You never even look at another woman."

Lion released a bark of laughter, as if I'd given him the funniest joke he'd ever heard. "Four years I've been schoolin' you, and you ain't learnt nothing?" He shook his head and guffawed harder.

When I narrowed my eyes at him, he sobered up, confessing, "T's my whole life. I'm nothing without her. I love her with every part of me. She's my queen. But, Kia, whenever I'm away from her for too long and I wanna fuck, I fuck. You don't see that 'cause I'm good at hidin' my shit. You can be the devil disguised as Jesus if you know how to keep things on 'da DL, Kia."

Mouth agape, all I managed was, "Wow. You're good. Lord knows you had me fooled."

He waved me off, saying, "Anyway, back to your earlier

question, yes the friend was JK."

"This meeting was about the dance show, wasn't it? Is he getting it?"

Lion dismissively waved the question away. "The job was JK's from the start. They're just holdin' off the announcement for publicity. Prolonging the suspense."

"You think so?"

The look he gave told me I had asked a dumb question. Of course, Lion knew everything. "The show needs JK to up their in-da -toilet ratings. Everybody's talkin' about him. He's young, he's got that look...you *ladies*"—he nudged me— "think he's 'fine as hell', and he can dance his ass off. They've gotta bring him in if they're serious about bringin' back the show."

He gave me a pointed look now.

"So this means, even if I wasn't touring, *he'd* be off traveling for auditions and acclimating to this new venture," I mused.

"Exactly," Lion said. "So the timing couldn't be more off for you two."

Sighing, I dropped my head on his shoulder. "But I can still hope, right?"

He chuckled. "Stop bein' so dramatic. Everything'll work itself out."

"Lion?" I mumbled, leaning into his side.

"Yeah?"

"Thank you. For everything."

Although he didn't do well in emotional moments, he patted my arm. "I try to make good on my promises."

I loved him more than I did my own delinquent parents. God knows, he looked out for me more than they were ever capable of doing. He was stern when he needed to be, gentle and comforting when that was fitting. He never once judged my obsession with Jahleel. He just guided me through it all. And just like he said, he did come through on his promises.

He promised me the world, and I had it.

I SPENT THE next couple of days wrapped up in Jahleel. Each day was the same: rehearsals, planning, and all things Jahleel Kingston.

Knowing and accepting the fact he would probably be unfaithful during my absence, I spent as much time with him as possible, leaving my mark, my scent, my imprint, so if he did cheat, he'd be thinking of me.

After taking some time to think about what Lion said, I

had to admit, six months was a long time for a *man* to go sexless. Sucks big time for me, nonetheless. But I figured it was better for me to know and anticipate possible unfaithfulness, than to worry endlessly about it while on tour, nagging him with suspicious questions and letting it affect my mood and focus when I should be giving my all on stage.

Le sigh. Sometimes it made sense for people in my position not to have relationships.

Jahleel was still an insensitive tosser sometimes, but his mood switches were far and in between. Anyway, I was getting used to him. Plus, for some inexplicable reason, it affected him greatly whenever I told him I hated him, so sometimes—and I chose those times wisely—I used it as a weapon.

Worked like a charm.

Two weeks slipped by faster than a cheetah in the night, and then it was the night before I left for tour. I had to board my bus by six the next morning. As a result, activities squeezed my day so tightly, I barely had time to breathe.

This was also the day Jahleel's position to judge on Dancin' 2da' Beat was announced. I got a whiff of this news through Amy and Jamie's giggles of gossip, but I hadn't been able to call or text Jahleel to congratulate him. So strung out, I didn't even have a clue where my cellphone was.

By the time all the rush slowed into quietness, it was

almost 11pm. Stacey, my assistant, brought me my cellphone and I spared not another second in having Thomas take me to Jahleel's.

On the drive there, I checked my notifications. From Jahleel, were 32 missed calls leading up to half-an-hour ago, and two text messages; one saying he got the position on the show, and the other saying he wanted to do something special with me before I left—sent earlier in the day.

Tried ringing him back a couple of times, but got no answer. Neither was his bike home when Thomas dropped me off at his house, so I let myself in with the spare key he gave me—*oh yes, he went there!*

Dumping my stuff on his bed, I made a beeline for the clinical all-white bathroom and had me a long shower, washing away the muck and weariness of the day. I was knackered to the point of drowsiness, but I had to spend my last hours in SF with Jahleel.

When I emerged from the shower, my phone was lighting up on the bed. I ran to snatch it up and saw five missed calls from Jahleel. When I tried ringing him back, he didn't pick up, even though his last call was less than a minute ago. Ridiculous.

A few minutes later while I dressed, my phone pinged with a message from him:

JK: What?

Me: Where r u?

JK: Out.

Me: K. When will u b home?

JK: Home? Leave.

Me: Wut?

JK: LEAVE.
I won't be there.

Did he really expect me to leave without seeing him? What was he out doing that he couldn't spare a few hours with me?

Dialling off his number, I rang him back, but he wouldn't pick up. I rang and rang until I started yawning.

Flipping back the covers on his bed, I slid beneath them and dozed off.

THE DIN OF my cellphone pulled me from semi-consciousness, but by the time I found the phone under the sheets, it stopped ringing. A missed call from Jahleel. Yet, when I rang him back, there was no answer.

Maybe it was because I was knackered, frustrated and needed him like a new-born needed its milk, or just plain pissed I wouldn't see him before I left, I don't know, but I sent him an irate message:

Me: *Am.tired.of.ur.shit*
So u kno wut?
Fuq.U!!!

JK: *Bitchy Sassy?*
U know how I feel about her.
Breathe easy.

Raging like a bull about to take off, I paced, ringing him again and again. No answer. Eventually, I collapsed on the bed and nodded off.

From the depths of my sleep, I heard the loud rumbling of Jahleel's bike pulling up outside. He was home. The anticipation jolted me upright.

Springing out of bed, I ran out of the room like a kid on Christmas morning to meet him at the door. But as I turned the hall corner, I skidded to a halt in shock at seeing Jahleel all but crashing through the front door.

With Krissy.

My heart fainted.

Unaware of nothing but themselves, they were a fever of lips and tongues and hands. Voraciously grabbing and mauling each other.

Krissy gripped his jacket and dragged him with her, walking backwards into the kitchen from the front entrance.

"Your room," Jahleel muttered before they disappeared from my line of sight.

Unsure of how my feet were even functioning, I stepped into the kitchen from the bottom entrance.

"No," Krissy said, a deep urgency in her soft, deceitful voice. "Can't wait. I want you now."

Both still oblivious to me standing at the other end of the kitchen—because they were *that* lost in each other—Jahleel pulled back from her a little. "Krissy, not like this."

"We can make love later," she insisted, moving in to close the slip of distance Jahleel put between them. "Right now, I want you to fuck me."

A lump the size of a baseball clogged my throat, but I ignored it, too riveted, painfully so, on what unfolded before me.

"Dammit," Jahleel swore under his breath. "I don't want—"

"Please, JK," Krissy begged in a voice heavy with need, but lacking true, genuine passion. She didn't love him. She was using him. The manipulative bitch. "Just...just let me feel…you."

As if finally sensing me, Jahleel's eyes flicked up over Krissy's head and landed on me.

Dumbfounded, heartbroken, immobile, I just stared at him staring at me, revealing all I was feeling, while he revealed nothing but apology.

An apology.

He was choosing her over me. He never fucking got over her. He'd lied. And the first chance he got, he was going to take her and ruin what we had. Now there I was, the fool.

Hadn't I known all along I was second to her? That I was his standby?

The man I loved closed his eyes and turned his head to the side, shutting me out. He was wishing me gone, clearly dismissing me. That easy, he made his choice.

From somewhere deep down, past my unconscious heart and the sick, gutted feeling roiling in the pit of my stomach, somewhere in the tsunami of pain, I found the strength to move.

I wouldn't fight. Every fight I had in me was gone. Used up by him. What I *would* do was grant him his wish: be gone when he opened his eyes.

Absconding from the kitchen, not wanting to alert his beloved Krissy, I quickly fetched my belongings from his room as silent tears streamed.

I shouldn't have cried. Crying was weak, and I needed to be strong. I needed to walk away and never look back. I could do it. I knew I could. I hadn't always been an idiot. I used to be strong once. And tonight, I willed that side of me back.

Contending with Krissy was futile. A battle I would never win. She owned him. Like a fucking puppet on a string. She used him whenever and however she pleased, taking advantage of his feelings for her, and later indifferently pretended to be oblivious to his feelings.

From now on, she could jack his heart up with a butcher knife. I didn't care. Not anymore.

Tears, hot tears, stubbornly disregarded my order and streamed down my face as I slipped out the front door without a peep, blocking out the sounds in the kitchen.

I rushed hurriedly down the driveway while texting Thomas and ran smack into a tall, hard, wall of a man. He had a powerful but heady scent of new leather and an undertone of olive bar-soap.

Not wanting be recognized, a sobbing broken-hearted fool, I kept my head down and muttered my apologies as I moved to get around him. But his firm fingers clasped around my arm in a sturdy grip and kept me where I was.

When I glanced up, recognition hit.

Krissy's mogul.

Oh, crap. Hell was about to turn over and I did not want to be around to get burned. So as his intense blue gaze narrowed in on me and his mouth opened to no doubt inquire what was wrong, I warned him, "You might not wanna go in there."

Thomas pulled up just then.

The hot mogul looked to the house with a frown, letting me go, and I lingered not another moment, making a beeline for the Phantom, and slid in the back.

"Home, Miss Day?" Thomas asked.

"Just drive."

Leaning back in the car seat, the tears flowed as I fought off all thoughts of him and Krissy together. I had to do something to purge him from my mind. But there was no one to go home to. Amanda was spending her nights with Zane due to the tour, and Ferbie, who'd opted out of coming on tour with me this time, had been seen once every couple of days, as Sade had taken him over, all to herself. Jealous I was, yes, but he was happier than I'd ever seen him, so I no longer interfered with his life.

Lion wasn't in SF, and Jamie or Amy's shoulder was out of the question.

Saskia Day was alone and heartbroken.

But I brought this on myself, didn't I? I persisted and

397

forced something that wasn't supposed to be, and in the end it backfired. Of course, he never wanted me. He used me as a distraction from her. And at the first chance she presented, he leaped. Saskia who?

Reaching into my bag for my cellphone, the bitter part of me took over, tapping out a quick message:

I hope she hurts you
Face to the dirt you

I hope she uses you
Spits on & refuses you

I hope she crushes you
Shits out & flushes you

I hope she breaks you
Pricks and deflates you

I hate you.
Hate you.
I hate you.
Hate you.
I do not wish you all the fucking best.

I do not wish you find foreva happiness.

All I have are curses.
Curses
Curses
With no fucking reverses.

I. Hate. You.

Thumb hovering over the send button, I contemplated sending it, asking myself if that's how truly I felt.

Yes.

I hit send.

That was it. Jahleel Kingston and Saskia Day were finished. But then, there never was an 'us' to begin with.

Thomas drove me around town for about an hour, until someone came to mind. Remembering how weird he'd been about his phone number the last time, and his strict instruction not to text back when he messaged me, I decided to text him instead of calling.

Me: R u here?
S.D.

Five minutes later:

Chad: *Good timing. Just got in. You OK?*

Me: *Can I c u?*

Another five minutes passed.

Chad: *Yes. Where are you?*

Me: *Send me ur addy & I'll come 2 u.*

Aptly so, Chad resided in Russian Hill, in a high-rise building that looked quaintly charming on the outside. But when a tall, muscular, dark-skinned man met me outside to escort me into the building, the modern décor inside contrasted sharply to the outside with its solid colours, stainless steel, glass and sharp angles.

The escort entered a code in the lift, and I was reminded Chad was a Niiveux.

The lift doors soon opened to the foyer of a magnificent open-floor-plan penthouse. I stepped out and the doors closed, swallowing up the big man and shutting me in.

Designed with a deep brown and beige colour scheme, the space gave off a warm, masculine vibe. The only touches of colour showed up in wall paintings and decorative tchotchkes.

There was no one in sight, except for three large, girly pink suitcases sitting upright near where I stood. As I stepped further into the apartment, a tiny Hispanic woman looking to be in her mid-thirties materialized.

"Hello—" she started, then stopped, eyes widening as she pointed a finger at me, "Oh, oh, you Saskia Day!"

She slapped a hand over her mouth and glanced around nervously, as though she'd be in grave danger if caught losing her composure.

Clearing her throat, she regained her poise, turned and signalled for me to follow. "Right this way, Miss Day."

She led me through the impressive penthouse and out to a balcony where Chad was talking on his phone in a language neither English nor Russian.

With a nod from him, the housemaid turned and exited.

I was left with the man I knew I should steer clear of.

But, why? Jahleel broke his promise before I even left for tour, so it was only fair I could break mine. Promises meant nothing anymore.

Fresh and simple as usual, Chad was semi-formal in jeans and a white button-down shirt. Except, the buttons were all undone, exposing a hard chest of tattoos. Cuffs were also undone, left flapping open at his wrists. Barefoot.

His hair had grown longer, almost meeting Jahleel's normal length, but not nearly as thick or perfect. Chad's was thinner, with loose, wet-like waves. He was half the cool, suave Chad I knew, and half the square-shouldered, power-possessed man I'd glimpsed in L.A.

As his eyes narrowed, scrutinizing me while he spoke on the phone, I anxiously shoved my hands in my short's pockets.

What the hell was I doing here?

In a finite tone and unidentifiable language, he ended the call. We stood watching each other for a moment, until he took a few steps to close the short gap between us. "You were crying."

"Maybe I was."

Instead of asking the reason, he asked, "Don't you leave for tour in a couple of hours?"

And instead of asking how he knew that, I answered, "I do."

Chad was a man who a woman couldn't stand within his radius and *not* think about sex. The man was sexually attractive in every way. In the way he spoke, walked, focused.

So, having his inked chest right there in my face, there was no way I could not move further in and touch his hard heat of ink artistry with the tips of my fingers. Fascinated, I rubbed my whole palm over his pecs, and he caught my wrist to stop me.

As he made to say something, a female's voice cut through, "Cousin?"

I turned my head to see a slender, raven-haired girl, pretty, but no older than seventeen, standing at the entrance to the balcony.

Her obsidian eyes landed on me first, and her mouth dropped open. "Oh. My. God. You're Saskia Day!"

"Yep. That's me," I smiled at her exuberance.

"I was just unpacking while listening to your latest album. I have all of them! I like love, love, love you! You're super-duper awesome! And you're—"

Same as the housemaid did earlier, she slapped her hand over her mouth and shifted her gaze nervously to Chad behind me.

He must have shown his approval because she removed her hand and grinned. "It's okay if I ask her to sign my albums and posters?"

"You may," Chad said from behind me. "But not now. Later. What is it you wanted?"

Scooping her long hair to one side, she mumbled, "I was just going to bed...and wanted to tell you...thank you. For everything."

Moving by me, she went to Chad, tipped up on her toes

and gave him a peck on his cheek.

Chad returned a kiss to her forehead and jerked his chin to the door. "Get some rest, Alina."

She glanced at me, then back at him. "I want her autogra—"

"You'll get them."

Taking his word for it, she spared me another giddy grin and left.

Without thinking, I stupidly blurted, "You're not in love with her, are you?"

Chad raised a brow at me and I immediately apologized like an idiot. "Forgive me. I don't even know why I asked that."

"Yes, you do," he said knowingly. "Alina's my aunt's daughter. *Real* blood. Her parents just got...killed. I'm her guardian now."

"Oh," I murmured. "Sorry about your aunt."

I knew all too well about taking over with siblings. Even now I found it hard to let go of Timber and Ferbie.

Chad shrugged, as if it was nothing. "Shit happens."

Taking my hands in his, he brought them up between us and squeezed them. "I assume you were crying because JK was, well, himself. You were hurt. Now you're here."

Lowering his head, he gave me a soft, soothing kiss, then

drew back and continued, "But I'm no rebound fuck. I'm not a man who screws around. Whenever I engage in a relationship, I take it seriously. I only pursue women I can have something meaningful with. Because my time is valuable. Each and every second of it. So I never waste it on mindless, meaningless shit." He paused and studied me. "You're hurt. You're broken. You're fragile. And I'm not some horny, starstruck teenager dying to stick my dick in you."

He released my hands and cupped my face, his tone switching to one that warned against rebuttals. "So, here's what we're going to do: you're coming to bed with me, and I will hold you because you need to be held. You'll fall asleep in my arms because you're weary and worn. I'll wake you up at 5am and you'll leave to do what you must do to head out on tour. You'll forget about me, you'll forget about *him*, and channel all your energy and focus into your work. Block your mind to all irrelevancies, like *love*. In six months' time, you'll return with a fresh mind and a clear head. If you still want me then, come to me. Because I'll still have the taste of your kiss imprinted on my brain."

A warm feeling flowed through me and I sighed. For the first time, I felt something other than sexual attraction for him. I could grow to love this man. Chadrick Niiveux. He was what I needed. Controlled, calm and calculated. No nonsense, no bullshit. While Jahleel was a fuck-around, full of shit.

"Okay," I agreed in a breathy voice, watching his lips, wanting to kiss him, but knew it was off limits…for now. Six months from now, I could taste those lips.

Chad retrieved his cellphone, dialled off a number, and told whoever answered on the other end, "Retiring. Shut down."

Then he wrapped an arm around my waist, led me to his bedroom, and we did just what he decreed.

Chapter 22

Dreams have ended
In the black of the night
Tears she cried
Let her heart die

Hopes have faltered
When blue velvet skies
Swallowed whole a silver line
Fate's far, no more

Tonsils swollen
Eyes undead

Her tears for her
Her curses for him

Nose engorged
Eyes rim red
Her tears for her
Her curses for him

Is he happy?
She doesn't fight.
Is she happy?
He doesn't fight.

Fortune and her wheel
Icarus and his sun
Nature and her wind
Moth and his flame

Tonsils swollen
Eyes undead
Her tears for her
Her curses for him

Nose engorged

Eyes rim red
Her tears for her
Her curses for him

Curses for him
Curses for him
Her tears for her
Her curses for him

But who?
WHO gives a fuck?!

I belted out the last line with a feral roar, putting heavy emphasis on the swearword then dropping it in the mike with a sharp, abrupt end, the electrical waves of that last line traveling in echoes over the arena.

The crowd waited with bated breath, unsure if that was the end of the song, or something else was coming, as this was yet another new song I dropped at the end of a show.

One, two, three seconds passed, and when the audience realized this was the end, an uproar of screaming and whistling erupted.

I grinned out at the crowd, at the masses of fan-made posters with my name on them. 'We love you Saskia Day!', 'You are my idol!' 'You fucking ROCK!' 'Be my BFF! Please!' were just a few of the praises I could make out.

Crossing my forearms, I gave them my signature bow and started off stage. "Now, you all know how I say goodbye, don't you?"

The crowd raved, bellowing my signature goodbye before I even began. I waited until the clamour abated, then began, "Sweden, this was…"

The crowd picked up, "Bloody awesome!!"

"This was…"

"Bloody awesome!!!"

Moving back as the spotlight dimmed on stage, I shouted, "Sweden, I *said*, this was…"

"MotherfuckingAwesome!!!!!!"

The lights went out, the crowd went nuts, and I bounced off stage.

The microphone was immediately pried from my hand. A hand-towel replaced its position, and a water bottle was shoved in my other hand, while roadies fussed around me removing ear-mikes and wirings.

Once I was free, the tour manager, Mikael, took me by the elbow and propelled me down the hall heading to the exit with Thomas and John flanking us. We couldn't linger a second longer if we wanted to make it to our next destination in time for tomorrow night's show.

"Did Manda make it back?" I asked Mikael as we got to the back door.

The guards there promptly opened it, and Mikael guided me out as he answered, "Yeah. Zane dropped her off an hour ago. She's out cold on the bus."

At the sound of his voice, a contradictory combination of gravelly and velvety, I peeked up at his profile and smiled.

My usual tour manager was a lanky lesbian brunette named Melissa. But this time, it was Mikael, hired behind my back by Lion. All the time Lion and I planned this tour, I thought he was passing on my requests to Melissa, so one might imagine my surprise to see Mikael the morning before we left.

Lion had some underlying intention when he hired Mikael, I believed.

At around six four, Mikael was a sight. He was all muscles, not the steroid-ridden type, but the scrumptious, I-want-to-rake-my-nails-all-over you type. He had buzzed dark hair, dazzling blue eyes, perfect white teeth and a commanding alpha attitude. He wore black, only black, and spoke only when necessary.

But surprisingly enough, even though his attraction to me was obvious, I kept things on a professional level, disregarding his hot bod and good looks, remembering Chad's command to focus on work and block out all irrelevancies. So that's what I did for the past three months I've been on tour.

"I can feel your eyes on me, you know," Mikael said in that damn arousal-awakening voice as we approached the bus.

Thomas and John split up behind us, going around the bus to check the tires and for lurking lunatics.

"So?" I shot back. "I can't look at the badass in black who's guiding me by the elbow? Maybe you should consider wearing a mask like Batman." I twisted my mouth to the side, "Hmm, but people would stare twice as much then, wouldn't they?"

Like hell if I couldn't look at a hot guy! Not after being single and stuck on the road with absolutely no intention of getting entangled. I was, of course, looking forward to going home to Chad. We could be something together. But that was three months from now. So until then, I pleasured my eyeballs with whatever eye-candy was in sight, going by the rule 'look but don't touch'.

In the darkness of the night, I might have glimpsed the mighty Mikael roll his eyes, but I wasn't sure.

To change the topic, he said, "Lion said to tell you, and I quote, 'save those fuckin' new songs for the next album'." We reached the bus and he opened the door. "You've sang about fifteen new songs since you started the tour. And they're all incredibly good. Billboard potential."

My turn to roll my eyes. "Tell Lion not to worry. When you have a broken heart, lyrics come to you in abundance."

When I made to enter the bus, I only got one step up, because Mikael was still holding onto me. I peered over my shoulder at him to find him staring at his hand on my arm.

Catching himself, he let go of me and cleared his throat.

As I got another step up, he called, "Saskia?"

"Yeah?" I turned around.

"Whoever he was," he said, staring me in the eyes, "he didn't deserve you. And he doesn't deserve those songs you keep singing for him. He doesn't even deserve your curses."

He does.

Breaking eye contact, I lied, "I know."

Mikael looked down at his scuffed black boots and stuffed his hands in his front pockets, then looked back at me. "You were amazing tonight."

"Thanks."

We stood without a word for another awkward minute until he cleared his throat again. "You go get some sleep. I've gotta help Thomas and John prepare to get outta here."

I continued on into the bus and he closed the door behind me. Loud snoring came from Amanda, Jamie and Amy's sections as I moved down the aisles and went straight to my room at the back, diving into bed, clothes and all.

Feeling inexplicably content.

Going on tour immediately after you've had your heart broken was probably the most curative prescription there was. God bless those who's got the luxury to do so.

See, after watching the man you love choose another woman, leaving you feeling worthless, pointless, without value, with a bruised ego and shattered confidence, nothing could be more therapeutic than getting up on a stage where people, masses, strangers, admirers, are all chanting *your* name, screaming and hollering their love and devotion for *you*. Reminding you of your worth, your value, inflating your ego and boosting your confidence. Feeling fucking *loved. Idolized.*

So what if one undeserving asshole didn't?

Forget him. He was nothing. Something small, minuscule in a life that was great, awesome, grand and extraordinary. Damn straight I didn't need him for my happiness.

About a month after I left for tour, I received an email from him, titled, 'You Were My Sheba.' In the body of the email was a link to the film *'Solomon',* which he abridged to focus on just the love story between Solomon and Sheba.

Apparently, King Solomon, a man of great wealth, had 700 wives and 300 concubines, but only one woman whom he truly loved: Sheba, Queen from another land. Solomon gave her everything she desired, except the one thing beyond his control: making their son heir to the throne. So Sheba left him and went back to her land.

Highlighted below the link in the mail, was a line Solomon spoke to Sheba, *"You are the Queen to my King. I sought you ever since I was a youth. Without knowing what it is I was seeking."*

What did he mean by that email? I had no idea. Or maybe I didn't care. He chose Krissy over me. With nothing but an apologetic glance. The email held no tone of apology, nor intimated he wanted me back. Therefore, I didn't see its purpose. My days of trying to figure him out were over.

Everyone had a breaking point, and that was mine. There would be no reconciling.

Even as I came to this resolution, I fumbled under my pillow for the iPod I kept there, one song on repeat for the last three months. Sticking the earplugs in, the sweet melody of A Great Big World's *'Say Something'* lulled me to sleep.

A month later, we were all lounging and idle chatting about

nothing of relevance during our long drive to Tucson.

Amanda was cross-legged on a sofa, and I laid with my head in her lap. Amy and Jamie were sitting across from us—Jamie staring unabashedly at Mikael, where he sat working at a table at the front of the bus.

Jamie had a serious crush on him, but he hadn't so much as smiled at her. Poor girl. I knew all too well what it was like to be ignored.

Somehow the conversation landed on whose name? Yep. Jahleel Bloody Kingston. Thanks to frigging Amy.

With a groan, I turned on Amanda's lap and pressed my face to her stomach.

Please, no. I did not want to hear his name. But Jamie and Amy kept babbling, because, of course, they had no clue what happened between us, and telling them was out of the question. So I kept quiet while they babbled on about the show he judged on.

"...and TMZ wrote, JK owns that show like Michael Jackson owns the moonwalk."

Tired of people giving undue credit to that arseshit, I flipped over and glared at them. "He can't own a show that's not about him. It's about the goddamn contestants! He just sits behind a bloody desk giving opinions nobody gives a crap about, because he's *no one*."

Jamie and Amy blinked at me, looked at each other, then back at me. "You haven't been watching the show, have you?"

"Ah, I thought about it once, twice max," I said in sarcasm, "but then I just carried on living my *fabulous* life."

For the sake of my sanity, I avoided watching that show at all costs.

"That explains it," Amy said, rolling her eyes. "You know how everyone watches *The Voice* just to see Adam Levine?"

"Hoping he'll take his shirt off?" Jamie added.

Amanda snorted and I stared, far from amused.

But the chatty wenches continued, "Well, since that audition in Denver, the show ratings skyrocketed. Everyone's watching—

"Hoping he'll dance...or take his shirt off," Jamie filled in.

"Oh yes!" Amanda joined in. "That audition was a talk about."

Groaning, I slapped my hands to my face. "Uh Jesus. Not you, too."

"No, Kia," Amanda said, "you should see it. Seriously. He was amazing."

"That's exactly why I don't wanna see it," I hissed at her.

She shrugged and backed off, but before I knew it, Amy flipped open her laptop and shoved it in my face.

417

YouTube video. 42million views. Nice.

Amy hit play, and there was the a-hole. In all his steami-licious glory. A stab of pain impacted my heart, but gratefully, it was fleeting.

His hair had grown much longer, caught in a messy pile on top of his head, as if he didn't give a damn, but it loaned him a pretty boy vibe. Maybe the stylists on the show decided to go with his usual don't-give-a-shit vibe or he insisted on it. Knowing Jahleel, I'd bet the latter.

With him being behind the table, I could only see his up-per half, clothed in a red hoodie. Another stab of pain.

Red Hoodie Guy.

Sitting next to him was Siria Les, a fierce Native Ameri-can who could dance her socks off. Her right hand was unnec-essarily close to Jahleel's on the table, their pinky fingers touching. Hmnh.

On the other side of her was Grey Tomlin. He was a vet-eran, but up in age, his fifties, and probably should be done with this life by now.

Lots of chattering from the host who called the next per-son up for audition, Jared. Young, fit, good-looking and quite good, in my opinion. Had I been a judge, I would've no doubt given him a pass.

Grey and Siria gave their opinions, which were good, of

course. But when it was Jahleel's turn, he was, well, Jahleel, and stated, "You're not ready for this competition."

That, of course, caused an outburst from the crowd.

Grey, who'd being wearing a sullen expression from the get-go, was incensed. He leaned forward and looked past Siria to Jahleel. "Are you serious? What on earth is your problem?"

Quite clear that Grey was no fan of Jahleel. Huh.

Instead of acknowledging Grey, Jahleel looked at the guy on stage, who looked as if he was about blow. "One, two, three of us have travelled from state to state searching for talented contestants. And one, two, three of us have said 'yes' to all the contestants chosen. So one, two, *three* of us know that the talent we already have in this competition will eat you alive. I'm only saving you from embarrassment and disappointment, Jared. You're not ready."

Grey looked as if he wanted to flip the table over and punch Jahleel to a pulp, Siria kept her eyes downcast, while the guy onstage went off the grid.

"Man, what the hell do you know?! I've never even heard of you until now. You're just some talentless pastor's boy!"

Grey tittered, while Jahleel remained impassive. Two securities materialized to escort the pissed-off guy from the stage, but Jahleel stopped them.

To the guy, he said, "Alright. Let's make a deal."

419

As Grey started to object, Jahleel talked over him. "I'll come onstage and show you the level of dancing from the weakest contestant we've got, and if you still believe you can beat that—remember, this will be the level of the *weakest* dancer in the competition—then I'll give you your third yes and let you hang yourself."

The guy beckoned with his hands for Jahleel to 'bring it'.

Jahleel stood up from the table, shrugged out of his hoodie and tossed it on the back of his chair, which Siria wasted no time in fixing properly so it didn't fall off.

Now he was left wearing a white wife beater, white sneakers and close-fitted faded jeans with a wide ripped out hole at the right knee.

At the stage, instead of taking the stairs, he made one large leap and back-flipped right on top of the stage. The very *high* stage.

The crowd gasped, as if they expected him to fall and break his neck. When they saw he survived, a great cheer erupted.

Impressive.

"Play anything," Jahleel said.

Almost immediately, fast paced club music blared and Jahleel moved at the utter first beat. Like he was a marionette and the music pulled his strings. Together, he and the music were one.

Effortlessly, he moved in time with every beat, twisting his limbs in ways I didn't think were possible. The music bled into break dance music and that's when the crowd's noise brought the roof down.

Mouth open, dumbfounded, I watched as he danced like a Cheetah chasing its own tail. The man was nothing but a blur of white and denim.

"Bees knees," I whispered to no one in particular. "Is he even touching the ground?"

"Dope, right?" Jamie said across from us, though she was still staring at Mikael.

The music abruptly stopped, and marionette to the music, Jahleel abruptly suspended his movement in the middle of a break dance position, his whole body balanced slant up in the air on one hand, his muscles rippling with sweat.

The crowd went ballistic.

Righting himself back to his feet with a quick frog-flip, he turned to Jared who gaped at him, awed. Through laboured breathing, he said, "That is the weakest level. Say the word, and that yes is all yours."

Running to edge of the stage, he backflipped off and went back to his seat. Siria magically produced a red hand-towel and handed it to him with a massive grin on her face. When he

421

took it from her and sat back down, she leaned over and whispered something in his ear. Jahleel gave her sidelong glance, looked at her face a little too long before nodding.

He redirected his attention back to the stage, then leaned into the mike. "You have your yes if you want it, Jared."

But the guy stared agape at the crowd, who were still screaming their heads off, with shrills of 'JK!!!' 'Ohmigod, you're so hot, JK!', 'Dance for us again, JK!', while Grey's face was as sour as unripe grapes.

Finally, Jared pointed his finger out to the crowd's frenzy and dazedly said, "No. I want *that*."

Jahleel nodded, pleased. "Go home, then. Train harder. Surround yourself with dancers who're ten times better than you and strive to be better than them. Challenge yourself, try new things. Don't try to control the music, let the music control you. Be the music's bitch, be submissive to it. Move at its command. Come back next year, and maybe then you'll get..." He trailed off, turned, and looked out at the audience.

Just when I thought they couldn't have gotten any louder, they did. Jahleel turned back around, leaned into the mike, and with his signature crooked grin, he said, "*that*."

"Thanks, man. Thanks. I'll work harder. Come back and rip it, man," Jared babbled. "Maybe you could train me, you know. I'd be so much better with your help. We could do—"

"That'll be all, Jared," Siria cut in.

Jared rattled around a dozen more thank you's before he finally backed off the stage. The video ended and I wanted to scream.

No. I wanted to see more. Oh my God. Why hadn't I been watching this before? Jahleel...

Snapping a lid on my thoughts, I stopped myself before I relapsed into obsessing about him again. He was what I couldn't have. He broke my heart. I had to remember that. Had to remember that I hated him.

"It came out later on a talk show that Jared is Grey's nephew," Amy informed me. "Apparently there was some agreement that Jared would get an automatic pass into the competition. Seems JK didn't get the memo, or he just disregarded it. That's why Grey and Jared were so furious, and why Siria kept quiet."

Jamie piped in, "Grey denied all of it of course, even with proof they're related. So now people only look forward to JK's opinion on the show—"

"Because he didn't just talk the talk. He walked the walk. Credibility," Amy said, taking back the reigns. "Last week, one girl broke into tears when he walked out. Like he's fucking Michael Jackson or somet—"

"Saskia," Mikael's deep and deadly voice broke through,

traveling in thick waves down the bus. "Can I borrow you for a minute?"

Handing Amy her laptop, I rolled off the couch and trundled up to where Mikael was, sipping a cup of coffee and entering data in a spread sheet. I plopped down across from him at the table.

He was wearing his focused face, with those slim reading glasses he used whenever he worked on his computer. That face always made me smile, because he looked so different and business-like in them, his blue eyes piercing, a mile from the tough man in black.

Without even looking at me, he warned, "You laugh at my glasses again, Saskia, I'll pinch you where it hurts. I only called you up here to save you from being drowned in details of the man you curse each time you sing."

How did he know JK was the ex? Not once have I mentioned Jahleel's name, to anyone, ever since that night. Unless Lion told him—

"You say his name in your sleep. All the time," Mikael said in a quiet voice, answering my unasked question, his eyes still on his computer screen, fingers typing. "Only took me a second to piece it together just now."

Tears pricked at my eyes, and I dipped my head, studying my fingers. I wouldn't let the tears flow, though. Nuh uh. I didn't love him. I hated him. He didn't choose me. For three months I'd managed not to think of him, and I would successfully continue in that vein, staying focused on going home to Chad—the better suitor.

Putting all poignancy and irrelevancies aside, I slapped on a smile and stretched across the table to playfully tap Mikael's glasses in the middle where it met his nose.

He chuckled lightly and swatted my hand, avoiding direct eye contact with me. "Saskia...behave."

But I kept teasing him, until I glanced over his shoulder and caught Jamie staring at us, her expression forlorn.

Pulling back, I eased down in my seat and lowered my voice, "She likes you, you know."

"Good for her, whoever she is," he said dully, still typing.

"Jamie," I whispered.

Mikael said nothing in return.

Jamie and Amy were two girls who cared about naught, not even relationships. They were materialistic, shallow and self-absorbed, albeit loyal. So I knew, by the way Jamie stared at Mikael from a distance, day after day, that she liked him on a different level. Like a *serious* level.

Shallow Jamie would've been shoving her tits in Mikael's face ages ago, relentless until he had sex with her. But this lust, it was different. She might have even made an immense error in letting herself fall in love with him. A man who may never notice her, who will ignore her, never returning her feelings. Ever.

Even if she changed her hair colour and became a superstar, the world in her hands, chanting her name. Even if she stalked him around the world and eventually got close to him, got him in her bed. Still, he'd use her and discard her. He'd never want her. He'd never requite her love. And she would never, ever be whole.

She'd try to move on and wrest her happiness, but it wouldn't be real. None of it would fulfil her. So she'd forever walk around life half-empty, with half of a heart, her other half in someone else's grasp.

"You know," I whispered, mildly melancholic, convincing myself that the sadness was on Jamie's behalf, "nothing hurts more than being ignored. When the one person you want more than anything in this world, doesn't want you."

For the first time since I came to sit across from him, Mikael looked up from his computer screen, his blue gaze meeting mine. "That's a hurt I can identify with." He stared at me a moment longer, before lowering his gaze from mine and whispered, "Even now."

Chapter 23

I was Chad's.

At the tour's end, I went straight to him, as directed by his mandate.

That was four months ago.

We dated under the radar because Chad didn't care for the media, plus he was private to the utmost, even with me. We spent a lot of time together, and I got to know him... but at times it felt as if I didn't know him at all.

There was the Chad I knew—smooth, suave, with undeniable sex appeal. Other times, it was Chad, the authoritarian—in command with a different posture, different aura. I wasn't sure which Chad was the real one.

High instincts told me he lived a double life, but I was too caught up with my own demanding life to pay attention to small details. A girlfriend who cared would've dug into it, right? Well, I didn't care enough to dig or ask questions. In addition, the man had a certain air of intimidation that deterred people from confrontation.

Did I love him? Maybe.

He was amazing. Attentive, most of all, and serious. Probably too serious sometimes. But we were great together. No drama, no complications. He loved having me at his place and I loved being there, not just because of him, but Alina, too.

For my birthday two months ago in May, he took me to Bora Bora. Stole me from the world for an entire week. Work and technology left behind. Just us. It was heaven.

Sexually, things were off the charts—as I'd always suspected it would be with him. Chad could make me speak in languages that didn't exist. He even topped my best-sex-ever ex, Tex. And Tex was damned hard to top.

Emotionally? Well, it was quite possible feelings were being forced. The raw, natural connection wasn't there like it was with...*him*. But that was irrelevant. Real love isn't something we fall into, it's something we grow into. Right?

Right.

Weird enough, for the four months we've been together, I

never once ran into Jahleel—not that I wanted to run into him, but they were best friends. Chad assured me all was well when I questioned if their friendship was still intact.

So, that was that.

At present, I was in Chad's living room, bonding with Alina, eating Honey Nut Cheerios from the box, while he engaged in never-ending conference calls in his office. He did that sometimes, stayed wrapped up in phone calls that went on for hours.

Alina was watching some new adult crap show on T.V. while she filed her nails with a bright pink nail file in her *LOVE PINK* pyjama set and pink toenails. Typical teenager.

She stopped filing her nails and breathed out a dreamy sigh, "Ian Somerhalder is sooooooo hot."

My eyes rolled. "What is it with you girls and this bloke? I don't get it."

Alina gaped at me in horror, as if I were some monstrous creature about to eat her alive. "You can't be serious."

Popping a handful of Cheerios in my mouth, I spoke around them, "I mean, sure, he's undeniably good-looking in the face. Striking even. That jawline, wow. *But* he's short, and puny, and probably couldn't lift up a woman who weighs over a hundred pounds without farting or shitting himself."

Alina snickered.

429

"Now if you're talking about a real man," I went on, "hot both in looks and body build, you're talking men like Henry Cavill."

Alina scoffed. "You're just bias because he's British."

"Maybe," I said around another mouthful of Cheerios. "But what about Chris and Liam Hemsworth? Now those are *men*."

"Oh yeah," Alina agreed in a swoony voice. "I'd definitely want Liam to lift me up in those long, strong arms."

I grinned at her, then glanced around to see if Chad was anywhere nearby to overhear us. He was strict with his staff and especially Alina, and I knew this was a conversation he wouldn't want me having with his cousin. "You have a boyfriend, Alina?"

She resumed filing her nails and remained silent for a long while before answering. "Guys are afraid to date me."

"What? Why?"

Alina shrugged, but it was a shrug that told me she couldn't, or shouldn't talk about it.

"But there's someone at school you have a crush on, right?"

It wasn't normal for a girl her age to *not* have a crush. Or at least sneaking around with someone.

"Not at school," she spared. "Guys my age repulses me.

They're brainless idiots. Think they can tell me anything and I'll drop my panties for them. They're hairless, muscle-less, half-brained fucknuts—sorry for swearing."

I laughed as I stuffed more Cheerios in. I seriously loved the fuck out of her and contemplated kidnapping her and moving her in with me, what with Ferbie and Timber all on their own now. "Oh. I was worried for a minute there. Thought you were some abnormal weirdo."

She giggled, then fell silent, leaving me no choice but to watch the pointless vampire crap on T.V. Until she whispered, "JK."

Wondering if I heard her right, I shot her a side long glance. "What's that?"

She kept her voice in a quiet hush, "Cousin's best friend. He's my crush."

Oh. "Oh."

"You should see him," she gushed, eyes twinkling. "He's so freaking hot. He has tattoos and his hair is, like, long and perfect. And his eyes, oh God…you should really see him."

Trust me, I've seen him. And felt him. Fingers, tongue and cock.

"Oh, wait!" she said, snapping her fingers.

Uncrossing her legs, she leaned to the side to lift up the sofa cushion, pulling out a magazine hidden beneath it and handed it to me.

GQ.

And who was on its cover?

JK.

In all his panty-burning glory. How on earth did he land this one? Lion, no doubt.

Jahleel was a ball of steam, smoke and testosterone on the cover, in well-faded jeans with rips in both knees, no belt holding up his jeans, leaving it to hang tantalizingly, illegally, temptingly, dangerously low on his hips, showing off that V.

Oh, for the love of all things perilously sinful...

With that, he wore just a black biker jacket, no shirt beneath, leaving his glorious abs and pecs on display, designed to drive women right out of their minds, burning holes in their knickers. He had his asshole face on—fierce, no hostages—gold eyes mesmerizing, lips parted, both hands raking back through his hair which had grown a descent length past his shoulders.

Swallowing past the giant lump in my throat, I handed the magazine back to Alina. "Does he feel the same?"

Her eyes widened, staring at me as if I just asked her the world's dumbest question. "God, no! He *can't* know. Did you not hear me say he's Cousin's best friend? If he knew I had a crush on him, it would most likely make him uncomfortable, and he would stop coming around. I sure don't want that to happen."

Alina was a lot smarter than she appeared. She was definitely from Chad's lineage. "He comes here? Huh. Strange, I've never seen him here."

"You know how private Cousin is. Whenever JK stops by, it's either before you come here or after you leave," she informed me. "I guess Cousin plans it that way."

Seemed Chad was sparing us from awkwardly running into each other. Good thinking.

Just as I was about to bombard her with more questions, Chad sauntered into the room. Tall and sexy, in nothing but a silk, champagne-coloured pyjama bottom, the dragon tattoo tail on his back wrapped around his left side, the tip disappearing just beneath the waist band.

This ridiculously scrumptious man was mine, and mine alone.

His presence shifted the energy of the room in a major way, and he looked to Alina. "Can I steal her for a bit?"

Alina rolled her eyes as she stood up, deftly hiding the magazine behind her back. "All yours, Cousin. I was just heading off to bed, anyway."

Chad watched her retreat from the room, then without warning, he lunged at me, scooping me up from the sofa, throwing me over his shoulder like a sack of potatoes, and raced off to his bedroom.

At the sudden and unexpected action, I squealed.

Chad smacked my bum. "Stop being such a girl."

"I am a girl, caveman!"

Entering his bedroom, he kicked the door shut and threw me down on the bed. His weight was on me next, tongue plunging into my mouth, rubbing against mine.

When we parted for air, he husked out, "I missed you."

"You're the one who thought work was more important than me."

"Ah," he hummed, tracing the curves of my lips with the tip of his tongue. "I had the television muted on *Late Nite with Dee Jones* while in the middle of a conference call. This gorgeous dark-haired beauty walked out on stage to perform, provocatively dressed, with a riot of stubborn raven curls billowing around her. Her smile, like sunshine. Her voice, like an angel's. Her legs, to murder cold-blooded for. And there I was, deaf to the conference call, thinking, 'Fuck, she's fucking hot.' My cock hardened as I swore, 'I'd give *anything* to have her inner thighs pressed on either side of my face, to have her clit on my tongue.'"

He tore my top off.

"Then it hit me. I *can*." He trailed slow kisses down my

neck, down my stomach, hooking his thumbs in the sides of my shorts and knickers, peeling them off in one go. "Because that fiery hot, raven-haired minx is only a room away…waiting for *me*."

Pushing my legs further apart, he sprinkled pepper hot kisses along my inner thighs then stopped where I was aching for him, wet for him, impatient. "So, what do I have to give to have her?"

Fighting to speak through ragged breaths, I said, "Nothing. I just want you…your tongue…on me."

A swear word, a groan, and then his tongue was on me.

CHAD AND I, the following night, with much time on our hands, attempted to bake a cake for Alina who had passed her End of Term exams with bright red A's. The cake was Chad's idea, because I would've just ordered one.

We had no idea what we were doing. But the fun part was in trying. I could cook well, but was inept in the baking department. Chad had no culinary skills whatsoever. All we did was laugh and make a mess of the kitchen like two idle teenagers. Flour everywhere, all over us.

When we got bored with it, Chad set me up on the countertop, standing between my thighs with the bowl of batter between us. We dipped in, licking the batter from each other's fingers, forgetting completely that the cake was supposed to be for Alina.

As Chad brought my chocolate covered index finger to his mouth, sucking and licking it clean, I heard the elevator doors open. Alina had been out, so I knew it was her returning.

Except, she wasn't alone.

"Stop teasing, JK!" she whined, in a voice that had an underlying *'tease me, tease me, please don't stop teasing me'* tone. "I so hate you right now. Like, totally abhor you."

"And I think you're an adorable nerd. Straight A's, Ally?" Jahleel's voice teased. "Seriously, who uses the word 'abhor' anymore? Oh, that's right, *nerds*."

Both Chad and I froze, listening to Alina and Jahleel bicker, their voices getting closer and closer to the kitchen.

Chad looked at me, suddenly disconcerted and uneasy. "I, uh—do you want to go to the bedroom until he's gone," he asked quickly. "I'm sure you won't feel comfortable seeing him."

Knowing it wouldn't do me well to see Jahleel in person, now or anytime in the future, I nodded and set the bowl aside.

But it was too late.

As Chad placed his hands on my waist to help me down from the kitchen counter, Alina breezed into the kitchen with Jahleel dragging in behind her. His head was down as he typed on his cellphone.

The next second, my cellphone vibrated on the kitchen counter, but too much was happening in the moment to check it.

Alina stopped when she saw me, and her eyes widened in fear. She was so afraid of Chad and I was yet to understand why.

"Oh my God, Cousin. I'm so sorry," she rushed out. "I didn't know she was here."

But Chad said nothing, staring guiltily at Jahleel, who, at Alina's sudden rush of apology, turned his attention from his cellphone and glanced up. Saw us.

Chad, shirtless and worn jeans. Me, in a sports bra and Chad's boxers. Sitting on the countertop with my legs apart, Chad wedged between them.

For about a million minutes, there was nothing but intense silence.

Jahleel glared at Chad, never at me. Myriads of painful expressions flitted across his face, betrayal more prominent.

Chad looked away first, and no one uttered a word.

My brain ceased sending out messages to my organs the

437

second my eyes landed on Jahleel. My heart, I heard it crack again. My eyes, they burned with forced-back tears. My hands, they shook with the need to touch him. If only with just the tips of my fingers.

He was Jahleel Kingston. He was everything. He was my happiness, my meaning, and my purpose. He owned me. Body. Mind. Soul.

Just one sight of him, *one*, and every piece of fake happiness I'd carefully manufactured, shattered. Into a billion tiny pieces. None of it was real. *He* was my real. I loved him. I never stopped.

I needed…I just needed to touch him.

Jahleel began backing out of the kitchen, while nodding his head and repeating, "Okay...Okay...Okay...Okay…"

And without sparing me a single glance, he turned and walked away.

Confused, Alina looked between us and stuttered, "Wha—What's going on?"

Before anyone could answer, Jahleel stormed back into the kitchen, temples flaming red. "You know what, it's *not* fuckin' okay."

Faster than anyone could react, he slammed his fist into Chad's face. Chad's head bobbed back at the unexpected attack.

Alina let out a little scream, while I sat there, unable to move.

Chad moved back a step and wiped his mouth. Staring at the blood smear on his hand, he said, "I'm not gonna fight you, JK."

At 'JK', Jahleel punched him again. "Nah, fight me, Chadrick. C'mon, man. You're good for it. You got a Red Belt, don't you? I'm not afraid to lose. I'll take a beat down and lose like a fuckin' *man*. C'mon. Fuckin' fight me!"

Chad blinked, that second hit rattled him a bit. Still, he refused to fight. "I won't. You're my frien—"

Jahleel moved in and chucked him hard, hissing, "You got no business using that word. You're no fuckin' *friend*."

When Chad didn't react, he began backing out of the kitchen again. But something caught his eye, and his gaze snapped in my direction—well, to my feet, which were covered in red socks.

He froze for a bit and stared at my feet, until he turned suddenly and swept a long muscular arm across the counter. Cake batter, sugar jar, flour jar, all the utensils we'd used clattered, crashed, or splintered to the floor.

Damage done, he stormed out without another word.

Alina bolted after him, calling for him to stop. "JK!"

Inert, speechless, I listened for the sound of the elevator

439

doors. When they finally opened and closed, I looked to a bloody-lipped Chad, who wore a contrite expression.

Then it hit me…"You never told him, did you?"

The expression on Jahleel's face just now, he couldn't have known Chad and I were together. He'd avoided looking at me. Glaring only at Chad, accusing him. He'd had no idea his best friend was dating his ex.

Chad's non-answer to my question verified as much.

"Why?" I demanded. "Why would you hide it—*us* from him?"

"Because I didn't want to see that look on his face." Stepping back from me, he raised his eyes to my face. "And I didn't want to see this look on yours."

There were no words I could convincingly use to deny still having feelings for Jahleel, and Chad watched me closely as he waited to hear something, even a squeak of denial.

When a few minutes passed and I said nothing, he shoved a hand through his hair, turned and left the kitchen, leaving me alone, heart splattered in my chest like the cake batter on the floor tile.

Hopping off the counter, I scooped up my cellphone, and right there on the screen, was the text message *he* sent a mere second before he caught me with his best friend:

I want it all back...

CHAD DISAPPEARED INTO the depths of his house for the rest of the evening. I didn't know where he was, and I didn't search for him.

It wasn't until around midnight, while I was lying in his bed staring off into space, that the bedroom door opened, a flood of light from the hall spilling into the darkness of the room, and Chad's silhouette filled the door frame.

He moved, walking up to the nightstand to switch on the lamp, and looked down at me in utter bewilderment.

"You're still here..." he mused.

As he sat down on the edge of the bed, I flipped onto my side. "You want me to leave?"

"No, I..." He stopped, ran a hand down his face. "I thought you'd—"

"Go after him?"

"I'm...it's just that...he never fights. He's not a fighter. Walking away with a shrug is more his style. Yeah, back when we just became friends, I taught him how to fight. I trained him. But he still wasn't the one to push fights. Never. He...he

441

S. ANN COLE

knows I can kill him instantly with my bare hands, yet he punched me, provoked me. Twice."

Instantly? Bare hands? And why did his voice sound so...scary?

"*Really*? You can do that?"

Chad gave me an odd glance, wary, as though he'd revealed too much. "That's beside the point."

On a sigh, I sat up and scooted over to him, wrapping around him, one arm over his shoulder, the other around his torso. I kissed along a Russian inscription on his shoulder blade. "I'm with you, Chad. It doesn't matter what I feel—felt for him. None of it matters. *You* matter. To me. I want to be with you. I want to be yours. So, I'm *here*."

Chad said nothing in return. What sucked the most was that he was utterly unreadable. I could never tell which Chad was with me, the suave Chad or the power-holder Chad.

I sprinkled kisses along his shoulder, up the side of his neck, and waited for him to speak to me.

"You never told me what happened with you two," he said finally.

"You never asked."

"What happened?"

"Why do you want to know now?"

He turned and faced me full on. "Because I need to know

if what he did to you was so bad, you'd never…put yourself in a position like that again."

He needed assurance I'd never leave him for Jahleel.

"He decidedly cheated. In front of me," I divulged, ignoring the ginormous pain that jabbed me just by saying those words. "He *chose* her."

Chad didn't question who 'her' was. Anyone who *knew* Jahleel, knew who I spoke of.

He sighed, and I wasn't sure if it was a good sigh or a bad one. Was that enough to appease him or not?

Tipping his head to the side, he leaned in and kissed me. I curled my fingers in his hair and pulled him in.

We fell back on the bed in a feverish heap.

THE ANSWER CAME two months later.

Heading back to my hotel from a press conference in Australia, I was starved and knackered. As my team and I stepped inside the lobby, Chad materialized in front of me. Impeccably dressed in a crisp, well-fitted black suit.

Six months ago, I would've been surprised to see him here, popping up at a location I gave no hint I'd be at. The first three times he did it, I demanded to know how he knew my schedule and he flat-out refused to tell me, so I stopped asking. The man was simply an enigma.

Amanda leaned in to whisper in my ear, "Honestly, Kia, your boyfriend needs to be illegal. Scratch that. He *is* illegal. Lethally illegal."

Giggling like a proud girlfriend, I moved towards Chad.

Before I could hug or kiss him, he tersely uttered, "Can we talk? I'm not here for long."

He flew all the way to Australia to see me, yet he wasn't here for long? "Uh, okay?"

Pressing a hand to my lower back, he guided me through the lobby, over to the hotel bar.

"Want something to drink?" he asked, once we were seated on two barstools.

"You said you weren't here for long, no?"

"I've got time for a beer." He turned to the bartender, "Two Coronas."

We were both fans of the same beer.

"Lemon with that?" the bartender asked.

"Yeah."

Chad patiently waited for the bartender to serve us, while I studied him. On the norm, it was difficult to tell which Chad was with me, but this time I could.

This was the Chad I didn't know well. The brusque, intimidating man with power and leadership. The Chad who had a glint of evil in the dark pools of his eyes.

The bartender served us our beers and moved on to the next customer, and before I lifted my beer to my mouth, Chad announced, "I'm ending us."

As if I'd just been slapped across the face, I froze, staring at him, mouth agape.

I searched his face, eyes, for any kind of emotion whatsoever and found none.

"Why?"

Careful to maintain his hard, invulnerable exterior, he took a long sip of his beer. "I don't love you. I could. But I won't allow myself to."

"Why?" was all I managed again.

A speck of emotion flitted across his face for one brief second. A minute, almost imperceptible crack in his composure. "I can't do this anymore, Saskia. Being with you and worrying if one day you'll just leave and go after him. I can't keep investing my time in a relationship my gut tells me won't last."

Setting down my beer on the bar, I leaned forward and took his free hand in mine. "I won't, Chad. I promised you I wouldn't."

He shook his head. "I can't live with your promise, Saskia, so I won't make you keep it. I love that you're a woman of your word, but your promise can't be the only thing keeping us together. I have no peace of mind in knowing that."

"But I want *you*," I tried to assure him. "I'm with *you*."

Chad's gaze dropped to my hand holding his, watching them for a beat before he pulled his hand away. "You're with me, but you're not mine. You never were. And you won't ever be. I should've known better than to fuck with nature."

I forced myself to feel some semblance of pain or disappointment from this breakup. Maybe some tears would be convincing. But nothing came. Nothing.

Chad couldn't leave me. Our relationship was the only thing keeping me from going after Jahleel.

Staying focused on Chad and his promise to be with me had kept me whole on tour. Ever since that night, he was the one person who kept me from going absolute barmy. If he left me, I'd drive myself to ground with the love, the pain, the anger, the obsession of Jahleel Kingston.

I needed Chad to keep me sane and levelled. And no, I wasn't being selfish. Because no one had even an inkling of how *deep and desperate* my love for Jahleel ran. It terrified the bejesus out of me what I'd do if I couldn't ever have him.

"Chad, that's not tru—"

"You repeat his name in your sleep, Saskia," he told me, voice empty. "You lie in my bed, in my arms, and dream of *him*."

"So, if this is a problem, why'd you continue with me?"

"It happened for about a month when you returned from your tour. But once we started spending time together, it stopped. Completely. Now…" His voice trailed off, leaving me to fill in the rest.

It started again when I saw him eight weeks ago.

Holding on to myself for support, I clasped my hands around my arms. "That's not fair, Chad. I can't control what I do or say while I'm *asleep*."

"Well, I can control what passes through my ears, and I have to preserve and protect myself from possible heartache in the future. I have to end this, Saskia."

Although he kept his true emotions under wraps, I knew it had to be hard for any man to sleep next to a woman who's dreaming of another.

No, I didn't want him to leave me, but I couldn't continue being selfish by begging him to stay. So, I accepted with a quiet, "Okay."

Chad studied me for a minute, searching for who-knows-what. Then he rubbed his palms together and smiled. "Great. Now that that's out of the way, I need a favour."

"*Really?*" I stared at him in utter awe. "You flew around the world to break up with me to my face, and in your next breath, you ask me a favour?"

"I only ended our sexual relationship, not our friendship," he chastised. "You're one of the strongest, loyal, most down to earth women I've ever met, Saskia. Of course, I have to keep your friendship."

I blew off his compliment by waving my hand. "What's the favour?"

"You still got security at your place, right?"

"Yeah."

"How many?"

"Still three." I picked up my Corona and took a sip. "The two securing the residence and the one who follows me around."

When he raised a brow, I laughed. "What? You forgot about *The Bling Ring*? I don't leave a key under the mat like Paris Hilton. I leave burly human securities who can break your neck with a snap."

"Perfect," Chad said, nodding in approval. "I have to do some traveling for a couple of weeks. The only other person I trust isn't speaking to me at the moment. You're next in line, so I want you to keep Alina for me until I get back. I can't leave her alone at the penthouse. She's already packed and waiting for your call. If she asks to go anywhere than the norm, run it by me first, and always set a security tail on her whenever she leaves the house. She's disciplined, malleable and smart, so she shouldn't be much of a problem."

"Okay. I'll have someone pick her up," I agreed, ecstatic. I could abort my long-time plot to kidnap her now that she was being turned over to me with no effort on my part. "But it sounds more like you're telling me instead of asking. How were you so sure I'd say yes?"

Chad flashed me a dazzling smile before leaning in to kiss me softly. "Because you're awesome, Saskia Day," he whispered, then kissed me again. "Unbelievably awesome."

"You just broke up with me and broke my heart, so I'm saying yes because I like *Alina*, not you."

He stood up from the barstool, buttoning his jacket. "Sure you are." Coming to a stop beside me, he lowered his head to whisper in my ear, "Just so you know, that was fucking hard for me to do." His lips pressed a kiss to my temple. "I'll miss the fuck out of you."

Then he left me.

I was alone again. Dumped.

Swear it, I had the crappiest luck with men. Or maybe no man would ever stay with me because I would always be in love with someone else.

Jahleel *Bane-Of-My-Existence* Kingston.

Chapter 24

"KIA, I'M WORRIED about you."

My head slowly turned in the direction of the person who spoke. Amanda.

She was sitting beside me in the back of the Phantom, and I couldn't, for the life of me, remember where we were going or where we were coming from. But who cared, right?

Ever since Chad broke up with me seven weeks ago, my life has been the same: wake up, get dressed, eat, be a superstar for the world, smile when I didn't feel like it, sing when I didn't feel like it, get high on 'what could've been' thoughts of *him*.

What the hell else did people want from me?

"*Why*, Manda?" I demanded out of sheer annoyance.

"Why are you worried?"

The edginess in my voice didn't faze her. "Because your body is here with us but *you* are not. You've been like a zombie for the past seven weeks. Your movements are just…formulaic and mechanical. Your smiles are plastic. Your eyes are…Jesus, Kia."

"I'm doing everything I'm supposed to, right? Making everyone happy, putting money in everyone's pockets. Sure I am. So, what the fuck more do you all want from me?"

Shifting over on the back seat, she moved in, getting all up in my face, but her intimidation tactics weren't working on me, because I was barely restraining myself from punching her in the eye. "I want my bloody friend back."

"She's here."

"She's not."

"Piss off, will you, Manda?" I leaned forward to tap Thomas. "Make a pass by Pacific Heights."

"Sure, Miss Day."

"You're wasting your time," Amanda mumbled, shifting back to her side, but I ignored her.

A glimpse of his bike. A glimpse of his Jeep. A glimpse of his house. A glimpse of him. *Anything*. I just wanted to glimpse something of his to stop myself from losing it completely. Because I could feel me losing it. Slowly.

With Chad leaving me, I'd been left with nothing to keep my focus off *him*, so each day I fought a losing battle to keep my thoughts Jahleel-free.

Things felt a lot different because he wasn't a fantasy anymore, because I'd gotten close to him, felt him, known him on a deeper level. Before that, it was easier to love from afar for five years and still maintain a healthy, successful life, becoming an icon.

Never before had I allowed him, or what I felt for him, to affect my work. But getting close to him had intensified my craving, my obsession, my need, my love.

And now? Now I got jitters. Now I trembled when no one was around. Now I cried through the nights. Now I popped sleeping pills. Now I wrapped my arms around myself like an asylum patient to prevent myself from calling or texting or watching videos of him.

This place, it was a horrible place to be, and I had no idea how to get myself out of it.

Thomas turned the vehicle up Jahleel's steep hill and I grasped the door handle, holding my breath as we got nearer and nearer to his house. I wouldn't go in, of course. I only wanted to see something related to him. I hadn't been to this place since I ran out a blubbering mess over a year ago.

The house was dark-out when Thomas pulled up at the

curb. No bike, no Jeep, not even Krissy's.

A car drove down the other side of the street, then swung around and began reversing up a driveway. Their headlights illuminated Jahleel's driveway, and that's when I spotted the 'For Sale' sign.

"Told you it was a waste of time coming here, didn't I?" Amanda droned in a bored tone. "But of late, you haven't been listening to anyone but the voices in your head."

Dragging my gaze away from the dark, vacated house, I turned to face her, but she was staring out the window on her side.

"He moved," she apprised me. "Things got a little crazy since he judged on that dance show. Stalker sluts and papa-razzi. He's hot shite, and he hates it. Hates the attention and lack of privacy. He got worried about his daughter's safety so he—"

"Wait, what?" I paused her, my heartbeat kicking up a frantic speed. "He has...a d-daughter?"

Amanda turned from the window to face me now, her ex-pression commiserative. "Oh, Kia. You've blocked out all things Jahleel Kingston since you started dating Chad that, for a first, you're behind on his status and I'm abreast. Don't you ever listen to Ferbie? Amy or Jamie?"

"Like you said, I blocked him out," I replied, voice

hoarse. "So, he knocked-up Krissy?"

"No," she shook her head, "Krissy married the mogul, like, a month after we went on tour."

What?

"So who—"

"Her best friend," she filled in. "But here's the soap opera part of it…" Amanda trailed off and dipped her chin, looking at me under her lashes, a smile dancing on her lips. "You ready to hear this complete and absolute *ridiculousness*?"

"Just tell me already!"

Amanda leaned in as if she were about to divulge some top secret, "She stole his sperm."

Then she burst out laughing as if it was the sweetest joke in history.

But I was confused. "I'm not sure I understand."

"Simple," Amanda said with shrug. "He had sex with her, she stole the condom with his semen, went home, drained it in a turkey baster and knocked herself up."

"Wha…Are you bloody well *kidding me*?"

The expression on my face must've been a mixture of horror, shock and incredulity, because Amanda clutched her stomach and howled in another fit of laughter.

"Your obsession with JK is nothing comparing to this bitch's," Amanda said, hiccupping. "This wench took things to a whole 'nother level."

"When did this happen?"

"The little girl's four, so…"

"And he's just finding out?"

"Apparently, she hid it from both him and Krissy, and when Krissy found out, she threatened to tell JK if she didn't. So the best friend came clean. JK 'lost his shit', I heard. But whether the baby was deceivingly conceived or not, she's still his. So…"

Five years ago, someone was far more obsessed than I was. Jahleel had a daughter. A four-year-old daughter. Could things get any worse? And I was sitting outside his dark, empty house like some fucking pathetic lunatic.

I tapped for Thomas to drive on.

"So, where did he move to?"

Amanda sobered, smile disappearing as she turned back around and looked out the window. "I don't know."

"You do."

"I don't."

"Stop lying to me, Manda."

She spun to me in utter irritation. "Why do you want to know, Kia? Look what he's done to you! With all the melee going on with him you *still* want to join in? Can't you see that JK and everything regarding him is a crazy mess? Insanity?

Un-fucking-healthy?"

"Can't you see that *I'm* a crazy mess? Insane? Un-healthy?" I yelled back. "Can't you see I'm lifeless without him?"

"You need to let go, Kia."

"You don't think I've tried that, Manda?! Nothing works!"

To cool down my boiling temper, I shifted around and stared out of the window at the lights and automobiles zooming past us. "If I let go of him, I'll let go of life."

Silence grew as thick as a brick wall between us. I was beginning to hate everyone. Everything. Even life. There was no point in anything anymore.

"Closer to you." Amanda's quiet whisper broke through my wild reveries.

I frowned and cocked my head slightly in her direction. "What?"

"Look, I'm not saying this means anything, yeah?" she said without looking at me. I could tell she hated herself for telling me, thinking she'll regret it. "It could simply be because he likes the neighbourhood, but he bought a house about five minutes away from yours."

"Okay," I said, slowly, as I contemplated my next question. "Can…can we go there? Just to see."

Amanda closed her eyes, sighing heavily. "I'm losing you,

Saskia. *We're* losing you. The world is losing you. So whatever it takes to make you come back to us…"

Shuffling over to her, I threw my arms around her and hugged her tight. "It won't get any worse, Manda. I promise."

She didn't hug me back, neither did she look at me when she said, "I wish to God I could believe that."

THOMAS SWUNG UP outside Jahleel's new house. A house I drove past each and every day and didn't even know it was his.

Had Chad been so perfect a distraction I didn't pay attention to anything at all concerning Jahleel? Why did he have to leave me? Next time I saw him, I was going to slit his face open. Something I should've done when he dumped me in Australia.

Jahleel's new house had more charm and less modernism. An impressive two storey bungalow with shapely shrubs, a green lawn, palm trees, colourful flowers, cobble stones and even a lit-up fountain. If non-bachelor was what he was going for, he nailed it.

None of it reflected him, but then I remembered what he told me about who he was, and who he'd forced himself to be.

Maybe he'd stopped forcing and was letting the original Jahleel reign.

The place was gated, but they were wide open, as was the garage door. His bike was there, next to a newer one, along with his red Jeep and a white Beemer. The Beemer sure wasn't his; he wasn't a car man.

"You okay with just looking, right?" Amanda asked from beside me.

"The gates are open," I mused.

She sighed. "Want me to come with you?"

"No."

I opened the door and stepped out. Palms suddenly clammy, I rubbed them down my denim-covered thighs, took a deep breath and trekked through the gates of Jahleel Kingston's property, down the cobble-stoned pathway, around the gushing fountain, up the limestone steps and came to a halt in front of the big black door. As black, hard and impenetrable as his heart.

Exhaling a slow, steady breath, I rang the doorbell and promptly stuffed my hands in my back pockets to prevent me from doing anything embarrassing when I saw him.

A few seconds ticked by before the door swung open, but it wasn't Jahleel who stood in front of me. It was the woman who'd tumbled through Jahleel's front door with Krissy on the first day Jahleel brought me to his house.

She was more beautiful than I remembered and could easily pass off as a member of that Armenian family famous for their big bums. Bobbed black hair, bow-shaped lips, voluptuous curves and a big round bum. She had to be the sperm stealer.

I hated her.

She looked at me with a rather off expression, one I couldn't point out. Was that fear, or worry?

Before either of us could utter a word, a little girl ran up to the woman's side in the doorway, tugging the woman's hand in earnest and pouting. "Mommy, Daddy says I can't have another gum ball. Can I have another gum ball?"

The mechanics of breathing eluded me as I stared down at the little girl. One couldn't deny she was Jahleel's child. She was the spitting image of him. From her thick sandy brown hair to her golden eyes, her straight nose, her lips. Everything was from him. I couldn't stop staring.

"Sure, Claire," the woman said, her voice frail. "Give Mommy a minute, okay?"

She pushed the little girl back a bit and stepped out, closing the door behind her, which forced me to take a couple steps back. Her hands remained behind her, holding fast to the door handle.

459

I blinked a few times, then cleared my throat. "Is JK—"

"I just got him back," her voice cracked as she cut me off.

Confused and taken aback, I stuttered, "W-what?"

"He's trying with us. Me, and Claire. And now you're here to fuck things up," she rushed out. "I *just* got him back. I can't let you take him."

"I never had him to begin with," I told her, watching the dread on her face, the annoyance and inconvenience of me being there.

Did this woman really think getting Jahleel was as easy as showing up on his doorstep? It took me five bloody years, and it took her a stolen condom of sperms and a turkey baster.

"Look, I'm just here to—"

"No!" she hissed, as quiet as she could. "He can't see you."

"I—"

The door handle rattled, but she kept her hands firmly gripped on it, tears springing to her eyes. "Please," she pleaded. "You're rich and famous and….you have *everything* in the world. I just have this one—"

The door handle rattled again and the woman struggled to keep it from opening.

"The fuck?" I heard Jahleel's voice say on the other side. "Marsh?"

"Please, don't let him see you," she continued to beg in a whisper, tears streaming down her face now. Real tears, not faked or forced. This woman genuinely loved him. "*Please.*"

"Marsh, you okay?" came from the other side.

In the midst of the door handle rattling, my desperation to see Jahleel and this woman's teary plea, it dawned I was the one who needed to do right here.

If she was terrified of Jahleel seeing me, then she knew something I didn't. Something such as, say, I had power over Jahleel as much as he had power over me. If I fought, I stood a chance of getting him back. But did I want to break up a family? No.

Undeniably so, I loved, wanted, needed Jahleel, but the woman in front of me seemed more desperate than me.

As she began losing the battle with the door handle, I nodded in agreement to her plea and bounded down the steps. By the time I got to the bottom, the woman lost the battle completely and Jahleel came out, questioning her.

My feet moved faster.

"*Sassy?*"

I stopped sharply for just a second, my shoulders tense, palms sweaty, heart pounding. If I turned and saw his face, I wouldn't leave. The sight of him would weaken me. So instead of turning around, I ran forward.

461

Tears blinded my vision as I sprinted down the cobble-stoned path, almost tripping.

"Sassy!" I heard his bare feet slapping on the stones behind me. "Fuck. Shit. Sassy, wait!"

But I kept running until I got to my ride, diving straight in the back. "Drive!"

At the sound of palms slapping on the windows, accompanied by a muffled, "Sassy, please. Wait. Please!" I squeezed my eyes shut and buried my face into Amanda's bosom, her hands curling around me.

I didn't want to see. I didn't want to hear.

The vehicle drove off, no sounds of palms slapping against the car, no muffled pleas to wait. Just the sweet melody of Zedd's *Clarity* flowing through the speakers.

Only when I knew we were a distance from his block did I allow myself to look out the back window. All I could make out was his silhouette standing in the middle of the road, watching me slip farther and farther away.

"SASKIA? ARE YOU alright?"

I blinked. My blurry vision became clear and revealed the

sight of Gildene Matthews, her bright green eyes watching me with concern, the light above our head suddenly too bright.

Reality clocked in as I glanced around, and I remembered I was in the middle of a live talk show. I'd zoned out again. A frequent occurrence of late.

"Yes, yes, I'm fine." Making a show of pressing a palm to my forehead, I told her, "Just a light headache. What was the question?"

Gildene smiled sweetly. "I asked you how it feels to be nominated for Best Album three times in a row. But since you're not feeling well, I think we can cut this short." She turned to the audience. "Can't we?"

The audience clapped and cheered in agreement, and she turned back to me. "Are you still up for performing?"

"Of course!" I exclaimed, forcing exuberance. "Plus, I will be singing a brand-new track. Exclusive. Right here on Late Night with Gildene, you'll hear it here first!"

The audience cheered, while Gildene grinned at what this would do for her show ratings.

Standing up from the armchair, I hugged her tight, smiling when she whispered, "You are awesome."

After embracing, I walked over to the stage prepared for my performance. And sang my heart out. Because it would be the last song I sang.

463

Untold stings from a golden arrow
Our tragic ending, you knew
And still...
I love you more

Pencil lead scratches on white paper
Our worthless memories, you drew
And still...
I love you more

Me shattering before you
But her loveless kisses, you choose
And still...
I love you more

365 repeated at 5
365 repeated at 5
Hated you on each breath
Loved you more the next
365 repeated at 5
365 repeated at 5

Go, wonder what would be

Had you chosen me
And think...
Do you love me now?

Go, grab a glossy image
Next to an incomplete sketch
And think...
Do you love me now?

A black silhouette in the dark
Watches a Phantom hot on wheels
And you think...
I love you now.

365 ended at 6
365 ended at 6
Loved you on each breath
Hated you more the next
365 ended at 6
365 ended at 6

To what you never wanted
I say goodbye
To what we never were

I say goodbye

365 ends at 6
365 ends at 6

The ride home was quiet and heavy. Amanda kept quiet, but judging from the wringing of her hands in her lap, I knew she wanted to say something. She wouldn't, though. Because I wouldn't care for her words.

I got up each morning and lived as everyone expected me to. Lion expected me to keep up appearances, and I did. Being the 'awesome' everyone thought I was. However, I couldn't help zoning out in the middle of interviews and talk shows.

The night I ran away from Jahleel, I died.

We are told to do right in this life, so I did the right thing for him and his family. But I killed myself in the process.

He'd inundated me with calls and text messages since I ran two weeks ago, but I ignored them all. I wouldn't be a self-ish Krissy and let him break another woman's heart.

That woman regarded me in the same light I had regarded Krissy when I was with Jahleel. In her eyes, I recognized the same desperation I had, so I knew the pain she would feel if I were to barge in and let him choose me over her. I couldn't do it. I couldn't.

Therefore, I rejected his calls and deleted his messages and emails without opening them. This was the end of my obsession. The end of who we weren't. The end of me.

ALINA AND FERBIE were lounging and joking around in the living room when I got home. Her leg tossed on his lap while he drew something like a bracelet around her ankle with a pen.

She grinned at me, babbling something about the late-night show earlier, but her voice was a tunnel echo as I ignored everyone, kicked off my heels and went straight into the kitchen to grab a bottle of Vodka.

As I made a U-turn in the kitchen with my Grey Goose Vodka, I felt Amanda's stare eating into me from behind like maggots on fucking carcass, as she tailed less than two feet behind me.

With my arms spread wide, I spun and announced to the house, "*No one* disturbs me for the rest of the night. I need to be alone."

Still, as I marched off, Amanda followed me. "What're you going to do?"

In a fit of pique, I whirled on her. "It's almost midnight, Manda. I don't have a man to fuck my brains out or massage me to ease my stress. So, if you really wanna know, I'm going up to *my* room, in *my* house, to strip naked, pop in a porn DVD, empty this vodka bottle, then fuck myself with it." I tilted my head to the side. "That okay with you, *Mum*?"

Without waiting for her reply, I turned and continued up the stairs.

Once in my bedroom, I snatched up my iPod and headed to the bathroom, hauling a chair behind me. After closing the door, I turned the lock and jammed the chair up under the handle, then stripped naked.

Setting the bottle of vodka and iPod on the side of the bathtub, I plugged the tub and turned on both the shower and the lower pipe.

While the bath filled, I went over to the cabinet and bundled up all the bottles of pills I found in my arms, then tossed them into the bathtub before climbing in and lowering down into the water.

Picking up my iPod, I stuck the plugs in my ears and set Jack White's version of U2's *Love is Blindness* on repeat.

Next, I reached for the bottle of vodka, screwed off the cover, sipped some, then poured some in the rising water. I selected a random bottle of pills from the scads floating on the water, screwed it open, popped a pill in my mouth, and sipped a mouthful of vodka to wash it down. "365 ends at 6."

I popped another pill, took another sip of vodka, Jack White screaming in my ears.

"365 ends at 6."

Pop. Sip. Swallow. "365 ends at 6." Pop. Sip. Swallow. "365 ends at 6." Pop. Sip. Swallow. "365 ends at 6." Pop. Sip. Swallow. "365 ends at 6." Pop. Sip. Swallow. "365 ends at 6." Pop...Sip... Swallow...

Chapter 25

THE LITTLE BLONDE girl dipped her head under the gushing river stream.

Where did she go?

A further distance down the stream, her head popped up. "365 starts at 6," she sputtered, before allowing the water to swallow her whole again.

"Hey, where are you going? Come back!"

I tried wading into the river, but as cool, clear and fresh as the water looked, it burned through my soles like hot coals, forcing me to jump back on the riverbank.

I couldn't enter. I couldn't catch her. I couldn't save her.

The little girl's head bobbed up once more, her wild

blonde curls dry as dirt even though she'd just been under water. The stream carried her even farther away from me, but her eyes were like wide grey disks, glistening, her face a blinding sunray of hope.

One tiny hand rose out of the water, and in it she held a microphone too large for her proportion. Her other hand came up next, and in it she held planet Earth, rotating slowly in her palm. Bringing it to her lips, she blew, and like a suds bubble, planet Earth floated towards me.

I caught it, now rotating in my palm.

"365 starts at 6!" she repeated.

Rearing back her hand with the microphone, she pitched it towards me, and allowed the river stream to wash her down the falls. Gone.

The microphone she threw came at me in full force. I held up my free hand to catch it, but it careened on its own and slammed me straight in the stomach.

Bloody hell, that hurts!

As I made to clutch my stomach to fight against the pain, I found I couldn't, my hand wouldn't move. On its own, the microphone drew back and jabbed me in the stomach again, and again, and again.

"Please!" I cried, "Stop! It hurts!"

But the inanimate object continued its torture. I felt as if I were being ripped into two halves.

"Make it stop, please!"

Pain. Pain. It hurt so much. So much pain. "Make it stop!"

"She's talking...talking...talking...talking..." a voice echoed all around me.

It was so damn loud. My head hurt. My throat. My eyes.

"Success...cess...cess...She'll live...live...live..." that loud, grating voice echoed again. "Continue...tinue...nue..."

The microphone came at me again, ramming me in the stomach, brutally hurting me, over and over. The pain became unbearable. No more. No more. I could take no more.

I gave up, dropping the rotating Earth and falling into the river which was now boiling hot.

Then, nothing.

"...YOU EVER FUCKIN' talk to me? Are you even real? My whole life, all I hear is how good you are, all about the many fuckin' miracles you perform, you're this and you're that, and if I seek you, you'll be there. But even when I did everything I was taught, you still hated me. You never speak to me, you never answer me, you never help me, you never do jack-shit.

I ask for one thing, just *one*, and this is what happens? And here I am talkin' to myself like I'm fuckin' crazy. Because you aren't real. There's no You, is there…?"

The ranting voice, I recognized even in death. It belonged to the person who'd been so far away from me. The person who made me want to be far from everyone. From life.

Now the voice was *so* near. Right…there. Here.

Although my eyes felt like sandbags, I forced them open. After a few ponderous blinks, blurriness faded and Jahleel came into focus. He was sitting on a chair beside the narrow hospital bed I laid in, hooked up with drips.

He held my left hand in both of his, forehead lowered to them as he continued on with his rant—to God, I assume— oblivious of my consciousness.

Dragging my gaze away from him, I glanced around the plain, clinical room, a monitor beeping annoyingly on the right. Swallowing past the acridness in my throat, I pondered whether it was fortunate or unfortunate I survived my suicide attempt.

I was supposed to be dead. Not lying here, with the man who induced it in the first place holding my hand. No, I didn't want to be alive, because now things were going to be far worse than before.

Did I not jam a chair under the bathroom door handle to

ensure no one would get to me in time? Yet here I was. Alive.

Not even Death wanted me. Fuck my fucking fuck of a fucked-up life.

Bringing my gaze back to a still ranting Jahleel, I tried speaking past the rock in my throat. "Maybe if you tried omitting the plethora of swearwords from your prayers, he'd respond."

Jahleel's head snapped up, and only for a fleeting moment did I discern a look of relief and elation in his eyes, as his features immediately hardened, his bloodshot eyes narrowing with something resembling anger.

His face was shadowed in days of facial hair, which looked comely instead of shabby. His hair a perfect mess around his face and shoulders. Full and bouncy.

He was beautiful. Like a tanned, untouchable, incontestable, magnificent Greek god who had untold riches of gold and silver and copper, diamonds and pearls and rubies, large fields of violets and roses, kisses in abundance and love enough for the whole world. He was all that, and more.

I. Love. Him.

Jahleel turned his head to glance briefly at the door, before pushing up from his chair to lean over me.

My eyes followed him.

Pressing his lips to my ear, he whispered with vicious

stings, "See, everyone's gonna be all nice and sympathetic towards you. They'll say they understand when they fuckin' don't. They'll shed tears and offer words of comfort. *I* won't. If there's anything I want to do, it's *strangle* you so you can die a proper death, you selfish fuck. If you thought I hated you before, you were wrong. *Now*, I do. I fuckin' hate you so fuckin' much for tryin' to leave everyone...leave *me*. I. Hate. You, Saskia Day."

Slowly, he moved back and sat down, still clutching my hand even with all the venom he just spewed.

Unsure of how that acrid statement made me feel, I blinked at him for several minutes before asking, "You're not family, not even a friend, so how are you in here?" ...*And if you hate me so much,* why *are you in here?*

"I'm your fiancé," he said in a flat tone. "And the only family you have here is an imbecile."

Aiming to moisten the dryness in my throat, I swallowed. "I thought you liked him. How could you say that?"

"Would've said just about anything about anyone to get in here. They weren't making it easy," he said, shrugging. "You thirsty?"

"Yes."

"I'll go get the nurse, but..." he paused and glanced back at the door again. "Someone leaked that you 'committed' suicide, so yesterday it was all over the news that you're dead. Then it switched to 'attempted to commit suicide', while some say you're a drug addict and overdosed. It's mayhem. You've been the topic on every news channel for the past 48hrs. If people think you're suicidal, that's it for your career. No one will look up to you anymore. They'll try to move you to a psych ward to get help so this doesn't reoccur." He stopped to rub his eyes, obviously knackered. "Chad found a guy who'll take the fall for—"

"Take what fall?"

He glared at me. "Just shut up and listen."

Maybe he wasn't conscious of it, but his thumb was rubbing circles in my lifeline, even as he glared in hate at me.

He continued, "The guy's in some deep debt at the expense of his family's lives. We cleared his debt. In a couple of hours, the police will get a tip about a homicide attempt, giving the name and address of the guy. They'll pick him up. They'll find valuables belonging to you in his apartment. In his cellphone, they'll find messages from an untraceable number tersely discussing your hit, with strict instructions to make it appear as a suicide. He'll admit to executing an unsuccessful hit, how he forced you at gunpoint. But in 'fear for his family's lives', he won't reveal who ordered the hit, and no, he doesn't know why they want you dead.

"At his sentencing hearing, you'll give a speech about forgiveness and how this near-death experience has changed your perspective on life yada yada yada. Then you'll ask the judge to be lenient, so they won't give this innocent man a fuckin' life sentence."

He watched my expression for a moment, exhaled, then told me, "The act starts the second a nurse walks through that door. You're a victim, not suicidal. Got that?"

Averting my eyes, I croaked, "I don't like it."

"I don't care if you like it or not," he snapped. "Were you seeking attention when you did this? 'Cause if that was your motive—as if you didn't already have it all—now the world's fixated on you. And not in a good way. What did you think would happen? You think if you'd succeeded, at some point you could decide you no longer want to be dead and make yourself un-dead? Once you're dead, you're *dead*. There's no turning back. You wanna maintain your rep, you do as I say and act your fuckin' ass off. You wanna selfishly give it all up? Be my guest, Suicidal Sassy."

His warm hands left mine, and a shiver ran through me as he stood to his feet.

"Does Lion approve of—"

"He'll get on board. Last time I told him to do something, someone became a star and locked in his cred. Smart as he is,

Lion couldn't come up with a better plan to salvage this mess you created. Thank Chad."

There, he was distancing himself as if he had nothing to do with it and it was all Chad. But I knew Jahleel more than he thought I did, and his fingerprints were all over this plan.

As he started moving towards the door, I groaned when a sharp pain lanced me in the gut. "My stomach hurts *so* bad."

In a dull, apathetic voice, he tossed over his shoulder, "It was pumped. That's what happens when you swallow over two dozen mixed pills." When he got to the door, he placed his hand on the handle, then looked back at me and said, "It sucks, right? But damn, I was hoping you'd wake up feeling a shit lot more pain than this."

He gave me a hateful, repulsed look that hurt more than my stomach pain before he left.

Now I really wanted to die.

CLAUSTROPHOBIC DOESN'T EVEN begin to describe how I felt with everyone crowding around my hospital bed, giving me sympathetic gazes, pursed lips and small head shakes, as though I were lying dead in a bloody casket.

Lion stood at the foot of the bed, cellphone pressed to his ear as he divided his attention between me and whoever was so important on the other end. The one person I expected to be raging mad at me was him. However, he was uncharacteristically commiserative.

Was this the part where people sucked up to me because they thought I was unstable and fragile, so they avoided saying anything that would probably send me swallowing pills again?

Everyone talked all at once, but it was all white noise to me, because I didn't really want to hear from, or see, anyone. Jahleel's venom was preferable to their empathizing. As much as I was curious about who found me and how, I haven't uttered a single word to a soul since they entered.

Jahleel never returned since he left the hospital room the day before, so that could very well be the reason behind my mood. Maybe he *really* hated me for what I did.

All had gone as he'd said. The man taking the fall was picked up with evidence that tied him to my attempted murder—including my 'engagement ring'. He confessed, and it hit the news with a jaw-dropping twist to the 'Suicide Day' story.

Detectives came in earlier that morning to question me. Alina came in an hour before them, sent by Chad to relay word for word the story given to the cops, just so my story would align. I was positive Jahleel would deliver the message to me and not Alina, but it was clear he was avoiding me, distancing himself.

He came to the hospital several times a day, but didn't see me. This I knew, because whenever I heard his name mentioned through the white noise, my ears would perk up like a damn watchdog.

At this very moment, my auditory nerves were heightened and keened to the left, where Amanda, Amy and Jamie were blabbing about how good of an actor Jahleel was.

"…unbelievable how well he plays the devastated fiancé," Amy chattered.

"Don't you mean believable?" Jamie pitched.

"I think he's in the wrong profession," Amanda agreed. "I swear he has me so convinced, the only time I'm reminded he's acting is when the doctors turn their backs and he's a sweary arsehole doucheshit again."

"Well, he's made bread out of stone. God forbid how things would've turned out if this was left in Ferbie's hands."

They cackled, and, of course, that ticked me off.

"Get out," I said out loud, speaking for the first time since they'd gathered in like gossipers at a crime scene. "*Everyone.* I need to be alone."

No one budged, as if what I said no longer mattered.

"Last time you said that," Amanda whispered, "you were

found half-dead in a tub of water."

Shooting her a glare while tilting my head in Amy and Jamie's direction—who didn't know the suicide attempt was a *real* suicide attempt—I gritted out, "I wish the attempt on my life had been successful. At least I'd have privacy in death. A golden casket all to myself? Fuck yeah. Buried six feet under where I can't be disturbed? Le sigh."

Blinking rapidly, she turned and started out of the room, tossing over her shoulder, "You're already disturbed, Kia."

"I bet a million bucks it was you, you nosy bugger," I said to her retreating form.

She whirled around, tears filling her eyes. "You're a pain in my arse, Kia! I don't know why I...I should have just..." She trailed off, frustratingly flashing away the tears from her eyes. She *never* cried—at least not in front of others.

"Yeah, Manda," I bit out. "You bloody well should've. That's the *point*."

Instead of perpetuating the argument, she stormed out of the room, and like the leader she was, when she moved, everyone else followed suit.

Except Lion, who was still planted at the foot of the bed, mumbling into his cellphone while watching me with concern.

"You, too, manager," I snapped, glowering at him.

Arching a brow, he mumbled for a moment longer into

the phone before hanging up. "You don't get to give me orders, Kia."

"Out."

Refusing to acknowledge my request, he slid his cell-phone in his pocket, and gripped the steel barring on the hospital bed as though he needed something to hold him up.

I'd never seen him like that before: hurt, confused, help-less.

And for the first time since yesterday, I spared a sliver of thought on the ripple effect my selfish actions might have on the people close to me.

Lion loved me like his own, so of course something like this would leave him gutted. He was probably beating himself up for not paying close enough attention. But then, the few people close to me knew I had issues. And they knew precisely what my issues were. Or *who* my issue was. Lion and Amanda were two people who didn't even have to question why I did this. They just knew.

"You know," he said in a low, remorseful voice. "If I'd known things were this dysfunctional between you two, I would've opened up my damned mouth and said somethin' sooner."

"Oh, spare me," I said with a quick eye roll. "You knew everything from the very beginning. There's nothing you could've done. He's the only one with that power."

Lion dropped his head, and he looked down at his hands still gripping the steel barring. "You right 'bout me knowin' everything from the jump. But I kept both your secrets, sat back and watched a fuckin' train wreck in motion that coulda been stopped if everybody had just kept it one hundred."

"'Both'? What are you talking about?"

Letting go of the barring, he ran a hand down his face and sighed. "It's a long fuckin' story, Kia. And I have to go before I miss my flight. Tonight's the Awards, and I've gotta be there both for my nominated artistes and to collect *your* awards. You wanna record a 'thank you' message from the hospital bed? Fans aren't too happy about you not performin' tonight, so a recordin' would make up for it. I could get—"

"How do you even know if I'm going to win anything?"

A proud grin split across his face instead of the cocky eyebrow lift I usually got whenever I fired 'how-do-you-know' questions at him. "Because you're *you*, Kia. You always win. Not only that, but you've been nominated for *eleven* different awards. You have to win at least one."

Did I always win? Awards? Sure. But the battle of love and obsession? Nope. This hospital bed proved it.

"No," I replied. "Just speak on my behalf. Say I'm too confused and beside myself or some shite like that."

"Cool. I should really be stayin' here with you, but I easily feel confident leavin' you in *his* hands."

"Confident?" I squeaked, eyebrows shooting up. "He was mean as shite to me when I regained consciousness. He hates me, Lion."

Lion waved a dismissive hand. "He's been mean to everyone. He barked in my face and even chucked me, blamin' me for lettin' this happen. He hasn't spoken to me since. But I let him be angry and allowed him to take over because I know well enough, this is his way of dealin' with his shit. He's blamin' everyone around you, as a matter of fact."

"Everyone but himself," I muttered. "The *real* reason."

"Kia...don't hesitate to do as he suggests. I'll approve. He's a smart dude who never fails. And even if he comes off as an asshole, it's because he's...because he means well."

"Okay," I agreed. "But only because you, my manager, say I should."

"Right, *that's* why," Lion said, laughing as he walked up to the side of the bed. He leaned over to plant a kiss on my forehead. "The world loves you, Kia. Your friends love you." He straightened up then stared me in the eyes. "I love you."

It's not enough, I wanted to say. *Because the one person I wanted to love me, didn't.*

Chapter 26

EVEN IN THE dark depths of my sleep, I could smell him, taste his scent on my tongue. I kept my eyes closed, heart thrumming as I held my breath just to hear him breathe. For some reason, I *dreaded* him, having no idea what kind of acerbity I'd wake up to.

Along with the constant beeping of the machine stringing me up, was a scratching sound I've become familiar with after spending much time with him: pencil lead on paper.

He was sketching.

Me?

After a good three minutes ticked on, his voice floated over me in warm waves, "I know you're awake."

Busted.

On a sigh, I opened my eyes to see him turning the sketch face down on his lap. "How?"

He stood to his feet and dragged his chair closer to the bed so he could take my hand in his, thumb circling in my lifeline. "I can watch your heart, remember?"

Reaching up, he pressed two fingers to the dip at the base of my neck. "Your pulse here started beating an erratic pace the second you woke and figured I was here."

Like a blushful teenage girl getting high and flustered at the first touch of her crush, I shoved his hand from me. "That's a little arrogant, don't you think?"

"I'm only made arrogant by your sloppily concealed reactions towards me," he said with a small smile. "So, blame yourself."

I regarded him with a frown. His mood had changed considerably since the last 48hours. Had he decided he no longer hated me?

"When are they going to let me out of this damn place?"

"Tomorrow. Psyche ward, therapy, and all other complications from the failed suicide went away when the 'attempted homicide' came into play."

"Thank you loads for stepping in, JK," I whispered. "I really appreciate it."

"Oh yeah, Lydia can't make it here to see you because she's on a hospital bed herself..." Pausing, he squeezed my hand. "She's dying of cancer, Sassy."

A painful sound escaped me. "Oh my God. And she kept it from me? I have to get out of here and go see her! I can't...Oh my God. How could I have been so selfish?"

"Shh. Relax. One tragedy at a time, okay? Let's think about you first. Lydia has a couple more weeks to go."

"But—"

"Sassy, look at me." He pushed me back down when I tried to get up. I looked at him. "Calm down. Please. I promise we'll go see her before she..."

Dies. Before she dies! Lydia... I took a few calming breaths. He was right, if I was going to see her, I had to look hale and happy. Not like this. "Okay."

Satisfied with my acquiescence, he kissed the back of my hand. "Timberly...I tried gettin' hold of her...but nothing. I don't understand. I'm sure wherever in the world she is, she'd be aware, right?"

Timber was someone I practiced never to worry about. With her touring the depths of the world in strange countries with strange cultures, sometimes we didn't hear from her for weeks at a time. "She's probably in some part of the world where dinosaurs and giants still exist and technology is unheard of."

"You sure?" he asked. "Ferbz seems worried something might have happened to her."

"Probably," I mused. "But I'm ninety-nine percent sure she's safe. I'll give her another week to call before hitting the panic button."

He shrugged. "Well, that's it for your family."

His fingers flexed over mine, his eyes moving to our hands and staying there, as though he'd suddenly developed a fascination with hands.

As I watched him watch our hands, his tongue made a swift sweep over his bottom lip, and if I perceived accurately, he almost seemed…nervous. A nervous Jahleel? Wow.

"Who found me?"

Gaze shifting to my face, he answered in a voice so quiet, "Me."

"How?"

"Amanda." He swallowed hard, as though the memory was too much. "She called me. Crying. Said you'd been strange all week; that she had a feelin' you were gone. I was confused, not knowing what she meant by that. Until she screamed, 'I think she's trying to kill herself, JK. Now.'

"Of course, I told her both of you were sick fucks, and I didn't have time for your shit and hung up. But even as I said all that, I was already straddling my bike. I got to your house and ran upstairs. You weren't in your room, but I could hear the shower running. Thinking you were fine as I'd assumed, I was going to leave, but then I noticed water seeping under the bathroom door. I tried the door, but it was locked. I panicked and shouted for your men. We tried kickin' the door in, but it wouldn't budge. Thomas went and found an axe. We had to axe the fuckin' thing open…"

Pausing, he let go of my hand only long enough to rake his fingers shakily through his hair. "You really wanted to die, didn't you? A chair under the door handle?"

"Yes," I whispered in reply to his rhetorical question. "Life no longer made sense without you."

His head dipped low, and he sucked in a sharp breath. "Fuck, Sassy. I don't know how it's even possible you're here—alive. In that big ass tub, your head under water, you were hueless, cold…dead. I still can't believe it. Not even the doctors—I think it was one of the docs who saw your lifeless body when you first came in who leaked shit news that you're dead. But I wouldn't accept that, and insisted they do whatever the fuck they had to do to bring you back, and…here you are. Unfuckingbelievable."

I now understood his anger towards me the day before. His anger both to me and to God. He was gutted. I couldn't even begin to pretend I understood what it must've felt like for him to find me like that. To think I was really gone. Poor Amanda must've lost it, yet I treated her like complete crap earlier today.

Jesus, I was truly selfish.

Naked silence descended. I had no excuse or plausible words for what I did. For hurting the people around me.

I raised my eyes to the clock on the adjacent wall and watched ten slow minutes tick by, while Jahleel kept his head lowered, eyes on our hands again. It was 1:34am, and I idly wondered how the Awards went, and if Jahleel's new family was waiting up for him.

"Does she know you're here?" I blurted.

"She who?"

"Marsh, if I remember correctly."

"My life's none of her business."

"Isn't she—"

"Marsha led you to believe something that isn't true," he said, eyes snapping up to mine. "We're not together. We never were. She was already on thin ice with me for what she did, then she went ahead and fuckin' lied to you."

"So…" I swallowed, "you don't live together? As a family?"

"No," he said, slowly enunciating the word so I'd get it.

"Claire's not used to me. She's almost five, for shit's sake. Never knew her father until now. She doesn't understand my role in her life yet, so whenever I admonish her, she doesn't listen. She's fuckin' rude, feisty and answers only to her mother. Drives me fuckin' crazy.

"I understand I can't just shove this father thing down her throat and expect her to adapt, so I let Marsh come over sometimes and we spend time together so Claire can get used to me. That's all it is. After what she did? You kiddin' me?"

Shaking his head, he ran a hand through his oh-so-amazing hair again. "Swear to God, ever since I learned about Claire, it's like my cock went into repulsed mode against women. I'm afraid to fuck again. Because apparently not even condoms can protect you. Women are sick fuckin' creatures."

I couldn't help smiling. "Maybe you should try the dick-to-dick route then. To avoid us 'creatures'."

He dipped his head to hide his own smile, brushing his thumb over my knuckles. "I'll think about it."

This smile wasn't his usual arrogant, crooked one, but a sweet, shy smile that somehow made him appear boyish and innocuous. How misleading, eh?

"Oh," he murmured, removing his hand to dip into his front pocket. "Picked up your 'stolen' stuff from the station today. Including your engagement ring…"

"Ah," I groaned with a roll of my eyes. "The act. Blimey. How long do we have to play this through?"

No answer came while he got the ring out—an ornate titanium goth-like ring with a not-too-large baguette black diamond, outlined with red stones. Very *me*. I couldn't have chosen a better ring for myself. Hell, this man *knew* me.

Lifting my ring finger slowly, caressingly, he slid the ring onto it. He raised his eyes to mine, answering with a question, "Forever?"

Not a peep came from me. I couldn't breathe let alone speak. My gaze left his and dropped to the ring on my finger, then back to him, then back to the ring, then back to him. *Ohgodohgodohgodohgodohgodohgodohgodohgodohgodohgodohgod...*

Did he just...? Oh. My. God.

"Sassy?" he questioned, when several long minutes passed and...nothing.

My mouth opened and closed like a fish gagging on bait.

Releasing my hand, he reached up and touched the tips of his fingers to my cheek. "Breathe, Sassy, breathe."

Doing as he suggested, I let out the breath I held in, and the ability to speak returned. "Are you doing this because you think I'll try killing myself again?"

"No."

"Are you *lying* to me right now?"

"No."

"Do you have any idea what this means?"

"Yes."

"So you *do* know you have to be committed to me and me only, right?"

"Yes."

"And you, a whore and more, have absolutely no problem with that?"

"No."

"And you'll never, ever, cheat on me again?"

"*No.*"

"Do you *love* me, Jahleel Kingston?"

His lips tipped up in that damned crooked smile. "Yes."

I forgot to breathe again. "You...Oh God...For how long?"

"Six years."

Wait, what? "What?"

Standing up, he set his sketch pad down on the chair and ordered, "Scoot over."

When I shifted over on the bed to make room for him, he cuddled up beside me. Reaching a hand up to my hair, he captured a wild raven curl, twirling it around his finger. "This, this is fake. Naturally, you're blond."

"That's true," I admitted in a whisper.

"A blonde that glistens when the light hits it. A blonde far more luminescent than an angel's. An unusual blonde I've never seen before, and will probably never see again."

"How do you—"

"Six years ago, I was backstage at a concert in Manchester, heading back from the restroom after a break in warm-up rehearsals. This gorgeous blond went up on stage. She was opening for my boss, and the second she began singing, I stopped moving. Her voice, it did something to me, and like magnet to steel, I went straight to the foot of the steps at the stage where I could see her better. Every inch of her taunting curves.

"And she sang on, *'How do you know it's real? Does he make you paralyzed? When he's there, do you see only him? Does he suck you in? Consume you? Overwhelm you? Does he make you forget to think? How, how do you know it's real? Is there a pull? The brain still works? Thoughts jumbled together? Nothing makes sense? You feel but don't understand? Knows right but do wrong? You explode in a song? How, how do you know it's real?'*

"I couldn't move. Her voice wrapped around me like barbwire and trapped me in a painful trance. I fell in love with her voice. I fell in love with her curves. I fell in love with her hair.

494

I fell in love with *her*. Right there. Back stage. Seeing and hearing her for the first time in my life. I fell in love."

A stray finger traced the outline of my lips.

"When I finally got my damn legs to work, I practically sprinted to my boss. Lion. I asked him if he'd heard her sing. He hadn't. But I believed in what I heard, her voice, so I badgered and badgered until he gave in, saying, 'Alright. I'll send for her and feel her out if it'll get you to shut the fuck up.'"

Jahleel paused to have a good long laugh, as if remembering how much of a pain in the arse he'd been.

"When she came into the room after her performance, my hands literally shook. Fuckin' ridiculous, right? My hands trembled like a bitch, heart raced like a teenager, and I bopped my head to muted music, pretending to mind my own business, all the while listening to the conversation to see if Lion would offer her a deal...or something. Now that I look back at it, the whole thing was ridiculous," he said, laughing out, while I grinned so wide my face hurt.

As his smile melted, his expression became regretful. "But then I thought, *what the fuck is wrong with me? This ain't me. Practically obsessing about a girl who, up until fifteen minutes ago, I didn't know existed. What if she has a boyfriend? She lives in the UK. How would this even work?* The whole fuckin' thing was pointless. So I unmuted my iPod and tuned out everything, deciding to forget it all.

"Except, I couldn't. When we got home, I nagged Lion to take you on. He wouldn't. Said you're British, managing you from the U.S. would be costly etcetera etcetera. So I gave up. Worse, I didn't even know you." He chuckled again. "Then one day I noticed Krissy watching this reality show about a Brit girl group who went to L.A. to pursue their music career."

"Stingers?"

"Yeah, them," he confirmed. "No hesitation, I pounced on Lion with that idea. He bitched around for a while, but finally relented, 'cause I was relent*less,* and of course, because he respects me—the only reason he tolerated my nagging in the first place."

"So, basically, *you* are responsible for me becoming this famous superstar?"

"No," he said, face serious. "You are. *Your* talent, *your* voice and *your* hard work. I only believed in that voice, sat back and watched you bloom like a fuckin' sunflower."

A great sigh tore through me. As much as the small bed would allow, I turned over and stared up at the ceiling, a migraine approaching.

This had to be what Lion was talking about earlier. *"I kept both your secrets…"*

He'd known all along Jahleel loved me as much as I loved

him, and he said nothing, watching me suffer day after day. But that was Lion, he'd die before he betrayed a confidence.

"None of this makes sense, JK. I'm sorry. All the pain and heartache, for what? You were an unapologetic arsehole. You loved Krissy. You chose her over me. You let me get with your best friend…I just…it's too hard to believe."

For a long moment, he said nothing.

I kept my eyes trained on the ceiling. This was too much to digest. All the unnecessary crap could've been avoided had he refrained from being an arse all the damn time and told me how he felt.

"What I told you that day in the shower was true," he said at last. "I wasn't ready to be owned. The way I felt when I was around you, when I looked into those wide grey eyes, or when you touched me, I knew you held a certain power over me and I hated it. When you're near, I see no one else, I get nervous, my heart races, I'm aware of nothing but you. And it terrified me. That's what brought out the asshole in me. I knew if I let you in, that would be it for me, I'd be done for. Owned. So…that's why I acted the way I did, fighting off the inevitable. I wanted you but I didn't. I loved you but I hated you. And it was so fuckin' immature."

"Then what was the deal with Krissy?" I asked, getting inexplicably irked. "You couldn't have loved both of us,

Jahleel!"

Wrapping his arms tight around me as if afraid I'd bolt, he sighed. "I *thought* I loved her. I *knew* I was *in* love with you. It was two completely different feelings, and I knew without a doubt which was real and which was forced. But I felt, somehow, that my loyalties lied with her. Maybe because I've felt responsible for her since she first came to us when she was six? I dunno. I just always felt guilty whenever I tried putting you above her. So even though I knew she was selfishly using me that night, I let her. Plus I was monumentally pissed at you.

"For one, I just got news about the show and wanted to share everything with you, but you were completely unavailable. And two, you were going on tour *the next day* and I didn't want you to go." He lifted up my hand and tapped the ring. "This was delivered to me the day before."

Rolling back to my side, I faced him, wide eyed. "You were going to *propose*?"

"Yes."

"So because you rang me a couple times and couldn't get through to me, you acted like a sulky toddler who got dog-shit thrown in his sand box and just decided to rip my heart into a million pieces instead? How fucking mature of you!"

"And I have regretted it every single day since," he confessed, looking abashed.

"Did Chad know all of this?"

Face hardening, jaw clenching, he ground out, "From the get-go."

"Really?"

"*Really*," he affirmed. "At first he was just flirting with you to feel you out. But then you fuckin' *kissed* him. After that, the fucker decided to make the shit real. 'May the best man win' he'd told me."

"He almost did."

"He couldn't win when there was no contest," Jahleel scoffed. "You belonged to me, even then. I owned you, just as you owned me. He knew that. I knew that. You knew that. God knew that. So that 'relationship' couldn't last. You can't force love. I've learned as much with Krissy. You have to go with what's real. And what we have is one hundred fuckin' percent real. What Chad did..." He trailed off, sighing heavily. "He sat and listened to me beat myself up every day. Listened to me talk obsessively about you. Tellin' me to move on, when all the time he was...with you."

My exasperation dissipated, and pure, undiluted contentment settled in as I let the scruff on his face abrade my palm. "I-I just can't believe this is happening. That this is real. Are you sure I'm not dead? Life doesn't usually offer these delicious twists."

"It's real," he assured me, smiling. "I, Jahleel Giovanni Kingston, am in love with you, Saskia Valencia Day. I've loved you since you were blond. I've loved you since your first song. I've loved you as you grew, evolved. I loved you even as you've loved others. I loved you all over again when you sauntered through my studio doors. I loved you hard when you climbed onto the back of my bike. I loved you even harder when you begged me to kiss you. I loved you something fierce when you took care of me when I was ill. I loved you on a brand-new level when we made love. I fell fuckin' deep when you told me you were in love with me. I've loved you for every second of every day since you left me. And I love you even more now."

"But, that night when I told you I loved you, you didn't want to hear it. You were cruel. You made me feel so…worthless."

"Didn't want to hear it?" he gaped. "Sassy, those words made me whole. You have no idea. I reacted the way I did because I was mad, not at you, but at myself. See, I tried to hold off being intimate with you until you came back from tour. I knew once I had you, I'd fall hard then have to turn around and let you go. I didn't have a problem with fallin' hard, I had a problem with you going on tour.

"So I was pissed for letting myself have you that night,

knowing you were going away in two weeks. Then the minute you said those words, I felt pain like I've never felt before at the thought of you leaving me. For *six* fuckin' months. So…yeah, I reacted, instead of tellin' you my true feelings."

"You're still forgiven." I leaned in and kissed him, fingers curling into his hair, and then it hit me. I drew back, grinning at him. "I'm Headless Singing Girl!"

A laugh rumbled through him, as he caught my hand and touched the tattoo on my forearm. "And I'm Faceless Hoodie Guy."

He turned, stretching off the bed to nab his sketch pad from the chair and turning back to me. He held up the sketch so I could see it. It was the same sketch of Singing Girl, except now she had a head. My head. I looked fierce, dominant, like I had the world spinning in the palm of my hand.

"So, this means I'm constant now?" I asked, grinning like I swallowed too much happy pills. *Oops. Forgot. I did, didn't I?*

"Now, you're mine, *constantly*," he told me.

Moving in closer to him, I pressed my body tight against his, just to feel his heat, to smell his scent, to breathe his air.

Jahleel set the sketch pad on the pillow above our heads and pressed us together even closer, wrapping his arms around me.

His lips touched mine, and I parted them, inviting him in.

Before his tongue slipped inside, he whispered, "365 starts at 6."

He'd watched my bloody goodbye performance.

My lips curved against his as I agreed, "365 starts at 6."

Also by S. Ann Cole

About the Author

S. Ann Cole is an exaggerator, a laugher, sometimes overly chatty, sometimes overly shy. She's afraid of cats, dogs, snakes—heck, she's only tolerable to gold fishes in a tank.

She *hates* fireworks, schmaltz and arrogance.
She *loves* carbs, full moons and humility.
She lives nowhere and everywhere.
Jokey people are her favorite people to be around, as laughter is the way to her heart.

When Ann's not abusing her computer keyboard, you can find her nosing a novel, watching anything on television that makes her laugh until she breaks into hiccups (*loves* Disney, TBS, and *Impractical Jokers*!) studying the Bible, or sipping red wine.

VISIT **WWW.ANNCOLE.NET** FOR MORE INFORMATION ON
S. ANN COLE'S BOOKS AND UPCOMING RELEASES.